Young adult novels by Kate Hattemer

The Land of 10,000 Madonnas
The Vigilante Poets of Selwyn Academy

HERE COMES TROUBLE

KATE HATTEMER

Alfred A. Knopf
New York

THIS IS A BORZOI BOOK PUBLISHED BY ALFRED A. KNOPF

Visit us on the Web! rhcbooks.com

Educators and librarians, for a variety of teaching tools, visit us at RHTeachersLibrarians.com

Library of Congress Cataloging-in-Publication Data
Names: Hattemer, Kate, author.
Title: Here comes trouble / Kate Hattemer.
Description: First edition. | New York : Alfred A. Knopf | Summary: Soren is famous for his pranks, but with his best friend gone and well-behaved cousin Flynn visiting for a year, he tries to mend his ways.
Identifiers: LCCN 2017028599 (print) | LCCN 2017040461 (ebook) |
ISBN 978-1-5247-1846-6 (trade) | ISBN 978-1-5247-1847-3 (lib. bdg.) |
ISBN 978-1-5247-1848-0 (ebook)
Subjects: | CYAC: Practical jokes—Fiction. | Schools—Fiction. | Family life—Fiction. |
Cousins—Fiction. | Behavior—Fiction.
Classification: LCC PZ7.H2847 (ebook) | LCC PZ7.H2847 Her 2018 (print) | DDC
[Fic]—dc23

The text of this book is set in 12-point Chaparral Pro.

Printed in the United States of America

May 2018

10 9 8 7 6 5 4 3 2 1

First Edition

for Henry

CHAPTER ONE

OUR MISSION: to see out the window without anyone seeing us.

Difficult, sure, given the whole windows-made-of-glass thing. But Ruth and I have had a lot of experience with spy work, and we instantly saw the potential in the long white curtains. She swaddled herself in one and I took the other. We couldn't move, and we couldn't retaliate when our brother, Ivan, who's two and terrible, hit us with his Barbie. But we would get the first look at any car coming down our street.

"They better get here soon," said Ruth. "I feel like a mummy."

"Mummies can't feel," I told her. Ruth is only in fourth grade, and sometimes her lack of education shows. As her big brother, I feel it's my duty to enlighten her. "Their brains have been siphoned out—ah-*choo*!"

"Don't tell Dad how dusty these curtains are," said Ruth. "He'll make us vacuum."

"Ah-*choo!*" I wiped my nose on the fabric. "What if I'm sneezing and I miss the car? I'm keeping my eyes open next time."

"No! Soren! No!" The white column that was Ruth swayed in panic. "If you keep your eyes open when you sneeze, they explode out of your head."

"No way."

"I read it in a book."

"I don't believe it."

"Fine," said Ruth. "Try. See if I care." She stared dourly out the window. "See if *I'll* pick up your bloody eyes from the floor. See if *I'll* put them on ice while we wait for the ambulance. See if—"

"Okay! Okay! I'll—ah-ah-ah-*choo!*"

I'd closed my eyes.

"*Thank* you," said Ruth.

It wasn't fun, being burrito-wrapped in a curtain that was rapidly coming to resemble the inside of a tissue, but I needed to get a look at Flynn before he got a look at me. A newcomer is big news when you live in a tiny town. And I mean *tiny*: there's not a single person in Camelot who doesn't know me, my parents, and how old I was when I last wet the bed.

(Too old.)

You see, Flynn's mom, our aunt Linnea, is an artist. She won a prize where she gets to study in Paris for a year, and she doesn't have to work in a restaurant, too, the way she does in New York. It was a big deal. Probably a bigger deal,

2

though, was that our cousin Flynn was coming to live with us for the entire school year. It was the most exciting thing to happen in Camelot since Mr. Flick's pig made it to the Sweet Sixteen of the Northern Minnesota Hog Farmers N-C-Double-Oink March Madness Tournament.

"My new best friend is about to get here," I said to Ruth, "and I don't even know what he looks like."

Flynn and I hadn't seen each other since we were Ivan's age, nine years ago. I had no memories of the visit, but Mom sure did. "You didn't get along," she'd said. "You had entirely different senses of fun."

"What do you mean?"

"Flynn was calm. He would sit in a corner and page through books, even though he couldn't read. His favorite toy was a child-sized yoga mat."

"He did yoga?"

"He'd be in downward dog," said Mom, "and you'd be sprinting circles around him, *whumpa-whumpa*-ing, pretending you were a helicopter."

"I bet Flynn's more fun now."

"People are different, Soren. People have fun in different ways."

She'd kept talking, but I'd tuned out. The thing was, Flynn couldn't have been coming at a better time. Alex, my best friend and partner in crime, had moved away at the beginning of the summer, and I was lonely without her. Ruth and I were pals—we'd really bonded since Ivan was born; nothing like a common enemy—and I had other

3

friends at school. But a *best* friend is different. A best friend is your default. Your other half. If you've had a best friend and then not had one, whether because of moves or new schools or betrayals, you know. You know how much it stinks.

"There!" squealed Ruth.

I peered out the window. Ruth did the same. Even Ivan attempted a pull-up to boost himself above the windowsill.

Dad's Honda crawled down the street and stopped in front of our house. Our eyes were trained on the passenger door.

It slowly opened.

A bowling shoe emerged.

An argyle sock.

A cuffed pair of—

"Are those *skinny jeans*?" said Ruth.

Then the other leg, and then the torso: a purple plaid shirt, a black bandanna tied in a jaunty, cowboy-like V.

Longish brown hair, topped by—

"Is that a *beret*?" said Ruth.

And under the beret, a face that looked way too much like mine—

"Is that *Flynn*?" said Ruth.

That was Flynn.

FLYNN HAD TWO pieces of luggage: a messenger bag and a trunk. He handled the messenger bag. Dad heaved the trunk up the walk to the house, his lips pursed into the face that I privately call *if I weren't a dad, I'd be cursing right now.*

Flynn followed, his mouth moving fast. Dad dropped the trunk on the porch and crumpled against a pillar, wiping the sweat off his shiny bald head. As Flynn reached for the doorknob, Ruth and I jumped to get untangled from the curtains.

"Greetings!" Flynn called into the house.

Ruth and I looked at each other.

"You have dust on your forehead," I told her.

"Well, there's *something* hanging from your nose," she told me.

We wiped our faces on our curtains.

"Are we good?" I said.

"We're good."

I'd expected some kid in gym shorts and a ratty T-shirt.

Someone like Alex.

Someone like me.

We went into the entry hall.

"Flynn," said Dad, panting slightly and gripping his lower back, "you remember your cousins. Soren and Ruth."

Flynn extended his hand with a dramatic windmilling move. "Delighted."

"Um," I said, gingerly shaking his hand, "me too."

"Absolutely *delighted*."

"Same," said Ruth.

We stood there. I kicked my left shoe with my right. Ruth fiddled with her pigtail. Dad, who is oblivious to awkwardness, and in fact creates it whenever possible (do not, under any circumstances, allow this man to chaperone your school dance), said, "A family reunion! What a day, what a day!"

Ivan charged into the entry hall, still wielding the Barbie.

"And this," said Dad, "is—"

Ivan crashed into Flynn's legs.

"—Ivan."

"The Terrible," Ruth and I added in unison.

Dad scooped him up. Ivan hates being restrained—strollers, car seats, cribs, he sees them all as the prisons they are—so he started howling. "Oh, shush," Dad said crabbily. "I'm not letting you maul your cousin on his first day."

Flynn flinched. "Don't worry," I told him. "Ivan's relatively harmless. He'll throw food, sure, and toys, especially pointy ones, and he's got really good aim, which is weird, since he'll run right into a wall if there's nothing in his path, but he's not that bad. . . ."

"Lies," whispered Ruth.

"Well?" Dad asked Ivan. "Do you promise not to attack Flynn?"

"WON'T!" hollered Ivan.

Personally, I'd have asked Ivan to specify: Won't attack, or won't promise? But Dad, a hopeless optimist, set him down. Ivan growled in satisfaction.

"Well, well, well, Flynn!" Dad said. "We'll have dinner when your aunt Lucinda gets home, but what would you like to do now?"

"Ruth and I can give you a tour!" I said.

We'd practiced that morning. I was the tour guide, and she was Flynn. She kept saying things like "Wowzers!" And "We don't have chicken coops in New York!" And "How amazing is it that you have a pet piglet?"

It had made us both even *more* excited for his arrival.

"I don't know," said Flynn. "How extensive is this tour?"

"Very," I assured him. "The house, the garage, the chicken coop, the vegetable garden, the tree platform, the clubhouse, the dock, the pigpen—"

"You keep pigs?"

"One piglet," said Ruth. "One adorable, roly-poly piglet."

When our neighbor Mr. Flick had offered us Jim Bob, the runt of the litter, the idea was that he'd live a typical piggy life: gain four hundred pounds, turn into sausage. Then Ruth had gotten attached. She'd rather eat her own arm than a Jim Bob patty.

Her expression had gone all hazy and lovestruck. "One darling pork dumpling, cuddleable, snuggleable—"

Flynn shifted from foot to foot. "I'm not sure about touching a live pig."

"Let's go introduce you two!" said Ruth.

He glanced up at Dad. "It's just, I've been traveling all day. . . ."

Dad jumped in. "Come on into the kitchen. We'll relax, catch up, get reacquainted. May I offer you a Coke?"

RUTH, IVAN, AND I will do anything for Coke. We never get it except for holidays. So we followed Dad into the kitchen like ants following a sugar trail, which I guess we kind of were.

"You pour and we'll choose," I told Ruth. She got down four glasses, and I monitored her to make sure she wasn't pulling the ol' ice cube trick. (You put less ice in your own glass so you get more drink. Ruth is known for it.) "You can have first choice," I told Flynn, like the gracious host I am.

"Actually," he said, "I don't consume corn syrup."

"You mean—"

"I don't want any. Thanks, though."

Ruth, shocked and appalled, stared at Flynn. I must have looked the same way, because Dad said, "*Children!* Manners! Do we stare at our guests?"

"But he doesn't want Coke," Ruth told Dad.

"A healthy choice!" said Dad, clapping Flynn on the back. "Maybe we should *all* cut out corn syrup."

Ruth and I shot each other identical looks of dismay.

"I'll stir up some lemonade instead," said Dad.

"Actually," said Flynn, "I don't consume any sugar. No white sugar, no brown sugar, no corn syrup, no rice syrup, no dextrose, no sucrose, no evaporated cane juice—"

"What's left?" said Ruth.

"I used to eat honey, but then I became concerned for bee welfare. Uncle Jon, may I use the kettle?"

Dad, clearly gobsmacked, gave a nod.

"Would anyone like a hot cup of Japanese green tea?" Flynn rustled around in his messenger bag and pulled out a bag of brown twigs. "It's sourced directly from Mount Fuji."

"DIRT!" cried Ivan. "STICKS!" He beamed—he's used to receiving massive amounts of positive reinforcement every time he uses a word other than *no, won't,* or *don't*—but nobody paid him any attention. We were watching Flynn measure twigs into a tiny strainer.

"I get this at a specialty store called Sereni-Tea," he said. "Back in Brooklyn, of course. I can walk there by myself."

"We're allowed to walk around Camelot by ourselves too," said Ruth.

"It's next door to Spinster, my favorite record shop. And down the street is L'Éléphant—they sell vintage luggage; that's where I got my trunk. Ooh, water's boiling!"

He poured the water into the strainer and set an hourglass on the counter. The sand trickled down. "It steeps for five minutes."

"Couldn't you use the microwave timer?" I said.

"I like to keep the tea ceremony pure."

"I have a feeling this family will learn a lot from you," said Dad.

Flynn smiled in a way that reminded me of this angel ornament we have. Ruth and I call him Little Angel Two-Shoes, and every Christmas Eve we have a secret contest that involves beaning him in the head with peanuts.

The last grains of sand slipped through the hourglass. Flynn crouched to photograph the tea. "Who wants a sip?" he said.

He looked so eager. Round eyes, raised eyebrows, a hopeful smile. He looked from Ruth to Ivan, and I thought,

Fat chance in *those* quarters. They were sucking down Coke like they were being paid by the ounce.

"I'll try it," I said.

I lifted the cup. The steam hit my nose. I nearly heaved. I had to set it down so I could swallow the saliva filling my mouth. The tea smelled, no joke, like a barfy toilet.

But I couldn't back out now.

I took a sip.

"BLECH!"

A warm mouthful of Japanese green tea, sourced directly from Mount Fuji, splattered across the kitchen.

"Soren!" said Dad, wiping droplets from his face.

"Gross!" said Ruth, rubbing her eyes.

"BLECH!" said Ivan in imitation, spitting out a glob of Coke and drool.

I sprinted to the sink and stuck my mouth under the faucet.

"Want me to brew you a full cup?" said Flynn.

"That tasted like pig pee!"

"Manners!" said Dad.

"How do you know what pig pee tastes like?" said Ruth.

"Disastrous game of truth-or-dare—let's not get into it. Flynn, you *drink* that?"

"I think it's good."

But for the first time since he'd arrived, he sounded hesitant.

"It's dead-on pig pee," I said. "Come out to Jim Bob's pen and I'll prove it."

"Unacceptable," said Dad. "Soren, apologize to your guest."

"Sorry, Flynn," I said, "but it's got that *tang*, you know?"

"To your room, young man!" said Dad.

"I don't *have* a room anymore," I reminded him.

"Soren Ebenezer Skaar. *Immediately*."

I whirled around and left.

"Please excuse us, Flynn," I heard Dad say as I stomped up the stairs. "Soren needs to work on his manners."

"I listen to an etiquette podcast I could recommend to him," Flynn said. "Maybe it would help."

CHAPTER TWO

"COCK-A-DOO-ARGH-ACK-ECK-EH!"

I was released from solitary confinement just as Martha, our rooster, decided it was dawn.

"COCK-A-DOO-ARGH-ACK-ECK-EH!"

He starts out with your standard crow, but then he switches to a terrifying hacking noise. It's like he's puking. Or dying. "Good afternoon, Martha," I called, giving the coop a wide berth.

He snarled at me. His wives pecked at invisible bugs. When he was a chick, he looked like our most adoring great-aunt, all fluffy-haired and wrinkly-ankled, so we named him Martha. Then he turned out to be a scrawny old rooster and she stopped being so adoring. Oops.

I dug around in the garage and found the old soccer ball I use for shooting on the woodpile. I shot—*thwop*—and the ball bounded back. The woodpile's almost as good as a friend. Alex and I used to spend a lot of time out here on the driveway, kicking around and plotting our next prank.

Thwop.

It had been sunny earlier, but now clouds were blowing in. Ruth came outside. "Where's Flynn?" I said.

"Taking a nap."

"Voluntarily?"

"He said he wants to be rested for the first day of school tomorrow."

"Oh. Weird."

I passed to her. She did a nice trap and passed back. "Will you tell me?" she said. "Please?"

"Tell you what?"

"I'll keep it a secret. I promise."

"I don't know what you're talking about."

"Tomorrow's the first day of school, Soren." She gave me a significant look. "The *first* day of *school*."

"Do you have to rub it in?"

"Just tell me what you're planning! I'm old enough now. I won't spill to Mom and Dad."

I hit my pass too hard. It went wide, and I had to jog to the chicken coop to get it. When I came back, I said, "Nothing."

"Come on, Soren. What are you going to do?"

"Nothing. I told you. Nothing."

"But you always have an epic prank for the first day of school!"

"Well, not this year."

It had been a tradition, the epic welcome-back prank. Alex and I used to spend all summer planning. We'd had our share of failures (when the thousand live crickets we'd bought online had escaped in her bedroom a week early), but people still talked about our successes (when the trophies for the Kick-Off Kickball Game had been found mysteriously encased in Jell-O).

But now that she'd moved three hundred miles south . . .

"I might have retired from pranking," I told Ruth.

"Yeah, right," she said. "I saw what you put in the salt-shaker last week."

"That wasn't a prank. That was a modest joke. How am I supposed to pull off an epic prank without Alex?"

"I could help," she said.

"You're only nine."

"You pulled off Tapegate when you were nine!"

I smiled despite myself. We'd replaced all the toilet paper at school with rolls of duct tape. "Everyone got stranded," I said reminiscently.

"Not Connor Carraway," said Ruth. "He wiped."

The sky had gone a yellowish gray, and we heard a clap of thunder. "Kids!" Dad yelled out the window. "Tarp the chicken coop before it rains, would you?"

Ruth and I groaned. Our coop's sort of ramshackle. It doesn't have a real roof, just a wire grate. You probably think throwing a tarp doesn't sound too bad, but that's because you haven't met Martha.

The thunder clapped again, a lot louder. "Don't dilly-dally!" yelled Dad.

Ruth shot me a dark look. "Let's get this over with."

We got the tarp from the garage. The chickens, sensing the coming rain, had huddled on the roosts and in the nesting boxes, but Martha was eyeing us. "COCK-A-DOO-ARGH-ACK-ECK-EH!" he screeched.

"He saw the tarp," said Ruth.

I felt a drop of rain on my cheek. As bad as it is to tarp the coop, it's worse to clean it once it's gotten wet. The bedding gets all mildewy, and the chicken poop liquefies and makes paste with the dirt. "Hurry," I said.

We stretched the tarp between us. It was really raining now, drops hitting the packed dirt so hard they spattered up on the rebound.

"Ready?"

We approached the coop. This is the part that's terrifying. Martha *hates* being tarped. So when he sees it coming, he hurls himself against the wire walls of the coop.

And yeah, the walls are going to hold. (Probably.) But if a twenty-pound rooster with ferocious claws and a pointy beak and a high-decibel crow is hurling himself at you, you're going to want to fling yourself out of danger.

The part of your brain that's evolved for survival doesn't think much of chicken wire, is what I'm saying.

"One," we chanted. "Two. Three—"

Martha attacked just as the tarp was sailing toward the coop. Ruth dove to the ground. The tarp got all wadded up. "Sorry," she said.

"I was about to go down myself," I admitted.

"It's a simple task, kids!" yelled Dad. "Just get it done!"

"I'd like to see Dad face down Martha," I grumbled. Our parents don't believe us about how mean he is.

"One," said Ruth after we'd gotten into position. "Two. Three—"

"AHHH!" I launched myself to the ground. I couldn't help it. He'd flown right at me.

"Think about chicken fingers," said Ruth, who looked as pale and shaken as I felt.

"How did we end up with a rooster who's claustrophobic *and* a psychopath?" I said.

"We *dominate* you, Martha!" Ruth shouted into the coop. "We have your kind for *dinner*!"

"One. Two. *Three!*"

We threw the tarp. It landed. We could hear Martha freaking out inside—flapping his wings, pitching himself against the walls, and cock-a-doodle-vomiting while his poor wives clucked—but we were safe. "Come on," said Ruth. We ran through the pouring rain to the house.

CHAPTER THREE

"WHAT A NIGHT!" said Dad over dubious-looking plates of eggplant, couscous, and something stringy and orange. The storm was wailing outside. We had the lights on in the kitchen. Every so often the rain was interrupted by the roar of thunder, the snap of branches, and the distant, haunted screeches of Martha. "We've got a lot to celebrate!"

"A lot to *mourn*," Ruth corrected him. "School starts tomorrow."

"Yes, school starts tomorrow!" said Dad in exactly the opposite tone. "And this morning, Ivan went to music group and didn't hit anyone with his tambourine!"

"DID!" Ivan insisted.

"Well, only me."

"Progress," said Mom, patting Ivan on the head. "Good boy."

"But most importantly," said Dad, "we're welcoming our dear nephew and cousin to Camelot!" He raised his glass. "To Flynn's year studying 'abroad'!"

"And to my gracious hosts!" said Flynn. They clinked glasses. "This reminds me."

He stood.

"I just started playing the banjo." He whipped it out from under his chair.

"Very cool!" said Dad.

"And as a small gesture of appreciation to you—you're so generous, taking me into the bosom of your family—"

I gagged. The combination of eggplant and the word *bosom* was just too much. Flynn waited till I was done coughing.

"—I wrote you a song on the plane. It's to the tune of 'O Little Town of Bethlehem.' I'm a huge fan of using religious songs for more inclusive purposes." He strummed a chord. "May I?"

"Of course, Flynn!" said Mom. "We're honored!"

Another chord, and he began.

> "*O tiny town of Camelot,*
> *Thy fields have lured me in.*
> *This city mouse has found a house*
> *With country mice, his kin!*
> *I'm already enchanted*
> *By rustic, homespun charm.*
> *My city grit, my jaded wit,*
> *Are sweetened on thy farm.*"

"We don't live on a farm," said Ruth.

"Shush," said Dad.

"O peewee town of Camelot,
Where all is sky and tree,
No subway trains mar these great plains,
There's nothing to do but be.
How quaint the prairie seemeth,
When I think of whence I roam,
Yet earthy scents and dirt-cheap rents
Make this my home, sweet home!"

He strummed one final chord and looked up eagerly. "What do you think?"

IF I WERE starting at a new school, I'd be nervous. So after dinner, after Dad told Flynn to skip the dishes, after Ruth and I did the dishes, after we got into a splash fight over the dishes, after we got yelled at for getting water on the floor, after we mopped, I went to his room. Which, until yesterday, had been my room. Now I was sharing with Ruth and Ivan.

I did a double take when I walked in the door. "You rearranged the furniture," I said.

"Do you like it?"

"It's different."

"Thank you."

I didn't really mean it as a compliment, just a comment. He'd put the bed at a diagonal, and the room seemed off-kilter. It reminded me of these Mondrian paintings we'd learned about in art. They're white with lines and blocks, but they aren't symmetrical at all, and though I'm not a neat freak—kind of the opposite, actually—it bothers me.

Flynn was arranging mason jars on the windowsill. "I like to keep these filled with seasonal plants," he told me. "Lilies in the summer, goldenrod in the fall, et cetera."

"I guess that's goldenrod?"

"Your dad took me out to pick it after dinner. You don't know the plants in your own garden?"

Flowers have petals. Weeds are ugly. Don't step in poison ivy. That's about the extent of my plant knowledge. "Why are you doing all this decorating, anyway?"

"I'm very sensitive to my surroundings. My mom says so."

I plopped down on the diagonal bed. "This angle would make me seasick."

"Good thing I'm sleeping here, not you."

It was weird hearing that about my room, but I guessed I'd get used to it. I'd have to. "Listen, about tomorrow," I said. "We're in the same class, so stick with me. I'll introduce you to all the teachers."

"I can introduce myself."

"Sure, but they teach fifth grade too, so I know them really well already."

"In Brooklyn, we start middle school in sixth grade."

"Well," I said, kind of annoyed at his interruptions, "Camelot's not big enough for a middle school. So we have K to six and seven to twelve. Any other questions?" He shook his head. "Okay. Teachers. Ms. Madigan is math. If you raise your hand for the bathroom, she acts all disappointed, so what you've got to do is make a thoughtful comment and *then* ask to go. Ms. Hutchins is science, and she's super intense about lab safety, so I know it'll be tempting, but if we do anything with acid, do *not* pretend to drink—"

"I'm good with teachers," said Flynn. "Adults like me."

"Still, I wouldn't suggest fake-chugging acid in front of Ms. H."

"I've been going to school in New York. I think I'll be able to handle it here."

"But you don't even know where the cafeteria is!" I wasn't halfway through the fundamentals of survival at Camelot Elementary School. "You don't know where detention is!"

"I'm not planning to get detention."

"Yeah, that's what I always say too," I said grimly. "You don't even know which teachers *give* detention. Or which stall doesn't flush, or which water fountain tastes like blood. You don't know what we do at recess!"

"You have recess?"

"You don't?"

"It's considered passé."

I didn't need to ask him what *passé* meant. If he'd let me finish my teacher intros, he'd have known our Language Arts teacher was obsessed with context clues. "I'd quit school if we didn't have recess," I said. "We play pickup soccer. Do you play soccer?"

"I'm on a club team. Well, I *was* on a club team. At home."

"Really?" I said, excited. "That's perfect! I'll draft you for my side."

He had to be good, if he played club. Maybe *really* good. And Billiam Flick wouldn't know how good, and my team would win. And Flynn and I could play on the driveway every day after school, and sometimes maybe we'd get Mom or Dad to take us down to the high school so we could shoot on a real goal. He could show me tricks he'd learned from club, and I could show him tricks I'd learned from YouTube, and I'd have someone to play with all the time. Someone who weighed more than fifty-four pounds, unlike my sister. Someone whose idea of "defense" wasn't smearing the ball with deer poop, unlike my brother.

Someone who lived in Camelot. Unlike Alex.

This school year wasn't going to be so bad after all.

"It's still light out," I said. "Let's go kick around on the driveway!"

"I don't know," said Flynn. "I'm tired. Tomorrow's a big day."

"Oh."

"Hey, um," he said, twiddling a goldenrod stalk, "what are the other kids in our class like?"

"Normal. Well, mostly normal. Some of them. Sometimes."

He twiddled more. Finally, he said, "Do you think I'll have friends?"

"You'll have me."

"Is that it?"

"There haven't been any new kids since the Andrezejczak triplets came in first grade. Everyone's going to be very, very interested in you."

I wouldn't have guessed he was the shy, retiring type, not after what he'd done to that Christmas carol, but he looked terrified.

"Soren!" Mom yelled. "The shower's unoccupied! Now's your chance!"

"What if I don't need to shower?"

"Not an option!"

"But I don't smell!"

I could hear Mom laughing from two floors away. Flynn followed me to the door. "The bus ride tomorrow morning—can I sit with you?"

Maybe he *was* nervous. Or maybe he just wanted to sing me a song. *We three kids of Camelot are / On the bus we travel afar.* "Sure," I said. "You can even have the window if you want. Full disclosure, though: I get carsick on the aisle."

CHAPTER FOUR

CAMELOT ELEMENTARY SCHOOL is a big redbrick building. It has round towers at each corner, and it looks like a castle, except with a playground instead of a moat.

Flynn's banjo case knocked against the seats as we walked off the bus. I hitched up my backpack and gave my hair a quick rub. Mom likes to lick her palm and smooth it down before I leave the house, and this morning I hadn't dodged quickly enough.

"Move faster," Ruth grumbled from behind us. "Some of us have friends we want to see."

I took a deep breath and stepped into the playground, which was already teeming. Ruth shot off.

"Where are *your* friends?" said Flynn.

"Um," I said, "I'm looking."

There was Ruth's pack of fourth-grade girls, already playing double Dutch. There were the cool kids, who all wear the same socks. There were the tetherballers and the monkey-barrers and the climb-the-firepolers and the fun-sized replicas of human beings known as kindergartners.

But where was—

Oh.

Ever since kindergarten, I'd gotten off the bus and looked for Alex. I guess I was so used to it that I'd . . . I'd forgotten.

"Come on," I said to Flynn. Over by the flagpole, I saw guys from my grade: Jéronimo Luna and Freddy Firkins and Marsupial Jones. We play recess soccer together. I go to their birthday parties, and they come to mine.

They're fine.

They aren't Alex.

But they're fine.

They were in a tight bunch, examining something in Freddy's palm. I joined them. Flynn hung back. "What's in there?" I said.

"Mexican jumping beans!" said Freddy. "My uncle gave them to me!"

I craned in. Six brown beans were sitting on his palm. I opened my mouth to ask what was so special about them, and then one of them jumped. It jumped half an inch, right before our eyes.

"Are they mechanical?" I said.

"They've got moth larvas inside," said Jéro.

Another jumped, and another. It was so weird. Just when you thought they were normal dried beans, they'd twitch.

"Wow," I said, imagining the possibilities. "You know how Ms. Hutchins always has that big salad for lunch?"

"So?" said Soup. (His mom is a naturalist; that's how he got named Marsupial. But everyone calls him Soup.)

"So I've got the perfect plan," I said. "We'll send Flynn to the teachers' lounge. If anyone asks, he got lost looking for the bathroom. He opens the fridge, finds her salad, dumps in the beans, and no one's the wiser."

They stared at me. Flynn had edged closer when he heard his name, and he was the first to speak.

"Isn't there a sign on the door of the teachers' lounge? Wouldn't I know it's not the bathroom?"

"You're not going to get in trouble on your first day at Camelot. Oh, hey, everyone, this is Flynn. My cousin. Flynn, meet Jéro, Freddy, and Soup."

They nodded.

"Back to the plan," I said. "Flynn? Try first period, because that way if you're redirected, we'll have three more chances before lunch—"

"I'm not feeding my beans to Ms. Hutchins," said Freddy.

"She wouldn't eat them. She'd be *about* to eat them. They'd be on her fork, and then ..." I gave a sudden, twitchy hop in my best impression of a Mexican jumping bean. "Imagine her face!"

"I like my beans," said Freddy. "I want to see the moths hatch."

"They're pets," said Soup.

"Would you put a dog in Ms. Hutchins's salad?" said Jéro.

"Besides," said Flynn, "I think I can find the bathroom."

"You're all missing the point," I said.

Alex would have understood. Alex would have called my

idea and raised it. Who *knew* what would have happened? Things tended to spiral out of control when Alex and I worked together.

How would I ever prank again without her?

PHWEEET! PHWEEET!

Mrs. Andersen whistled on her knuckles to call us inside.

"HELLO, HELLO!" said Ms. Hutchins. She's our homeroom teacher and our science teacher, so we have her for seventy minutes first thing in the morning. I like Ms. Hutchins. She's pretty chill, except when it comes to veganism and science. "I hope you all had a wonderful summer." She smiled, pretending she'd missed us the way they make teachers do. "Who did something exciting?"

"I went to Washington, D.C.," said Jeremiah Johnson.

"I went to the mall in Duluth," said Goldie Grandin.

"I got Mexican jumping beans," said Freddy, spoiling the prank once and for all.

"I got chicken pox," said Tabitha Andrezejczak.

"Chicken pox is extinct," said Jéro.

"Not for me," Tabitha said proudly.

"I always knew you were a mutant," I whispered.

Tabitha rolled her eyes and whispered back, "Nothing's as mutant as your face, Soren Skaar."

"Soren!" said Ms. Hutchins. I jumped. "I believe something exciting happened to *you* this summer!"

"Uh . . ."

My summer: Kicking a ball against the woodpile. Playing

27

Settlers of Catan with Ruth. Seeing what Ivan would and wouldn't eat. Rereading Harry Potter, all sad because the Fred to my George had moved away.

What was Ms. Hutchins talking about?

"Would you introduce our new student?" she said.

Oh!

Flynn was perched on the edge of his seat, his feet tucked up on the rung. "Yeah," I said, "so that's my cousin."

"Soren! Where's our Minnesota politeness? Let's hear a real introduction!"

I coughed. "Ladies and gentlemen, please allow me to present *the* Flynn Skaar, straight outta Brooklyn." That got a laugh, even though Alex would have said it was overused. "Flynn likes . . ." Uh-oh. What *did* he like? "He likes banjo, green tea, soccer, and—"

"Science!" said Flynn. "I love science!"

Ms. Hutchins beamed. "Flynn," she said, "why don't you tell us a bit—"

He was already on his feet. Here was something else Flynn liked: an audience. "Hello, everyone!" he said. "I'm thrilled to be here in Camelot for my sixth-grade year! I hail from New York, and I'd be happy to answer any questions you might have about life in the city."

The class was staring, openmouthed. So much for him acting nervous last night.

"Soren's right, I'm currently a banjo-tea-soccer kind of dude, but my passions change a lot. Let me give you my usernames so you can keep up."

We aren't allowed to have phones or iPods or anything in school, but he spelled them out, and Goldie wrote them down. And if Goldie does something, other girls do it too.

"Long story short," said Flynn, "Adidas over Nike, pita chips over potato chips, Yankees over Mets. That about sums it up! That's me!"

He popped into his seat. "I like pita chips too," Goldie whispered.

"Well, *I* like the Yankees," said Freddy.

"You do not," I reminded him. When they'd swept the Twins last year, Freddy had bought a Baby Ruth bar just to smash it to a pooplike pulp on his driveway. "You hate the Yankees."

Nobody paid attention to me. "Pinstripers, unite!" said Flynn, giving Freddy a high five. He turned to Goldie. "Potato chips are just too greasy, right?"

Goldie and Freddy looked extremely pleased with themselves. Everyone else looked jealous.

"The grease is the good part," I said. I was ignored.

Luckily, nobody was paying attention to Ms. Hutchins, either, and she had a lot more power. "Class!" she called, clapping her hands. "Class! Quiet, please! No video announcements today since we'll have an assembly later, so let's dive into our course material. This is our sixth-grade theme!" She gestured to the banner strung above the whiteboard: THINK LIKE A SCIENTIST! "Who can tell us what that might mean?"

Dead silence.

Finally, Soup raised his hand. "Do we get to wear safety goggles this year?"

"We'll see," said Ms. Hutchins wearily. "Anyone? What does it mean to think like a scientist?"

"Follow the scientific method," said Emily Garcia. "Ask questions, gather background information . . ."

"Absolutely." Ms. Hutchins turned to the whiteboard. "Let's start with a quick review of the scientific method. And yes, you should be writing this down."

It was going to be a long year.

CHAPTER FIVE

WE WERE WELCOMED home by Martha. "COCK-A-DOO-ARGH-ACK-ECK-EH!"

"Is that normal?" said Flynn.

"For Martha, yes," I said. "For roosters, no."

"I've got to visit Jim Bob," said Ruth. "He's been missing me all day. Want to come meet him, Flynn?"

"The hog?"

"The American Yorkshire piglet," she corrected him. "He'll love you! He's so friendly."

"I don't like pigs," said Flynn.

"You've never met a pig like Jim Bob."

He hesitated.

"Are you scared?" I said.

"No!"

"Come on!" said Ruth. "I'll let you feed him his bottle!" She grabbed Flynn's hand and began dragging him to the pigpen. He looked at me the way a shipwrecked rat looks at a piece of floating timber.

"Flynn probably needs a snack," I told Ruth. "I'm starving."

"Me too," said Flynn, shaking himself free.

"Your loss!" said Ruth.

We turned toward the house. "I was a bit scared of Jim Bob before I met him," I said. "Because you should see his mom, Mr. Flick's prize sow. Her name's Hercules Mulligan and she weighs six hundred pounds and snorts like a rhino."

"Stop," Flynn moaned.

"But Jim Bob's nothing like that." I considered the facts of life as I opened the kitchen door. "Well, not yet."

In the kitchen, Ivan was banging a spoon on his high-chair tray. Dad was reading a seed catalog, which he threw down upon our entrance. "Soren! Flynn! All hail the conquering students! How was school? Tell me all about it!"

After a day at home with Ivan, Dad gets way too excited about humans who can talk in full sentences. "It was fine, thanks, Uncle Jon," said Flynn.

"Details!" cried Dad.

"Our classes were good. But I think I've already learned a lot of the stuff we're doing in science."

"Flynn won Scientificopardy!" I said.

"Bless you!" said Dad.

"No, Scientificopardy! A review game Ms. Hutchins invented. *Jeopardy!* plus fifth-grade science, minus prize money."

"Well, well, well!" said Dad. "Congratulations!"

"The questions weren't that hard," Flynn said modestly.

Maybe not for him. *I* found them hard. Over the summer, I'd forgotten everything I'd ever learned about igneous versus sedentary-or-whatever rocks. I couldn't name a single parasite besides Ivan, and I knew King Philip Came Over, but for what, who the heck knew? But Flynn had nailed every one.

"And guess who's my lab partner?" said Flynn.

"Who?" asked Dad.

"Hint: she assigned them alphabetically by last name."

"And that means . . ."

"Dad," I said, "me and Flynn have the same last name."

"Oh!" Light dawned. "The Skaar Science Squad! Eh? How's *that* for a team nickname?"

"Love it," said Flynn at the same time as I said, "Yeah, I don't think so."

"Lucky Soren," said Dad. "Partnered with the champion of Scienti-Scientifo-Scientisto—er, the review game! So what else happened? Outside of the science classroom?"

"We had auditions for music groups," said Flynn, patting his banjo. "Mr. Brandoon was very impressed, he said, but I guess there aren't banjo parts in band music, so I have to do Intermediate Choir."

"I got Intermediate Band," I said from inside the refrigerator, where I was digging for after-school sandwich ingredients. I play the trombone. Badly.

"I'm going to ask Mr. Brandoon if the choir and band can work together to perform one of my original songs." Flynn strummed a chord. *"Roosters we have heard on high / Sweetly crowing o'er the plains."*

"Maybe for the holiday concert!" said Dad.

"My goal is to have a full concept album by the end of the year. *O Strum, All Ye Faithful,* I think I'll call it. What do you think?"

"I can't wait to hear the whole thing," Dad said. "Ivan! Play with Gloria or eat your tomato soup! Not both!"

"SWIM!" yelled Ivan.

Dad, sighing, took away the soup, but not before Ivan had dipped in his favorite Barbie headfirst. I lidded my sandwich. "This is a work of art," I said.

"Soren," said Dad, "offer your cousin half your sandwich."

"I think it has corn syrup."

"Offer," said Dad through gritted teeth.

I had just taken a massive bite. "Ouldoo ikaffuh myanditch?"

"Huh?" said Flynn.

I stuck my jaw forward and, feeling like a rattlesnake who'd done well for himself, swallowed. "Would you like half of my sandwich?"

"That's okay." He eyed it. "I've lost my appetite."

I didn't see the problem, myself. Peanut butter, banana, marshmallow, and pickle on sourdough. Every major food group was represented.

"PLAY!" yelled Ivan.

"I'll play with you," said Flynn. "Hi, Barbie!"

"BARBIE NOT BARBIE!"

Flynn didn't even know what the Barbie's name was. "He calls her Gloria," I said. "After the baby sister in the Frances books. Right, Ivan?"

"IVAN NOT BABY!"

"Uh, you missed the point, dude."

Flynn leaned in. "Hi, Gloria!"

"He likes to throw her," I said. "I'd be careful if I were you." Ivan glowered at me.

"Will you play with me, Gloria?" said Flynn.

Ivan regarded him suspiciously.

"Glo-Glo-Gloria!" said Flynn. "Will you take me on a tractor ride?"

We don't even own a tractor.

"Will you give me a farmland tour?"

Ivan giggled.

"I can play too," I told Ivan. "Gloria! Want to go for another swim in the tomato soup?" I tugged at the Barbie's leg, but Ivan only grasped her more firmly. "Come on, Ivan. Give her to me. Swim time, Glo!"

"NO!"

I yanked. Ivan yanked back.

"Fine." I returned to my sandwich.

"Oh!" said Flynn. "Soren—watch out—"

I glanced up just in time to see Ivan's eyes narrow and his arm rear back in a windup. Gloria winged through the air. She spun toward me, limbs akimbo, drops of soup pinwheeling from her hair—

She hit me right in the eye socket.

"Gloria!" said Flynn, all fake shocked. "Who taught you to fly?"

And Ivan, that little traitor, he giggled. Again.

CHAPTER SIX

OVER THE COURSE of the next week, my black eye went from black to purple to blue to orange to green. "*What* happened?" said Jéro at lunch on Tuesday.

"I told you. I got kicked." I hadn't mentioned that a Barbie had done the kicking. "But you should have seen the other guy."

I'd broken off Gloria's leg.

When we got freed from the cafeteria, we all milled out to the—well, I won't say *field,* but it's a field*ish* thing, 90 percent dirt, 10 percent scrappy weeds that try so hard but get stomped down every day at 11:35 a.m. Recess soccer's fun, though sort of stressful because there's no ref. That means when there's a dispute, whoever yells the loudest wins.

We rotate captains. That day it was me and Billiam Flick. He said, "I'll take Freddy."

"Hmm," I said. I tried to look like I was deciding, even though I already knew. "I'll take . . . hmm . . . Flynn."

"*Him?*" said Billiam.

After a week of school, I'd finally convinced Flynn to make his recess soccer debut. Nothing he'd done so far would make anyone think he'd be good at soccer. He'd worn a lot of skinny jeans and swirly shirts and caps, and he'd won another review game, Who Wants to Be a Scientistionaire?

"Him," I repeated.

"O-*kay*," said Billiam, skeptical. "I'll take Randall."

"Goldie," I said. She jogged over and low-fived Flynn. They were friends now.

We picked the rest of the teams, and I took the kickoff. I tipped it back to Jéro, who dribbled a couple of yards and paused, looking up for the pass. Freddy and Randall converged.

"Look at Soup!" I yelled.

Jéro passed. Soup thinks he can dribble, but Kiyana stole the ball from him in about half a second. She took it up the line. Then, in a streak of paisley, appeared Flynn.

I don't know how he did it. One second Kiyana was whizzing up the wing; the next, Flynn was whizzing in the opposite direction. He dodged Randall, and he dodged Freddy, and he glanced up even while he kept moving full tilt ahead. Poppy Moore was posted in the center. He crossed the ball to her. All she had to do was stick out a foot. The ball ricocheted into the goal.

I blinked.

"Goal!" shouted Goldie.

"Goal?" said Poppy. "I—I—scored?"

"You *scored*!" yelled Flynn.

"I *scored*!"

Usually she spends the whole game braiding clover.

"Get back in position," I called. "No time for celebration."

Billiam kicked off with a long pass to Jack. Jack tried to get it to Randall, but again Flynn intercepted. He dribbled around Randall like Randall was a cone—they do kind of look the same—and he crossed a high floater to Soup, who'd been keeping pace down the field. Soup leapt and headed it into the dead center of the goal.

"Brilliant!" cried Flynn.

Next he assisted Goldie, then Jéro, then me. We gave up one on a penalty kick after Poppy accidentally handballed, but we were still winning 5–1.

PHWEEET! That was the two-minute warning. Billiam kicked a clod of weeds. "Let's quit now."

"We're playing to the end," I said.

Jack tapped it to Freddy. Flynn, with a burst of speed, was on him. He had the ball. He took off toward their goal, the ball staying on his toes like it was glued there. Billiam approached. With a flick of his foot, Flynn megged him. Billiam tripped over his own feet and crashed to the ground. Flynn didn't even look back. Randall and Jack were advancing, but Flynn threaded the needle between them.

"Yeah, Flynn!" yelled Jéro.

He reached the grassy spot near the goal. In a last, desperate attempt to stop him, Freddy went for the slide tackle. Flynn wasn't fazed. He jumped over Freddy, caught the ball on the other side, and casually slotted it into the corner of the goal.

"FLYNNIE!" cried Goldie in glee.

"I've never seen moves like that in real life," said Soup.

"He's related to *you*?" Billiam said to me.

PHWEEET! PHWEEET!

My team gathered around Flynn. *Both* teams gathered around Flynn. They were beaming. They tugged at his sleeve and slapped him on the back. That's what you want to do when you see something amazing. You want to touch it. If you see a cupcake frosted like a Lego or a caterpillar that looks like a squishy string of beads, you want to reach out and touch it with your very own hand. Touching it makes it real.

We tromped back inside, pushing sweaty reefs of hair off our foreheads, jangling into a line for the water fountain. Everyone was happy and excited but me. I hung to the back.

CHAPTER SEVEN

"HE'S REALLY GOOD," I told Alex when we video-chatted that night. It was the first time we'd talked since school started. "He's way better than the rest of us. Which could be bad, but he's not a ball hog."

"At my new school there's not enough playground space for soccer," said Alex. "Everyone just hangs out by the fence."

"There aren't monkey bars or anything?"

"Well, there are, but sixth graders are too old."

"That's a school rule?"

"No. That's just what everyone says."

It sounded awful. "Do you miss us?" I said. "I mean, Camelot?"

Alex scowled. Our Internet was being slow, so she got all jerky whenever she moved. "Well, obviously."

"Oh. Sorry."

"My new school's a lot bigger. There's like three hundred sixth graders. I only know a few people."

"Weird." I knew all the kids at Camelot. I knew their birthdays. "Do you have any friends?"

"Kind of." She adjusted her screen. Her face turned into a pixelated mess. "Mostly people don't even know my name. I'm just the new kid. But there's this nice girl who's in my reading group. Her braid's so long she can sit on it."

Seemed to me that could cause trouble on the toilet. "Cool."

"I'm going to see if she wants to be my new pranking partner."

That made me feel weird. It wasn't like I wanted Alex to be alone, but I didn't want to be replaced *that* fast. "What are you guys going to do?"

"Probably we'll start with some good old-fashioned Post-it-ing."

"Classic." We'd done it to Ms. Hutchins last year. What you do: You take a couple of packs of Post-its and you cover the teacher's whole desk, like it's a fish and the Post-its are scales. Cover the chair, too, if you have enough. And the lamp. Everything. It looks hilarious. Even Ms. Hutchins had laughed. "That's nice that you get to do all of our old pranks over again."

"It's the only good thing about moving." She pushed her glasses up her nose. She'd gotten new ones, purple and thick-framed. "I'd be really bummed out if it weren't for that."

I almost told her I wished she'd move back—like, I *really* wished that, all the time—but I figured (a) she knew and (b) it wasn't like she got any choice in the matter. So instead I said, "Everyone'll know your name as soon as you do a prank."

She straightened and smiled. "True."

"I think I'm retired from pranking, myself."

"What? Soren! No!"

"It's no fun without you. And too hard."

"Have you even tried anything?"

"I need a new team first," I said. "Or at least a new partner."

She frowned, her eyebrows blundering down in slow motion. Stupid Internet. "Who? One of the soccer guys?"

I remembered how Freddy and Soup and Jéro had reacted to my idea with the Mexican jumping beans. "I don't think so. No."

"The Andrezejczak triplets?"

"I don't know."

"They like making trouble. And they live next door to you."

"But they're mostly friends with each other." Not to mention, they were intimidating. They moved in a pack and had their own language made up of eyebrow raises and weird acronyms. It was common knowledge that you didn't want to find yourself on their bad side. Get one Andrezejczak, get gotten by all three.

"Well, you should find a new partner. You're not going to feel like yourself unless you're pranking." She was being so encouraging. It was the total opposite of my automatic jealousy of Nice Butt-Braid Girl. "What about your cousin?" she said.

"Flynn?"

"Could he be your new partner?"

"Soren!" yelled Mom from the other room. "Time to get off the computer!"

"You said I could have it till eight!"

"Flynn needs it for homework," she called. "You know the rule."

This is the rule, which is terrible: whenever someone needs to do homework, they can kick you off immediately. What Ruth does, she does five minutes of online math and then switches to a game, and unless you stay to watch over her shoulder you don't even know.

"But we don't have any computer homework!" I yelled.

"At my new school," Alex said from the screen, "we always have computer homework."

Flynn appeared in the doorway. "I want to type my Language Arts answers," he told me.

"Mom! He could just write them! I'm talking to Alex!"

"It's the rule, Soren!" called Mom.

"I like to go above and beyond," said Flynn. "Typing is more professional."

"You know that question you just asked?" I said to Alex. *What about your cousin? Could he be your new partner?* "The answer is no." I x-ed out of the chat and left the computer, and the room, without meeting Flynn's eyes.

WHEN WE WERE in third grade, Alex and I were caught planting plastic ants all over the teachers' lounge. Mean Ms. Rue was the one who discovered us, and it turned out she had an ant phobia. We got dragged, actually dragged, to Principal Leary's office.

Want to know what kind of friend Alex was? "It was all me, Principal Leary," she said. "My idea, my ants. Soren was in there because he was trying to stop me."

I started to protest. She pinched me under the desk. "I take all the blame," she said.

Later, she didn't even let me thank her. "It was the sensible move," she said. "*One* of us should have a clean record."

"I'll pay you back someday," I said, but we were never caught again, so I never had the chance. Now I probably never would.

That was Alex. My best friend. Nobody would ever replace her. Nobody would come close.

CHAPTER EIGHT

"GUYS! GUYS! SIXTH GRADERS!" Ms. Hutchins is nice, so nobody's on best behavior in her class. "Sit down, Kiyana! Marsupial, now is not the time to hop around the room!"

She finally got everyone settled. Fanning her armpits, she said, "What's our theme for the year, class?"

"'Think Like a Scientist,'" read Emily and Poppy from the banner above the board.

"Precisely!" said Ms. Hutchins. "And to practice the scientific method, we're going to do a class experiment where we'll all investigate this question."

She clicked on the projector.

DO PLANTS GROW TALLER WITH WATER OR WITH COKE?

We got with our lab partners to make hypotheses. "What's our background information?" said Flynn.

Finally. Something I knew more about than he did. "Once I saw Ms. Hutchins and her wife at the grocery, and they were buying fifteen pounds of kale. Plus a bag of carrots so big Mr. Karlssen was keeping it with the livestock feed."

"So?"

"They *juice*."

"And?"

"Ms. H is a vegan foodie health nut. There's no way she'd have her class do an experiment that makes Coke look good."

"That's your background information?"

"Mark my words. The plants that get water are going to do way better. Look at her desk! Just look!" Among the bazillion photos of her dog and her wife, Ms. Hutchins had two huge metal water bottles. One said FOR THE PLANET and the other said BECAUSE PLASTIC WILL KILL US ALL.

"A pure scientific experiment," Flynn began, "is unbiased, not going for one outcome or another. . . ."

I snorted. "So you want to hypothesize that Coke is better for plants?"

"Well," said Flynn, backpedaling, "all that acid in soda, it can't be good for their roots."

"Great. We agree." I grabbed our worksheet and wrote, *Hypothesis: Coke will kill the plants, but water will make them grow big and tall.*

"When you're done, guys," yelled Ms. Hutchins above the din, "come fetch your seedlings!"

The baby bean plants were growing in cardboard egg cartons. Each lab group got two to repot in cottage-cheese containers. The classroom became pleasantly chaotic. Dirt was flying everywhere. Flynn labeled masking-tape strips *COKE* and *WATER*. He had cool handwriting. He even gave the letters little feet, like a font on the computer. "Decision time," I said. "Which plant do we doom with Coke? And which plant gets to thrive with water?"

"Technically, we shouldn't know which is which," said Flynn.

Soup poked me with his ruler. "What'd you guys put for your hypothesis?"

"Duh," I said. "Water."

"We put Coke," said Jéro, his partner.

"Coke had better win," said Soup. "Then my mom'll have to let me drink pop all the time."

"Um, humans aren't plants," said Flynn.

"Yeah?" said Soup.

"So you can't take a plant-based experiment and apply the results to humans. By that logic, we'd do best if we stood around in dirt, facing the sun."

"Plenty of people spend recess that way," I said.

"Take your initial measurements!" Ms. Hutchins shouted. "Be precise!"

Everyone hunkered down over their plants. Flynn and Soup and Jéro could think what they wanted, but I *knew* Ms. Hutchins, and right now, that was way more important than knowing about sugar or acid or photosynthesis. She'd never do an experiment that made Coke look healthy, and she wouldn't care that it was just plant-based, either. We'd probably have to write a whole paragraph on the prompt "If Coke can kill a hardy bean plant, what do you think it can do to you?"

Unless.

Unless the experiment somehow turned out the other way.

"Soren!"

I jumped. My eyes had gone out of focus. Flynn gave me a strange look. "I said your name like six times!"

"Sorry. Daydreaming, I guess."

"Here." He handed me a beaker. He'd just returned from the fluid station with our two-ounce allotments of Coke and water. "Let's feed these guys."

"Wait," I said quietly. "Wait."

HERE'S HOW IT would have gone with Alex.

Me: "Wait. Wait. I have an idea."

Alex: "Oh. *Oh!*"

I wouldn't have even had to explain. It was an obvious prank. Simple and brilliant. We'd sneak into the classroom and sabotage the plants. We'd make the Coke plants grow, feed them water and fertilizer. We'd slowly kill the water plants. Pinch their stems.

I could imagine the whole thing: getting all nervous and excited and heart-poundy while we sabotaged, trying not to laugh in class when we heard things like "I don't know why my water plant is dying so fast!" and "Wow, Ms. H, plants really like Coke, huh?"

It would have been amazing.

I GUESS I was tricked by how amazing it *would* have been, because even though I 100 percent knew it wouldn't work, I tried it out on Flynn.

"Sabotage?" he said. *"Sabotage?"*

"Keep your voice down, okay?"

"But—Soren—this is *science*!"

"Shush!"

Ms. Hutchins was roaming the room like a hungry vulture, on high alert for illegal activity. "Milton DeVoe!" she yelled. "That Coke is for your bean plant, not for you!"

Flynn waited for her to pass. There were blotchy pink splotches on his cheeks. He gestured at the banner. "Think like a *scientist*, Soren. Science is about truth! What would happen if scientists faked experiments?"

"Never mind," I said.

"Medicine! Engineering! Food! Technology! We wouldn't be able to rely on anything! The modern world is built on trust in science—"

The splotches were getting worse. "I get it," I said quickly. I didn't want Ms. Hutchins to catch wind. "It was a bad idea."

"You can say that again."

"It was a bad idea."

Flynn groaned. But even that only cheered me up a bit. What I was thinking as I counted leaves: How had everything changed so fast? I used to have a best friend who'd have happily killed plants with me, but she was gone. As far as my life was concerned, she was a bunch of choppy pixels on a screen I wasn't even allowed to use very often. She was off in Minneapolis with a new pranking partner, and me? I was here. I was here with Flynn.

CHAPTER NINE

IF YOU'RE A bug, the last thing you want to do is fly past a hungry frog. Well, that was me walking through the kitchen on block-party day. Mom flicked out her long tongue and I was stuck.

"You can either peel the oranges or open the cans of pineapple," said Mom. "But you have to do one."

"Pineapple." At least opening cans involves a cool gadget. Peeling oranges is death to my thumbnails. "What are you making?"

"What are *we* making. Jell-O salad. A lot of it."

Jell-O salad, in case you don't know, is the best salad, because there's nothing green in it (unless you're making lime). It's basically a lot of canned fruit suspended in Jell-O—like those insects that got caught in amber at the end of the dinosaurs—that you douse with whipped cream. "Did you get Reddi-wip? Can I do the spraying?"

"If we ever get to that point," said Mom, who was boiling three pots of water. "I've never made Jell-O salad for a hundred. But how much harder can it be than making it for ten?"

"Probably ten times harder."

"Thanks, Soren. Very helpful. Hey, where's your cousin?"

"No clue," I said morosely.

"What's all this?" Mom always picks up on tone. Sometimes it's nice, like if you want some attention and your other parent is busy keeping your baby brother from eating a matchbook. Sometimes it's annoying. "Something on your mind?"

"Nope."

"School okay?"

"Yep."

"You've done your homework for the weekend?"

"Of course . . ."

She turned on the faucet to run cold water.

". . . not," I whispered.

She turned off the tap. "How's school treating Flynn?"

"He loves it," I said. "And it loves him."

"Good. Here. Stir." She dumped in the boiling water, and I stirred in the powder. We were making the Jell-O in the biggest pot we had. It was practically a cauldron. When Ruth and I played Baba Yaga with Ivan, we made him sit in it so we could pretend to cook him. "This year must feel very different to you."

"Yeah. Even though I have the same teachers."

"Sometimes when things stay the same, the big picture feels even more different."

How did she know? "Maybe."

"Is Alex planning a visit soon?"

"I don't think so. Because of her mom's job." Mrs. Harris cuts hair. Here in Camelot she'd worked in a salon, but the reason they'd moved to Minneapolis was so she could start her own business giving haircuts in people's homes. It was called Ubercut. There was an app and everything.

"Right," said Mom. "It's hard to take time off when you're just starting. Have you talked much with Alex?"

"We *were* talking. But the computer got snatched. We haven't been online at the same time since." I gave the Jell-O water one last stir while Mom ripped open a huge bag of ice. "It'd be a whole lot easier to keep in touch," I added, "if I had a phone."

"Not a chance, whippersnapper. Nice try."

"Flynn has a phone."

"That's his mother's decision. *Your* mother says no."

"*Mo-om* . . ."

"You see that contraption on the counter over there? Black? With the buttons? Specially engineered to fit from ear to mouth?"

"*Mo-om.*"

"Free to use, anytime you want."

"That's not a *real* phone."

You'd think Mom would be pro-technology, given that she designs websites for a living. She tossed in the ice. The Jell-O water sloshed and overflowed. "Darn it," she said, grabbing the spoon. "That'll be sticky. Listen. Soren. Your whole life doesn't have to change just because Alex moved. I'd bet you she's still doing the things she likes to do down in Minneapolis. And you can keep doing what you like to do up here."

What Mom didn't get was that to do the things I liked to do, I needed Alex. I couldn't pull off a massive prank alone. I couldn't even pull off a micro prank alone. And nobody wanted to work with me. Look how fast Flynn had shot me down on the first day of the plant experiment.

"It's okay to be sad. Someone's gone who was a big part of your life, and now your life's different. That's tough, honey."

Things had been weird the past few months. I guess tough. Nothing was wrong, but nothing was that fun, either. Like a Pop-Tart with no frosting or sprinkles. Better than nothing, but.

"Give me back that spoon," I said. "I can stir."

"First," said Mom, "come here."

She squished me in to her. It made me feel like a little kid again. Mom doesn't touch us much. Which I appreciate, honestly, because so often as a kid you just get prodded, patted and petted and poked, so it's nice to have someone who gets that even though I've got a mini body, it's still *my* body.

But the occasional Mom hug is gold. It always makes me cry. And the other great thing about being hugged really tight is that you can wipe your eyes and/or nose on the person's shirt and they never even know.

"Okay," she said. "That's enough. Stir."

CHAPTER TEN

WE LIVE ON a dead-end street, not a block, but we've been having this party for as long as I can remember. It's a good time. Some adults grill, and some get competitive with desserts, and there's a bike-decorating contest and a watermelon-seed-spitting contest, both of which Ruth dominates, and there's chalk and bubbles and cornhole and Bruce Springsteen. The grown-ups are too busy chatting to keep track of how much pop you're drinking, and the food is amazing. Last year Mrs. Andrezejczak made this thing that was like s'mores in a casserole dish, all these layers of chocolate pudding and graham crackers and marshmallows. I had so much that I threw up in Mr. Flick's pigpen, and then his pigs ate it, but, frankly, it was so good I didn't blame them. And it's not like it was all that digested.

"Oooh!" squealed everyone when Ruth showed up with Jim Bob. "He's *so* cute!" Some of the boys tried to hold back, the ones who care about being tough and not-so-secretly think boys are better than girls, but you could tell they wanted to ooh and aah too.

Jim Bob was lying stomach-up in Ivan's old stroller, and Ruth had dressed him in baby clothes: a ruffled bonnet with holes for his ears and a onesie that said *iPood* under the Apple logo. He looked highly pleased with himself.

"Can I hold him?" asked Goldie.

"Sure." Ruth hauled him out of the stroller.

"How much does he weigh?"

"Eight pounds," said Ruth, chucking him under the chin. "Still a wunt, aren't woo, my wittle sparewib?"

"I *need* a picture." With her spare hand, Goldie wriggled her phone out of her back pocket and handed it to Flynn. "Smile, Jim Bob!"

"Stunning," Flynn pronounced. "Give that a classic filter and you won't believe the number of likes you'll get."

Flynn was as popular as Jim Bob, and he didn't even have to wear an *iPood* onesie to get there. He'd made friends. Real friends. He'd gone over to Goldie's after school on Friday, and they'd eaten pita chips, he'd said, and watched this old movie called *Clueless.*

"I want a picture too!" said Kiyana.

"I already called next!" said Evelyn.

The ladies-in-waiting follow Queen Goldie—that's what Alex used to say. So Flynn was automatically friends with Kiyana and Evelyn and Tori. *And* all the boys liked him. He made them look so good at soccer that he was impossible not to like.

"I'll be the official photographer," said Flynn. "And if you don't have a phone, I'll get them on mine and send them to you."

Flynn was fine. Flynn was great. I just didn't need to line up to get my photo taken with Jim Bob. I lived with Jim Bob. We could do an uncle-nephew picture anytime. I dropped back and sat on an overturned recycling bin. "Are we even going to play Spud this year?" I wondered.

"Why would we want to do that?" said Olivia, the smallest Andrezejczak triplet. She's randomly two inches shorter, even though they're supposedly identical. That's because Lila and Tabitha were stealing her food back in the womb.

"Because we always play Spud at the block party? Because it's fun?" said Tabitha. "Round them up, Lila."

Lila's lips were drawn. "They're busy. We'll wait."

Me and the Andrezejczak triplets were the only ones not into the photo shoot. "Maybe we're getting too old for Spud," I said. I got the feeling the *Vocabulary Workshop* book calls *melancholy*. The block party would be over soon, over for a whole other year, and it wasn't even that fun anyway. It was like a banana-flavored Tootsie Roll. Gross but also too small.

"They'll want to play soon," said Lila.

"The only thing they want to do is take pictures with Flynn," I said.

"They just have to get the newcomer out of their systems," said Lila.

"I wish I could get the newcomer out of *my* system," I said without thinking.

"That's mean," Lila told me, but Tabitha looked interested.

"I thought Flynn was a good guy."

"He *is* a good guy." I wished I could take back what I'd said. "I meant Jim Bob."

"Oh," said Lila. "Yeah, I bet it's no fun to have to shovel out his pen."

"Exactly," I said. But Tabitha gave me a laser-like look, one of those beady-eyed beams of observation straight out of an alien movie, the kind that does a quick brain probe and knows just what you're thinking and why. That's the thing about Tabitha: she's an alien. Just kidding. The thing about Tabitha is that she notices. Everything.

"Flynnie!" cried Goldie, so loud that I looked over. "Your turn for a pig pic!"

"That's okay," said Flynn.

"You *have* to! It'll be *such* a great photo!" She thrust out Jim Bob. Flynn shied away. Jim Bob squawked.

"Whoa!" said Ruth. "Support his neck!"

"I don't want to hold him right now," said Flynn.

"But when else would you use the pig emoji?" said Goldie. "It's your turn!"

"I just don't want to."

He was turning red, a blush that trickled all the way down the collar of his black V-neck shirt. I decided to save him. And myself.

"Hey, everyone!" I yelled. "Who wants to play Spud?"

"Me!" said Tabitha.

"I call captain!" said Billiam.

"You can't *call* captain!" said Jéro.

In the hubbub, Ruth returned Jim Bob to his stroller. "I'm taking him home," she told me. "He needs a rest."

"Good idea," I said. "You're not bringing him back, right?"

"Nah," said Ruth. "Enough excitement for one day." She tucked a baby blanket around his head so only his snout and eyes showed. "Right, my wittle bacon bit?"

"Soren!" called Tabitha. "You just got picked! You're on Billiam's team!"

I ran back over. Flynn poked me. *Thanks,* he mouthed.

"Huh?" I said. "Come on. Do you know how to play Spud?"

CHAPTER ELEVEN

THE BELL RANG. Ms. Hutchins pulled down the projector screen. We have announcements in homeroom, and a few years back they switched to a live video broadcast. It was supposed to be a great technological innovation, but all it really means is that we have a daily betting pool on Principal Leary's necktie.

Today it was patterned with tiny pencils. "Good morning, students and teachers," he said from behind his desk. "Lots of announcements this Friday morning. The Safety Patrol will meet after school in Mr. Doyle's room. . . ."

Jéro flipped through his records. He wants to be a bookie when he grows up, so he runs the Video Announcements Necktie Betting Pool. You propose your bet to him ("Red on Tuesday," "New tie any day this week," "Three consecutive days of stripes"), and he calculates odds and keeps a massive spreadsheet with the running totals.

". . . anyone interested in playing basketball this winter should see Coach Compton for a training schedule. . . ."

I hadn't made any bets yet this year, so I wasn't too invested. But it's always fun to watch my classmates' faces as they win or lose fortunes. Chloe Ting looked really upset. She's the worst gambler in the class, and I think she's addicted, too. Meanwhile, Milton DeVoe was bouncing lightly in his seat, looking pleased with himself.

". . . and the Rubik's Fanatiks will meet during lunch in Ms. Rodney's room for a special cube-greasing event," Principal Leary said. "WD-40 will be provided."

He set down the paper. "One final note regarding behavior in the lunchroom." I sighed and tuned out. I know *how* to behave in the lunchroom, even if actually behaving in the lunchroom is sometimes a different story.

Alex and I never got to do this prank we'd imagined, where we'd hack into the school network and interrupt Principal Leary's announcements with some other video. We hadn't decided what we'd show: she wanted a call to revolution; I wanted baby pandas on a slide. We hadn't figured out how to hack the network, either, but the Internet has instructions for everything.

I sank down in my seat. I'd never pull it off without her.

"Food is to be eaten, *not* thrown," said Principal Leary. I probably couldn't even pull off a food fight without her. I looked around the classroom. Chloe was frantically sorting a pile of nickels and pennies. Jéro was scribbling odds on his bookie notepad. Flynn was patting his hair, which he'd gelled this morning, I'd noticed, and Goldie, Kiyana, Evelyn, Olivia, and Tori were all sneaking looks at Flynn. Everyone else looked bored.

Nobody else looked like they missed Alex.

That, I thought, was the weirdest part of this year. It was like I was the only one who'd noticed she'd left.

"Bus your tray when you're done eating," said Principal Leary. I'd heard this lecture so many times I could mouth along. "And check around your seat for debris," we both said, him out loud, me with just my lips.

I'd never make it through a year like this.

Something had to change.

Your whole life doesn't have to change just because Alex moved, Mom had said. *Keep doing what you like to do.*

Fine, I thought. I would.

AFTER SCHOOL, WHILE Flynn and Ruth were still stuffing their faces with Dad's special stovetop pepper popcorn, I went to the computer. Alex was online. "Hey," I said, feeling a rush of relief even to see her face. *"Hey. So."*

"What's up?" she said. She was eating a granola bar.

"I have to prank. I have to."

"I knew you'd get there," she said. "It's like pooping. You can only hold off the urge for so long."

I kind of wanted to keep exploring the comparison—school was obviously the toilet, but what was the toilet paper? What made it smell? Did Alex and I have prankarrhea?—but I had more important things on my mind. "I had an idea in science," I told Alex. "Help me figure out how it'll work?"

Alex set down her granola bar. "Gladly," she said.

It felt like riding a bike on the first warm-enough day in

the spring. Back at it, and it was just as good as ever. I told her my plan. "You need detention," said Alex.

"Right!" Detention means you have to clean whiteboards. "Brilliant."

"You'll be alone in the classroom—"

"Left to my own devices—"

"Do something bad enough that you get detention twice a week," she said. "For, say, three weeks. It's got to be pretty bad, but don't accidentally get suspended."

"Good point."

She gave a happy sigh. "This is awesome."

"Yeah, I just wish—"

I shut up, but not fast enough. We both knew what I was going to say. It killed the mood. It reminded us that this was *actually* like riding a bike on a random warm day in February, when a blizzard's on the way.

"How's *your* prank?" I said.

"Oh," she said, "fine. I guess. You know the girl in my reading group?"

"Ol' Butt-Braid?"

"Yeah, her. *Sophia.* I told her about it, but she didn't even get excited. She was just like, 'Oh! Goodness gracious! I can't risk getting in trouble!'"

"She actually said that?"

"Pretty much. Not those words, but you know."

"Weird."

"No, I like her. But I'm not pranking with her." Alex started crumbling the half-eaten granola bar.

"Go it alone."

"I don't know if it's worth it."

"You've got a great idea. It'll kick off the year."

"I don't know."

"Just do it. You've got the Post-it notes already, right? Sneak in during recess. I believe in you."

"Maybe."

"You can't hold it in. Remember? You said so yourself. Like pooping."

That got a small smile.

"It's unhealthy to hold it in," I said. "You'll get a stomach-ache."

"True," said Alex. "Constipation kills."

CHAPTER TWELVE

THE SETTING: A lunchroom in the basement of a school in Camelot, Minnesota. There's a hot-food line, tables, garbage cans, and signs Student Council made that say, in big bubbly pink letters, *Throw Out Your Trash or Else* You're *Trash!* It smells like ketchup and sweat.

THE TIME: 11:22 a.m. Smack-dab in the middle of fifth- and sixth-grade lunch.

THE ENEMY: Mrs. Andersen roams the room, and Principal Leary stands at the doors with his arms crossed. The rest of the teachers are at the faculty table, highly distracted by their conversation, which is probably about something super fascinating like, I don't know, mortgages.

THE HERO: Soren Skaar sits at a sixth-grade table. He—
I—

—said, "Hey, is anyone not going to drink their milk?"

"You can have mine," said Freddy, tossing me his pouch. We used to have milk cartons, but they switched to pouches to save money and room on garbage. You just poke in your straw and suck it down. It was weird at first—you felt like a

64

hummingbird stabbing its long beak into a flower—but we got used to it.

"Thanks." I punctured Freddy's pouch with his straw. I'd already set up mine.

"What are you doing?" asked Soup.

"Nothing."

"Is this . . ." His eyes lit up. "Does this have something to do with *Alex*?"

I told you. She's legendary.

"I don't know what you're doing, dude," said Soup, "but I know I'm a fan. Here. Take mine."

"Thanks."

I set up Soup's pouch right next to Freddy's. Now was the moment. Principal Leary and Mrs. Andersen were far enough away that I'd have some time before I got tackled, but close enough that they'd know it was me. Three weeks of Tuesday/Thursday detention, that was my goal.

I positioned the first straw.

Three.

Two.

One.

With the flat of my hand, I squished the milk pouch.

Thwsssst!

There was a faint whistling sound. A stream of chocolate milk shot out and arced through the air. My mouth fell open. I'd wanted to do this since day one of milk pouches, but Alex and I had a strict rule: we were never bad for bad's sake. We were bad only in service of the greater good.

"Ew!" squeaked Billiam from the other table. "Hey!"

"Whoever's doing that, *stop!*" cried Kiyana.

"There's milk on my shirt!" yelled Jeremiah, plucking it from his chest.

"THERE'S MILK," yelled Goldie at the top of her lungs, "ON MY *FISH STICKS!*"

That got everyone's attention.

The boys at my table were pointing and laughing, but I didn't let myself get distracted. Calmly, coolly, I squashed the next bag. The milk shot out. "AHHH!" yelled Poppy and Emily, leaping out of the way.

"SOREN!" bellowed Principal Leary. He and Mrs. Andersen were advancing upon me, but it was hard for them to get through all the chairs and legs that blocked the aisle as kids dove for safety. "STOP THAT!"

Three weeks of detention, I reminded myself.

Not one week. Not two weeks. Three.

I locked eyes with Principal Leary, and I squished the last bag.

The arc of milk wasn't pointed at him, but it crossed the path he'd have to take. There was no way around it. Mrs. Andersen hung back, but Principal Leary gritted his teeth and sprinted through the milk stream just like you'd sprint through a sprinkler. When he got through, he had a dribbled streak of brown across his white shirt.

"It's washable," I told him. "I checked."

"Soren," he said, panting from either sprinting or rage, "go to my office. *Now.*"

CHAPTER THIRTEEN

I HELD MY breath as we walked in the kitchen door after school. So far, everything had gone perfectly. I'd gotten my three weeks of detention, and I'd cleaned up the lunchroom during recess. I was just hoping Principal Leary hadn't called home.

Dad spun around from the stove. I was braced for him to tell me to report to their bedroom for a serious conversation, young man, do not pass Go, do not collect an after-school snack, but instead he said, "Hello, schoolchildren!" Phew. Normal. "Hello, rational speakers of English! I am *so* pleased to see you!"

"Hey," we said.

The whole room reeked of play dough. You know how. Like French fries except off. Dad was cooking up a new batch in the wok.

"PLAY WITH PLAY DOUGH!" Ivan shouted from the table.

"Ooh!" said Flynn, settling down next to him. "What color do I get?"

67

"FINNIE GET BLUE!"

"What do I get?" asked Ruth.

"ROOFIE GET RED!"

"What about Sorie?" I asked him.

Ivan eyed me, absentmindedly massaging a glob of purple play dough into his left eyebrow. Finally he said, "SORIE NO GET!" He cackled.

"Fine. I don't even want to play." I went over to the stove. "Hey, Dad," I said quietly. "I signed up to help Ms. Babbitt with sets for the winter play."

"Wonderful!" said Dad. "Thrilled to see you taking an interest in the theater!"

"Er, right," I said, shifting from foot to foot.

"Backstage, though? I wouldn't have expected a Skaar to shy from the spotlight."

"I love the spotlight," said Flynn from the table.

"We know," I muttered. Dad gave me a lips-pursed, head-tilted look, the one that tells you you're on thin ice.

"So," I said, looking at my feet, "I'll need to stay after school Tuesdays and Thursdays."

"Okay."

"For the next three weeks."

Before he was a stay-at-home dad, Dad was a lawyer. He says all his lawyerly skills are permanently encrusted beneath a layer of diapers and carpools and vomit and *Hop on Pop*, but sometimes they peek out. "Three weeks?" he said, eyebrows rising. "And then never again?"

Oops. I hadn't thought of how weird that'd sound. "She

wants to get most of the building done before the rehears-als really get going, so the actors won't be in danger. . . . Hammers, you know. . . ."

I've never been good at lying under pressure. Alex and I used to practice, but the practice hadn't helped. I still babbled.

Ivan saved me. "IVAN NEED BROWN!" he shouted.

"Just a sec, Soren," said Dad. The best four words in the world. "Ivan, you want me to dye the new batch *brown*? Are you sure? What about a nice, autumnal orange?"

"BROWN!" insisted Ivan.

"You could make autumn leaves! Or pumpkins!"

"IVAN NEED BROWN!"

"Fine," sighed Dad. "Soren, help. What primary colors make brown?"

"All of them," I said. "Just dump them in." If I've learned anything from art class, it's how to make ugly colors.

When we'd kneaded the new batch smooth and let it cool, I took it over to Ivan. I peered at their projects: Ruth was making a set of mini fruits; Flynn was making a dude playing a banjo; Ivan was making a mess. "Is that a self-portrait?" I asked Flynn.

"I'm thinking it has good potential for my album cover."

"Ah."

"You should make something, Soren," said Ruth.

"Am I allowed?" I asked Ivan.

"SOREN SIT!" he yelled.

"Really?" I was touched. My baby brother wanted my

company. Flynn was okay and all, but I guess it just wasn't the same without me.

"SIT!" Ivan said.

"I'm going to make a model of Lionel Messi," I said, pulling out the chair.

I sat.

Something squished.

Ivan cackled.

I jumped up and felt my rear end. It was damp with a huge clod of play dough, which, I saw as I attempted to peel it off, was from the new batch. A rich, fruity brown.

"Ivan!"

Ruth and Flynn howled with laughter. Ivan joyously banged a spoon. I scraped brown play dough off the seat of my pants.

"Did I get it all?" I asked Ruth.

"Spin. . . ."

As my butt passed Ivan, he yelled, "FEE SEES!"

"What?"

"SOREN FEE SEES!"

"What? You see fees? Fee sees? Who is Fee?"

"Oh," said Dad, abashed. "I'm sorry, Soren. I taught him that word today."

"Fee? Like an admission fee?"

"We were discussing polite language, but I'm not sure anything sank in except that one word. . . ."

"What word?"

"FEE SEES!"

"Um," Dad said delicately, "I believe he's saying *feces*."

Ruth and Flynn resumed howling, but even louder. "I'm leaving," I said.

"IVAN LIKE FEE SEES!"

"Ivan *is* a fee sees," I muttered.

I could hear them laughing all the way up the stairs.

CHAPTER FOURTEEN

MR. JACKSON, JANITOR and very nice guy, looks exactly like Andrew Jackson, the guy on the twenty-dollar bill. Hairdo and all.

He (the alive one) gave me a bucket of rags and a spray bottle of whiteboard cleanser. "Now," he said, "you do not want to ingest this board cleanser. Pure acetone. It'll eat you from the inside."

"I'm not going to drink whiteboard cleanser, Mr. Jackson."

"That's what they all say," he said darkly, "but I've been in this business for a few years. I knew a kid once—No-Hit Norman, they called him, best pitcher Camelot Elementary ever had. But he got thirsty cleaning the board, and instead of visiting the water fountain . . ." Mr. Jackson shuddered. "No-Guts Norman, that's how he was known ever after. He was a shell of his former self. Literally."

"Got it, Mr. Jackson."

"If it were up to me, the most dangerous thing you kids

would hold would be a No. 2 pencil. Not that No. 2 pencils can't cause serious damage. Are you old enough to recall Perfect Pamela? No? On track for sixth-grade valedictorian, quite a student—until, that is, she became Perforated Pamela. . . ."

If I didn't start now, I'd never get to Ms. Hutchins's classroom. "I'll be extremely careful, Mr. Jackson," I assured him as I headed off down the hallway.

"And you watch out for those rags!" he called after me. "The stories I could tell you about rags!"

I gave him a wave as I turned the corner into the kindergarten zone. The teachers were gone, their rooms dim and dustily quiet. I worked my way up the classrooms, youngest to oldest, cleaning the boards as fast as I could.

Finally, I got to Ms. Hutchins's room.

I was nervous. But it was a familiar feeling. I'd felt the same way before every prank we'd ever pulled. My hands quivered. My knees melted. My stomach churned like a washing machine, and my heartbeat went as hard and fast as Tabitha Andrezejczak on the snare drum. Everything was sharper, brighter, like the world was a YouTube video that had suddenly adjusted to HD. Alex used to feel the same way.

We both loved that feeling.

I went straight to the windowsill. A tidy line of forty-eight bean plants leaned toward the sunshine.

I darted a glance over my shoulder.

No movement, no sound from the hallway.

73

I lifted the spray bottle. I hit the first plant labeled *WATER* with a good spray of cleanser. "Pure acetone," Mr. Jackson had said. If it could destroy the intestines of a star pitcher, what would it do to a twiggy bean plant?

One after another, working quickly but carefully, I sprayed every water-fed plant. Then I got a watering can and watered every Coke-fed plant. Done.

I headed to the side board with the cleanser, and not a moment too soon.

"Hey there, Soren!" said Ms. Hutchins.

I jumped. "Where did you come from?"

"Oh, just grabbing—now, where did they go—aha!" She waved a manila folder of quizzes. "Almost forgot them, but what's an evening without a stack of grading? Come on, I'll walk you out. Leave the supplies. I'll get them to Mr. Jackson tomorrow."

Phew. Close call.

"That's your dad picking you up?" she said once we were outside.

"Yep."

Dad rolled down the window. "Evangeline! Hello."

"Good to see you, Jon! Angelica and I have missed you at yoga class lately!"

"Yeah, I've had my hands full with this one." He nodded back to Ivan, snarling in his car seat. "Takes after his big brother."

"Uh-oh," said Ms. Hutchins. "Well, come to yoga anyway. Ditch the kid; get your Bikram on—"

"IVAN NOT KID!"

"Really, sweetie?" said Ms. Hutchins. "What are you?"

"IVAN TIGER!"

"It's a phase," Dad said wearily.

"I understand why your yoga practice is—er, on hiatus."

"Eighteen-year hiatus."

"You know," mused Ms. Hutchins, straightening to stretch her back, "there are definite perks to being a teacher."

"Sending them home?"

"Exactly." She waved. "See you tomorrow, Soren. Don't let your brother bite anyone's leg off!"

She thought that was pretty funny. I think it hit too close to home for Dad and me. He turned on the radio, but it didn't drown out Ivan's growls.

CHAPTER FIFTEEN

"NEVER, IN MY ten years of teaching," said Ms. Hutchins, "has an experiment gone so poorly."

Nobody was supposed to hear that, I don't think. She muttered it to herself as she walked among us, watching us measure our Coke plants (as green as a rain forest) and our water plants (the gray-yellow that Ruth turns when she reads in the car). "Are you *sure* you've been treating your plants according to the labels?" Ms. Hutchins asked me and Flynn. "The Coke one's getting Coke? The water's getting water?"

"Of course," said Flynn, his face cloudy. He gently shifted a leaf to measure the water plant's full height, but the stem was so brittle it broke. The leaf wafted to the floor. "I don't understand it."

"I don't either," said Ms. Hutchins. "It's almost like someone—but no. Couldn't be."

Flynn shot me a look. I put my face close to the ruler I was using to measure the Coke plant. "Seven inches," I said, "and one, two, three, four, five of these little tick marks, um, so, five-sixteenths—"

I could feel myself blushing. Alex always told me I needed to control my blush better. We used to practice that, too, throwing accusations at each other and seeing how long we could make it before we cracked. I was never very good.

"I guess it's just one of those things," said Ms. Hutchins.

"Guess so," said Flynn, but even with my face buried in the ruler, I could tell he was still looking at me.

I GOT AN email from Alex that night:

> So, I took your advice and just did it. I snuck in during recess. The math room was empty. I covered half the desk in Post-its, and then the teacher walked in.
> Not good.
> I hate this place.
> I really hate this place.

That was the whole thing. I checked, but she wasn't online. I wrote back:

> WHAT?!?! NOOOOO!!!!!!

She wasn't online the next night either, and she hadn't responded to my email. I kept checking all weekend, and she never wrote back and never signed on.

. . .

WHEN I LEFT my last Tuesday detention, Flynn was alone on the playground, juggling a soccer ball. Left knee, right knee, right heel, up and over, bump from the forehead, left knee, roll down the shin to the toe— "Oh, hey," he said, doing a little jump move to catch the ball between his knees.

"Why are *you* here?"

"Same as you. Waiting for your dad."

"Yeah, but why are you *here*?"

"Mr. Brandoon was helping me arrange one of my original songs for choir and band. He's pretty into the idea."

"Cool."

"Yeah." He passed me the ball. We kicked around for a few minutes, ranging over our weedy-dirty field. When my pass went wide, he ran for it and dribbled back, but he didn't pass. "Hey," he said. "Mr. Brandoon and I were in the Fine Arts office."

"So?"

"So," he said, still not passing me the ball, "I was giving him a preview of 'Jim Bob, the Red-Nosed Piglet,' my latest. You want to hear it?"

"Not right now." The way he was holding on to the ball, it was making me nervous. I did a few butt kicks just to have something to do with my body. "Then what happened? Pass."

He passed. "Well." I trapped the ball between my feet. "This lady walked in. Tall and really pale?"

I kicked him the ball. "I think you're talking about Ms. Babbitt. She's the drama teacher."

"Figures. Because she said, 'What a day, Barry, what a day! Children! *Children!* I am exhausted!' Then she collapsed onto the table. Not really collapsed. It was all fake."

"That's Ms. Babbitt for you. She's very dramatic."

Flynn started to juggle again. "She stayed in the office for the rest of our meeting. She ate a whole king-sized chocolate bar and moaned occasionally, but mostly she was on her phone."

"I'm not surprised." I couldn't figure out the point of the story. I saw our Honda at the stoplight down the block, and I said, "Dad's here."

Flynn tucked the ball under his arm. I slung my backpack over one shoulder and we walked to the pickup circle. "Well, *I* was surprised," he said delicately, "because I thought you were staying after school to help Ms. Babbitt build sets."

Oh.

Oh.

"I—I was—she told me what to do and then left, probably went straight to the Fine Arts office. . . ."

There I went again, babbling whenever I tried to lie. That was my main tell. Alex always fiddled with her glasses. Hers was more obvious, but mine was harder to stop. All she had to do was sit on her hands.

Dad pulled up. "Don't tell Dad," I said hurriedly. "Please, Flynn."

"What have you been doing, then?"

"I got detention. You know. The milk thing. I didn't want to tell Mom and Dad. I've been cleaning classrooms."

"Alone?" said Flynn. "Have you cleaned the science room?"

He was looking straight ahead, his profile tipped to the sky, but I could tell he knew.

"I don't care what you tell your parents," he said. "But the *science*, Soren. How could you?"

"It's funny," I said weakly.

We were right by the car. Flynn stopped. "You have to tell Ms. Hutchins."

"No!"

He wrapped his fingers around the handle to the front door. I guess he was getting shotgun. "Either you tell her," he said, "or I do."

"Flynn! You *can't*!"

"What I can't do is let someone mess with a scientific experiment." He opened the door. "Uncle Jon! Thanks so much for the ride! How are *you* today?"

CHAPTER SIXTEEN

TUESDAY IS EXPERIMENTAL Food Night at our house. I dawdled over Dad's latest: broccoli slaw with peanuts, tofu, and a spicy peanut-ginger dressing. It wasn't as gross as it sounds, but it involved a lot of chewing. "My voice teacher in New York gave me a bunch of exercises that strengthen the facial muscles," Flynn told me as I massaged my jaw. I was still at the table with half my dinner while everyone else bustled around me, cleaning up the kitchen. "I can pass them along if you'd like."

"Soren's just trying to get out of cleanup," said Ruth, shooting me an evil glare from the sink.

"Am *not*!" I said.

"To ensure domestic tranquility," Mom said smoothly, "we'll leave Soren the drying and putting away."

They were all in the living room by the time I finished eating. It sounded like they were playing charades. It sounded fun. I marched over to the mountain of clean, wet dishes stacked by the sink, and the same questions that had been racing around my head for hours did another lap.

Was Flynn actually bothered that I was messing up the experiment? Or was he a tattletale looking for an excuse?

Would he tell Ms. Hutchins? Or should I call his bluff?

What would Alex do?

And what had happened to Alex, anyway?

I glanced at Dad's laptop. I was risking trouble—I hadn't asked permission *or* finished the dishes—but before I knew it, I'd abandoned the sink and dried my hands on my pants and signed in. (Everyone knows Dad's password is "fr33d0m" plus the year Ivan graduates from high school.)

Finally! She was online. I clicked on her name and she picked up right away. "Where *were* you?" I said. "Oh my gosh, Alex, I have so much to tell you. Are you okay? What happened?"

"I got caught."

"Right, you said, but—"

"My parents took away my screen time. Since grounding wouldn't make much sense for someone who has no friends."

"That's not true! You have friends!"

She ducked closer to the screen. "I hate it here, Soren. I. Hate. It. The math teacher, she got all mad at me for wasting Post-its! Which I bought with my own money!"

"What better use for Post-its *is* there?" I agreed.

"She made me stack them neatly so they could be reused. And then the vice principal called my mom."

"What did the other kids think of the prank? Did they laugh?"

It was probably the Internet being crappy, but her eyes looked all blurry, and there was a tiny chance she was crying, or about to. "She caught me too fast. I had all the Post-its restacked by the time they came in. All they saw was me being sent to the office."

"It's okay," I said. "It's a minor setback. You'll do something better."

"You only get one first prank, one time when no one suspects you, no one's on the lookout—and I wasted it."

That first part was true. After Alex had confessed to the plastic ants, she was always at the top of Principal Leary's suspect list, and some suspicion rubbed off on me because I was her friend. Luckily, my parents were oblivious. Once, my mom had to wash Silly String out of my hair, and she didn't say a thing.

Alex said, "My mom's training new employees right now, but she says that as soon as she trusts them with Ubercut, we can drive up for a visit."

"Really?"

"It'll be short, she said, but I can spend the whole afternoon with you. We should prank together. Since I'll never pull off anything here."

"Yeah, maybe," I said. "Unless I've been caught out too."

"How are the bean plants?"

I took a cautious look around, but all I heard was guessing and laughing and clapping from the charades game in the living room. "Fine. Except. Well. What would you do if . . . if someone found out about your prank?"

"You're getting blackmailed?"

"He said he'll tell Ms. Hutchins unless I tell her first. But I don't even know if he's serious."

"Who?" said Alex. "Soup?"

"No, no—"

"Billiam Flick? He *would* be a blackmailer."

"He would," I agreed, "but no, not him—"

"Well, then, who?"

"It doesn't matter. What should I do?"

"Poison," said Alex. "Just kidding. Pay him? Persuade him not to tell? Blackmail him back? If you'd tell me who it *is*— WHAT, MOM?"

She turned away. I heard footsteps from my end too. Flynn popped into the kitchen. "Just getting a special treat for the charaders!" he trilled. "Wait. Why are you on the computer?"

Alex came back. "It'd be a whole lot easier for me to help if I knew— OKAY, MOM, JUST A SEC—"

"I thought you were drying the dishes," Flynn said.

"I *was*," I told him. "I *am*."

"Great," he said. "I'll keep you company."

"Soren?" said Alex. "My mom's making me get off. Quick, tell me who—"

Flynn came up behind me to peer into the screen. "Who's that?"

"Yeah, who's *that*?" said Alex.

I had no other option: I slammed the computer shut.

"Was that a girl?" said Flynn.

I glared at him. "I don't need your company."

He straightened. "Okay. I'll leave."

Every time I'm mean, I feel awful about it two minutes later. It's that two-minute window that's the problem.

"Do leave," I said. "Stay out of my life."

He left. I finished the dishes. Two minutes passed, and I felt awful. I went upstairs and lay on my bed. Our house is small and the walls are thin, and I could hear them playing charades, rounds of clapping and laughing, Ivan yowling in joy. He probably got to act out being a tiger. That's his favorite thing in the world to do, especially when he gets to bite Mom's leg. The five of them, they sounded like a family. I looked at the cracks in the bedroom ceiling. In my old room there was a turtle, but here I didn't know the animals yet. I bet Flynn didn't see the turtle. It took a while to find it. You had to squint. It was the kind of turtle that only came out if it really, really felt at home.

CHAPTER SEVENTEEN

PRINCIPAL LEARY APPEARED on the projector screen. "Good morning, students and teachers. We've got several announcements this morning. Art Club will meet during lunch in Mr. Rilling's room. . . ."

Soup whispered, "*Stunning* tie."

It looked like a blackboard, and down the front it said *A B C* in wobbly, chalked letters.

"He's worn it before," whispered Tabitha. "Last April, I believe."

Jéro busily tabulated the Video Announcements Necktie Betting Pool results. "Ouch," he said, glancing at Chloe. "She's got a problem."

I peered at his notes.

"She's down like seven bucks," he said. "She should just cut her losses. But no . . ."

He pointed to her name. *Polka dots all month,* it said. *Odds: 80–1.*

"I think she's trying to win back all her money at once," said Jéro.

Chloe was slightly teary as she scrawled a note for him. *Put it on my tab. New bet: Christmas tie tomorrow.*

It was only October.

"Five hundred fifty to one," said Jéro.

Leary was still droning on. "If you'd like to audition for the winter play, *Alice in Wonderland,* you can sign up in Ms. Babbitt's room. The Library Helpers will meet after school today for a fun hour re-alphabetizing the picture books. That's all. Thank you. It's a lovely day for learning."

Ms. Hutchins snapped up the projector screen. "Class," she said.

Her left eyebrow had a slight twitch.

"We need to have a serious discussion," she told us.

I couldn't believe it. Flynn had told her.

"A *serious* discussion."

We all sat up straight and opened our eyes wide and solemn, trying to look innocent. Ms. Hutchins angrily paced under the THINK LIKE A SCIENTIST banner. I wished she'd decided to talk to me alone instead of calling me out in front of the whole class. "I have received information that's *very* disturbing," she said. I craned forward to see the paper in her hand, but it was folded too small to see the writing. "Someone in this class—one of our very own—has made a disastrous decision."

I tried not to squirm. She was really building this up.

"The results of our Coke-versus-water experiment have been severely compromised. *Someone*"—she waved the paper—"has tampered with the bean plants. *Someone* has sabotaged our experiment."

"Who?" asked Billiam.

I could feel the flush starting. I'd gotten in trouble before, of course, but always with Alex. This was different. I was all alone, and soon everyone in the class would turn toward me—

"I don't know," said Ms. Hutchins. "It was an anonymous tip and it named no names. But I've done a quick soil survey, and I have reason to believe it's correct."

"But why?" said Poppy. "Why would someone do that?"

"All I can say, guys, is not everyone cares about scientific integrity," Ms. Hutchins said sadly. "Science speaks the truth, and that's why I love it. It has no agenda, no motives. And scientists have a sworn duty to add their contributions, however tiny, to the mass of human knowledge, to what we have learned to be true about the universe."

The class was enthralled. She sounded like a teacher in a movie. I wondered if she'd written out the speech beforehand.

"But," she said, and took a long pause, "*but,* this can't happen when someone chooses to spoil science for everyone else."

She had the whole class shaking their heads.

"We'll need to abandon our bean-plant experiment. What a waste of time and resources. It's a shame."

She turned to find a whiteboard marker, and I glanced at Flynn. He was gazing forward, so innocent-looking it didn't even seem like he was trying to look innocent. He probably thought I'd be grateful that he hadn't told her it was me.

Well, I wasn't. I wouldn't get in trouble, sure. But my prank was still ruined. My harmless, hilarious prank.

Ms. Hutchins wrote *Scientific Ethics* on the board. "Who can explain why ethics play such an important role in a scientific experiment?"

There was a strip of air between Flynn's seat and Flynn's butt; that's how hard he was raising his hand. "An experiment without ethics means nothing," he said. "If scientists cheat on their results, we can no longer trust science."

"Exactly!" crowed Ms. Hutchins. We all relaxed. She'd come down from that red zone of teacher anger. "And if we cannot trust science, then what, class?"

"We're no longer human," intoned Soup.

Ms. Hutchins gave him a weird look. "I was thinking more along the lines of losing confidence in the medicines we take, the foods we eat . . ."

"Right," Soup said quickly. "That's what I meant."

"Ethics are essential in science," said Ms. Hutchins. "And sadly, unethical procedures are rampant. Many experiments are sponsored by someone who is set to profit. Did you know that nearly every study about the benefits of milk is funded by the dairy industry?"

Ah, the vegan agenda we'd come to know and love. Flynn nodded along.

"I've changed the plans for our next unit," Ms. Hutchins

told us. "We'll be exploring scientific ethics! It's a fresh look at our theme, 'Think Like a Scientist.' We owe a lot to our anonymous informer."

What about our anonymous culprit? I wanted to ask. We owed a lot to *him,* too.

CHAPTER EIGHTEEN

THAT NIGHT WAS Make Your Own Taco Night. I filled three shells with meat and dumped on cheese and sour cream and salsa. Dad had put out some vegetables, but I never bother with those.

I risked the target seat next to Ivan's high chair, since he seemed too busy packing his nose with guacamole to throw anything at me. "Flynn!" Mom called up the stairs. "Dinner!"

Flynn scooted into the kitchen. "Ooh! Is this farm-fresh zucchini?"

"Picked it today," said Dad. Gardening is his stress relief. He hauls out the playpen, plops in Ivan, and weeds for hours. "We had a bumper crop."

"Tragically," said Ruth.

Dad eyed her. "What was that, young lady?"

"*Magically,*" Ruth said smoothly. "I've always thought zucchini has a magical taste, you know."

"Really," said Dad.

91

"Magical like Bertie Bott's Every Flavour Beans," I said, trying to help her out.

"Yeah, the booger-flavored one," Ruth muttered to me.

"Excuse me?" said Dad.

"The *sugar*-flavored one," said Ruth.

"Zucchini *is* a rather sweet vegetable," said Dad. "You've got a very sophisticated palate, young lady."

Ruth basked. Flynn filled his tacos with so much zucchini he'd never get them closed. I'd been avoiding him since science class. I'd played Quidditch instead of soccer at recess, even though running around with a broom between my legs was obviously not going to end well, and I'd dawdled on the walk home from the bus stop so he and Ruth could get ahead.

"Well, Flynn," said Dad, "your mother Skyped me while you were at school today."

I watched Flynn. He didn't even perk up. He just swallowed his bite and said, "Oh?"

"She misses you, but she's doing well. She sold another tapestry."

"Yeah, she texted me," said Flynn.

There were times when I wouldn't have minded being thousands of miles away from my parents, but Flynn always seemed weirdly nonchalant about the whole business. Maybe he was used to it since his dad moved to Berlin when Flynn was a toddler. I guess Ruth was thinking the same thing. She said, "When's the last time you saw your dad?"

"He visits New York every year, just about," said Flynn. "But we're not really that close."

"Are they still officially married?" I said.

I got a scowl from Mom, but Flynn didn't seem to care. "Yep," he said. "I guess why bother getting a divorce if you don't have to."

"Would you guys bother getting a divorce?" Ruth asked our parents.

"That's not in the picture, honey," Dad said at the same time as Mom said, "Yes."

He glared at her.

"Hypothetically," she added. "If we were in the same situation as Flynn's parents. Which we're not, Ruth."

"Hmph," said Dad.

"I see," said Ruth.

Dad turned grumpily to Ivan. "Ivan, we don't put salsa in our ears."

"IVAN LIKE SALSA!"

Grimly, Mom began to excavate Ivan's ears. A strained silence fell. Flynn was the only one who didn't get the message. He hummed as he drizzled hot sauce over his zucchini mountain.

The tune sounded a lot like a Christmas carol.

"So!" I said. "I have a question. A hypothetical question."

"Some of us," Dad said pointedly, "seem to enjoy hypothetical thinking."

"*Honestly*, Jon," huffed Mom.

"Say you see someone breaking a rule," I said. "But it's not hurting anyone. Would you tell?"

"Ooh," said Dad. Nothing cheers him up like a good ethical dilemma. "Is there such thing as a victimless crime?"

"Never," said Mom.

"Well, *that's* simplistic," said Dad.

"Maybe it seems like you're not hurting anyone," she said. "But when you dig a bit deeper, you'll no doubt find that you are."

"But what if you're making people happy, too?" I said. "More people than you're hurting?"

"And what about questioning authority?" said Dad. "Civil disobedience? Principled rebellion? Do we *want* to raise a child who unthinkingly accepts every rule handed to him?"

"I don't think we're in any danger of that," said Mom, just as Ivan cackled.

Stupidly, I looked over.

"Hey—no—don't throw tha—" I said.

He nailed me in the forehead with a loosely packed ball of ground beef and sour cream.

"Ivan!"

A rivulet of sour cream trickled down my cheek.

"Straight to the bathtub, boys, both of you," said Dad, his voice tight. "And I am putting *you*, Ivan, straight to bed after that."

"NO! DADDY WON'T!"

"I'd like to see you stop me," said Dad. He stripped off his shirt in preparation for handling Ivan. I took off mine and used it to wipe my face. I was furious. At Ivan, technically, but really at Flynn. As I walked by him on my way out of the kitchen, I gave his chair leg a good hard kick. He jolted forward. Zucchini fell off his fork into his lap.

"Oops!" I said in a totally fake voice. "Sorry! I'm such a klutz!"

Dad was busy getting Ivan into an armlock, but I was sure Mom saw. She didn't say anything. Moist chunklets of meat slid down my neck. I got to the shower as fast as I could.

CHAPTER NINETEEN

"RUTH, SOREN," said Dad when we got home the next day, "I'd like you clean the chicken coop this afternoon."

"Nooooo," Ruth and I wailed in unison.

"Do not whine," said Dad. "You two took responsibility for the chickens, and part of responsibility is not whining. In fact, I'd like you to do it now. Before snack, before homework."

Flynn slunk around the corner. "I'll help."

"Thanks," said Ruth, "but you don't want to do this job. Help us some other time."

"But I want to help you guys now," said Flynn. He glanced at me. Did he look nervous? Eager? Both? It reminded me of him with the green tea, right before I'd taken a sip and spewed it across the kitchen.

"We don't need you," I said. "We don't want you either."

Do you ever get like that? Where you're mad at someone but also—or mostly—mad at yourself because you're acting so mean? And since you're mad (at yourself), you act worse (to them)?

96

It makes no sense, and I do it all the time.

"Come on, Soren," said Ruth. "Don't be a butthead."

"Don't *call* me a butthead."

"I won't call you a butthead if you'll stop acting like a butthead." She put her hands on both sides of her head and pressed inward, so it kind of looked like there was a crack going down her face. "Butthead!"

I didn't want to laugh but it made me. When you do that right and you have puffy enough cheeks (heh heh), you *do* look like a butthead. "Fine," I said. "He can come."

We trudged outside. Flynn headed straight for the coop. "So how do we do this?" he said.

"Wait!" said Ruth. "Wait. Wait. Wait."

Flynn froze, his fingers wrapped around the door handle.

"Back away," said Ruth.

Flynn reversed. When he was safe, Ruth shook her head. "That was a close one. *Never* get close to Martha without armor."

The coop is right next to the garage, where we gathered the necessary supplies. Ruth put on her bike helmet while I got my garden gloves. She gave some Rollerblade pads to Flynn.

"Knee pads?" he said. "To deal with a rooster?"

"Any little bit helps," said Ruth.

I turned to her. "You want to take Martha duty or poop duty?"

This was a tough decision. She bit her lip. "I'll take Martha."

"What about me?" asked Flynn.

"You can watch," I said, not looking at him.

"I want to help," said Flynn.

"You can," Ruth assured him. "Right, Soren? But watch the first round so you get the hang of it." She tightened the straps of her bike helmet. "Ready?" she asked me.

"Good luck, soldier," I said.

"Good luck, pooper-scooper," she replied.

We shook hands, squared our shoulders, and marched into the line of duty. The first step was to get the other chickens out of the way. That wasn't hard, since they're literally birdbrains. I had the garage-door remote, and Ruth had a bag of frozen corn. "Open the coop door, Flynn," said Ruth as soon as Dotty waddled near it. "Just an inch or two."

He opened it. I nudged Dotty out the door onto the grass. Ruth rattled the corn kernels and Dotty perked up instantly, following Ruth on the short walk to the garage. We repeated the process for Potty, Hatty, Eugenie, and Betty II. As soon as we had all five hens in the garage, Ruth jogged out and I hit the close-door button. The hens looked around in confusion: *Where is our corn? Why is that large object descending from the sky? Wait—why is it all dark in here?*

They started squawking, but they were no longer our problem.

But Martha, remember, can't handle being penned up. The coop is see-through, so he doesn't mind that, but the garage? He goes nuts. The one time we'd tried to stick him in there, he went on a homicidal rampage. (We ate most of Betty I, and buried the rest of her in the vegetable garden.) So we have to get him out in the yard for long enough to clean the coop.

"Here, Martha!" said Ruth.

He looked at us suspiciously, wondering what we'd done with all his wives.

"Here-here-here!" Ruth clucked like a chicken. Martha seemed interested. Ruth made her arms into wings and flapped them invitingly. "Martha! BAWK-bawk-bawk-bawk!"

Martha jumped at her. Ruth took off across the lawn, Martha in pursuit. I dove into the chicken coop with the shovel and began shoveling out the old bedding. I was going so fast I stirred up a cloud of dirt and cobwebs and feathers and poop. I tried not to breathe in. Chickens are gross.

"BAWK-bawk-bawk-bawk!" I heard Ruth say.

I popped my head out. They were on the other side of the lawn, Martha's beak mere inches from Ruth's backside. "COCK-A-DOO-ARGH-ACK-ECK-EH!" he cried.

I ducked back in. Shovel, shovel, pant, pant, pant. I'd almost emptied it.

"AHHH!" Ruth shouted. "CODE RED!"

I shot out of the coop just as Martha shot in. "So much for advance warning," I said, my heart pounding.

"He's getting smarter," Ruth said defensively. "He faked me out and changed direction."

"Well, be on the lookout. You know what happens when you're alone with Martha in the chicken coop."

"Scars," she said.

She didn't mean emotional scars, either.

At least we had a break: the next step was to hose it down, and Martha can stay in for that. We took turns spraying the walls. Pebbles of hardened poop turned into trickles of poop water. Martha hunkered down in the corner and glared at us.

"Can I have a real job now?" said Flynn.

I swapped out the shovel for an ice scraper and trowel.

"I want to help," he said.

"You don't have to," said Ruth.

"You really don't," I said, relenting. "I wouldn't wish this job on anyone."

"It'll go faster," said Flynn.

Ruth's eyes met mine. "He's right. And given Martha's ever-sharpening wits—"

"True," I said. "Very true." I gave Flynn the scraper. "This round's for all the little crap. You scrape; I'll trowel it into the bucket."

"And be careful," said Ruth. "Get out when you hear—"

"*Code red,*" said Flynn. "I was listening. I know."

We did a ritual group hug in case one of us didn't make it.

Ruth cried beguilingly, "Oh, Martha! I am waiting out here! Waiting just for you!"

Martha stuck his head out of the coop.

"I am a beautiful chicken lady, Martha!"

She flapped and did a sort of shimmy. Martha, intrigued, took a step forward.

"Come here, Roosterlicious!"

He took the bait and started chasing her again. Flynn and I leapt into the coop. "Martha doesn't like being tricked," I panted as I dumped leaves and poop chunks into the bucket, "so each cleaning stint gets shorter and shorter."

"Got it," said Flynn, scraping busily.

We'd done three-fourths of the floor. I heard Ruth clucking. "You know, Flynn," I said, shoving some sweat off my forehead with the inside of my elbow, "this goes a lot faster with you helping."

"CODE RED! *CODE RED!*"

Flynn and I dove for the door. I let him go out first. We made it just in time.

This time Ruth was the one who looked traumatized.

"Guys," she whispered, "I think he really thought I was a chicken."

"Isn't that the point?"

"He had an expression that was all . . . *lovey-dovey,*" she said in horror.

Flynn put a hand on Ruth's shoulder. "I'm so sorry."

"Thanks, Flynn." She took a deep breath. "Okay. Okay. I'll be okay."

"We're so close," I said. "One more time."

"You better clean fast," she said grimly. "I am not having an egg with Martha."

Squawking, she took off across the lawn. As soon as

Martha started chasing her, Flynn and I launched ourselves back into the coop. We worked fast. With a grunt, he scraped the last section. "Go ahead and get out," I told him. "I'll just get this into the bucket—"

"No, it's okay." With his bare hands, he helped me dump the scrapings into the bucket. It was brimming with disgustingness.

"Thanks."

"No problem," he said, tossing in a half-dead worm. "I think we're done."

We were. The plywood floor practically sparkled. "Let's get out of here," I said. "Go ahead—no, after you—"

"AHHH! SORRY! CODE—"

Martha was in the coop.

He stalked toward us.

We were cornered.

"Holy mother of . . . ," Flynn muttered.

I clutched the bucket to my chest. "Nice rooster. Nice Martha."

Martha took two slow, ominous steps toward me. I glimpsed Ruth's terrified face, peering through the wire grate. "Save yourself, Flynn," I whispered out of the side of my mouth. "I'll distract him."

"No," said Flynn, tightening his lips. "We escape together, or not at all."

Martha's beady little eyes were fixed upon me.

"Oh God," said Flynn.

I, too, turned to prayer. *Dear God,* I thought, *save us.*

Please save us. I'm sorry for all my sins. I'm sorry for being a jerk to Flynn. I'm even sorry for the Urine-Filled Squirt Gun Incident in fourth grade. I will be a better person, I promise.

All I ask is that we get out of here unscarred.

No.

All I ask is that we get out of here alive.

Martha minced another step closer.

"*Do* something!" hissed Flynn.

We needed to calm Martha down. "Marthie," I cooed, "don't you want to take a nice little nap?"

He didn't.

"Aren't you sleepy?"

He wasn't.

Panic jolted my stomach. He took another step. We needed to get him to sleep. What puts things to sleep—*think*, Soren, dang it, *think*—aha!

"Martha want a lullaby?" I said encouragingly.

Another step closer.

"Rock-a-bye, Martha, in the treetop . . . ," I sang. I was tuneless, my voice shaking.

His sharp beak trembled in anticipation of the kill.

"When the wind blows, the cradle will pop . . ."

Wait. Were those the right words?

"The cradle will . . . bop?"

That didn't sound right either. *Plop? Drop?* I did remember a certain grisly touch to the song, but—

"Soren," said Flynn. He stretched his left hand far to the that side of the coop. "When I snap, go for it."

I saw the brilliance of his plan.

Martha's tiny head swiveled to follow Flynn's hand. With his arm fully extended, Flynn snapped his fingers.

Martha's whole body jerked. He fluttered his wings and dove to the left corner of the coop.

Flynn and I made a break for it.

Ruth was ready. As soon as we cleared the door, she slammed it shut. Martha hit the grating and hit it again, throwing his body against it, furious that his prey had escaped. "COCK-A-DOO-ARGH-ACK-ECK-EH!" he screamed in rage.

It was a near-perfect escape.

The only hitch, actually, was that I'd tripped over Flynn on the way out. The bucket flew out of my arms. I fell splat on my face, and bits of chicken poop rained down all around us.

CHAPTER TWENTY

"I SEE WHY Ruth warned me away from this job," said Flynn. She'd gone inside, but we'd stayed out to hose down the coop one last time.

"Thanks for helping," I said. "You saved my life."

"I'm sure the lullaby thing would have worked eventually."

I made a noncommittal "hmm."

"You want a turn with the hose?" he asked.

We fell silent, watching Martha stalk around the coop, dripping wet and highly resentful. We couldn't put in fresh bedding until the floor had dried overnight (the chickens slept in the garage; Martha just had to deal), so our job was done, technically. But I wasn't ready yet to go back to the house. "Hey," I said. Mom says it's better to talk about stuff than to simmer in resentment. She always says that, *simmer in resentment,* which I like because (a) it's a real-life example of metaphor, and once I told it to Mr. Pickett, our Language Arts teacher, and he said I had *an excellent ear for idiom,* which is another metaphor, and (b) it's a *good* metaphor, because that's what it feels like when you're angry but not saying anything: you're a pot and you're bubbling, boiling, low enough that people'll only notice if they come really close, but *you*, pot you, can't relax. You're on constant heat.

So I said, "Hey."

"Hey what?"

All in a rush, since just because it's good to talk about stuff doesn't mean it's easy, I said, "Hey, I wish you hadn't told Ms. Hutchins about the prank because first of all it was going to be really funny and second I worked really hard on it and you ruined it and I know it's probably stupid to work hard on something like a prank but I used to have this friend and that's what we did together and I miss—"

That's the thing with talking in a rush: sometimes stuff comes out that you don't expect.

"What I mean," I said, "is I think pranks are important. I think they're like mini protests. Tiny ways of saying, *We're here!* And I'm careful. I always think about whether they'd hurt people, and if they would, I don't do them. I'm not that kind of prankster."

"I know," said Flynn. "I know you're a good guy, Soren."

I don't know why I cared so much about hearing that from Flynn.

"But I still disagree," he said. "You think pranks are important. Okay. But I think science is important."

"So do I!"

"And messing with an experiment, it's . . ." He wiggled

his mouth like he couldn't get the right word out. "It's like Ms. Hutchins said. Science is all about truth. So making science say something untrue—that's just not right. Science *is* truth."

The look on his face, I'd seen it before. I'd seen it on Ms. Hutchins when she talked about animal rights and on Dad when he talked about equal justice under law and on Mr. Pickett when we'd had that metaphor chat.

Maybe that was what I looked like when I talked about pranks.

"Do a different prank," said Flynn. "One that doesn't mess with a science experiment."

"You think so?"

"Sure. You think pranks are important, right? You like doing them? So do a prank."

I thought, I bet that's why I've been walking around all gray and gloomy. Not because I was mad at Flynn, but because I missed the prank. I missed having something to look forward to, something to think about when I was falling asleep or bored in math.

"Will you help?" I said.

"I don't think so," said Flynn. "I just don't like breaking rules. It's not fun for me."

What *was* fun for him, then?

"But maybe there's someone else who'd help."

Did he even *have* fun?

"And I'll cheer you on from the sidelines."

"Let's go in," I said. "I've got some planning to do."

                                    .   .   .

DAD WAS AT the stove, stirring something that looked sickeningly similar to the contents of Ivan's diaper after he tried cauliflower for the first time. "Dad," I said, "what are the lyrics to that one lullaby? 'Rock-a-bye baby, in the treetop . . .'"

"'When the wind blows, the cradle will rock.'"

"Rock?" I said. "That doesn't even rhyme!"

"'When the bough breaks, the cradle will fall—'"

Ivan looked up from the floor, where he was using silverware to build a prison camp for Gloria (now sporting a leg cast) and his other Barbies. "WON'T!" he shouted.

"'And down will come baby—'"

"IVAN WON'T!" He hurled a fork across the room.

"'Cradle and all.'"

"IVAN *WON'T* GO TO BED!"

"That's a weird lullaby," I said.

"Perfect for weird kids," said Dad, smiling. "You used to love it." He poked me with a wooden spoon. "Dump in those peas for me, would you?"

CHAPTER TWENTY-ONE

THE NEXT MONDAY, Ms. Hutchins kicked off the new Ethics in Science unit by making us talk about what *ethics* was, which turned out to be a good idea because someone, I'm not going to say who, thought it was a type of cheese.

"What's a synonym for *ethical*?" said Ms. Hutchins.

"Good," said Goldie.

Ms. Hutchins wrote *good vs. bad* on the board. "Give me another pair."

"Right versus wrong," said Flynn.

"Fair versus unfair," said Lila.

They got on the board too. Then she counted us off into groups of four for case studies. I got Tabitha, Olivia, and Flynn. Flynn, of course, grabbed the group worksheet as soon as it floated onto our desks. "We have to read the situation, discuss the ethical issues, and then do a skit for the class," he said. "Want me to read the situation out loud?"

"Yes!" said Olivia. "Please do, Flynn!"

"Sure," said Tabitha, one hundred times less enthusiastically.

I hate being read to, but Flynn and I were getting along, so I wasn't about to protest. "'Case number four,'" he read. "'Sam is working on an electrical-circuit lab in science class. Sam is a good student and knows he's doing everything right.'"

"Arrogant slimeball," whispered Tabitha, catching my eye. I laughed.

"'But when Sam does calculations to see if his data match the formulas in his science book, he discovers that his data must be wrong.'"

"Ha!" said Tabitha. "Serves him right."

"'He suspects the equipment is not working properly, but his teacher, Mr. Volt, is helping a clumsy fellow student.'"

"That can be you in the skit, Soren," said Tabitha.

"Hey!" I said. "No!"

"Typecasting," said Olivia. They giggled.

"One of *you* can be the clumsy student. I'm Sam the Science Star."

Flynn glared at us. "I'm trying to read." We quieted down. "'Instead, Sam does the math to figure out the correct set of data and simply changes his own data to match what he has calculated.'"

"Now what?" said Olivia.

"We have to talk about whether there's anything wrong with what Sam did, what his other options were, and what we'd have done if we were Sam."

"And we have to plan our skit," said Tabitha. "I feel like this story could be way more exciting."

We didn't have much time to practice before it was our turn to present. I actually ended up volunteering to be Clumsy Student because it was the smallest part. It's funny: I don't get nervous talking in front of the class, but if you turn it into a skit and make me pretend to be somebody else, I instantly get butterflies. Flynn was the teacher, and Olivia was Sam.

"It was a bright and sunny day," said Tabitha, the narrator, "when Sam the Science Star and his klutzy friend walked into the science lab."

Olivia pranced onstage, shoving imaginary glasses up her nose. I took one step and tripped over my own feet. Already people were laughing more at our skit than they had at anybody else's. Success.

"I love science," said Olivia. Ms. Hutchins crossed her arms and frowned, probably because this lover of science was talking in a super-nerdy chipmunk voice. "And today's the electrical-circuit lab! Hurray!"

"Get to your lab stations, class!" said Flynn, who made a very believable teacher. "We've got a lot to do today!"

"The class began to work with the circuit," said Tabitha. "But the other student was having trouble."

"May I help you, uh, Bob?" said Flynn.

"Wait, my name is Bob?" I said, forgetting I was supposed to be in character. Everyone laughed. "Uh, yeah. Help! I dropped all the batteries!"

"I love this lab!" chipmunked Olivia. "And it's so simple, too!"

"While Mr. Volt was busy helping Bob," said Tabitha,

"Sam the Science Star was putting together the electrical parts. But then—*ZZZZZZZ!*"

This had not been rehearsed, but Olivia went with it. She flopped to the floor and twitched violently.

"Sam the Science Star was being electrocuted!" Tabitha cried. "He thought he was good at science, but he thought wrong! *ZZZZZ! ZZZZZ!*" Olivia convulsed on the floor. The class was in hysterics.

"I'll rescue you, Sam!" I yelled.

"But little did Bob know," said Tabitha as I did a slow-motion run toward Olivia, "that electricity can be conducted through the human body. When he made contact with Sam"—I touched her—"*ZZZZZZZZ!*"

Now both of us were flopping around on the floor. "*ZZZZZ! ZZZZZ!*"

"*Cut!*" yelled Ms. Hutchins, marching to the front. "Cut! Now! That is *not* what's supposed to happen in your skit! What about your ethical issue?"

"We were getting there," said Tabitha.

"We were just livening it up a bit," said Flynn.

Flynn? Defending bad behavior?

Wow.

I twitched one last time, just for fun, and got to my feet. Olivia and I brushed off our pants. "You've wasted your classmates' time," said Ms. Hutchins, "and they don't appreciate that."

"Yes, we do!" said Soup. "That was the best science skit ever!"

"Marsupial, I didn't ask for your input," she said, her lips tight. "Now, the four of you, let's get on with the lesson. Please explain your ethical issue for the class."

"Should we continue the skit?" said Olivia hopefully.

"*No.*"

LILA CAME OVER to our group after the bell rang. "Well played," she told us.

"We got cut off way too soon," said Olivia. "Ms. H has no appreciation for the arts."

"Well, she's a scientist," said Tabitha. "What do you expect?"

"Not true," said Flynn. "Look at me. I'm into banjo, drawing, *and* science."

"That's because you're weird," I said. In a nice way, though. The way you tell your friends they're weird because you like them. I hoped he'd get it. He smiled and flushed and focused far too hard on sliding his science folder into his messenger bag, so I was pretty sure he did.

"Get to Language Arts, kids!" said Ms. Hutchins. "Chop, chop! Mr. Pickett will blame me if you're late!"

Flynn edged behind me in the scrum at the door. "You know how you were looking for new pranking partners?" he whispered. "I don't think you have to look any farther."

CAUTION
CAUTION
CAUTION
CAUTION
CAUTION
CAUTION

CHAPTER TWENTY-TWO

"YOU'RE GOING TO prank with the triplets?" said Alex when we video-chatted after school. "Well, okay."

" 'Well, okay' *what*? You're the one who suggested them."

"True."

"And you should have seen them in science class. They're funny."

"I know they're funny. Remember their mystery video for Language Arts last year?"

It had involved their golden retriever, a trampoline, a fedora, a trench coat, and at least four ketchup bottles' worth of fake blood. Ruth and I still watched it on YouTube every few months. It was a modern classic.

"They're not epic pranksters like us," I said. "Not yet, anyway. But they like to stir things up. Plus they live next door. They're perfect."

"Perfect," echoed Alex, but her voice was flat.

"So what's your problem?"

"I don't have a problem."

"Fine."

We were quiet. She tugged one of her braids. Finally, she said, "Have you asked them yet?"

"No. I wanted to run it by you first."

She perked up a bit. "Oh."

"What's wrong?"

"I don't know," she said. "Nothing. I guess—I don't know. It's weird for me to imagine you pranking with people who aren't me."

"You're the one who suggested it!"

"I know. It's just weird. That's all I'm saying." She shrugged. "But go for it. Ask them. They'd be good."

"And the two of us are going to prank when you visit, right?" I said.

"If you even want to."

"Of course I want to!" She had no idea, I thought, how much I missed her. No idea how much her leaving had screwed up everything about this school year. "You're the best person to prank with. I'd never even consider the triplets if you were around."

She smiled. One of those post-tears smiles, shaky and hopeful. I peered at the screen, but the sucky Internet plus her glasses made it impossible to tell if she'd actually cried.

"How's Ol' Butt-Braid?" I said.

"Her name is Sophia, Soren. *Sophia.*"

She'd always be Ol' Butt-Braid to me.

"She came over after school last Friday."

"What'd you guys do?" I said.

Alex flushed and started fiddling with her glasses. "Um, we watched some stuff online, and then my mom let us make trail mix, and then, um, we just sat around." She wiggled the frame of her glasses so her nose got battered from side to side.

"Why are you messing with your glasses?"

She ripped her hand away from her face. "I'm not."

"You were." I was grinning broadly now. I'd caught her. "Looks like someone's telling a lie."

"I was adjusting them."

"You were straight-up playing with them. That's your tell. Fess up. What'd you *really* do with Bu—Sophia?"

Alex slumped. "Rats. I'm out of practice. Er, we . . ."

I saw her hand sneak up to the side of her face.

"Don't even think about lying."

"Um. Wemadepaperdolls."

Had I heard what I thought I'd heard? "Say that slower."

"We. Made. Paper. Dolls."

I stared at her in both horror and glee. She shook her head. "I know. I know."

"You go from a life of crime to a life of making paper dolls?"

"Sophia really likes them. She's good at them too. She taught me this trick for making the clothes stay on—and you know what, Soren? It was fun. It was actually fun. I'm not even embarrassed. It was *fun*."

. . .

THE TRIPLETS COMPLAIN all the time about how they're allowed online only on weekends. Their parents are the strictest in the class. Dad and Ivan were outside, harvesting (curses) even more zucchini, and Flynn and Ruth were sprawled out on the living room floor with Settlers of Catan. I had an opportunity. I grabbed the landline.

The last time I'd touched it was when Alex and I had recorded the outgoing message to say, "Greetings! You've reached Slinky Sally's, the Best Snake Vet in the Midwest!" Then we posted fake advertisements on a lot of reptile-enthusiast message boards. My parents got so many random voice mails.

I couldn't believe Alex had a new friend.

Now *I* was the one who felt weird. I wanted to be in Minneapolis, cutting out mini blue jeans and ball gowns. Making up characters and voices and plots. And I didn't want Ol' Butt-Braid around either.

I shoved away those thoughts and dialed the phone. It rang four times. "Hello?" said a male voice.

"Um, hi. This is Soren Skaar. May I speak to the triplets, please?"

"Which one?" said the person at the other end, who sounded too young to be their dad.

"Doesn't matter."

The other end laughed. "They *do* have separate personalities, you know."

"Right. Yeah."

"So which one do you want?"

"Uh, all three? Do they do conference calls?"

He snorted. "For a fee, probably. Hold on." I heard a clank and a muffled shout: "HEY, DOOFAE, YOU'VE GOT A PHONE CALL!" With a rustle, he was back.

"They're on their way. Do you go to their school?"

"Yeah."

"Cool. Listen. Do you have any dirt on them?"

"Dirt?"

"You know. Stuff I'd find useful."

"Useful?"

"I'm Ethan. Their big brother. Home for a visit. Look, those girls have been tormenting me for eleven years, three months, and seventeen days."

"You did that math quick."

"They announce their age every morning at breakfast. You know how they are. Imagine what it was like to live in the same house as them. Outnumbered, outsmarted, out-maneuvered."

"I'm so sorry."

"Thanks, man," he said, sounding touched. "So—they're coming—quick—a little blackmail fodder?"

I scrolled through my memory. The triplets were constantly causing trouble, stirring the pot, but they stayed under the radar. The teachers thought they were angels, mostly because they were blond and round-faced and girls. "Just say the words Noodle Incident," I said. "They never got caught for that one. They'll flip."

"You're my hero. Here they are. Shh. Nice chatting."

"What were you *chatting* about?" I heard one of the girls say suspiciously.

"Oh, nothing," Ethan said airily. "Here's Soren."

"Soren? Soren Skaar? He called? On the phone?"

"Quaint, no?"

A pause.

"Hi," said a voice into the receiver. "It's Tabitha. What do you want?"

"I want to collaborate," I said.

CHAPTER TWENTY-THREE

WHEN FLYNN HAD first arrived, he and Ruth had stuck together on the walk to the bus stop, mostly talking Settlers of Catan strategy. I'd trail behind, partly because I'm never in a hurry to get to school and partly because there's something about know-it-all-ness that turns my stomach in the morning, and Flynn, frankly, is a know-it-all when it comes to Catan.

Walking alone had given me a lot of time to think about how it used to be. There'd been three kids then, too, a pair and a spare, but back then it was Alex and me together with Ruth trailing behind, since we never let her in on our pranks. It had been a depressing walk this year. It was when I missed Alex the most.

But lately, ever since the chicken coop, all three of us walked together. And ever since the triplets and I had started planning a prank together, they'd wait on their porch until we came by. So we were this huge pack, throwing pinecones and rating Halloween decorations and practicing our *cock-a-doo-argh-ack-eck-eh*-ing. It was different. I liked being part of a pack. It was fun.

Even if Flynn was still a know-it-all.

On the day of the class spelling bee, he was crabby. "No reason," he said when I asked why he wasn't laughing at Olivia's spot-on Principal Leary impression.

"Are you mad at me?"

"No."

"Then why are you in a bad mood?"

"It's not all about *you*, Soren."

"Then what's it about?"

"I'm just crabby, okay? It happens. My mom says it runs in the family. Artists are moody, she says. It's the way we are."

I went up ahead with the triplets and Ruth.

At the spelling bee, I nailed *apologize* and had a lucky guess on the number of *c*'s in *recommend,* but then I stuck an *e* in the middle of *orchard.* I wasn't upset. My only goal was not to be the first one out.

Flynn was still in. And he was still in when it was down to three, and still in when Tabitha misspelled *scepter.* (She "accidentally" kicked an empty chair on her way back to her seat, just like me at dinner that one time.) He was still in when Kiyana messed up *pandemonium,* and he spelled it right to win.

"Our champion!" said Mr. Pickett. "Congratulations!"

Everyone clapped the way you're supposed to clap in class, a.k.a. quietly so it doesn't go through the walls and make other classes jealous that you're having fun, but I whooped. "That's a Skaar!" I yelled. "That's my boy!" Soup and Jéro and Freddy laughed.

"Indeed," said Mr. Pickett, frowning at me. He put the alphabet crown on Flynn's head. "Flynn will be our representative to the school bee next month, and we'll all be rooting for him!"

I whooped again. Finally, Flynn cracked a smile.

AT RECESS, I had a job: scoping out whether it was possible to sneak into the gym during recess. The triplets and I were getting ready for P-Day. That's Prank Day, of course, but the *P* also stands for something else, because the only way to talk your way inside from recess is to convince Mrs. Andersen that you have to twirl some chocolate soft-serve onto the big white cone. If you know what I mean.

I staggered over to her. "I need to use the bathroom," I said.

"You can't wait?"

I tried to look strained. "It's an emergency."

Mrs. Andersen tilted her head to the side.

"It's just, egg sandwiches at lunch, and after last night's burrito—"

She winced. "Go. Go."

I lurched into the school. As soon as I was out of view, I started walking normally, but fast, to the gym. There was an all-school assembly next Thursday. It'd be after lunch—they always were—so if the triplets and I could infiltrate the gym during recess . . .

Would it be locked?

I tried the doors.

Nope.

Bingo.

I peeked in, expecting to see nothing but a shiny sweep of floor. But Flynn was sitting on the stage. His legs were hanging off, and his ankles looked all bony and knobbly, poking out from the bottom of his skinny jeans. He wasn't on his phone or reading or doing last-minute homework or anything.

"Hey," I called. The sound echoed in the big empty room.

Flynn looked up. "Hey."

"Why aren't you out at recess?"

"I don't know."

"You won the spelling bee."

"Yep."

"I didn't know you were that good at spelling."

"Guess I am."

"Winning didn't cheer you up?"

"Guess not."

Weird. If I'd won—well, that would never happen. Not in the real world. So yeah, if I'd won, I'd have been *extremely* cheerful, because it would have meant I'd slipped down a wormhole to an alternate universe, which is a major dream of mine.

"You were right about the triplets," I said. "We're planning something good."

"I don't even want to know."

Just as well. If he didn't know, he couldn't tell. "Won't you come outside?" I said. "Jéro's trying to get a soccer game going. We need you."

"Don't feel like it."

"Are you homesick?"

"I just want to be alone."

"Momsick?"

"Bye, Soren."

"Oh." I stood there sort of awkwardly. I watched the laces dangle off his one untied shoe as he swung his feet against the stage. "You have a lot of friends here," I tried. "Everyone likes you. Goldie and Kiyana and those girls, and Jeremiah, and all the teachers—"

"Do you know what *alone* means?"

Fine. If he wanted to sit in the gym, missing the best part of the day, probably about to get in trouble for skipping, well, I'd let him. If he was uncheerupable, I wouldn't try. "Your shoe's untied," I told him, and I left.

CHAPTER TWENTY-FOUR

IT WAS P-DAY. My secret alarm went off before the sun rose. I stumbled out of bed, pulled on a sweatshirt while Ruth and Ivan snoozed, and tiptoed down to the garage.

The triplets were already there, with their identical squashed noses and wispy hair and bleary, early-morning eyes. "Hey," said Olivia.

"No time for politeness," said Lila, swishing a legal pad through the air. "We're here for a reason."

"Oh, stick it up your ear, Lila," said Tabitha, who is not a morning person.

"I don't know about you," said Lila, glaring at her, "but *I* am trying to make sure this plan goes smoothly."

"Yeah, I'm sure nobody else wants that. . . ."

Lila licked the end of her pencil. "I'm taking the high road," she said. "I can't hear you down there. Let's run through the checklist. Backpacks?"

"Check," we all said.

With a totally unnecessary flourish, she made a check mark. "Duct tape?"

"Check."

"Thirty-seven alarm clocks, each set to 12:37 p.m.?"

We'd had to raise money for this prank: two lemonade stands and a weekend spent raking leaves for old Mrs. Olson. Then we'd gone to Goodwill and Salvation Army and three garage sales and bought up all the alarm clocks that blasted out *BRRRING!* Now they were synced to the second in the corner of the garage.

"Check."

"Load 'em," said Lila with satisfaction.

Our backpacks were chunky and jangling with clocks. We were ready.

IT WAS KIND of embarrassing to claim a number-two-related emergency during recess for the second week in a row. I didn't want Mrs. Andersen to think I had particularly high-maintenance intestines. Actually, I didn't want Mrs. Andersen thinking about my intestines at all. But I sacrificed my dignity, described breakfast (Raisin Bran) and lunch (three-bean chili), and got permission to hobble inside the building.

The triplets were waiting for me at our lockers. "How did you all get in at once?" I said as I retrieved my clock-filled backpack. "Did you *all* say you had to—"

"Ew!" squealed Olivia. "No!"

"They let us move as a unit," said Tabitha, shrugging. "It's a triplet thing."

We headed to the gym. "Walk with purpose," I told

them. "Like a teacher sent you on an errand." That was another thing Alex and I used to practice. We'd stride down the second-floor hallway in her house. . . .

I felt a pang. She should have been here.

The gym was empty. Folding chairs were already set up for the assembly. "Go, go, go," muttered Lila. We scattered across the floor. With a strip of duct tape, I attached the first alarm clock to the underside of a chair. When I stood, it was invisible. I laughed aloud. Somebody'd be in for a big surprise when their butt started ringing at 12:37 p.m.

We stashed twenty clocks in the audience and tucked ten on the windowsills. Two we put in the ball closet; two we camouflaged near the scoreboard timer; two we tangled in the soccer nets. Olivia, holding the final clock, hesitated. "I know we planned to put it in the lectern," she whispered urgently, "but what if Principal Leary sees it before 12:37?"

"Stop thinking!" hissed Lila. "Start acting!"

"Won't he be suspicious?"

"Just *put* it somewhere!"

Olivia shoved it under a chair in our sixth-grade section. I lunged in with a strip of duct tape.

Our work was done.

BECAUSE OF THE all-school assembly after recess, we hadn't had video announcements that morning during homeroom. The gambling crowd all groaned when Principal Leary took the stage: his necktie had normal, boring gray-and-blue stripes. "The house won today," said Jéro as he did the calculations. "Nobody expects normal. Not from Principal Leary."

Supposedly, the reason for the assembly was to celebrate our first-quarter achievements. Leary started by giving straight-A certificates to every single kindergartner. It went on from there, with smaller and smaller percentages from every grade. They said that was because school got harder, but had anyone asked, What if actually we were getting dumber? What if school was backfiring?

Maybe there was an experiment you could do to figure it out.

Oh no. Was I *Thinking Like a Scientist*? I hate it when teachers get into my head.

I'd gotten a B in Language Arts because I'd started my book report at ten p.m. the night before it was due and a C+ in math because fractions, so I clapped while Flynn, Jéro, all three triplets, Goldie, Kiyana, and a few other people accepted certificates of merit. "And now," said Principal Leary, "I have several reminders about how to conduct yourselves within these hallowed halls."

That was the real reason we had these assemblies: so Principal Leary could lecture us about rules. He likes a captive audience. That's probably why he's a principal.

It was 12:23. Fourteen minutes to go. "In fact," Leary said happily, "I made a slide show."

The first slide said THE A TO Z OF RULES, REGULATIONS, AND REMINDERS. I got comfortable. Thirteen minutes left.

I'd missed *A*, whoops. "*B* is for *Bathrooms*," said Leary.

"No horseplay or gossip in the bathrooms. Bathrooms are to be used for one thing only."

"We shouldn't wash our hands afterward?" called out Sam Goldberg, a third grader.

"You know what I mean, Sam," said Leary. "*C* is for *Cafeteria Conduct. . . .*"

I swiveled around to find the triplets. Olivia was gazing in Flynn's direction. Lila was admiring her certificate, and Tabitha was folding hers into a paper airplane.

"*F*," said Leary. "*Fights,* whether of *Fists* or *Food,* are strictly *Forbidden.*"

Seven minutes.

"*H* is for *Hallways,* where students should be seen and not heard," said Principal Leary.

Two minutes.

"*L* is for *Lockers.* No food is allowed in lockers, as well as no drinks, no electronics, and no biohazardous waste."

One minute.

"*M*," Leary began, but he didn't get to say what *M* was for, because—

BRRRRRINNNNGGGGGGG!!!

Everyone leapt out of their seats. Principal Leary bobbled the wireless microphone, which hit the floor in an explosion of static. Mr. Pickett let loose the highest, shrillest shriek I've ever heard.

I basked.

It was chaos. It was like a fire alarm but better. The noise came from the windows, the chairs, the closet, the timer, the nets. Everyone's reactions only made it more chaotic. The younger kids, on mats at the front of the gym, were rolling around, or yelling, or both. The third and fourth graders practiced their murder-victim screams. Lila and Olivia were on the aisle, and they jumped up to knock the big red exercise balls off their racks. The balls bounded across the gym, bouncing off the heads of anyone who'd stayed sitting down.

Flynn gave me a pointed look. I widened my eyes and opened my mouth in shock: *Me? Why on earth would you look at* me?

He cracked the tiniest of smiles, and I cracked one back. We'd done it.

CHAPTER TWENTY-FIVE

"IT WORKED?" said Alex.

"Yes!"

Those new purple glasses plus the lurchy Internet made it hard to read her expression, but I could tell that she was nowhere near as excited as I wanted her to be. "It was *chaos*," I said again. "The clocks wouldn't have been that noisy by themselves, but once everyone started screaming—you know how little kids are, one screams and the rest have to scream too—"

"Yep."

"It was like flicking over a domino. Just starting something and watching what goes down. Remember what that feels like?"

"I remember."

"You know what *I'd* forgotten about pranks?" I was grinning like a goofball and going on way too long, but I was feeling so great. Even tarping the chicken coop before this afternoon's rainstorm hadn't brought me down. "I'd forgotten the adrenaline. It's like a roller coaster. But way better, because you're the one who designed it."

Alex nodded.

"And Leary actually called me into his office to 'discuss a few matters'—you know, how he always did with you. . . ."

Ever since those blasted plastic ants.

"But I said I was innocent and he believed me. He said that without your influence, he doubted I'd try anything. So it's actually—"

"A good thing that I'm gone?" Alex said flatly.

"No! That's not what I was going to say!"

I was going to say it was *kind* of a good thing.

A very, very small good thing. That obviously I would trade in a flash to get her back.

"We're driving up on Saturday," she said. "If you even want to prank with me anymore."

"Of course I do!"

"You don't like the triplets better?"

"No. *No.* We should prank all together. All five of us. It'd be epic."

"I'm only there for an afternoon. We don't have time for anything epic."

"It'd be fun anyway."

"I don't know."

Ruth knocked on the dining-room door. "Sorry, Soren," she said, "but Dad says I have to do my online math stuff now."

"Dad says?" I said suspiciously.

"He does!" yelled Dad from the kitchen.

"Okay. I gotta go, Alex. Bye."

"Bye!"

I x-ed out.

"Why didn't you argue?" Ruth asked me.

"Did you want me to?"

"Well, it would give me more time not doing math."

I shrugged and stood up. I didn't even push the power button, which is an annoying but satisfying thing that Ruth and I traditionally do to each other when we get kicked off the computer. "All yours."

I wandered to the living room. I looked out the same window where we'd waited for Flynn to arrive. It was still raining. If the prank was a roller coaster, now I was at the end, where you have to pry yourself out of your seat, when your head's rattled and the ground's not as solid as it used to be. I watched the rainwater wash brown leaves into a clump at the bottom of the driveway. The reason I hadn't argued, I could have told Ruth, was that I hadn't wanted to talk to Alex anymore. She was acting like a drip, and I was a bit sick of her. I'd never felt that way before. She was my best friend.

AROUND NOON ON Saturday, Alex's mom texted Dad to say they were half an hour away. Mom had taken Flynn and Ivan to the farmers' market, and the quiet house made me feel even jumpier. I went out to kick on the woodpile until their car pulled up and Alex got out.

"Alex!" cried Dad, jogging out of the house. "Alex Harris! What a sight for sore eyes! Welcome back!"

"Hey, Mr. Skaar."

He went over to the driver's window. Alex and I nodded at each other. It wasn't like we were going to shake hands or hug. I bobbled the ball between my feet. "Yep," I said.

"Yep."

"What's up?"

"Not much. You?"

"Not much."

It was a tad awkward, you might say.

Meanwhile, Dad was shouting into Mrs. Harris's window, "Welcome back to Camelot! Your home away from home! Smell that clear country air! Soak in these prairie vistas!"

Dad claims he doesn't act different after his Saturday-morning run. Ha. He basically transforms into a human exclamation point. A sweaty one, too.

"Your dad's sure in a good mood," said Alex. She quirked an eyebrow. "Might I guess—runner's high is involved?"

I grinned. There she was. The person who got me. I didn't have to explain the backstory because she'd been around for the backstory. "It's Saturday morning," I said. "Nothing's changed."

"Well, well, well!" Dad was saying. "So Ubercut is a success! I can't say I'm surprised. My follicles miss your scissors, Marilyn!"

I rolled my eyes at Alex.

"See you around six!" said Dad. "And you"—he did a little spin move and pointed at Alex—"you must be hungry! Come on in, dudette!"

Usually parents make things more awkward, but sometimes they're just so over the top and weird that they have the opposite effect and destroy everyone else's awkwardness, like when a comet gets absorbed into the sun. Well, that's what happened. Dad grilled ham-and-cheese sandwiches and then he grilled Alex about her new life. Ol' Butt-Braid, apparently, took a class in "scissor art" and was trying to get Alex to sign up too. "How nice!" said Dad. "How civilized! I wish Soren had a hobby that was so . . . so *quiet*."

"Soccer is quiet," I said.

Ruth slunk around the corner. "The whole house shakes every time you miss the woodpile. Oh. You're here. Hi, Alex."

"Hi, Ruth."

They've never gotten along. Well, that's not true. Really, Alex has never accepted that Ruth is a person. Alex doesn't have little siblings, so she sees them as tiny and annoying beasts who are always underfoot and/or trying to butt in. And sure, they're annoying, but what your friends don't see are all the times your siblings *are* your friends. They're always around. They're better company than real friends, sometimes. I feel like in books and movies the person with siblings despises them, and the only child wants to play with the other family's babies, but in my experience, anyway, it's the opposite.

"Want to go outside?" I asked Alex.

"The great outdoors!" said Dad. "The freedom of child-hood!"

"Can I come?" asked Ruth.

Alex grimaced and shook her head at me as if we were behind Ruth's back, which we weren't. Ruth saw the whole thing.

Darn.

But what could I do? Alex was only here for the afternoon. "Sorry, Ruth," I said. "We've got something we're working on."

"Let them have their time!" trilled Dad. "Ruth, come with me. Ivan's about ready for big-boy underwear, and I think I remember where we packed away Soren's. You can help me organize it."

"Dad!" I said. "Stop talking about my underwear!"

"Though we might have to buy some new pairs, to be honest. Soren was so big by the time he finally got toilet-trained that Ivan might not fit—"

"Da-ad!"

"Not to mention the stains— What, Soren? Something wrong?"

I groaned. "Forget it. Come on, Alex. Let's go outside."

CHAPTER TWENTY-SIX

FROM THE TREE platform, we could see the triplets in their backyard, rummaging around in a longish patch of grass.

"What are they doing?" said Alex.

"Let's ask them," I said.

"I don't know—"

"ANDREZEJCZAKS!" I hollered. They jumped and looked up, but they couldn't find us. The tree platform has a lot of camouflage, mostly because it's half-finished. That's why we don't call it a tree house. Dad and I were building it together, but then Ivan got born.

Alex said, "Do we have to—"

"YOO-HOO! UP HERE!"

Tabitha pointed, and Lila's and Olivia's gazes followed. They jogged toward the tree platform. "Trust me," I told Alex quietly. "They're fun."

I unfurled the rope ladder, and Olivia grabbed it first. "Don't mess with my ankles while I'm going up," she told her sisters.

"Of course not!" cried Lila.

"We would never!" said Tabitha, wounded.

Olivia rolled her eyes and flew up the ladder like she didn't believe them at all. "Oh my gosh!" she said when she saw Alex, who'd sat with her back against the trunk of the tree. "It's you!"

"Hey."

"Wow. Alex Harris. I always knew you were good at pranks, but Soren's been telling us *how* good." Olivia reached out her hand. "It's an honor to be in your presence."

The corner of Alex's mouth twitched into a smile, and I could have kissed Olivia. (In a totally non-gross way, like on the back of the hand or something. And only if nobody was watching.) "What's he been telling you?" said Alex.

"Well, a lot is still classified, he says," said Olivia, and Alex gave me an approving nod, "but he told us a few details. Like that you were the one who got the kickball trophies out of Leary's office."

Alex would put that on her college application if she could.

"And how you stockpiled duct tape for months before Tapegate."

Alex grinned. She couldn't help it. Nobody in their right mind would call any Andrezejczak triplet "the nice one," but Olivia is as close as it gets. "I heard about the Alarm Clock Incident," said Alex. "Very impressive."

"Thanks!" said Olivia. "Though we really should be thanking *you*."

138

Alex's expression soured. "Because if I hadn't left, you wouldn't have gotten to work with Soren?"

"No! No! Because you trained him so well."

"Soren's taught me a lot too," said Alex.

"Aww," said Olivia.

"Aww," mimicked Tabitha.

Quick as a snake, Olivia reached out and pinched her neck.

So much for the nice one.

"You'll regret that, Olivia," said Tabitha.

"You'll regret mocking me, Tabitha."

"You'll regret making me regret it, Olivia."

"You'll—"

Lila clapped her hands. "People! People! It's time to get to work."

"True," said Tabitha, instantly switching gears. "Look at the collective prank power in this tree house."

"Tree platform," I corrected her.

"We'd be stupid not to take advantage of this opportunity."

"That's what we were thinking too," said Alex.

Yes. *Yes.* I knew she'd come around.

"How much time do we have?" said Lila.

"Just this afternoon," said Alex.

Just an afternoon. It was a crumb, and I used to have a cake.

Lila whipped out a legal pad. I don't know where from. It's one of her special talents, whipping out legal pads from nowhere. "I'll take notes while we brainstorm," she said. "Ideas, please!"

WE WERE LONG past brainstorming, deep into details, when Ruth and Flynn wandered over. "What are you guys doing?" said Ruth.

"Quick!" said Alex. "Pull up the ladder!"

"Who's that?" I heard Flynn ask Ruth.

"Alex, Soren's friend," Ruth said. "Hey! Guys! What's going on up there? Can we come up?"

"You mean, *may* we come up," said Flynn.

Alex was rolling up the rope ladder, so the answer to both questions, obviously, was no. "Not this time," I said, feeling a punch of guilt.

"Oh, come on," said Olivia. "Can't they?"

Olivia likes Flynn. Plus she has a soft spot for younger sisters because she's the runt.

"You guys will make the platform collapse," said Alex. "Five is as many as this thing can hold."

That was honestly true. I could hear ominous creaks every time anyone shifted position. "Let's play Catan tonight," I called down. "The three of us."

Ruth lifted a shoulder. Flynn didn't say a word. They beat their retreat back to the house.

"I feel kind of bad," said Tabitha.

"Me too," said Olivia.

"I play with them all the time," I said. "Seriously. All the time. And Flynn doesn't even like pranking. He told me."

"The thing about pranking," said Alex, "is that if you let everyone in on it, there's no point. There's no *prank*."

Lila fluttered the pages. "Back to the plan."

I'd be extra nice to Ruth and Flynn tonight, I thought. I'd make it better.

But not now.

CHAPTER TWENTY-SEVEN

HERE ARE THE instructions for our small, domestic prank:

1. Sneak into the kitchen and find a box of uncooked macaroni. You also need Scotch tape. And one sandwich bag for each toilet you want to target.

2. Put a little handful of dry macaroni in each bag. Maybe ten pieces. Not much.

3. Go to the bathroom. Close the door like you're actually, you know, going to the bathroom.

4. Tape the bag to the underside of the seat. Make sure the macaroni's spread out enough that the seat looks flat when you close the lid.

5. Wait.

With five experts, it didn't take long to hit every bathroom in both houses. Mom popped in just as we'd all met up in our living room for step 5. "Alex!" said Mom. "We've missed you so much!"

"Speak for yourself," I said.

Alex looped back her leg and nailed me behind the knee. I crumpled to the floor. "Gotcha," she said.

"Nice one," said Mom, high-fiving her.

"Thanks for supporting your child," I told her.

"You deserved it," she said. "How *are* you, Alex?"

I waited for their chatting to die down. "Where are Ruth and Flynn?" I asked Mom as soon as it did.

"They're walking to Coneheads," said Mom. That's the ice cream shop in town. "They took Jim Bob in the stroller."

"Flynn agreed to get near Jim Bob?"

Mom gave me a look. "Don't be mean, Soren."

"I'm not. I was just wondering. So they'll be gone for another hour?"

"At least," said Mom.

Good, because I had a feeling they would not take it well if they were the ones who fell for the prank.

"Let's play Pictionary Telephone," said Tabitha. Before long, we were howling over how demented our drawings got. It was so fun I wished Ruth and Flynn were there too.

We almost missed Dad lumbering down the hall, the newspaper folded under his arm.

"There he goes!" I hissed. "P-Day! P-Day! The moment has come!"

"*Shh!*" said all four girls together, so hard that the breeze from their mouths practically knocked me over.

"Keep playing," said Tabitha. "It'll look suspicious if we don't."

Luckily, we were at a naturally quiet part in the game,

everyone sketching the phrase that the person next to them had written. Nobody was paying much attention to drawing, though. We heard the bathroom door close. The fan whirred on as Dad turned on the light, and then there was silence.

And then—

"AHHHH!"

We were wide-eyed, trying not to laugh.

"LUCINDA!"

Dad rushed down the hall, holding up his pants with his hands.

"Yes?" said Mom. "Is there a problem?"

"I—I'm—"

"What's going on, Jon?"

"Nothing like this has ever happened before—"

"Nothing like *what*?"

We tiptoed into the kitchen and peeked around the doorframe. Mom was peering up at Dad, her work laptop open in front of her.

"Jon?" she said. "Are you all right? And why aren't your pants zipped?"

"Well—"

"One of those scalawags clog the toilet? Well, the plunger's where it always is. Unless Ivan had it up in his crib again—"

"It cracked," Dad whispered urgently.

"The plunger? That clogged, huh—"

"The seat."

"The *what*?"

"I cracked the seat."

"You *what*?"

"Lucinda," said Dad in despair, "I must have sat down too hard—I was in a bit of a hurry—or maybe it was on its last legs—but I sat, and the seat, well . . . It broke."

"You broke the toilet seat?"

I made the mistake of looking at Tabitha, who was bright red and quietly shaking. I had to stuff the collar of my shirt into my mouth.

"Yes," whispered Dad. "I don't know what to say, Lucinda. I heard it crack."

THE DOWNSIDE TO this prank: it's clearly a prank. Mom marched right in to check out the damage, and it was pretty obvious that a bag of macaroni hadn't casually strolled over to the toilet and taped itself under the lid.

But the upside: nobody can be that mad. We were doubled up laughing, flopped on the floor, when Mom and Dad came storming into the living room with the macaroni. "It just crunched, right?" I managed.

"I sat down," Dad said darkly, "and that crack—it was dead-on the sound of a toilet seat breaking." The ends of his belt were still flapping around his thighs. "You should have seen me. I was up like a shot."

That was enough to send us into another gale of laughter. Mom and Dad started laughing too.

"Why didn't I think of this one myself?" said Mom.

"Did you booby-trap any other toilets?" said Dad. "No. You know what? Don't answer that question."

"Maybe we'll go over to the Andrezejczaks' for a while," I said innocently. "See what's going on over there."

Mom lifted her eyebrows at Dad. He shook his head, but not like *no*. More like *why even bother?*

"Be back before dinner," said Mom.

"Have fun," said Dad.

"I don't think you have to tell them that, Jon."

ALEX SAID THERE was a hope that when her mom came back at six, we could persuade her to stay for dinner, and we'd eat really slowly, and it'd end up too late to drive to Effie, where they were going to stay with Alex's aunt, and they'd have to spend the night with us.

No such luck.

Mrs. Harris whipped into the driveway at six o'clock sharp. She came up to the door to get Alex and thank my parents, but you could tell she wanted to hit the road. She was bouncing on her heels and she kept glancing at her phone. "I trusted my new stylist," she told my mom. "I left my whole business in her hands. And now I've got a text that she snipped a man's ear!"

"Snipped it, or snipped it off?" I said.

"Given my luck, snipped it off," said Mrs. Harris. "Why did I leave for a day? Who up and leaves the thing they care most about? *Abandons* it?"

"But what about the ear? Can they reattach it?"

"Probably not," she said gloomily.

I *knew* it. Those haircutters always get way too close with the scissors, and Mom never believes me when I tell her I'm in danger. "I am never getting my hair cut again," I said.

"I'm positive it was just a nick," Mom said to both me and Mrs. Harris. "Everything will be fine, Marilyn. Give him a coupon for a free haircut and he'll settle down."

"He'd better," said Mrs. Harris. "Go take one last bathroom run, Alex, because we're going all the way to Minneapolis and we're not stopping."

Mom ran her hand through the back of my hair. "You're getting pretty scruffy, Soren. Thanks for reminding me. I'll make an appointment for next week."

Ugh.

"Bye," I told Alex when she got back. "See you—see you next time."

"Bye," said Alex. "Yeah. See you. Bye, Soren."

This was the second time I had to watch Alex drive away, not knowing how long it'd be till I'd see her again. It didn't get any easier.

CHAPTER TWENTY-EIGHT

THAT NIGHT IT rained, and it kept raining straight through to Monday morning. That didn't stop Dad from making us walk to the bus stop. "You know the rule," he said. "Skaars walk unless . . ."

"It's below zero with gale-force winds," Ruth and I recited glumly. Dad has a lot of call-and-response sayings like that. "Trash goes in . . . ," he'll say, and we'll chant, "The proper receptacle!" Or, "Skaars are too nice to . . ." "Act exclusive!" He's trying to mold us in his image.

Flynn and Ruth and I set out together, but they started speed-walking right away. They were sharing Flynn's Metropolitan Museum of Art umbrella. I didn't have an umbrella, just a hood, and Dad had made me wear these janky, too-big rain boots I couldn't go fast in. "Hey," I yelled. "Wait up."

Flynn's head bent toward Ruth's, and I heard her giggle. They started walking even faster. "Guys!" I called.

No response. I kicked a wet bundle of leaves. All that did

was throw a bunch of water down the boot, so now my sock was soggy too.

The triplets weren't on their porch. I thought about waiting for them, but I was worried I'd miss the bus and Dad would be mad and I'd be late and Ms. Hutchins would be like, "Your *cousin* was on time." So I sloshed on, getting farther and farther behind.

When I got to the bus stop, the triplets and Ruth and Flynn were all clustered under the gigantic umbrella. "I can't wait to change into my tennis shoes," I announced. Nobody looked up. I elbowed my way in. "How'd you get here so fast?" I asked Lila.

"Mom drove us," she said. "Look."

They were huddled around the worm in Ruth's palm. "I saved him," said Ruth. "He was stranded on the sidewalk."

"Ruth," I said, "there were hundreds of stranded worms."

"Yeah, but only one was Mr. Wiggly."

He was definitely wiggly. That much I'd give her. "*You* like worms?" I asked Flynn quietly.

"Nope. That's why my hands are in my pockets." He shook his hair off his forehead. "Yours are too."

I looked down. Yep. I gave Flynn an embarrassed grin. "Guess so." I couldn't be squeamish—I had a reputation to maintain—but honestly, I don't like worms much either. It was those pink, pointy ends they had. No thanks.

"I think Mr. Wiggly knows you're the one who saved him," Olivia told Ruth. "Look, he dances a bit whenever you get your face near."

The bus pulled up, clanking and splashing. Flynn wrestled with his umbrella and the rest of us lined up to get on. "If Mr. Wiggly's so smart," I told Ruth, "we should use him in a prank."

"No! He's my friend!"

"What better fate for a friend than to be used in a prank?" said Tabitha.

"You guys have one-track minds," sighed Flynn.

"Don't even think about touching Mr. Wiggly," said Ruth.

The bus was damp and steamy, and my socks were so wet I could feel my toes pruning, and all the seats were gone so I had to sit with Billiam Flick. But I found myself in a good mood. It was fun to get along with people. It was a lot better than fighting. We rattled to school. What if Mr. Wiggly ended up in Principal Leary's pocket? Or in a teacher's microwave lunch? Not that any of these pranks would happen, but there was no harm in imagining.

FLYNN WENT TO Goldie's after school to work on their science presentations, so Ruth and I went home alone. "How's Mr. Wiggly?" I asked her.

"He died in math."

"Me too," I said. We'd had a polygon quiz.

"Mr. Snyder let us bury him in the hamster cage. We had indoor recess so we did a whole funeral. Wallaby sang 'Tears in Heaven.'"

"Wow. Sounds sad."

"Nah, it was fun. Hopefully I can find Ms. Wiggly on the way to school tomorrow."

That reminded me. "Do you think Dad would let me have the triplets over?"

"No. No way. It's a school night and you haven't done your homework."

"How do *you* know I haven't done my homework?"

"Have you?"

"Well, no."

"Ha. Told you. Why can't you meet them on the tree platform?"

"Because it's pouring rain."

"I could help you sneak them in," said Ruth, perking up. "Call them up. I've got just the plan."

TABITHA PICKED UP after one ring. "Hello?"

"Oh, hey," I said, relieved it wasn't some weird relative. "I want to do another prank."

"Me too."

"But we've got to be inside—"

"Tell him we can't have friends over on school days," said Lila in the background.

"I *know* that, Lila," Tabitha said snippily. "We want to plan too, Soren—"

"Tell him I've got a new legal pad," I heard Lila say.

"I can talk to him myself—no—quit it—"

There was a bump and a lot of staticky feedback.

"Hello, Soren," said Lila smoothly into the receiver. "*Ouch!* Tabitha!"

"Can you guys get out of the house?" I asked.

"Sure, we're allowed outside. But it's raining, in case

you didn't notice. And maybe we could get an exception and invite you over if we'd done our homework already, but we haven't even started Ms. Hutchins's giant presentation, and that's due the day after tomorrow."

"I don't even know my topic." I paused, distracted. But I had to shake it off. I'd worry about the presentation later. "No, but listen. What I've been trying to tell you: Ruth can sneak you in."

"Really?"

"She's got a plan."

Another bump. More static. "Tell Ruth she's amazing!" Olivia shouted into the phone. "Ouch, Lila! Stop that—*ow*—"

Lila was back. "Hi again. We'll be over straightaway."

"Give us thirty minutes," I said. "And come to the front door."

"But you guys never use the front door."

"Exactly."

TWENTY-TWO MINUTES LATER, Ruth rambled into the kitchen. Dad was cleaning out the cabinet beneath the sink, and Ivan was whizzing around in his baby walker. He uses it even though he can walk now, I'm sure because he can get up some serious speed.

"Can I make scrambled eggs?" Ruth asked Dad.

"Sure."

Ruth whisked a few eggs, turned the stove up to the max, and gave me the thumbs-up. I sidled out of the kitchen and went to the front door.

"WHEEEEEE!" I heard Ivan shout.

"Ivan!" said Dad. "Ruth, could you corral him on that side of the kitchen? I've got a lot of dangerous household chemicals out over here."

I couldn't see, but based on the furious screaming and revving of wheels, Ruth was holding Ivan by his collar. I peeked in. When I saw a wisp of smoke from the stove, I ducked back to the front hall.

"SET IVAN FREE!" Ivan yelled.

"Just a sec, Ruth," said Dad. "Let me get the bleach onto a high shelf—"

"He's really pulling," panted Ruth.

"One second—"

And there it was, the smell of burning eggs. If you've never smelled it, don't. It's kind of like the yolk of a hard-boiled egg plus a fart, but it's all warm and smoky too.

"Your eggs!" shouted Dad.

BEEEEEP! BEEEEEP! That was the smoke detector.

"Oh no!" cried Ruth, sounding only the tiniest bit fake. "I totally forgot!"

"Get that pan off the stove!"

BEEEEEP! BEEEEEP!

"Should I let go of—"

There were pounding footsteps, clattering wheels, and a clang.

"WHEEEEEE!" yelled Ivan.

I opened the door. The triplets darted in.

"Up the stairs," I muttered. "And step on it."

BEEEEEP! BEEEEEP!

They started to run upstairs, me on their heels, but our plan had one major flaw:

Dad sprinted to the front door to fan out the smoke.

We were caught red-handed.

"Do not move," he said.

The triplets and I froze midstep.

Dad fanned the door back and forth. Cold air rushed in, and a raft of raindrops. With one last, drawn-out, resentful beep, the smoke detector fell silent.

Ruth peeked into the hallway. "Oh," she said sadly. "Caught."

Dad surveyed me and the triplets, stock-still on the stairs. Ivan, smirking, wheeled out to the hall. After automatically checking Ivan's tray for the bleach bottle, Dad looked back to me. "I guess I knew that someday you might try to sneak a girl up to your room. But I always thought it'd be one, not three."

"School project," I said weakly.

"You know what?" Dad said. "I'm done. I'm just done. I throw up my hands."

Ruth and I shot each other alarmed looks. Ever since Ivan was born, we'd worried that Dad might crack. "Daddy . . . ," said Ruth.

"I'm fine," he sighed. "Ivan and I will have a nice bracing glass of pomegranate juice. You go work on your"—he paused—"school project."

CHAPTER TWENTY-NINE

"ALL THE WAY UP," I told the triplets on the stairs. "We'll use Flynn's room." The room Ruth and Ivan and I share was filled with dirty laundry and Duplo, and if you step on Duplo barefoot you basically die, it hurts so much.

"Where *is* Flynn?" said Olivia.

"He's at Goldie's. They're working on their science presentations."

Tabitha clapped her hands over her ears. "LA LA LA SCIENCE PRESENTATIONS ARE NOT A THING LA LA LA—"

"It only counts as procrastination if you feel anxious and terrible," Lila explained. "So we have this new strategy where we convince ourselves that major projects don't exist."

Olivia, tearfully twisting a lock of hair, said, "Yeah! It's great!"

"We'll get it done," Lila assured her. "We always do."

"Get what done?" said Tabitha.

"Nothing!" said Lila. "Nothing at all! No deadlines! No projects! We're free!"

Personally, I preferred feeling anxious and terrible. I opened Flynn's bedroom door. "Whoa," I said.

The room was totally different from when it'd been mine. He'd covered one of the slanted attic walls with a sheet of butcher paper, and it looked like he was in the middle of coloring and drawing and doodling all over it. It was like the cave paintings we'd learned about in social studies, except Flynn is way better at art than cavemen.

"This is super cool," said Lila.

"Flynn is amazing," moaned Olivia.

"Hey, look, Soren," said Tabitha. "There's you."

I looked. It was a cartoon of Ivan tricking me into sitting on play dough. There was me, yeah, and there was a clod of brown stuff on the butt of my pants. "Great," I said flatly.

Now that I was looking closely, I saw one familiar scene after another. There was Flynn steeping me that poisonous green tea. There was Flynn at the block party, holding his phone and surrounded by girls. There he was, grinning at his desk, as Ms. Hutchins read aloud the anonymous tip that'd ruined my prank. There he was walking to the bus stop with Ruth, and, yeah, if you followed the road like ten inches back, there was me, walking alone.

"I don't get how he's good at science *and* soccer *and* banjo *and* art," said Tabitha.

"*And* drawing every time I've ever looked stupid!" I said in a chipper voice.

"He's so amazing," said Olivia.

I sat on the floor so I'd have to crane way up to see the mural or whatever you wanted to call it. Those dumb pictures had made me crabby. "Moving on," I said. "Let's plan."

"What are we planning?" said Ruth, lingering by the door.

"We?" said Lila.

"I can stay, right, Soren?" said Ruth.

I shrugged. "If they're okay with it."

"Of course we are," said Olivia. "We wouldn't even be in here without Ruth."

"But can she keep a secret?" said Lila.

"I can!" said Ruth. Her back was ruler straight and her eyes were wide. "I'm good at secrets!"

"Prove it," said Tabitha. "Tell us something you've never told anyone else."

"Trick question," said Ruth. "I won't."

Lila and Tabitha nodded. "She can stay."

"I'll ask Dad if we can borrow his laptop," Ruth said, and shot down the stairs.

"Why?" wondered Tabitha.

I shrugged. When she came back, I said, "Ruth? Why the laptop?"

"To video-chat Alex," she said, like *duh*. "You weren't thinking we'd plan without her, were you?"

Well, yes. I was. Based on the nonplussed looks on the triplets' faces, they were too. Alex had called us the Dream Team after the Crackaroni Incident, but—well, we'd forgotten all about her.

Ruth hadn't forgotten, and Alex wasn't even nice to Ruth.

"We weren't sure she'd be online," I told Ruth.

But she was. I panned the screen so she could see the whole room. "The Dream Team is back!" she said. "Oh, and you, Ruth. Is this your old room, Soren? What happened to the wall up there? Are those drawings?"

"Never mind that," I said quickly, tilting the screen to center on my face. "We've got our next all-school assembly in a couple of weeks. Want to help us plan something?"

Alex frowned. Her glasses slipped down her nose. "My mom says we can't visit again until she's a hundred percent certain nobody's going to cut off an ear the second she leaves town."

"Oh."

"She said definitely not November. Maybe December."

"Oh. Shoot. Okay."

"So . . ."

"So what?"

"So let's plan a prank for then."

"Sure, we will," said Lila, neatly sliding in front of me, "but what about now?"

Alex bit her bottom lip. "Just, I think you should wait till December."

I grabbed the screen so I was the one in it again. "Alex. We can't wait till December."

"Why not?"

"Because it's only October! What are we going to do in between?"

"Plan the December prank."

"And pass up any other opportunity?"

"We're the Dream Team," said Alex. "Well, minus Ruth."

"Yeah, but—"

"And the Dream Team shouldn't prank when only four people are there."

"Five," said Ruth under her breath.

"You shouldn't leave me out," said Alex.

"You could do something down there."

Alex snorted. "Yeah, right. The way they secure this school? And Sophia hates pranking. She's always like, 'Why is that even fun?'"

I shook my head. If someone doesn't immediately grasp the joy of pranking, they're beyond hope.

"Listen," said Lila, taking advantage of my momentary lapse to regain control of the laptop, "we're pranking now. That's decided. So either you're cool with it and help us, or—"

"I just think you're being a little mean," said Alex. "You *could* wait for me."

But you moved away! I wanted to say. *I never wanted you to move, Alex, but you did, and what else am I supposed to do?*

Lila swiveled so Alex couldn't see her face. She mouthed at us, *What should I say?*

"I got this," said Tabitha. She scooched forward. "Alex?"

"Imagine how epic December could be—"

"We're having trouble hearing you." Tabitha frowned at the screen. She grabbed the top of the screen and shook it back and forth. "Alex?" she said in a faraway voice. "We're losing you—bad connection—are you—"

She slammed the laptop shut.

"Done," she said.

We all stared at the laptop there on the rug. A second ago it had been talking, it had been Alex's moving face, scowling, glasses shifting around—and now it was just a hunk of plastic. Technology was weird.

"That's what we do when our mom's out of town and trying to give us chores," said Tabitha.

"It's not very nice," said Ruth.

"Nope," agreed Tabitha. "We're Slytherins."

"Big picture, it *is* nice," said Lila. "She doesn't need to know we're pranking without her. She can think we're waiting, and we'll forget to mention whatever we do."

"I'd rather know the truth if I were her," said Ruth.

"But you're *not* her, are you?" I snapped.

What? Where did that come from?

"No," said Ruth, "but—"

"Go away," I said. "You're just proving you're too little to be here."

I guess I thought, At least I can do *one* thing Alex would approve of.

"Go away, Ruth," I said again.

"You said I could stay!"

"*They* said you could stay. But you're my little sister, so I get to decide." Right then it felt like everything had been better in the old days, and that's the most helpless, hopeless feeling. "And I decide no."

Ruth stomped her foot.

"Very mature," I told her.

She drew herself up as tall as she could. Her eyes got big as she tried not to let tears come out. There was no way she'd cry in front of older girls. Ruth has a lot of pride. "I am *extremely* insulted," she said. "If it hadn't been for me, you wouldn't have even gotten them in the house." On her way out, she whirled around to toss one more thing over her shoulder. "Don't think I'm going to wash that egg pan for you."

IF YOU'VE EVER been over to your friend's when they fight with their sibling, you know it's the second-most awkward situation in the world, number one being them fighting with their parents. I'd seen it plenty (Soup can't even ride in the same car as his sister Wallaby without name-calling), but I'd never been the one who caused it. Not because I'm noble. Just because Ruth and I are, usually, cool.

The triplets were tactfully silent. After a while, though, we started reliving the Alarm Clock Incident. That cleared the air. Olivia did an imitation of Leary when the clocks went off—"*M*, children, is for—AHHHHH! HELP!"— and we were all rolling around like the kindergartners on their mats.

"We've got to do another prank," said Tabitha. "That was the most fun I've had since we forced Ethan to go ice fishing for his boxers."

Lila's legal pad was scrawled with ideas by the time the door opened.

"Oh," said Flynn. "Hey, everyone."

"Oh my gosh," said Olivia, sounding like she'd been sucking on a helium balloon. "It's *Flynn*."

"Hi, Olivia."

She turned bright red and scooted back so she was half-hidden by the desk. "Hi!"

"I'm back from Goldie's," Flynn told me.

"We can see that," I said. "Um, is it okay that we're in here?"

"I guess." He didn't sound totally sure, but he perched on the windowsill and played the piano on the seams of his pants. "What's up? Are you working on your science presentations too?"

"What science presentations?" said Lila. "What in the world are you talking about?"

"Nobody here's started," I said.

"They're due in two days!" said Flynn.

"LA LA LA—" the triplets began.

"What are Dad and Ivan doing?" I asked Flynn. "Are they okay?"

"Your dad is lying flat on the kitchen floor. Ivan is driving trucks over his face."

"Back to normal, then," I said, relieved. "Er, did you happen to see Ruth?"

"She's reading *From the Mixed-Up Files of Mrs. Basil E. Frankweiler* on the couch." Uh-oh. Isn't that book about a girl who runs away from home because her brothers are so annoying? "She looks mad," Flynn added.

"I bet she does," said Tabitha.

"Poor Ruth," said Olivia.

"You don't know anything about it," I told them. "So don't pretend to."

There was an awkward silence.

"So," said Flynn.

"So," said Lila.

The awkwardness continued. Three other people thought about saying, *So*.

Finally, I glanced at the mural on the wall. "We *would* ask you to hang out with us," I said, "but you wouldn't like what we're doing."

"Oh."

I wanted him to leave. I wanted him to get the hint.

"So," I said at last, "you're kind of interrupting."

"Well," said Flynn, "you're kind of in my room."

As a unit, the triplets stood. "We're sorry!" said Olivia. "We'll go!"

"Let's go downstairs, Soren," said Lila.

"Don't boss me around in my own house," I told her. I turned to Flynn. "And you should remember that your room is actually *my* room."

"Whoa," Tabitha said. "Chill."

Didn't she know that the worst, the absolute number-one worst thing to be told is "chill"? I went from annoyed to mad to furious in about half a second, and I grabbed a corner of butcher-paper mural and tore it. I tore it twelve inches, a jagged diagonal rip that went right through a careful, colorful cartoon of Flynn playing the banjo while a bald dude and a ponytailed lady, obviously my parents, bowed in worship. "You can *have* this room," I said. "At least I'm living in my own house."

Flynn turned a deep red. I spun to leave, but not before I saw the way his eyes had gotten all watery. It was the second time that day I'd made someone cry. I knew I was supposed to feel sorry, but it didn't hit me right away. It didn't hit me for a while. For a while it felt like when you've won a soccer game, not just won but really pounded them, and you're walking off the field and you give your counterpart on the other team that little look, chin up, square in the eyes: *I'm better than you.* It was like the surge you get when you win a random arm-wrestling match at lunch and everyone shouts, "OHHH!" Until the sorriness hit me, I felt like a champion. Then it hit me, and I wanted to cry myself.

CHAPTER THIRTY

FLYNN HAD A stomachache and didn't come down for dinner. Mom went to check on him, and after we ate she took up a plate of food and stayed up there for an hour at least.

I figured I'd be in for a Big Talk, so I spent the hour preparing arguments in my head. He didn't like pranking, he'd *said* that, so I wasn't acting exclusive, and about the room, the thing is, as Mom knew, in a big family, or even a medium family in a small house, it's not a huge deal to use someone else's room. Sometimes there's just no other place to go. We hadn't snooped or messed anything up, well, except the mural that had gotten torn, but that was practically an accident—

But Mom didn't say anything about it.

Also, I would have asked whether she'd noticed that the most embarrassing moments in her son's life were depicted in graphic detail on her nephew's walls, and what did she think about *that*.

Nope. Nothing. She did make me wash the egg pan, though.

The next day, Flynn went over to Goldie's again. Her dad dropped him off right before dinner. He slid into his seat and said, "Wow, Uncle Jon! Homemade pizza!"

"Homemade *cabbage* pizza," Ruth corrected him. It was Experimental Food Night again. "Don't get excited."

"Cabbage is my favorite!"

"There's acorn squash and caper pizza as well," said Dad. "Have a slice of each."

"What did you and Goldie get up to?" said Mom.

"First we had snack," said Flynn. "Mrs. Grandin made Snickers salad. It was amazing. I'm really coming around to Midwestern cuisine."

I was having a tough time choking down the cabbage pizza, and I think what happened was that I took a way too big bite and actually clogged my ear canals for a few seconds. Everything's connected in there. By the time I managed a swallow, both Mom and Dad were glaring at me.

"Soren," said Dad, "Flynn says he and Goldie spent most of the afternoon working on their Ethics in Science presentations for Ms. Hutchins."

"Well, actually, we've been working for weeks," Flynn said. "Today was for the finishing touches."

"And they're due *tomorrow*?" said Mom, still glaring.

"I'll be fine!" I said.

"Flynn is done. Have you even started?"

"In a way," I hedged.

"What way?"

"Well . . ." I considered saying I'd made half the Power-Point already, but that was an easy one to check. "I know what my topic is."

That was *almost* true. I couldn't have named it, but I did know where I had it written down.

As long as I hadn't thrown away that piece of paper.

It had to be in the pocket of my Adidas soccer pants.

Unless they'd gotten washed.

"I thought you'd vowed to stop procrastinating," said Dad.

"No, I said *soon* I'd vow to stop procrastinating," I said.

Nobody even cracked a smile. That was how I knew I was in trouble.

I WAS LOCKED in the dining room with Dad's laptop and a cowbell. The laptop was for working; the cowbell was for ringing if I had to go to the bathroom. Then Mom or Dad would come grant permission and stand there scowling until I got back.

At nine or so, Ruth popped her head in. "Flynn's making Snickers salad," she said. "He found the recipe online."

"Cool," I said, not raising my eyes from my PowerPoint. I was still choosing a visual theme, but that was probably the most important step.

"Dad gave him Snickers from the Halloween stash, and he's microwaving them and mashing them up with marsh-mallows and peanut butter and Rice Chex."

Those were four of my all-time favorite foods. "That sounds disgusting," I said.

"Too bad," said Ruth, "because I was going to ask if you wanted me to bring you a bowl."

"Wait, really? Will you really—"

With her sweetest smile, she said, "Nope. Just kidding." She skipped off.

My mouth was watering.

"I guess Flynn's eating processed sugar these days," I called, and after a minute, "Who's acting exclusive *now*?" Nobody answered. But I could hear the beeps of the microwave and Ivan chanting "GLOOP! GLOOP! GLOOP!," so I bet they could hear me.

They could definitely hear me.

I couldn't believe they were taking *his* side.

CHAPTER THIRTY-ONE

IT WAS TWO a.m. by the time I finished *Fudging Data: A Very Big Problem in Scientific Research*, the worst PowerPoint I'd ever made. I relied heavily on animations, twirling letters, and GIFs to cover up the fact that I'd done hardly any research. To be honest, I had to fudge some data myself. I would have considered the irony, but I was too busy collapsing into bed.

Approximately ten minutes later, Mom yelled, "Flynn! Soren! Ruth!"

I flinched.

"Flynn! Soren! Ruth!"

I rolled over.

"Rise and shine!"

I squinted my eyes open. The sun seemed extra bright.

"Blerg," I said to Ruth, forgetting that she was mad at me.

"Blerg yourself," she said, obviously forgetting too. She hopped out of bed. "It snowed! First of the season!"

That was why it was so bright. The sun was glaring off it, like the world was carpeted with fluorescent lights.

"You think we'll get a snow day?"

"No. It's not much. I can still see grass blades." October snow is usually pretty wimpy. Besides, we're so good at plowing up here in northern Minnesota that it takes a major blizzard to get a snow day.

"CHILDREN!"

"I'm up, Mom!" called Ruth.

"Me too, Aunt Lucinda!" yelled Flynn.

I closed my eyes. I'd rest for one more minute, let Ruth take her turn in the bathroom—

"SOREN EBENEZER SKAAR! YOU'LL MAKE US ALL LATE!"

I jolted awake.

"IF YOU DON'T GET YOURSELF OUT OF BED WITHIN THREE SECONDS, I'M COMING TO GET YOU OUT OF BED MYSELF!"

That made me jump. You do not want Mom to get you out of bed. Once she literally picked up the footboard and dumped me out, like she was having one of those superhuman-strength moments that normal moms get when they're saving their child from a flipped car or something.

I got on the bus like, *Phew*. Sometimes you want to go from the frying pan to the fire just for the change of scenery.

MS. HUTCHINS IS always peppy on presentation days, mostly because she gets to use the bingo machine she bought at an antiques store in Duluth. It's basically a bird-cage full of numbered Ping-Pong balls, and you pull a lever and they all hop around like water bugs and then one ball falls down the chute. Ms. Hutchins loves it. She danced over and set them popping and sang out, "Our first victim is . . ."

The Ping-Pong ball glided down the chute. We held our breaths.

"Number . . ."

She drags this out, I swear.

"Nine!"

We're numbered alphabetically. Twenty-three kids breathed a sigh of relief. Goldie stood.

"Hi!" she said. Goldie loves presentations. She was wearing a blazer, total overkill but probably doing great things for her grade. "My PowerPoint is called *Why We Shouldn't Experiment on Animals.*"

I half closed my eyes. I meant to mentally rehearse my presentation, but I must have dozed off. I was jerked awake by the applause as Goldie bowed left, right, and center.

"Thank you!" said Ms. Hutchins, glowing. "What a *wonderful* start! I hope you all will take Goldie's professional, well-mannered presentation style as a model."

She pulled the lever on the lottery machine. "Number . . ."

I crossed my fingers and prayed for salvation.

"Seventeen!"

Me.

Rats.

Reluctantly, I pulled up my PowerPoint on Ms. Hutchins's computer. "Er," I said, "hello. My topic is . . ."

I blanked.

"Um . . ." I turned around to look at my slide. "Oh, right. Fudging data."

It went downhill from there.

I've blocked out most of it, so, sorry, you don't get all the grisly details. I do recall reading authoritatively from one of my slides, "Amazingly, 37.2 percent of scientific data is entirely made up."

"Really," said Ms. Hutchins dryly.

"Yup," I said, sensing imminent disaster and clicking onward fast. The next slide was the second to last. Thank goodness. "So if you ever become a scientist," I said, "you should never make up data."

"*That's* your takeaway for the class?" said Ms. Hutchins.

"Um," I said, "I think there's one more slide."

I'd made the last slide in a delirious haze at two a.m. I had no recollection of what it was.

"In conclusion," I said, hoping it was some sort of conclusion.

I clicked.

Oh no.

Well. I didn't have a choice. I had to go for it.

"Always remember," I read with gusto, "when you fudge data . . ."

I clicked, and the rest of the motto twirled onto the screen.

". . . you say 'fudge you' to the scientific community!"

The class exploded into laughter.

"Soren!" said Ms. Hutchins. "Utterly inappropriate! What were you thinking?"

"I guess I thought it was catchy."

"You should know better."

"Sorry, Ms. Hutchins."

Oops.

CHAPTER THIRTY-TWO

YOU ONLY GO into Mom and Dad's bedroom if (a) you're deathly ill or (b) you're in the biggest trouble of your life. Or, once, when I decided that having the flu was a great chance to stockpile vomit ice cubes, both (a) and (b).

"Sit on the couch, young man," said Dad.

"We've seen the online grade book," said Mom.

They loomed over me. I'll spare you the lecture—I'm sure you can imagine it—but basically, I was grounded until my science grade improved. "But it's not about the grade," said Dad, trying to make himself feel better about his parenting. "It's about attitude. It's about work ethic. We want you to do your best, Soren, and your best is not a presentation that gets a . . ."

He peered at the laptop.

"A seven."

"Ouch," I said involuntarily. It sounded really bad when you said it out loud.

"How is a seven even *possible*?" said Dad.

174

"Ms. Hutchins is a really hard grader," I said.

"Then how did Flynn get a ninety-eight?"

"Well, Flynn should have gotten a hundred, so—"

"You should have gotten a nine?"

IT'S HARD TO plan a prank when you can't leave the house. On Friday, when I should have been planning with the triplets, or playing on Jéro's dock with him and Soup and Freddy, or kicking it with Alex, my real best friend—on Friday, when Flynn went rollerblading with Goldie and Kiyana, when Ruth went to Wallaby's sleepover birthday party, when even Ivan, *Ivan the Terrible*, had a playdate— well, on Friday, I took the bus straight home, alone.

"It's just you and me, Soren!" Dad crowed. "And I've got exciting plans for us!"

"Really?"

"Father-son bonding!"

I hoped he wanted to play catch. We used to throw around all the time, but then Ivan was born. "I'll get the mitts," I said.

"It's time for the Great Chicken Migration!"

"Wait, what?"

"I've taken a deep dive into the chicken-farming blogosphere, and we're going to move them to the mudroom for the winter. It'll be good for both their egg production and their mental health."

"But the mudroom's full of our stuff!"

"That's where you and I come in."

"Must be nice to have a kid," I muttered. "Forced labor."

"You're referring to your life, or mine?" said Dad.

We started clearing out the mudroom. It was like an archaeological dig, a layer of boots and coats drifting over the summer rubble of deflated water wings, unpaired flip-flops, and the badminton net. Finally we got to the distant past: crumpled vocabulary quizzes and dried-out stink-bug corpses. "Whew." Dad surveyed the lawn, where we'd dumped all the stuff. "This is a bigger job than I'd imagined."

"Maybe we should take a break," I suggested. "Finish up tomorrow when everyone's home."

He eyed me. "What do we say? Chores build . . ."

"Character," I finished grumpily.

It took a few hours, but by the time we sorted all that crap and dumped in pine shavings for the chickens' bedding, I was actually feeling good. I'd never admit this to Dad, but there's something weirdly fun about working hard enough to sweat and get hungry, especially if you're working outside. "We'll keep their feeder out in the yard," said Dad, "so they'll get exercise and fresh air."

"Hopefully they'll do their pooping out there too," I said.

"We can always dream."

"*You* can. I have better things to dream about than pooping."

He laughed, and I felt a warm *pop!,* like I was a can of Coke that someone had just opened, like I was all fizzy and alive. "Look at this nifty heat lamp I ordered," said Dad.

"Why? Won't it be warm in the mudroom?"

"Not warm enough, and it's for light, too. We'll set it to turn on at four a.m. If the chickens don't get a fourteen-hour day, they'll go into a molt and stop laying eggs."

"Would that be so bad?"

"You know your mother," he said. "She won't buy feed if they aren't producing."

Mom grew up on a farm in North Dakota. She doesn't believe in pets.

"You lure them in while I set up the lamp," said Dad. "Then I think we'll be done."

I scattered a trail of feed from coop to mudroom. "Bawk-bawk-bawk!" I called. Pecking and chattering, Dotty, Potty, Eugenie, Hatty, and Betty II waddled along the trail. They hopped in, nipped around, and settled down. Chickens aren't easy to stress out.

But Martha was still lingering in the coop.

"Come on, Martha!" I said, keeping my distance. "Here, boy!"

"COCK-A-DOO-ARGH-ACK-ECK-EH!" Martha screamed. He didn't move.

"Martha! Martha! Don't you want to be nice and warm for the winter?" I said.

He swiveled his head, but only because Mr. Nelson's car had pulled into the driveway. Flynn hopped out. "Ooh!" he said. "Are we winterizing the chickens? I've read about this!"

I skulked back. When I'd seen him whispering with the

Goldie gang at recess, I'd gotten that being-talked-about feeling, which was confirmed when they spent all social studies shooting me evil looks. But he hadn't said a word to me. I'd also seen him taking the Scotch tape up to his room, probably to fix the mural, and probably, while he was at it, to draw another picture of me looking bad. He had several new options.

Dad was giving him a tour of the mudroom. "But we're having trouble getting Martha to recognize his new home," Dad said.

"Relocation is hard," said Flynn. "What about a treat? Something to soothe him?"

"COCK-A-DOO-ARGH-ACK-ECK-EH!"

"Excellent idea!" said Dad.

"I'll get some yogurt," said Flynn. "Martha loves it."

How would *he* know?

But sure enough, when he came back with a dish of plain yogurt, Martha hopped happily into the mudroom. "Wow," said Dad. "Flynn, what would we do without you?"

"Yogurt's good for his digestive health, too!" said Flynn.

Dad slung an arm around his shoulders and pulled him close. "*Thank* you."

I trudged after them into the house. You could really tell they were related from the back. Their hair lay the same way, and their shoulders, too. "We'll do an easy dinner," said Dad. "How do veggie burgers sound, Flynn?"

"With hummus?" he said. "And pickled red onion?"

"Wonderful!"

FLYNN AND RUTH were refusing to walk with me again. They'd speed-walk if I walked normally and they'd dawdle back if I tried to catch up. Flynn I could handle, I guess, but it really annoyed me that he'd gotten Ruth on his side. She wouldn't have even remembered she was mad at me without his constant reminders.

Luckily, the triplets stuck with me. "Let's make this spelling-bee prank happen," I said, eyeing Ruth and Flynn twenty feet ahead. We hadn't had any good ideas yet, but it wasn't till tomorrow.

"Whatever we do, let's be careful," said Olivia.

"Naturally," said Lila, rolling her eyes. She doesn't like her authority being questioned, especially by the runt. "Nobody wants to get caught."

"No, I mean . . . let's make sure we don't ruin the spelling bee."

"Why?" said Tabitha. "Because darling Flynnie's in the bee?"

"No!" said Olivia, blushing. Obviously, she meant, *Yes!*

Lila shrugged. "We'll do the prank at the end of the assembly. After the bee's over."

"But what's our prank?" I said.

Tabitha's eyes glinted. "I have the perfect idea."

She told us. Olivia shook her head. "Ruth would never let us borrow him," Olivia said. "He's like a pet to her. No. He's like a *son*."

"Who says we'll ask her?" I said.

"He'll be fine," said Tabitha. "He'll like it."

"And Ruth will think it's funny," I said. "Eventually."

"I don't know," said Lila. "She's already mad at us for leaving her out. And then if we use—"

"It's a great idea," I said. I looked ahead at Ruth and Flynn, trudging along with their heads bent close, his messenger bag bumping her giant green backpack. "Let's do it. Once she sees how funny it is, Ruth won't mind at all."

CHAPTER THIRTY-THREE

"SHUSH!" MS. HUTCHINS kept saying as we found our seats in the gym. "Silence, sixth graders!" It had no effect. The spelling bee hadn't started yet, though the fourteen kids who'd advanced from the classroom competitions were already seated onstage. There were about ten teachers up there too, trying to figure out how to turn on the mike.

"Anyone want to bet on the winner?" said Jéro.

"I'll bet a nickel on Flynn," said Olivia.

"Ten cents on Justice," said Soup. "He won last year."

"The winning word," cried Chloe, wildly waving a dollar bill in Jéro's face, "will be *reindeer*!"

"Soren?" said Jéro. "Want to bet on your cousin?"

I nudged my backpack, which was unzipped at the top, a bit farther under my seat. "I'm good."

Mr. Pickett must have bumped the right switch, because his words suddenly filled the gym. "This mike design is bullpoop"—he didn't say *bullpoop*, though—"that's what it is, absolute bu— Wait, is this working?" He turned bright red and thrust the mike at Principal Leary.

Leary shook his head at Mr. Pickett, who slunk back. It was nice to know that teachers could get on principals' bad sides. It made them seem almost human. "Welcome to the spelling bee," said Principal Leary. He explained the rules while I peered over Jéro's shoulder to see whether anyone had won big by predicting Leary's solar-system tie. Pluto was featured right down by the tip. I guess it was an old one.

Macintosh Avery had drawn the first seat. "Your word, Macintosh," said Principal Leary, "is *nonchalant*." Macintosh is a third grader who comes up to about my knee, but he nonchalantly whipped it off.

Next up was Gordon Spinner, a second grader. "*Scenic*," said Principal Leary. Gordon missed the first *c* and burst into tears, but he got a solid round of applause for being the first loser.

Nevaeh Diggs got *chandelier*.

Rob Diedrich Jr. got *patrician*.

John Lovinsky missed *imbecile*, which is kind of funny if you think about it.

Flynn, wearing a tuxedo T-shirt and pants that stopped in the middle of his calf, was next. He got *artisanal*. I zoned out. Spelling's boring even when it's you who's doing it. The spellers finally burned down to three: tiny Macintosh, reigning champ Justice, and Flynn.

I'd been zoning out on Tabitha's ponytail, which I didn't know until she turned around and I realized I'd gone kind of cross-eyed. "Is something wrong?" she said.

"No, I'm fine."

She raised her eyebrows. *But are you* ready? she mouthed.

I was. Three spellers left. It'd be soon now. The plan was to set off the prank the second the winning word was spelled, before anyone had time to leave.

Justice went down on *dromedary*. His eyes welled up. I quickly looked away.

Macintosh got *pachyderm,* and rattled it off like it was *cat*.

Flynn got *trattoria*. His voice was shaking, but he nailed it. Then Macintosh screwed up *fracas* pretty hard. There was a *q* involved. Flynn had to spell it right to win. He stepped up to the microphone.

"*Fracas,*" he said. "*F*—"

I lifted my backpack to my lap. Lila and Olivia were on either side of me, and they leaned forward to give me cover.

"*R*—"

I opened the backpack. Jim Bob, curled cozily inside, blinked as he woke up from his morning nap. He looked groggy. My greatest fear was that he'd go right back to sleep. The prank would fail, and fail hard.

"*A*—"

I set the backpack on the floor and nudged at the bottom with my foot. I figured it'd take him a minute to discover his escape hatch and make a move, but he nosed out right away. He took off down the row of seats. "Grab him!" I hissed at Lila, and she swiped at him, but it was too late. There was a flutter of squeals and laughter as he poked his way down the row.

"C—"

"Stop him!" I whispered, waving frantically, but nobody heard me. Jim Bob reached the center aisle. Like a midfielder who breaks out of a clump of defenders and hits his stride in the open grass, he took off across the shiny wooden floor.

"A—" said Flynn, and then he saw Jim Bob. "CATCH IT!" he shrieked into the mike.

Now the whole gym looked to where he was pointing. Some kids laughed. Some kids screamed. Amid the uproar, Jim Bob made a beeline for the stage.

Flynn was totally safe up there. No piglet can jump four feet, not even at a dead sprint. But he freaked out. He shrieked again and leapt off the stage, knocking over the mike as he went. It hit the stage floor with an earsplitting burst of feedback. Jim Bob was startled. He turned tail and charged the fifth grade. A few of them were so scared they scrabbled up the gym walls to get away, like he was a rat. Principal Leary rummaged for the mike on the floor. "Catch it!" he cried into the mike. "Teachers! Students! Someone! Someone catch it!"

Jim Bob darted back and forth, oinking. He'd panicked along with everyone else. Chairs were flying as kids dove for safety.

"CALM DOWN, EVERYONE!" yelled Principal Leary into the mike. At the noise, all four of Jim Bob's short legs left the floor. When he landed, he took off even faster in the other direction.

"CATCH THAT PIGLET!" Principal Leary shouted at the top of his lungs. "FACULTY, I AM TALKING TO YOU!"

But the teachers were standing against the walls of the gym with faces that were like, *Not* my *problem.* Principal Leary tossed the mike aside and left the stage with a flying leap that was actually pretty impressive for a dad-aged guy. He took off after Jim Bob, his face purple with rage, the solar-system necktie flapping behind.

Kids sprang out of his way. Jim Bob maintained the narrow distance between them for a while, but as they approached the fourth-grade section, Leary was gaining. He dove. He missed.

"HEY!" yelled a high, furious voice. "THAT'S MY PIGLET!"

Kicking and flailing, Ruth emerged from the mass of fourth graders. She took off in a trot toward Jim Bob. "Here, Jimmy!" she called. "Here, Jimmy-Jimmy Bobkins! Here!"

Jim Bob didn't hear her. He started sprinting back toward the front, eyeing Flynn.

Leary, grasping a side stitch, stopped altogether, but Ruth picked up the pace. So did Jim Bob. I bet he heard her footsteps and thought it was still Leary. He was heading straight for Flynn. Flynn tried to shove Macintosh in front of him, but since Macintosh was about as big as Flynn's left leg, he didn't offer much protection.

Ruth sprinted, but Jim Bob sprinted faster. Ten feet away from Flynn, Jim Bob hit another gear, bounding down the aisle. Flynn's face was pure terror. Jim Bob leapt into

Flynn's arms. For a moment, Flynn clutched him, and then Ruth caught up and snatched him away.

"My darling!" I heard her cry in horror, before the whole gym was overtaken with excited shouts and banging applause.

Ruth ripped her gaze from Jim Bob and turned toward the sixth-grade section. She stared at me. Even from fifty feet away, the stare burned.

"Oh dear," Olivia whispered. "She's not very happy, is she?"

I slowly shook my head.

CAUTION CAUTION CAUTION CAUTION CAUTION

CHAPTER THIRTY-FOUR

WE GOT DISMISSED to the playground for emergency recess. I tried to catch up with Ruth, but she (and Jim Bob) got whisked away to Leary's office. Then I went over to the triplets by the fence, but Tabitha said, "Go play soccer. It looks way too suspicious to have you here right now."

I got drafted onto Kiyana's team. Jeremiah passed to Goldie, who tapped it to Billiam, who took it on a quick run down the wing. I charged, but Billiam blew past me and shot on goal. Kiyana did this feetfirst dive thing and just managed to knock it out of bounds.

Jeremiah lined up for the corner. A scrum formed around the goal, all eight of us jockeying for position, and I marked Jack. Jeremiah's kick soared. The scrum exploded like a firecracker. Jack leapt left and scorched a perfect header into the goal.

Ouch. My fault. I wasn't playing my best. I was all twitchy and high-energy, and that's not right for soccer.

You have to concentrate. It was like my mind was still in the gym, like it had become a spooked piglet itself, bouncing from one wall to the next, in one direction and another.

My team jogged back up to midfield. We were only down one, and then we were tied when Kiyana scored on a beautiful floater from twenty yards out.

Goldie was about to take their kickoff when Flynn appeared. "You want to play?" she said.

He didn't say anything, but he nodded. "We get him," said Billiam. "We're down a man."

"A person," said Kiyana.

"Whatever," said Billiam. "As long as we get Flynn."

There wasn't really any arguing, not when it was five versus four, so Flynn jogged over to their right wing. Of course Goldie passed it to him. "Mark your man!" yelled Kiyana to our team.

"Person!" yelled Billiam.

She ignored him. "Spread out!" Flynn passed so much that we'd learned how to face him: let him do what he wanted and cover the rest of his team. Let them make the mistakes, basically.

I was left to mark Flynn. I ran up to him, expecting him to pass as soon as I got there, but instead he took off down the wing. And I mean took off. I'm pretty fast, and before that day I'd thought I could beat him in a race, but I'd never seen him go all out. He was flying.

A bunch of his teammates were open, open enough to

pass to, anyway, but he didn't even consider it. He hosed me—I was five feet behind, then ten—and swept the ball into the top left corner of the net.

"GOOOOAALLLLLLL!" Billiam screamed. He ran over to chest-bump Flynn, but Flynn wasn't having it. Flynn didn't even smile. He jogged back up to the line, barely winded, and he said, "Take the kickoff."

That was how it went for the rest of the emergency recess. If we'd ever wondered what Flynn was really capable of, now we knew. He scored on midfield shots, on dribbles, on headers. He scored with his right foot and his left. He didn't break a sweat and he didn't crack a smile. It was 8–1, maybe 9–1, when Mrs. Andersen knuckle-whistled us in. "VICTORY!" yelled Billiam, raising his arms in ninety-degree angles and doing this robot dance thing, but Flynn just slumped down, like he was a puppet and the game was his string, the only thing holding him up. He started back toward the school immediately.

"What's with him?" said Jéro.

I shrugged.

"He could go pro," said Soup. "He could get free cleats."

"Yeah, he's really good," I said. I wished I could be a good sport, the kind of loser Dad always says we should be, but I felt like the bad kind of loser, the kind who shouts about unfairness and kicks the dirt and never wants to play again. I said, "Too bad he's scared of piglets."

Jéro and Soup and Freddy laughed. I thought it'd make me feel better, but it didn't really work.

I'D TRIED TO keep a low profile after school, but I had to come down when I was called for dinner. I was nervous. Ruth knew it was me, and Flynn probably did too. What if they'd told Mom and Dad? Or worse, Leary?

"Set the table, Soren," Mom told me.

"For six?"

"I called your sister in, but Flynn has another stomach-ache. Five."

Ruth came to the kitchen door holding Jim Bob.

"You know the rule," said Mom. "No animals inside."

Usually when Mom says that, Ruth and I mouth *except Ivan* at each other. But she didn't look at me. "Fine," she told Mom. "I'll eat slops. I'm not leaving him alone until he feels better."

"Honey, he's just a piglet—"

"Lucinda," said Dad, "let her be." He gave Ruth a PB&J for her and some unsalted peanuts for Jim Bob, and the two of them went back outside.

"Four," Mom told me.

The door between the kitchen and the mudroom is glass, so if you had the right seat, you could watch the chickens from the table. They were boring—mostly they pecked at nothing and readjusted their feathers—but that evening, dinner was even more boring. Ivan's always quiet on spaghetti nights because he's busy painting his entire body orange. Mom talked about a work thing and Dad gave her advice that she viciously tore to shreds, which is a thing they both enjoy. I was just grateful they didn't ask me any tough questions about how, exactly, Jim Bob had found himself at the spelling bee.

Like I said: they were clueless.

I loaded the dishwasher without being asked. (Obvious sign of a guilty conscience, but I couldn't help it.) Afterward, I went to shoot on the woodpile. It was dark, but there's a light on the garage that helps a bit.

Pow!

Pow!

Pow!

Ruth heaved herself up the hill from the pigpen. "Hi," I said.

"Hi."

I shuffled the ball between my feet, mostly to have something else to look at. "Is he, um, okay?" I said.

"He's not back to normal. But he lost that wild look in his eyes after he got the peanuts."

"Oh, good."

"Here," said Ruth. "Pass."

I passed. She shot. "So," she said as it rebounded. "That was you, right?"

I cringed.

"Well?"

I wished I could lie. But I couldn't, and to be totally honest, it wasn't because lying's wrong; it was because I didn't think Ruth would buy it. "Me and the triplets."

"Wow," she said. Her voice was quivering. "Jim Bob is my favorite person in the world, and you *kidnapped* him? You kept him in your *backpack*?"

"I didn't zip it all the way!"

"He could have died!"

"I put a banana in there! Which he ate! He couldn't have been too unhappy!"

She kicked the ball at me, hard. I barely managed to snag it before it went into the street. "Are you mad at the triplets too?" I asked.

She considered. "Not as much. You're the one who stole him."

"That's unfair."

"Besides," she said, "that was really mean of you, what you did to Flynn."

I passed back. "It's his fault he's scared of a harmless piglet."

"No. With the bee. He was about to win. Now they have to replay the last word tomorrow."

"He'll probably win anyway."

"Maybe," said Ruth.

"Pass."

She set a firm foot atop the ball. "He knows it was you," she said. "And I bet he thinks you did it on purpose."

"Well, we didn't bring Jim Bob to the spelling bee by *accident*—"

"No. I mean. That you targeted him."

"Of course we didn't!"

"Well, he was about to win and you stopped the bee. And you knew he was scared of Jim Bob."

Obviously we hadn't targeted Flynn. How were we supposed to know he'd be the last speller? The real problem, anyway, was that Jim Bob had escaped one letter too soon. "What happened with you and Principal Leary?" I asked Ruth.

"He said that as soon as he found out who brought the piglet, they'd get expelled."

"Expelled?"

"He was really mad. He wrenched his knee on one of those diving leaps."

"Did you—did you tell him you thought it was me?"

She gave me a withering look. "Of course not."

"Oh. Good. Phew. Thanks."

"I told him it definitely wasn't you. I told him I saw inside your backpack on the bus and it was full of books."

"Ruth . . ." I was a bit overcome.

"And I told Mom and Dad someone must have snuck over here and stolen Jim Bob. I said maybe Billiam Flick. You know Mom's thing with him."

Billiam wrote his name in the wet concrete when we got our driveway repoured. Mom's held a grudge ever since. The poor kid was six.

"Well. Thanks, Ruth."

"You don't deserve a sister like me."

I really didn't. "I'll give you my dessert tonight."

"Just because I'm not getting you into trouble," she said,

"doesn't mean I'm not still extremely mad. And so is Flynn."
Abruptly, she turned and headed inside.

"Wait—Ruth—"

She didn't stop. She hadn't even kicked me the ball. It began to roll down the slight slope of the driveway. I started to jog after it, but then I stopped too. I didn't feel like kicking anymore.

CHAPTER THIRTY-FIVE

"GOOD MORNING," Principal Leary said on the screen.

"A new tie!" whispered Soup.

Jéro scribbled hurriedly. New ties always gave him a lot of calculations. This one featured a globe surrounded by the words *World's Coolest Elementary School Administrator.*

How much competition was there, anyway?

"We have several announcements," said Principal Leary. "The Lego League will meet after school in Mr. Rashid's classroom."

Beside us, Chloe had gone all pale and sweaty.

"Are you okay?" said Tabitha.

Chloe braced both hands on her desk to keep herself upright. She looked like she might faint. Or barf. I scooched my own desk a few inches away.

Principal Leary continued. "The Future Engineers of America will meet with Ms. Vicari after school at the circuit board."

"Chloe?" said Tabitha. "Did you lose another bet?"

"I thought he'd go with stripes," said Chloe weakly. "And I bet it all."

"Class!" said Ms. Hutchins. "Stop talking!"

"I bet it *all*," Chloe said again.

"Attention up here, please!"

"My iPod—my guinea pig—"

"Eyes open, mouths closed!"

"The shirt off my back—"

"Who won the shirt?" said Soup.

"*Shush!*" barked Ms. Hutchins.

"One final announcement," Leary said. His grim tone plus Ms. Hutchins's orange-zone anger made everyone shut up, though Chloe was still rocking from side to side. "Yesterday, our school community was disrupted. We lost several minutes of valuable instructional time and had to reschedule the final word of the spelling bee. Furthermore, on a personal note, your fearless leader injured his knee." He turned the webcam to a brace strapped over his pants. "If you were the one behind this inappropriate and disrespectful act," he said, righting the camera, "don't think you'll get away with it. And the rest of you, as upstanding members of the Camelot Elementary community—if you saw something, say something. It is your duty."

I went rigid. Most likely, someone *had* seen something.

And that wasn't even mentioning Flynn.

"If you have information," said Leary, "please speak with a trusted adult. The safety and peace of our school depend on each one of you."

He stared out at us for a length of time somewhere between "awkwardly long" and "Is the webcam frozen?"

"Thank you," he said at last. "It's a lovely day for learning."

DAD CAME BACK from his Saturday-morning run with his usual runner's high plus a box of doughnuts from Mamie's Donuttery. Mamie's doughnuts are basically clouds dipped in frosting. I had a cinnamon cruller while Ruth had a cream-filled. Ivan got pink sprinkles, and Flynn, who was reading a book in his lap, had a toffee crisp.

Our parents paged through the *Camelot Roundtable*. "Mateo Luna is running for town council again, I see," said Dad.

"And Gerald Flick's heirloom butternut squash won second place at the county fair," said Mom. "We should pop over for a look."

"Can we have the comics?" I asked.

A few minutes later, Mom said, "Well, well. Jim Bob made the paper."

We craned to see the headline: SOME PIG! HOG "SPELLS" DISRUPTION AT SCHOOL BEE.

"Let me see that," I said, my heart pounding. Had Leary sicced a reporter on the case?

"Looks like total chaos," said Dad.

Mom, skimming the article, said, "Flynn! You didn't breathe a word! How modest you are!"

Some Pig! Hog "Spells" Disruption at School Bee

BY HENRY DUCK, STAFF REPORTER

The annual spelling bee at Camelot Elementary School was given a "streak" of excitement when a piglet interrupted the proceedings.

Kiyana Nelson, 11, said, "Usually the spelling bee is really boring, but this year I loved it!"

As Flynn Skaar, 12, was at the microphone, spelling what could have been his winning word, the piglet was let loose. He or she (bystanders were unsure) streaked through the assembly with students and faculty alike in hot pursuit.

Louis Leary, 49, the school's principal, was not pleased. "We at Camelot Elementary take spelling very seriously," he said. "Whoever did this showed a lot of disrespect to the students in the competition, not to mention those of us who risked life and limb to chase the beast."

The piglet was eventually apprehended, but the perpetrator remains at large. The next day, a replay of the last word was given to the two finalists. When Skaar stumbled over *viscera,* Macintosh Avery, 9, took the crown. Beaming, he said, "I owe it all to my parents, my teachers, and my personal hero, Noah Webster."

This reporter would guess that none of the students will forget how to spell *pig* anytime soon!

"Well, I should hope not," said Ruth.

"I see no culprit is mentioned," said Mom. "Should I call Principal Leary? Tell him that it may well have been Billiam Flick?"

I gave a nervous twitch.

"*I* think we're focusing on the wrong thing here!" said Dad. He pulled Flynn into a side-armed hug. Flynn squirmed away, probably because Dad was still sweaty. "We are in the presence of greatness! Flynn Skaar, second place in the spelling bee!"

"Thanks, Uncle Jon."

"Spelling must not be genetic," Dad mused. "Why, I could barely spell my own name when I was your age. Always put an *h* in there. What an accomplishment, Flynn! Are you thrilled?"

"I should have won," he said. "All I had left on *fracas* was the *s*, but I was rattled during the replay. Macintosh kept jangling his lucky charm bracelet, the one with the tooth of Noah Webster—"

"Excuse me?" said Mom.

"He bought it on eBay. Certified authentic." Flynn shook his head. "It threw me off. I confused *viscera* with *vicissitude*."

"Still amazing," said Dad. "We should celebrate! We'll bake a Silver Medal Speller cake!"

Ivan perked up at the word *cake*. "IVAN LICK BOWL!"

"We don't eat raw eggs, remember, not after Daddy read the latest from the CDC—"

"IVAN LIKE RAW EGGS!"

"Raw eggs make us sick, Ivy, remember? Sick at both ends?"

"IVAN LIKE SICK!"

"I'm in no mood to celebrate," said Flynn. Without warning, he stood and left. His footsteps took the two flights to the attic.

"Oh dear," said Dad.

"He's taken it hard," said Mom.

"Soren and Ruth," said Dad, "I hope you know that your mother and I are proud of you whether you get first place, or second place, or dead last place."

"Honey," said Mom, "are you sure that's the message you want to send?"

CHAPTER THIRTY-SIX

THREE MINUTES AFTER I sat down at the computer, Ruth claimed she needed to do research for her social studies project. "This is what happened the *last* time I needed to use the computer!" I said.

"And it'll happen the next time too," she said sweetly. "And the next, and the next, and the—"

I stomped out. Not before pushing the power button, though. And a few hours later, while Dad was distracted with building Duplo towers for Ivan to demolish, I grabbed his laptop and took it up to our closet. I wasn't supposed to, but I didn't know what else to do. I had to talk to someone. Someone who got me.

"Alex?" Her face jumped onto the screen. "I have some things to tell you."

"I thought you might."

"Okay. So." I took a deep breath. "Let's start with the last time we video-chatted. . . ."

I told her everything. I told her we'd hung up on her on

purpose. I told her we'd pranked without her, and I told her all about the prank.

"Now Ruth's mad and Flynn's mad and you're probably mad too," I said, "and it's all my fault."

"What about the triplets?" she said. "Don't they deserve some blame?"

"They asked if Ruth would care about us using Jim Bob, and I said no. They didn't know Flynn's scared of him. And you—you're *my* best friend. I'm the one who's supposed to be watching out for you."

I squirmed, which was a mistake since I was sitting on a pile of toys. I got stabbed in the butt by a dump truck. "And here's the worst part," I said. "I *wanted* to make everyone mad. It wasn't an accident."

That's what I'd realized lying in bed last night. I'd looked at the dark contours of the furniture and listened to the slow sleeping breaths of my sister and brother and I'd finally stopped fooling myself. "I wanted to blow everything up," I said.

"But why?" said Alex. "That's not why we prank."

"I don't know. I guess it was easier to make things worse than to make them better."

"I'm not that mad at you."

"Even though we hung up on you?"

"Well, that was annoying. Tell Tabitha she's way too obvious. She needs to shake the screen more."

"And distort the audio. Mess with the volume button, maybe?"

We both paused, lost in thought, and I could tell that'd be added to our list of Things to Practice.

"But anyway," said Alex, "I was talking to Sophia about the prank thing, and she said that if *she* moved and told me I could only do paper dolls when she visited, I'd think that was stupid."

"Oh."

I couldn't decide whether to be grateful to Ol' Butt-Braid for making my case for me, or annoyed that she'd managed to convince Alex that paper dolls were as cool as pranks.

"Plus, now you owe me," said Alex.

"Yeah."

"I got my mom to promise me we'll visit in December. She picked a random Thursday, since apparently that's the day Ubercut gets the fewest clients. December thirteenth. I get to skip school and come to school with you. We've got a chance to do something amazing."

"Wait. One more thing, Alex . . ."

I hadn't gotten to my last point, the last thing I'd realized when I couldn't sleep. Which was this:

I'd retired from pranking.

Not fake retired, melodramatically mentally retired, like I'd kept saying at the beginning of the school year. No. This time, I was done.

I couldn't trust myself. I'd hurt too many people.

"Whoopee cushions?" said Alex. "Stink bombs? Water balloons?"

"None of them," I said. "I can't. Because— OW!"

The closet door had been ripped open, and I'd jumped, and I'd landed right on the dump truck.

"Soren, Soren, Soren," said Dad, sighing. "Where do we even start with you these days?"

"Oh. Hi."

"Computer, please."

I handed it over.

"Huh?" said Alex's tinny voice. "Because what, Soren? Why can't you?"

Dad righted the laptop. "Hello, Alex."

"Oh! Hi, Mr. Skaar."

"We sure miss you here in Camelot. But *this* guy"—he clumsily angled the laptop toward me—"has not been authorized to use technology in his bedroom closet. As he well knows. I'm not sure when you'll talk to him next, so you'd better say goodbye."

"Bye," I whispered.

Alex stared at me. "Because *why*?"

The laptop closed.

ON MONDAY, Ms. Hutchins said, "Now that you've wrapped up your Ethics in Science presentations—some of you more successfully than others—it's time to return to our study of experimental design."

"More bean plants?" said Goldie.

"More Coke?" said Freddy.

"If you want!" Ms. Hutchins gave a *wait till you see what's in store for you* smile. It's always a bad sign when you get one of those from a teacher. "Class, you'll really get to think like a scientist. Because it's time for . . ."

She paused expectantly, but nobody drum-rolled.

"Science fair!"

She explained each step. We'd have to ask a question, and do background research, and formulate a hypothesis, and design an experiment, and execute the experiment, and analyze the data, and make a trifold presentation board, and present to outside judges during a special evening event on December 13—

December 13!

Science fair was the day of Alex's visit. This was the best prank opportunity I'd ever have. Alex, the triplets, and me—and a hundred kids and parents packed into the gym, a gym cluttered with scientific apparatus and experimental animals and trifold boards—

"This is a huge project," said Kiyana.

But I couldn't prank. I'd retired for a reason.

"It is huge," agreed Ms. Hutchins.

Flynn loved science. Science fair would probably be the highlight of his year. If we pranked it, he'd never forgive me.

Nope. No prank. I'd gone too far before, and I couldn't go back now.

Retirement, I'd started to realize, meant saying *nope, no prank* for the rest of my life.

"You'll write an individual research report," said Ms. Hutchins, "but you'll share the rest of the work with a partner."

"Soren!" hissed Jéro. "You want to—"

"An assigned partner," she said.

"Maybe she'll put us together," I whispered.

"No way," he said.

He was right. Sometimes teachers put girls who are friends together, because they have this idea that they're nice and docile. Boys, though, never get put with their friends. Especially boys who maybe don't behave perfectly every second of every day. But I bet we'd behave better if we did work together. Ever think of *that,* teachers?

"Jéro and Lila," Ms. Hutchins read from her list.

They both groaned.

"Goldie and Kiyana."

They squealed in delight.

"Marsupial and Evelyn. Jeremiah and Emily. Olivia and Tori."

I looked around the class. There weren't a lot of people left. Billiam was unpartnered, which was bad, but so was Tabitha, and *her* I wouldn't mind—

"Soren," said Ms. Hutchins, "and Flynn."

I froze. I'd never expected this. Nobody else was with their original lab partner. And nobody else was with their cousin.

Flynn had been avoiding me hard lately. At school he was always with a group, always moving, and at home he was always in his room, adding scenes to the *Soren Stinks* mural, I guess.

"Your initial idea is due next Monday," Ms. Hutchins said. "Go forth and think like scientists together!"

CHAPTER THIRTY-SEVEN

I DIDN'T SEE how I was going to think with Flynn if he wouldn't even talk with me. Sometimes Ruth and I will try the silent treatment on each other, but it never works. What happens is we keep thinking of good insults and breaking the silence to say them, and at some point both of us accidentally forget we're mad. The funny thing is, that's how Mom and Dad fight too.

So to me the silent treatment had been kind of a mythical beast, the unicorn of getting mad. I'd read about it, but I was pretty sure it didn't exist in real life.

It does.

Flynn pulled it off for eight solid days. Eight! He refused to make eye contact and shunned me at school and ignored me at the dinner table. I couldn't even tell him I'd retired from pranking, because he refused to acknowledge me. Every time I thought I'd pinned him down, he'd get this distant, confused look and cup his hand around his ear and say, "What's that noise? It must be the wind."

207

Ruth was still mad at me too, but her madness was like our Internet connection. It went in and out.

"Do you have after-school plans?" Dad asked me on Friday morning.

"Nope." Though hopefully the question meant I wasn't grounded anymore. I'd been doing all my science homework plus participating with Flynn-like frequency, and although my grade wasn't going to get a certificate of merit, at least it was in the double digits.

"Then why don't you come with me to Ivan's new class at the rec center?"

I shrugged. "Okay."

"We can talk."

Uh-oh. The word *talk* was ominous these days. "Okay."

Flynn went home with Kiyana. Ruth got off at our bus stop, but when the triplets turned down their driveway, she followed.

"Wait," I said. "You're going *there*?"

"I'm teaching them how to play Catan," said Ruth.

"Ethan loves it," said Tabitha. "So the plan is, we're going to become secret experts and then pound him next time he comes home."

"He'll be so mad," Olivia said dreamily.

"That sounds fun," I said, kind of hoping I'd get invited. I paused. Nobody said anything. "Too bad Dad wants me to hang out with him," I said to save face.

"Too bad," said Olivia. "Otherwise you could have come too."

Darn. I should have paused longer.

"Have a good afternoon!" called Lila.

Ruth didn't even smirk at me. Maybe she felt a little bad for stealing my friends and leaving me out. Or maybe she was so happy she forgot all about me. Either way, I deserved it, but that didn't make it easier.

IVAN CHARGED ME when I got home. Well, I assumed it was Ivan, since it was three feet tall, had limbs, and was attacking me, but I couldn't be positive since a helmet with a mesh mask covered the whole head-face-neck region. "IVAN FIGHT!" the figure cried, smacking my thigh with a wooden spoon.

It was definitely Ivan.

Dad dove in and grabbed the spoon. "Say *en garde* before you strike!" he told Ivan. "Remember how we practiced?"

"EN GARDE!" Ivan chopped at my leg with his hand.

"Sorry, Soren," said Dad, scooping him up. "His new class is Fencing for Toddlers. We thought it might provide an outlet for his natural aggression."

"IVAN KNIGHT IN SHINING ARMOR!"

"You've had a lot of questionable ideas," I told Dad, "but this is the worst."

We sat with the other parents in the bleachers at the rec center. The instructor made the toddlers all line up and lunge across the gym (several fell over in the attempt), and then he gave them cardboard wrapping-paper tubes. "I'm glad they aren't getting real swords on the first day," Dad said.

"They're getting real swords?" I yelped. "When?"

"Once they've mastered the basics."

One small girl lay flat on the floor while two others battered her. Ivan, with a determined expression, was hitting himself in the head. "So, never," I said.

"Let's hope not," said Dad. He squeezed the back of my neck. "You know, you were exactly the same at that age."

"I was not."

"Luckily, you've grown up. You're completely different now."

Was he being sarcastic? He stared with a straight face at the instructor, who was wringing his hands and yelling, "Fencers! Fencers! You should be practicing your first-position stance!"

"Really?" I said.

"You should *not* be whacking each other!" said the instructor. "Or yourselves!"

"Sure," said Dad. "You don't cause any trouble at all."

"Sarcasm is the lowest form of humor," I said, which he says to us all the time.

"True. I guess I should just come out and say it. It was you with Jim Bob, right?"

I jumped. That was *not* what I'd expected. I'd thought the talk today was going to be about No Technology in the Bedroom Closet.

"Well?" said Dad. "Let's skip the part where you play innocent, okay?"

"Ruth told you, didn't she?"

Dad snorted. "Soren. Someone brings the Skaar piglet to school, releases it in the middle of an assembly, and causes total chaos. I don't need Ruth to tell me who did it."

He had a point. "When you put it that way . . ."

"I know you know this," said Dad, "but taking Ruth's piglet, that wasn't the nicest move."

"Yeah."

"You're going to need to make it up to her."

"I know. And Flynn. He would have won."

"Second place is wonderful."

"Not to Flynn."

The instructor had succeeded in getting all the kids to sit on the floor, nice and far away from each other. He wiped his brow. "Let's try that again," he called, "*without* the swords."

"Poor guy," Dad and I said at the same time. We laughed. I glanced over. Dad didn't seem that mad. In fact, he didn't seem mad at all.

"Are you going to tell Mom?" I asked.

"Eventually," he said. "In 2030, maybe. Or 2040. Not that I'm keeping secrets from my wife, but does she need to know *now*?"

"Definitely not."

"This guy I knew," said Dad, "his junior year of high school, as soon as he got his driver's license, he borrowed his brother's pickup truck. He drove it out to his best friend's family's farm, and they loaded it up with two pigs. On them, they painted '#1' and '#3.'"

"Then what?"

"They brought them to school. Released them. The admins rounded them up pretty fast, but everyone had to stay outside for three more hours while they looked for #2."

I laughed. "That's amazing."

"I guess what I'm saying," said Dad, "is that I should be blaming myself."

"Wait."

"Yep. That guy? That was me."

I stood up in the bleachers, I was so discombobulated. "*YOU?*"

"And my best friend?" continued Dad. "That was your mother."

"*MOM?*"

"It was her idea." He sighed. "We should have known better than to combine this sort of genetic material."

"But you guys are *anti*-prank!"

And then I thought about it.

How they drove me around to buy alarm clocks and never asked why.

How they looked to the side whenever I came home covered with Jell-O, and never interrogated me about how I'd gotten a whole can of Silly String in my hair.

How they gave me a twelve-pack of whoopee cushions for my sixth birthday.

How, when I rubber-banded the handle of the sink sprayer so it'd shoot water when you turned on the faucet, and Mom got it right in the face, *after* she'd put on her work makeup, she'd laughed.

"Whoa," I said.

My world was shaking.

"Even so," said Dad, "here's something I didn't learn till I was, oh, twenty-nine. There's a time and a place for pranking, and it's not always, and it's not everywhere."

"I know. I'm retiring."

"No! Soren! A prankster of your talent!"

"I've done too much damage."

Dad reached around my back and pulled me in. "You and Ruth and Flynn are going to be okay."

"Do you really think so?"

"I really think so." He squeezed me in to him, and I fit my shoulder in the warm nook under his arm. After bath but before bed, when we were little, Ruth and I got to settle into those nooks so Dad could read Narnia to us. He does voices but isn't annoying about it. I remembered the bristle of his cheek at the end of the day, and the waffley feel of the blanket. When I was little, I thought nothing would change. I thought I was a kid and that was the way it was. But everything that's now eventually turns into something long ago.

"I believe in you," said Dad. "You're learning. You're growing up. That's a good thing, Soren."

"What happened when you were twenty-nine?"

"My two-year-old filled my favorite shoes with ketchup," he said grimly.

"Oh," I said. "That would have been me. Oops. Sorry."

We watched the toddlers sprint around the gym, banging each other with wrapping-paper tubes. "Ivan's having the time of his life," said Dad.

"It does look fun," I said.

CHAPTER THIRTY-EIGHT

MOM NOTICED FLYNN'S silent treatment. "Give him time," she told me. "Keep trying, but give him time."

The problem was, we didn't have time. Our science-fair idea was due on Monday. Finally, on Sunday afternoon, I cracked and told her about our assignment. "Oh," she said. "Hmm. Well, what if we try neutral ground? Do you think you could work together at Mugshot?" That's the coffee shop in town. "I could drop you off now."

"I can't even ask him if he wants to," I said, near tears, "because he'll say I'm the *wind*!"

The silent treatment, man. It gets to you.

"I'll talk to him," said Mom. I don't know what she said, but Flynn followed her down to the kitchen a few minutes later. I gave him shotgun even though he didn't call it.

Mugshot was packed, as always. We went up to the counter. "One coffee, medium roast," said Flynn to Jo Ann, who's worked there since it was the Kwikky Stoppe & Diner, since before some California tech guy got a cabin up here for the ice fishing and decided what Camelot really needed was an espresso bar. He wasn't wrong.

"Sure, hon," said Jo Ann. "Cream and sugar?"

"No thanks. I take it black."

I stepped up to order. "Cream and sugar, please," I said.

"Coffee?"

"No thanks. I take it white."

"Every man needs a signature drink," said Jo Ann, twinkling as she handed me the cup.

We sat at the creaky table by the window. Flynn got out his notebook. He still hadn't spoken to me. I was starting to wonder whether we'd plan the whole experiment like charades.

"So," I said, twiddling the sleeve on my cup, "um . . ."

He opened his notebook and labeled the page *Science Fair* without looking up. Maybe this was a good time to tell him I'd retired from pranking. He'd be all happy, we'd be pals again, the project might even be fun—

"Just out of curiosity," he said, "are you planning to pull your weight, or should I expect to do the whole project myself?"

"I'm going to help!" I was highly insulted. "You've never worked with me. I'm good at science."

"Riiight," he said. I bet he'd snuck a look at my presentation grade. That rat. "You have any ideas, then?"

He said it like he wasn't expecting anything. "Actually," I said, "I was talking to Jéro's big brother. He said the experiments with people, like psychology, he said they don't do well. It's too hard to figure out what's going on."

"As in, it's too hard to isolate the variables," he said, all condescending.

"Sure."

"I'd concur."

Fine. If he was going to act that way, I'd concur too. Whatever *that* meant. "I was thinking we could do an experiment with bugs," I said. I liked bugs. I also liked that Flynn didn't like them. "And let's split up the work as much as possible. Let's make it like two individual projects, and we'll pretend we did it together when Ms. Hutchins asks."

"Perfect." He drew a line down the middle of the notebook page. "That's just what I want."

It was weird how Mugshot, which was so warm the windows steamed up, could feel so cold. I wanted to leave. Being around Flynn made me feel guilty and sad and mad all at once, and I guess being around me didn't make him feel too great either, because he didn't even bother raising a stink about the bug thing. We went with the first idea we had. We'd get two specimens—pill bugs, maybe—and raise them differently, and see if one did better. Done.

"How are we going to raise them differently?" I said.

"Different diets, maybe. Something like that. We can get full points for the initial idea even if we don't have all the details hammered out." Flynn was the kind of guy who knew where his points came from, so I wasn't about to argue. "Where are we going to get the experimental subjects?" he said.

"You mean the bugs?"

Jo Ann was sweeping around our chairs. "You need bugs? We've got bugs."

"Really?" I said. "What kind?"

"Silverfish, millipedes, stinkbugs. All in the kitchen, free for the taking. And Don caught a couple cockroaches this morning. They're still under a glass. He hasn't gotten around to squishing them."

"Can we have them?" I asked.

"I don't see why not, hon."

"You really want to experiment on *cockroaches*?" Flynn whispered urgently.

"Cockroaches are amazing creatures," I told him. "They're the only animals on earth who'd survive a nuclear holocaust."

"But they're . . . *cockroaches*."

"You do the data and graphs and writing. You do the board. And I'll take care of the experimental subjects."

"Actually," Flynn said, "that could work."

THE WHOLE RIDE home, I watched the cockroaches crawl around their jar, up and down and over each other. I already felt fond of them. They *were* amazing creatures. They were trapped in a jar with only a few holes for fresh air, but they didn't get depressed or bored. They kept on exploring. "Since they're experimental subjects, we should probably go with simple names," I told Flynn and Mom.

"What about A and B?" said Flynn.

"I'm thinking Cah and Croach."

"Don't expect me to remember their names."

"Cah's the one with the longer antennae."

"I don't believe in naming cockroaches."

"If you were a cockroach, I bet you'd want a name."

"What a great idea to make you two partners," said Mom. "I'm going to email that Ms. Hutchins and tell her so."

"Don't," Flynn and I said at the same time.

Mom just laughed.

CHAPTER THIRTY-NINE

THE NEXT FRIDAY, Mr. Pickett and Ms. Hutchins combined their class time so the whole sixth grade could watch *Hoot*. I love team-teaching days. Ms. Hutchins gives all these super-specific instructions about SILENTLY collecting a mat and SILENTLY crossing the hall and SILENTLY, CLASS, AND I MEAN SILENTLY finding our place in Mr. Pickett's room so we can start the movie WITH NOT A SECOND WASTED, CLASS, WE DON'T HAVE A SECOND TO WASTE; but sorry, Ms. Hutchins, if you cram fifty sixth graders and two non-scary teachers into one classroom—on a Friday!—it's going to get messy.

I reclined on my mat. Hubbub hummed around me. Ms. Hutchins and Mr. Pickett were in a frustrated huddle, trying to figure out which cable to plug in where. We had assigned places in alphabetical order, so I was next to Flynn.

"Let's talk about the experiment," he said, brandishing his science notebook, "since we're stuck together."

Ouch.

"We need to be very careful to choose just one independent variable," he said. We'd been learning about that. It's the thing you change, so, like, what kind of liquid in the Coke-versus-water experiment. You try to keep everything else the same so that you know why the results are the way they are. "How about having two different habitats? At first I was thinking two diets, but we might not see any difference, since cockroaches can survive on practically anything, right?"

"They can go without food for a month," I said. I knew a lot about bugs, mostly because I've always kind of wanted to *be* a bug.

"What if we split a fish tank into two parts, and fill one side with fertilized soil and the other with gravel?"

"Okay."

"*I'd* hypothesize that the roach in the dirt will do better, but I'm happy to incorporate your thoughts, if you have any."

"Nope."

Irritated, he snatched away his notebook and started scribbling on a page labeled *Materials*.

"Can Cah be the one in the rich soil?" I asked.

"I think it should be double-blind."

"I'm obviously going to be able to tell the difference between them."

"Or at least randomly assigned."

"Well, randomly assign Cah to the soil, okay?"

Croach was cool, but Cah was my *man*. The way he

wiggled his antennae when I gave him a chunk of old pizza—it was like he was thanking me.

"Maybe we should try to teach cockroaches sign language," I said.

"That's not a science-fair-style experiment," said Flynn.

"What if I'm thinking bigger than science fair?"

He ignored me. Ms. Hutchins and Mr. Pickett were red and flustered, wielding cables and barking out the occasional "Quiet, please!" I bet lots of people in the room could have figured it out, but teachers never admit their oldness and ask for help.

Flynn was lost in his notebook. We weren't supposed to leave our spots, but I decided I'd risk going over to the soccer guys. They'd borrowed a desk from one of Mr. Pickett's students so they could play paper-clip badminton, a game Jéro invented a few years ago. I'd never played much—Alex and I had mostly hung out alone—but I'd always thought it was fun.

"I've got winner," Freddy told me, "but you're next."

"Match point," said Jéro. Soup served the little bouncy ball onto the desk. Jéro, his regulation 28-mm untwisted paper clip held between thumb and index finger, returned it. They rallied back and forth a few times. Tension grew. Then Soup hit a zinger that rebounded off the corner of the desk. It seemed destined for the floor—but Jéro flung himself to the side and nabbed the ball with his clip.

"Ha!" he grunted.

But he hadn't gotten much wire behind it, and his soft

lob floated over to Soup's side. Soup slammed it back. Jéro was still recovering from his violent dive, so Soup got the point, and the match.

Freddy and Soup spun clips to see who'd serve first. "What's Flynn doing with that notebook?" Jéro asked, wincing as he massaged his ribs.

"Science fair. I hate this project."

"Dude, tell me about it," he said. "I got put with Lila Andrezejczak."

"I'm the one who should be complaining," said Lila. The triplets, as they often did, had popped up out of nowhere. "All you do is veto my ideas."

"Your ideas are stupid!"

"Just because you don't want to do psychology—"

"Yeah, I don't want to test what kind of music makes people subconsciously want to obey your orders, and I think it's creepy you *do*, actually—"

"It's not creepy!" said Lila.

"It's a little creepy," said Olivia.

"But very useful," said Tabitha.

"Got him!" crowed Soup, waving his victorious paper clip in the air.

"Soup-de-dupe! Nice!" I high-fived him.

Freddy sprawled dramatically onto the floor. "I'm over life."

"I'm going to take you *down*, Soup," I said.

Suddenly, there was a burst of music from the speakers. "It works!" cried Mr. Pickett.

"We did it!" said Ms. Hutchins.

They high-fived with both hands.

"Sixth grade! Quiet, please! The movie's about to start! Soren Skaar, why are you out of your assigned spot, and *why* are you holding an untwisted paper clip?"

"You could take someone's eye out!" whispered Tabitha in an uncanny imitation of Ms. Hutchins.

Trying not to laugh, I skittered back to my seat.

CHAPTER FORTY

FLYNN AND I each had to write our own research report. The rest of the project we divided right down the middle, just as we'd agreed. He drew a diagram of the fish tank while I built a wall between the two habitats. I found Miracle-Gro in Dad's garden supplies and Flynn read the instructions on how to properly fertilize Cah's soil.

"Done," he said as I dumped the gravel into Crouch's side of the fish tank. "Put them in."

"These habitats are kind of bare."

"What do you want to add? Paintings? A coffee table?"

"I don't know. Something." I petted Cah's head with the tip of my pinkie finger. He scampered away.

"Armchairs? Houseplants?"

I knew he was making fun of me. "I just think they might appreciate a sun rock. A few shrubs."

"As long as it's the same between the two," Flynn said wearily. "It has to be controlled."

It was thanks to me that they got varied diets, too. If

Flynn had his way, they'd have been eating bread and water every day, like in a dungeon.

"You may be experimental subjects," I told them, "but I still respect you. I'll treat you right."

Flynn eyed everything I did. "Did you weigh that?" he asked when he saw me feeding them melon for dessert.

"Yes."

"Did you log it?"

"Yes."

"What'd you give them for dinner?"

"One Frosted Mini-Wheat each and three cubes of cat kibble."

"Did you weigh—"

"*Yes.*"

He checked, though. He flipped through the marbled composition book we kept by the fish tank.

I still hadn't told him I'd retired, and I felt like I had to try.

"Just to tell you," I said, "I'm not trying to sabotage this experiment."

He *hmm*ed.

"In fact, I've retired from pranking."

"Have you ever heard the phrase 'too little, too late'?" said Flynn. "Do you know what that means?"

"I'm not dumb."

"Maybe you should have retired before you embarrassed me in front of the whole school."

"Nobody cares that you lost the spelling bee!"

"I panicked when Jim Bob ran at me," he said levelly. He shook his bangs off his face to look me straight in the eyes. "I *shrieked*."

"Everyone shrieked! Nobody remembers your shriek in particular!"

He shrugged. "I remember. I'm just saying, Soren, claiming you've retired isn't going to fix everything."

I VIDEO-CHATTED ALEX as soon as I was allowed on the computer again. She picked up. "Because *why*?" she said, as if we'd lost Internet connection for two seconds, not two weeks. "Why can't you prank with me in December? Do you know how hard it was for me to get my mom to promise we'd come? It's *science-fair* day, Soren. I looked at the school calendar. Think about the possibilities—our best one yet—"

"I'm retiring from pranking."

She opened her mouth like a goldfish looking for food.

"I'm taking a solid break, anyway. Pranks are not good for me right now."

"Oh," she said. "You decide to retire right before I visit. I see."

"It has nothing to do with that!"

"You prank with the triplets, but I'm visiting and suddenly you're done? How convenient."

I wasn't used to Alex dumping her sarcasm acid on me. "Alex—no—"

"I *knew* you didn't want to prank with me. Even last

time, you had to pull in the triplets. Are we even best friends anymore?"

"I'm retiring from pranking, not from being your best friend."

"Those are the same thing!"

"No, they're not!"

"But pranking's all we did together!"

That wasn't true. What about our secret code? What about all the hours we'd spent kicking on the wood-pile, or digging tiger traps in the woods? What about our don't-blush, don't-babble practice sessions? And okay, so maybe a lot of that stuff related to pranks, but that was almost a coincidence. Pranking was just the language we spoke together. We could have had anything in common—soccer, or science, or, I guess, yeah, paper dolls—and we'd still have been friends.

I liked Alex because she was Alex. Not because she pranked.

But why did she like me?

"You don't even want me to be your best friend," I said. "You've got Ol' Butt-Braid."

"*Sophia.*"

"I'll call her whatever I want."

Alex crossed her arms. "Fine. Sophia's my new best friend. So what? Do you even care?"

"No," I said. "I don't."

I moved to x out of the chat window, but she beat me to it. Her face swooshed away.

Retirement wasn't going to fix everything. It might not fix anything, I thought. It might make things worse.

THE WEDNESDAY OF Thanksgiving week, Ms. Hutchins gave up with half the period left and told us that she was going to her in-laws for the weekend and if she wasted one single iota of patience on us she wasn't going to be able to handle them and to please, for the love of God, give her thirty short minutes to forget that she had voluntarily chosen to spend her professional life with eleven-year-olds. Then she collapsed into the beanbag chair at the back of the room. Goldie and Kiyana brought her a cold washcloth for her forehead. "Do what you want, class," she called. "Just keep it to a dull roar."

Jéro and Soup and Freddy were already shoving desks into competition formation. Paper-clip badminton hadn't been big since third grade, but the games we'd played before watching *Hoot* had sparked a revival. I went over. "Can I play?"

"Yes!" said Freddy. He sounded so enthusiastic it was kind of exciting. What with Flynn loathing me, and Alex hanging up on me, and Ruth making my life harder whenever she remembered, I hadn't heard a lot of "Yes!" lately.

Soup beat Jéro while I narrowly edged out Freddy. "You know what?" I said as we swapped seats. "We have almost half an hour till Language Arts. We should organize a class tournament."

"*Great* idea!" said Freddy. He whipped out a sheet of paper. "Round robin or single elimination?"

"Probably elimination, to save time," said Soup.

"But then all the people who haven't played before are going to get out really fast," said Jéro.

"Isn't that the point?" said Soup. "One of the four of us will win."

"Let's have two brackets," I said. "Amateur and advanced."

"Genius," said Jéro. We bent over the paper to seed the brackets. "It's fun having you around, Soren," he added. "You have good ideas."

My neck got all hot. "I've always been around."

"It's different this year," said Jéro.

Freddy squinted at his list of the kids in our class. "Who's missing?" he said.

Alex, I thought, quick as a reflex. I glanced around. I don't know how it happened, but suddenly I got a zoomed-out look at the classroom, like I was God or a TV camera or something. I saw the triplets reading a big book about mythology on the floor behind the begonia. I saw Ms. Hutchins conked out on the beanbag, and I saw the piece of tissue stuck to her upper lip flutter every time she exhaled. I saw Flynn doing Language Arts extra credit with Kiyana and Tori, like any of them needed it. And I saw myself, too. I saw where I was and who I was with, and I saw the things I'd messed up and the things I'd gotten right.

Jéro wasn't wrong. This year *was* different.

"I should obviously be top seed," said Soup.

"Ha!" scoffed Freddy. "I just destroyed you! Nine to one!"

"Only because my paper clip was messed up!"

"Soren should be top seed," said Jéro. "He's got that evil slam move."

It was weird, missing Alex and also being glad she was gone. Those were two feelings that seemed like Harry and Voldemort: *one cannot live while the other survives.* But there they were, lodged in my rib cage.

"Let's flip a coin," I said. "All four of us are good."

CHAPTER FORTY-ONE

WHEN WE GOT home from school, Thanksgiving preparations were in full swing. Mom had taken the afternoon off to do a last-minute grocery run over the border. It's a Skaar Thanksgiving tradition to, once we're totally stuffed with turkey and pie, top it off with these delicious Canadian chocolates called Coffee Crisps, and we have to go to Fort Frances to get them.

"While Mom's gone," Dad announced, "we're all going to work on a holiday centerpiece for the table!"

"Maybe I'll go to the grocery with her," I said.

"Are you sure?" Dad extended a bowl of oranges and a tin of cloves. "I could sure use someone to clove these oranges!"

I inched away. My thumb still had a dent from the last time Dad tricked me into cloving oranges.

"Or," he said, "you could help Ivan finger-paint autumnal foliage on our Thanksgiving banner!"

A lot of people think Dad's a pretty smart guy, but sometimes all the evidence points otherwise.

"Yeah, I'm definitely going to the grocery."

"Grab your passport and let's hit the road," said Mom. "It's going to snow."

The border's only a few minutes away, and Mom does Zumba with the guard, so we got into Canada fast. We found a parking spot and trundled through flurries into the store. It was packed, even though Canada had their Thanksgiving back in October. Mom had me push the cart—"If I bump into someone they'll get mad, but if you do they'll see you're just a kid"—and she darted around and tossed in food. "Thanks for coming," she said once we were finally in line to pay.

"Frankly," I said, "it was the lesser of two evils."

She laughed. "Maybe so. But I appreciate your company. You're fun to be around, Soren."

What the heck? Twice in one day, Jéro and Mom, saying nice things out of the blue. I scuffed my toe on the wheel of the cart. "Oh."

"It's nice to have you spending more time around the family."

"I am?"

"You've been hanging around the kitchen a lot."

"Because half the time I'm grounded."

"Well, true." We moved forward a foot in line. "Even so."

"And because I'm taking care of Cah and Croach." Their fish tank was in the corner of the kitchen, as far from the food as Dad could get it.

"How's *that* going?"

"Fine."

"You're working okay with Flynn?"

"Yeah."

"Hmm." She shoved the cart forward and almost clipped the heels of the old lady just ahead, who turned and glared at her. "Sorry, sorry, ma'am!"

"That's all right," said the old lady in a long-suffering tone.

Mom grimaced at me. *Oops,* she mouthed, and then said in her normal voice, "I've noticed you and Flynn still aren't talking."

"We're talking about science fair."

"Hmm," Mom said again.

"The thing is," I said, toying with the bars of Coffee Crisp in the basket, "he's really mad at me. I can't explain why. It's too complicated." I hoped she'd buy that. "And I'm really mad at him, too." For the mural, sort of, but mostly I was mad at him for being mad at me. I doubted he'd even thought about what a sacrifice it was for me to retire from pranking.

"Hmm."

"You're going to tell me things would be better if we talked them out, I know, and I'm not supposed to simmer, I know, but he won't even let me try! He won't even talk to me unless it's about stupid *graphs*!"

I was glad Mom hit the front of the line just then because my eyes had filled with tears. Angrily, I swatted them away. I hate crying. You look dumb plus your nose gets all stuffy.

Mom was loading the belt, and I put my head down and helped.

It wasn't until we were in the car, bags loaded, windshield wipers shoving away the snow, that she said anything that wasn't about being careful with the eggs, darn it, Soren, I mean *careful,* do *you* want to stand in that line again, etc. "I know what happened at the spelling bee," she said.

"Dad told you?" The man had no loyalty.

"He didn't have to tell me." She rolled her eyes. "Why you two imagined I wouldn't figure out that one on my own . . . Anyway. You're not going to feel good about yourself until you make things right with Flynn."

"I tried!"

"Did you?"

"I told him I'm retiring from pranking. Which I am. I'm done."

Till I saw the look on Mom's face right then, I'd had trouble visualizing her as a prankster. But her forehead crumpled, and her mouth gaped, and she looked the same as Dad had when I'd made my retirement announcement to him.

Surprised. And sad.

Suddenly I could imagine teenage Mom loading two numbered pigs into a pickup truck.

Come to think of it, she'd come home from work once with a story about how someone had Saran-wrapped her boss's entire office. . . .

And that time she'd given us mashed potatoes and gravy in ice cream dishes with cherries on top—maybe that *hadn't* been an accident, like she'd claimed. . . .

And once I'd found five bucks in Ivan's diaper and she'd said that sometimes babies pooped cash—it was a phenomenon as yet unexplained by science—and for months afterward I'd volunteered to change his diaper in the hopes of finding more money. . . .

Mom!

"Soren," she said, unaware that I was rewriting the story of my life, "retirement aside, you *do* need to make it up to Flynn."

"But—"

"I know, I know. You can't apologize, because he'd just cup his hand around his ear and say, 'Is that the wind?'"

"Right!"

"So apologies won't work. The thing is, you can't control what he does. You can only control what you do."

"What *do* I do?"

"Act like the person you want to be. Be kind. Think about how it's hard for him."

"It's hard for me, too."

"It is. I know, Soren. It is." She leaned forward, concentrating on the slushy road. "It's hard for everyone. That's kind of the thing about life."

It was dark already. The snowflakes zoomed toward us and then caught the wind up and over the car, like mini skateboarders. I must have fallen asleep, because next thing I knew we were at the border, and then Mom was poking at me and Ruth was saying, "Just because he went with you doesn't mean he doesn't have to help carry in the groceries."

We were home.

CHAPTER FORTY-TWO

I WOKE UP the next morning to the smell of roasting turkey. Dad was happily pirouetting from sink to oven to countertop. He wore a floral apron, and his forehead was smeared with a large dab of something pinkish brown. "Happy Thanksgiving!" he said. "I am thankful for *you*, firstborn!"

"Yeah, same to you," I said, which was all the holiday spirit I could muster. Three minutes ago I'd been unconscious. I went to the pantry for some cereal.

"Ah ah ah," said Dad, waggling his finger. "We're fasting till the grand meal."

"Dad! I'm starving."

"Hunger," he pronounced, "is the best spice."

"What time are we eating?"

"Six."

"There's no way—"

"Chef makes the rules!" Dad seemed loopy. Probably from low blood sugar.

238

"You've got something on your face," I told him.

"Ooh," he said, scraping it off and examining it. "Giblets."

BY THREE, I was about to pass out. My stomach felt like it was eating itself.

The turkey was still in the oven. The other preparations were done. Dad's sister and her husband had arrived from Ely, and once Aunt Karen, Uncle Foster, Mom, Dad, and Flynn were deep in a game of Scrabble, I snatched a bag of pretzels and made a break for it.

Ruth was already by the pigpen. Her cheeks were as full as a squirrel's in October. "Sneaking food?" I said.

"Of course not." She swallowed. "I was visiting Jim Bob."

"Sure. Uh-huh. I got pretzels. What'd you get?"

"Hummus." She pulled it from behind her back. "I was desperate. I grabbed the first thing I saw. Thank goodness you got something we can dip. I was licking it off a twig."

We brushed the snow from the downed tree and sat. "I haven't been so hungry since the last time we got sent to bed without dinner," Ruth said. "Remember? The tinsel and the blowtorch?"

"Yes, yes," I said quickly. "No need to get into details." I stuffed food into my mouth. "Wow," I said, muffled. "This is *amazing*."

"Hunger is the best spice," said Ruth.

We munched. When we were finished, Ruth tried to pick up snow all subtly, but come on, I'm a native. You're not going to fool me. Before she even started to pack it,

I'd sprinted behind the pigpen to scoop my first snowball. It was a free-for-all. We were both panting, moving fast, snatching snow and packing it and flinging it at each other.

A small figure darted across my vision. I had just packed a giant snowball, and all my instincts told me to hurl it. I nailed the person in the head.

"Hey!"

It was an Andrezejczak. A very bundled Andrezejczak. I couldn't tell which one.

"Pause!" I yelled to Ruth. "Armistice!"

The Andrezejczak took down her hood. It was Olivia. "It's clear now!" she called back. Lila and Tabitha came out from behind the garage.

"Wait," said Ruth. "They stayed on safe ground while you went out?"

"That's me," said Olivia.

"You're like the one poor penguin that the others shove into the water to test for seals," said Ruth.

Olivia dumped a load of snow from the hood of her coat. "That's me."

Lila and Tabitha marched up. "Hello, Ruth. Hello, Soren," said Lila. "Have you guys eaten yet?"

"Nope," said Ruth. "Nothing."

"So why are you outside?"

"The adults and Flynn are playing Scrabble."

"Same at *our* house!" said Tabitha.

"It's awful," said Olivia.

"We aren't allowed to make any noise," said Lila.

"Us neither!" said Ruth.

"Ethan keeps bluffing," said Olivia, "but Great-Aunt Ermintrude would have to be the one to challenge, since her turn's after his, and she never does—"

"She keeps being like, 'I declare, this young man's vocabulary is *enormous*!' after he's played a word like *KINJROG*, which he claims is an Icelandic knitting needle—" said Lila.

"Our parents are furious—he's beating them by like six hundred points—" said Olivia.

"We had to escape," said Tabitha.

"How'd that thing go?" said Ruth.

"What thing?" I said.

"Just a thing they were planning," said Ruth airily. "A secret thing."

"It went perfectly," said Lila.

"He was so mad," said Tabitha, biting her bottom lip in a devilish smile.

"Come on," I said. "Tell me."

Olivia took pity on me. "Let's just say mayonnaise went in a place mayonnaise should never go."

"That doesn't narrow it down much."

"We put it in Ethan's shampoo bottle."

"Oh. Wow." I really hoped Ruth wouldn't take any little-sister inspiration. "That's bad."

"You should try it on your mom."

"About that . . ." I glanced at Ruth. "I'm retiring from pranking."

I have to admit, I was hoping the announcement would

go like it had with Mom and Dad. Shock, sadness, people telling me I was the talent of a generation, etc. But the triplets just got *aha* expressions. "So that's why Alex emailed us," said Olivia.

"She emailed you?"

"Complaining about *you*," said Tabitha.

"And also—" said Olivia, but Lila kicked her and she shut up.

"And also what?" I said.

"And also, Soren," said Tabitha, "on the way over here, I found something you might be interested in."

"Really?"

"Yeah. Come here."

"What is it?" I took a couple of steps toward Tabitha—

And she stuffed a massive snowball into my face.

I forgot about everything else. It was *on*.

Ruth took my side, Skaars versus Andrezejczaks. We ranged over the whole yard, our fort behind the pigpen, theirs in the vegetable garden. We're better at throwing but they're more vicious, so it was an even match.

We'd just called time-out to catch our breaths and stockpile ammo when we heard footsteps. It was Flynn, looking wan and pinched.

"Soren?" he said. "It's time to feed Cah and Croach."

"I'm in the middle of something."

"They need to be fed at four p.m. exactly. That's how the experiment works."

"*We* haven't been fed yet today."

"That's irrelevant. Do you know *anything* about science?"

And everything Mom told me about Being Kind and Acting Like the Person I Want to Be, all that stuff disappeared the way snow disappears in hard rain. It didn't even have a chance. Here I was, making the ultimate sacrifice, retiring from pranking, infuriating my best friend—and there he was, acting like a jerk.

I was holding a giant snowball I'd been working on, hard-packed with crunches of ice, and I threw it at him.

Not that hard.

Not that soft, either.

It hit him in the face. He wasn't wearing a coat. It exploded all over him. His hair was covered with drifts of snow. His mouth was a small, perfect O.

Everyone gaped, shocked. A few seconds passed. I guess they were seconds. It felt like a month.

In a very small voice, Olivia said, "You shouldn't have done that."

"I *know*." I kicked the snowball pyramid I'd built, and then I kicked its ruins. They were staring like I was an exhibit at the zoo. "Stop looking at me," I said.

"You're destroying all our ammo," said Ruth.

"I don't care. I'm done with this stupid game. I'm going to go feed my *real* friends."

I stomped toward the house. When I was almost in, I heard Tabitha say, "His real friends are cockroaches?"

"They have names," said Flynn. "And personalities."

They all laughed. I slammed the door.

CHAPTER FORTY-THREE

ON MONDAY, Ms. Hutchins's skin had the delicately crumpled look of an undershirt that's been in the corner of your room for a week. I guess I wasn't the only one who'd had a rough Thanksgiving. "Today," she said, "you'll be writing a reflection on how your science-fair experiment is going. And yes, it will be graded."

Jéro scooched his desk toward Lila's, but Ms. Hutchins lifted her hand. "Nope. This is an individual assignment."

"But what if our reflections don't match?" said Jéro, eyeing Lila.

"What if one of us has a much better reflection than the other?" said Lila, eyeing Jéro.

"What if one of us makes unfair accusations about the other's quality of work?"

"What if—"

"Class, you have the rest of the period to write," said Ms. Hutchins. "If you have a question, save it for tomorrow. If you have an urgent question, consider whether it's actually urgent."

She returned to her desk.

"If you need me, and you shouldn't, I'll be over here. Just me, my coffee, and my frayed sense of self, trying to forget that my in-laws . . ."

We couldn't hear her anymore, but her mouth was still moving. Nobody in their right mind would have asked her a question. Nobody would have even asked to go to the bathroom. Sometimes it's better to hold it.

I read the first prompt from the board.

1. What have you learned so far from your research?

For his individual report, Flynn was researching the chemistry of nitrogen fertilizers. I was writing a paper called *Indestructible: The Life and Times of the Modern American Cockroach.*

> I have learned many fun facts about cockroaches. For example, did you know a cockroach can live for a week without its head? Plus, they can run three miles an hour. And if you're thinking, "Hey, I'm faster," well, your legs are also a hundred times longer.
>
> I have also learned that cockroaches cannot twerk.

I read the next question.

2. What have you learned about working with a partner?

I untwirled the spiral of my notebook.

I didn't want to answer that.

Everyone else was working. Soup wore the constipated look he always gets when he has to think. Freddy kept digging around in his ear with his pencil, so it kind of looked like he was writing with a quill dipped in earwax. Jéro and Lila were each hunched over, scribbling fast and furious, trying to outdo—a.k.a. out-tattle—each other.

Flynn was rotating his pencil inside the Statue of Liberty–shaped sharpener he kept in an Altoids tin. A curl of shaving dropped onto his desk. He glanced at me. I jerked my eyes away, but I knew he'd seen me looking.

"Ten minutes, class," said Ms. Hutchins. "When you're finished, stack your notebooks on my desk."

I have learned many things about working
with a partner.

I always start by repeating the question. It makes your answer look longer.

Sometimes you have to compromise

I tried to erase, since we hadn't done much compromising. But my pencil had the worst eraser ever. All it did was smear pencil guck around my paper.

I scratched out *compromise* and wrote *split up the work*.

Evenly dividing the work is important. That
way, you can do your thing and your

partner can do theirs and you don't have
to talk.

"Five minutes." People had started to file past me to
turn in their notebooks.

Though it'd probably be way more fun if we
actually worked together, so it's kind of sad
the way it's ended up

Where did *that* come from? I tried to erase. But no, not
with this cruddy pencil.
"Two minutes."

and that's why you should let us choose our
own partners next time.

I looked hurriedly up at the board.

3. **If you could start over, what would you do**
   differently?

I scrawled:

What I would do differently would be

"One minute."
Rats. I scribbled as fast as I could.

to not get in fights with everyone. I actually
hate fighting. And if Flynn and my sister

hadn't already been mad at me, it wouldn't have been such a big deal when Jim Bob

I scratched out that last part so hard I made a hole in the paper.

when something unfortunate happened, but now Flynn will never forgive me. (Ruth has mostly forgotten.)

My handwriting had gotten really messy, and my hand hurt.

I also feel guilty because I get to do all the fun parts of the project, like taking the experimental subjects for walks around the garden, and Flynn is doing the hard parts, like graphs.

The bell rang. "Notebooks on my desk. Soren? Everyone else has finished—"

"Okay! One sec! Almost done!"

Also, I should have made sure I was alone before I tried to teach my cockroaches to twerk. Ruth saw it, and she will never let me live it down.

. . .

ONE WEIRD THING happened that evening.

"Have you finished your homework, Soren?" said Dad.

"I'm reading our Language Arts book."

"Reading? Or reading ahead?"

Darn. Dad knew me too well. I hated the way teachers made you read one chapter at a time—just when you were getting into it, the homework assignment ended—so I always read the books in one go. "I'm way ahead," I admitted.

"Do you have other homework?"

"Some math problems in the online textbook."

"Flynn's on the desktop, but I think Ruth has my laptop in the dining room. Tell her I said it's your turn."

Reluctantly, I put down *When You Reach Me*. I dragged my toes all the way to the dining room, leaving two jerky trails in the carpet. "Dad says you have to—"

Shwop! Ruth had slammed the laptop shut.

"What were you *doing*?"

"Nothing," she said, way too fast.

Usually she either messages her friends or plays this game where you build fortresses out of cat heads. Or both. But I was pretty sure I'd seen a video-chat window, and a familiar face. A face with purple glasses.

"Go away," she said, clutching the laptop to her chest. "I'll give it to you. Just let me close what I was doing."

I was too surprised to argue.

As I signed in to the textbook, I thought, Should I be suspicious?

CHAPTER FORTY-FOUR

FLYNN AND I didn't speak for the entire last week of our experiment. I fed the cockroaches and took them out for exercise and noted their measurements, and he worked on the board in his room.

The day before it was due, he stopped by my seat on the bus home. "Hey."

"Hey."

"After you feed them, update the log one final time and bring it up to my room."

I grunted. He headed back to the seat Goldie was saving for him.

"Awkward," said Jéro.

"That's the first time he's spoken to me in a week."

"I *wish* Lila would stop speaking to me. I wouldn't even need a week. I'd take an hour."

"Guess who's visiting tomorrow?" I said.

"Who?"

"Alex."

"Wow," said Jéro. "I remember her. Are you guys going to do something?"

"Like hang out? Of course."

I thought of how Alex had hung up on me. How she had a new best friend, and how she'd emailed the triplets to complain about me.

Probably we'd hang out.

Maybe.

"No. Like an epic prank."

"Oh. No. Not this time."

"What you should do," said Jéro, "is prank science fair. Destroy all the boards so Ms. Hutchins can't grade them. Dump Kool-Aid all over them or something. And I'm not saying you'd *try* to dump Kool-Aid on Lila, but if she ended up in the wrong place at the wrong time . . ."

I laughed. "Yeah, no, not happening. That kind of thing takes weeks of prep."

"You guys are experts. You could do it."

Squirt guns. Or, no, buckets. A few dozen packets of red Kool-Aid powder. And the basketball backboards would be pulled up against the ceiling, so if we could get buckets of Kool-Aid strung up on them ahead of time, all we'd have to do mid-fair would be push the button to lower the hoops. . . . "That'd ruin a lot of people's hard work."

"Isn't that the point?"

"Well, anyway." I wished the conversation were over. "Nothing's happening at science fair."

Jéro elbowed me. "If our board's getting destroyed,

I don't want to bother finishing it. So if you change your mind, give me a heads-up, okay?"

WE GOT HOME. Flynn went upstairs, and Ruth went out to build a snow castle for Prince Jim Bob, Duke of Pork. Dad said, "Soren, will you watch Ivan for twenty minutes while I rest my eyes on the couch?"

"Sure."

"Thanks. He wrecked me today."

"What'd he do?"

Dad shot a grim look at a pile of dirty laundry. "It began with the creamed spinach. . . ."

"IVAN LIKE FEE SEES!" yelled Ivan from the floor.

"Got it," I said. "Go lie down. Ivan, want to help me feed Cah and Croach?"

Ivan lifted a trusting, chubby hand to mine. I walked him over to the windowsill with the fish tank. "There's Cah, in the soil habitat," I told Ivan.

Ivan peered in. Cah (such a ham!) started doing push-ups on his sun rock.

"And this is Croach. He's shy, but really funny once you get to know him. Wave, Croach!"

He sized us up with his glossy black eyes and then scuttled behind his cactus plant.

"IVAN LIKE!" Ivan put his hands flat on the fish tank's glass. Cah twitched, glared at Ivan, and ran away.

"You're smearing their habitat windows," I explained. "How would *you* feel if someone messed up *your* room?"

"IVAN NOT LIKE!" he said, frowning at me.

Oops. Definitely the wrong question to ask, as I messed up Ivan's room all the time. His crib rails made an extremely convenient rack for draping dirty underwear and wet towels. "Let's feed them," I said. I went over to the fridge while Ivan stared at the fish tank. He'd gotten as glazed over as he gets with cartoons. "Leftover spaghetti? No, too hard to measure. What do you think we should give them?"

"CREAMED SPINACH!" said Ivan.

"Uh, no. I heard what that did to you."

"IVAN GO BOOM!"

I winced. "How about saltines with peanut butter?" I chose two saltines with identical salt patterns and used the lab scale to measure eight grams of peanut butter onto each one. "A classic snack."

Ivan watched as I opened the feeding hatch and set down the crackers. Neither Cah nor Croach ever finished their meals, but Flynn said it'd be an experimental no-no to remove the leftovers. This meant the food areas were gross. They liked it, though. They'd hunker there for hours, licking a splotch of yogurt here, a crumb of croissant there. Once I'd seen Cah squatting to take a poop right on top of all the food. I'd looked away as fast as possible. Scientific curiosity is all well and good, but there are some things you can't unsee.

Ivan thrust his hand down the hatch. "No!" I said. I snapped it shut so fast that I caught his hand, and he started to cry. "Sorry, Ivan! Ack, I'm sorry! But don't wake up Dad! Come on, Ivan, shh—"

He sucked his hand and scowled at me.

"Let's go play Barbies," I told him. "Where's Gloria? Is she still in physical therapy for her leg? Will you let me visit her?"

At last, he gave a sulky nod.

CHAPTER FORTY-FIVE

FLYNN DIDN'T COME down for dinner. Dad sent Ruth to find him while we waited, chicken potpie glistening on our plates. "He says he'll eat later," Ruth reported. "He's got too much work."

"Hmph," said Dad, who likes his cooking to be appreciated. We ate, and Ruth and I did the dishes while Mom cleaned around us. Ivan was playing with his tea set in the corner.

"What's Flynn working on?" asked Mom as she swept the floor.

"The science-fair project, I'm guessing."

"*Your* science-fair project?"

"Well, also his."

"The project you two are doing as partners?"

"Um, yes, that would be the one."

Mom stood there with the broom like a Roman soldier with a javelin. "Then why," she said, her voice steely, "are you down here, not up there?"

255

"Well, this was his part—we split up the work—"

"*Jon!*" Mom blared.

"Yeah?" said Dad.

"We need to talk to our son. Soren, go to our bedroom immediately." She turned to Ruth. "Do your half of the dishes, and then stop. Not a single fork more. Your brother will finish his half himself."

I THOUGHT I might get some mercy. "He still won't talk to me," I said, but Mom said, "And that means you don't have to do your own science project?"

"I already did my half!"

"Remember our talk at the rec center?" said Dad. "I'm worried you walked away thinking that we condone bad behavior. And that's not at all the case."

"And remember *our* talk in the car?" said Mom. "I know he's not treating you particularly well, but imagine, Soren. What if you had to go live in Brooklyn with Flynn and Aunt Linnea? For a whole year? Go to a new school, make all new friends, come home after school and it's not your *real* home—"

"He's made a ton of friends."

Mom sighed. "You're missing the point."

"What's the point?"

"Right now," said Mom, "the point is that you can't let him do that project by himself."

"Reheat his potpie and take it upstairs," said Dad.

"And don't even think about coming down until the

project's done," said Mom. I opened my mouth. "If you run out of ways to contribute," she added, knowing what I was about to say, "well, keep him company."

"I swear," I tried, "he *wants* to do it alone—"

That got me nowhere.

Mom and Dad stayed in their bedroom, doing this thing they do every few months where they pretend they're so disappointed in their children they can't resume normal life. Ruth had finished the dishes. "You didn't have to do that," I called into the living room, where she was reading *Ella Enchanted*.

"I wanted to," she called back. "I'm pretending I'm an oppressed stepsibling who doesn't yet know she's going to be a queen."

"Oh. Thanks." I actually was grateful, even though that meant I was an ugly stepsister. "Thanks a lot, Ruth."

"By the way," she said, "do you have any water balloons?"

"Yeah, in my sock drawer. Why?"

"Can I borrow them?"

"You can have them."

"Really?"

"Sure." I slammed the microwave door on Flynn's pot-pie. "I owe you."

"Cool. Awesome. Thanks."

"It's kind of cold outside for water balloons."

She shrugged and turned a page. Flynn's potpie spun in the microwave. I strolled over to the window—

"AHHH! Ivan!"

He waved. He was still in the corner, playing with his teacups.

"I didn't know you were in here!"

"IVAN QUIET!"

"I know. It was weird."

Beep! Beep! That was the microwave.

"SOREN PLAY!"

"I can't right now." I felt a rush of big-brotherly warmth. "But I wish I could."

"IVAN WANT SOREN PLAY!" he yelled, his chin quivering.

"Sorry, Ivan. I really can't." He clearly didn't understand why not. "Someday you'll get it," I told him. "Someday you'll be in this much trouble yourself."

"I hope that potpie is on its way up the stairs!" Mom yelled from the bedroom.

"Gotta go," I told Ivan. "We'll play later."

"I DON'T NEED ANY HELP," said Flynn.

"Well, my parents are making me stay in here until you're done."

"I'd prefer to be alone."

"Well, my parents are making—"

"Fine."

I lay on the bed and watched him enter measurements into Dad's laptop. After a few minutes, I rolled over. Now I was facing the mural. Nope. Not about to look at *that*. I rolled over again. I started mouth-breathing. Supposedly you can hypnotize yourself if you focus only on your breath, eight counts in, eight out—*ahhhhh—ahhhhh—*

"Gah!" Flynn exploded. "Could you *be* any more annoying?" He tossed a sheaf of papers onto the bed. A box of colored pencils followed. "As long as you're trapped here, you might as well color these graphs."

"Whoa," I said, despite myself.

"You won't?"

"No, I just mean, these graphs are really professional-looking."

Flynn ducked his chin. "They're okay."

"They're *awesome*."

I felt kind of bad my name would be on them. That's how good they were.

"How did you know how to do all this stuff?" I said.

"I googled it."

I colored one bar of the first graph a soft periwinkle. Usually I'm way too impatient to color within the lines, but these were too nice to mess up. I took my time. I shaded the way Mom shaded when she'd take pity on me or Ruth doing geography homework and sit with us and help color in the nations of South America. She taught us how to hold the pencil loosely, how to overlap the strokes so the shade came out even. Coloring. It took me back, back before geography homework, back to dinosaur coloring books, to our old kitchen with yellow walls, where I sat on a pillow for a booster and someone cut me silhouettes of Santas and stars so I could make ornaments for the Christmas tree. I'd had *memories* before, obviously, and I'd have been able to tell you that the past had passed and you couldn't dip back, but I guess I hadn't totally believed it until right then, when I wished I were a little kid and knew I never would be again.

The graphs took a while. Flynn paged through them. "Not bad."

"Thanks."

"No," he said stiffly, "thank *you*. Thanks for doing all the hard parts of the project."

"Okay," I said, "no need for sarcasm."

"No, that's what I wrote about for Ms. Hutchins's reflection thing," he said. "That I flaked and gave you all the tough parts."

"That's what *I* wrote about!"

"You've been tending *roaches*!"

"You've been making *graphs*!"

We stared at each other.

"I thought I was getting off easy," he said.

"So did I."

"ONE LAST STEP," said Flynn at midnight. The board looked amazing. Mostly because of him, but it was true I'd done a lot of coloring. "We're going to display Subject A and Subject B—"

"You mean Cah and Croach—"

"But we also need photographs of them in their habitats." He grabbed his phone. "I should have done this earlier, but, um, I didn't want to get that close."

"They're very friendly," I assured him.

We tiptoed through the sleeping house. Mom and Dad's door was shut. Ruth and Ivan's was ajar, but their room was dark and silent. Flynn flicked on the kitchen light. I went to the fish tank.

"Good evening, Cah and Croach!" I whispered. "Ready for your photo shoot? Wait—what—no—"

I sank to my knees.

The feeding hatch was open. Both habitats were empty.

Cah and Croach had escaped.

CHAPTER FORTY-SIX

"GONE," I WHISPERED.

"Gone?" said Flynn.

"They must be hiding," I said frantically. "Playing a trick. Cah! Croach! Come out, come out, wherever you are!"

Flynn rattled the fish tank.

"Careful!" I squealed.

But I knew they weren't in there. We'd designed the habitats to be observed. There weren't places to hide.

"How could they have escaped?" said Flynn.

I thought for a minute.

Oh.

"Ivan was playing here—by himself—and he watched me open the feeding hatch earlier today—"

"You think he set them free?"

"I know it. He was in here alone after dinner. They're smart, Cah and Croach, but they couldn't have opened the hatch themselves."

"Our project is going to be so messed up if we can't find them," said Flynn.

"*That's* what you're worried about?"

"It's due tomorrow! What else would I be worried about?"

"Their safety!" I said. "Cah and Croach are house pets! They're domesticated! Now they're alone in the wild!"

"I don't know how we'll present our project without them," said Flynn.

"They're going to get lost—"

"We don't even have photographs!"

"Or get eaten—"

"This is terrible," said Flynn.

"It *is*."

"Do you think we can catch some backups and fake it?"

"That'd be like Dad expecting nobody to notice if he swapped Ivan with some other two-year-old from fencing class."

Flynn and I made sudden eye contact, and I knew what we were both thinking:

I wish.

"Let's split up the kitchen and search," said Flynn. "You take under the fridge, I'll—"

"No. No. We'll never find them that way." I'd done a lot of research. "Did you know a cockroach can flatten itself out as thin as a dime? They might not be in the kitchen. They could have slid under the door."

"Great," Flynn groaned.

"You don't find a cockroach," I said. "A cockroach finds you."

"And how are we going to make *that* happen?"

"Flynn, you're an expert when it comes to designing an experiment. You can do data and graphs."

"So?"

"You can think like a scientist," I said. "But I can think like a cockroach."

LUCKILY, I'D BEEN observing Cah and Croach so closely that I knew just what food they liked best. "Cah loves beans and sugar and fruit," I said. Flynn found a jar of raspberry jam while I unlidded the Tupperware of last week's lentil stew, which was definitely fermenting.

"Good thing your dad never cleans out the fridge," said Flynn.

"Only when something stinks and it's definitely not Ivan," I agreed. "As for Croach, remember that day we got sushi from Misohungri? That new place on Main Street?"

"I loved that sushi," said Flynn.

"So did Croach. He rolled around in it like Jim Bob in slops."

Flynn arranged a rank California roll on a plate.

"Don't use a plate," I said. "Put it right on the floor. Easier access, and the scent'll travel faster."

"You *do* think like a cockroach."

"Thanks," I said, flattered. Flynn dumped lentil stew on top, and I added the jam.

"Are we all set?" said Flynn.

I surveyed the food. All their favorites. It made me miss them. My mild-mannered Croach, who shimmied his thorax whenever I filled the water trough. My wacky Cah, who'd do anything for a joke.

My throat grew tight. "What if they can't find their way back?" I said. "They've been out for hours, Flynn. . . ."

"They're just getting a taste of the outside world. They'll be back."

I flipped off the lights. The moonlight made the kitchen silver and gray. Flynn and I took up positions on opposite countertops, poised to pounce at the first sign of scuttling.

"I just want my boys to come home," I said.

"Shh," said Flynn. "They'll be here any minute."

THE WATER HEATER popped and bubbled. Snow made a *shirr-shirr* sound as it shifted on the roof. A board creaked, and a train hooted a dreamy, distant whistle. Flynn, crouched on the other counter, was a statue. I could hear the beats of my own heart. We had waited for a very long time.

I stared at the dark mound of food on the floor.

There was nothing.

But then—

There was something.

A twitch in the side of my vision.

I thought it might be eyestrain, or wishful thinking.

But the twitch became a shape. A small, dark shape under the baseboard of the dishwasher.

Flynn saw it too. He bent his head, and I nodded.

Suddenly, the shape made a break for it. A cockroach scurried across the floor. He leapt onto the food.

I eased myself off the counter. As soon as my feet touched the floor, the cockroach felt the vibrations. He tensed. His antennae wiggled wildly. I froze, and he returned to the food.

I couldn't risk another step. I'd have to catch him with one move. I tensed my thighs, ready to leap.

On three, I thought.

One—

Two—

"WAHHHH!" Ivan cried from upstairs.

The cockroach startled and darted left. I dove. He scampered toward the baseboard, but I launched myself at him—my foot slipped on something—I crashed down—but my hands were cupped over the floor.

"Got him," I gasped.

Flynn turned on the light. We both blinked. I peeked into my cupped hands. "I think it's Croach," I said. I put him into the gravel side of the fish tank, and made sure the feeding hatch was closed before I squatted to squint through the glass.

"Yeah, it's Croach." He ran a lap around his habitat and sighed in relief (I'm guessing) as he lay on the sun rock and closed his eyes. "Get some sleep," I told him.

"WAHHHH!" Ivan wailed.

"He's going to wake up your parents." Flynn looked nervously at the mess of cockroach bait. I'd stepped in it, and it was ground thoroughly into the floorboards. "What if they wake up and find us here?"

"That'd be bad."

Flynn turned for the stairs. "I'm fetching him."

"The last person we want here is Ivan!"

"WAHHHH!"

"No," said Flynn, "the last person we want is your mom. And that's what's going to happen in about four seconds. We'll get Ivan, we'll restrain him, and we'll calm him down."

He was right. Keep your friends close, your enemies closer, and your baby brothers closest of all.

A FEW MINUTES later, Flynn tiptoed down the stairs. Ivan, snuggled in his arms, was wearing his gorilla pajamas and holding Gloria. "Ivan understands," said Flynn, obviously for Ivan's benefit, "that we have to be *very quiet*."

"Yep," I said.

"Ivan, can you show Soren what *very quiet* means?"

Ivan put a finger to his lips. He said nothing.

"Wow," I said.

"No sounds from your parents' room," Flynn said. "They must be pretty conked."

"They usually are," I said. "They find their lives exhausting."

"Now what?" Flynn shifted Ivan to his other hip and looked at the trampled food on the floor. "More waiting?"

All three of us gazed at the crab-lentil-jam mush.

"Gross," whispered Ivan.

Flynn set him down. He toddled to the fish tank. I tensed, but all he did was wave at Croach, who waggled a lazy antenna back.

"Free," said Ivan.

"They don't want to be free," I told him. "Life is good in their habitats."

It hurt to think of Cah out there. Scared. Alone.

"Where would he have gone?" Flynn said.

"Out," whispered Ivan. He didn't sound like himself when he whispered. He sounded less like a monster and more like a kid. "Out."

"What?" I said.

Ivan pointed at the door to the dark mudroom, where the chickens slept on their roosts. *"Out."*

CHAPTER FORTY-SEVEN

THE THREE OF us peered through the glass door. Flynn reached back to turn off the lights so we could see more than our reflections. Slowly, our eyes adjusted.

The hens were bundles of feathers: five plump, sleeping lumps. And there was Martha, a spikier bundle on a roost near the window. The heat lamp was dark, but I knew it'd turn on soon.

"What time is it?" I said.

"Three forty-eight," said Flynn.

"We've got twelve minutes before they all wake up."

"Can't we just turn off the timer?"

I shook my head. "It wouldn't help. They've woken up at four a.m. for weeks now, so they'll wake up at four a.m. today."

"Out," said Ivan.

The mudroom floor was six inches deep in pine shavings and straw, all gray and tangled in the moonlight.

"We don't even know he's out there," said Flynn.

269

"I bet he is." Ivan was right. If I knew Cah—and I knew Cah—he'd have looked for adventure. And where else could he be? If he'd been anywhere in the house, he wouldn't have been able to resist the food on the kitchen floor. "He's out there. We just have to find him. Flynn, get another spoonful of lentil stew."

We stepped into the chilly mudroom. It was 3:53 by the oven clock. Flynn dumped the stew on the straw, and I breathed, "Cah! Cah, Cah, Cah!"

Martha twitched.

We froze.

This was the most dangerous thing I'd ever done in my life. Entering Martha's lair—in the dark—with no armor?

What were we *thinking*?

My body shook. Sweat dripped down my neck. I didn't dare wipe it.

It went against all my instincts to take my eyes off Martha, but I stared at the food. *Come on, Cah,* I thought. *I know you smell the food. Come feast.*

The minutes ticked away. 3:58, 3:59.

Cah. Cah. Cah.

The heat lamp clicked on, flooding the mudroom with warm, yellow light. Ivan jumped, but stayed quiet.

I glanced at Martha.

One of his beady eyes opened. Then the other. His head swiveled. He saw us.

"COCK-A-DOO-ARGH-ACK-ECK-EH!"

With squawks and fluttering, the chickens startled

awake. They flapped from their roosts to the ground. In a burst of feathers, Martha, enraged, launched himself at us—

And there he was! There was Cah! Scuttling madly toward the stew!

"CAH!" I yelled.

"COCK-A-DOO-ARGH-ACK-ECK-EH!" yelled Martha.

I lunged, but Martha was faster. He held Cah in his beak.

MARTHA EYED ME. "Let him go," I pleaded. "Please. I'll hunt you other cockroaches."

I hoped Cah didn't understand me.

"Nice Martha—sweet Martha—"

Martha took one step backward on his pickled legs.

It was a lost cause. He had never liked me.

My eyes filled with tears as he took two more steps back. Cah, frozen in his beak, was drawn farther and farther away.

And then Ivan strode forward. He flung his arms wide. Martha, startled, stared at him. His chubby arms quivering, Ivan yelled, "EAT IVAN!"

"Ivan!" I said. "No!"

"EAT IVAN INSTEAD!"

"Don't sacrifice yourself! It isn't worth it!"

"BABY!"

"Get Cah!" Flynn hissed to me. "Get him while Martha's distracted!"

I hesitated. "But—"

"TASTY BABY!"

Martha poked his head forward, his wattle swinging, his beak within inches of Ivan's soft arm.

I dove for Cah, and I plucked him from the jaws of death.

Martha, furious, wheeled around. "COCK-A-DOO-ARGH-ACK-ECK-EH!" he howled. He flew at me. I stumbled away, raising an elbow to protect my eyes, cupping Cah in my hands.

"Inside!" yelled Flynn, fumbling with the doorknob.

The three of us fell into the kitchen. Flynn slammed the door. Martha threw himself against it, but the glass held.

I slowly opened my palms.

"Are you okay?" I murmured.

Cah waved his antennae.

"Don't let him escape again," said Flynn.

"Oh," I said, depositing Cah into his habitat, "I doubt he'll want to escape anytime soon."

Cah flopped onto his sun rock.

"After all," I told Cah, "it's not every day that three heroes will step in to save your life."

"Tasty baby," whispered Ivan.

"We did it," said Flynn.

Ivan stuck out his right hand to me. It took me a second to figure out that he wanted to shake. I don't know where he got the idea, probably from a movie, but we shook hands.

He turned to Flynn, and they shook hands.

He looked at the two of us.

Flynn and I couldn't have avoided it if we'd wanted to,

and, you know, I don't think we did. We were awkward, like we were aliens who'd seen humans do this weird hand-rubbing sign of peace and wanted to try it out for ourselves, but we did it. We shook hands.

It loosened something inside me. I smiled at Flynn. He smiled back. "You know," I said, "you're actually—"

Footsteps thundered on the stairs.

CHAPTER FORTY-EIGHT

THE LECTURE WAS not fun. Mom and Dad tag-teamed it, so as soon as one of them ran out of steam, the other reared up. Sometimes I think they must rehearse those things.

They told us they'd need time to figure out appropriate consequences, so we were sent to bed. About five minutes later, we had to wake up. Dad drove us to school since it was negative fourteen and we were hauling the fish tank and the science-fair board. "And remember, boys," he hollered out the door, "behave today, *or else*! You're skating on thin ice!"

"Ooh," I heard from behind me. "What'd you do?"

I spun around. Purple glasses, brown braids sticking out of a red wool cap—

Alex.

We nodded at each other, but it was too cold to stay outside, or even talk outside. Opening your mouth made your spit get all gummy and your teeth hurt like you'd bitten into

274

an ice cream cone. In the too-warm entrance hall, radiators hissing overtime, I said, "Whoa. Hi. I didn't know you'd be here so early. Did you guys leave at two a.m.?"

"We stayed overnight with my aunt in Effie."

"Oh. Nice."

"ALEX!" I heard someone say.

Not someone. Three someones. The triplets hurried over.

"Andrezejczaks!" squealed Alex. "It's so good to see you!"

She was so high-pitched I almost thought she was faking it, but Olivia flung her arms around Alex's neck. Lila and Tabitha weren't the hugging types, but they were beaming too.

Flynn nudged me with the science-fair board.

"Who's that?" he said.

"Alex Harris. My best friend." She and the triplets had formed a tight little clump. "Well, she was my best friend until she moved."

"Is that who you're always video-chatting?"

"Yeah. Until a few weeks ago."

"Are you guys fighting or something?"

I shifted my weight. The fish tank was getting heavy, and I couldn't take off my mittens until I put it down. "Let's go to homeroom."

"Okay."

I turned to Alex. "Um, see you later, I guess? Are you here all day?"

"I have a visitor's badge. I can stay as long as I want

and I'm supposed to text my mom when I want her to pick me up."

"You have a phone? When'd you get a phone?"

"A couple of weeks ago." She flashed it. "There's a lot you miss when you don't talk to me."

"You're the one who wasn't talking to *me*!"

"Come on, girls." She linked arms with Lila and Tabitha, leaving Olivia to trail behind. "We need to find a private place to catch up."

"And we need to find Ruth!" said Lila.

I trudged to homeroom. Flynn followed me. He didn't say anything, which was nice. Ms. Hutchins's classroom was already crammed with projects, boards and plants and things built of Popsicle sticks. Flynn slid our board into a safe spot behind the begonia, and I checked to make sure Cah and Croach had survived the journey.

"Yes," I said to Flynn, "is the answer."

"Huh?"

"To whether we're fighting. Me and Alex. I guess we are, anyway. She has new friends. This girl at her school, and the triplets here. She barely knew the triplets before she moved."

"Well, you have new friends too," said Flynn.

"I do?"

Jéro ran up to us. "I saw Alex out there. Anything you want to tell me before tonight, Soren?"

"Uh, no."

"Come on. One little hint for your buddy Jéro? Your

favorite bookie? I won't tell anyone, I promise. They could torture me and I wouldn't tell."

Flynn eyed me. "Are you *planning* something?"

"No! I told you! I retired!"

"Because I worked really hard on this science-fair project."

"So did I! So did everyone!"

"Hmm," said Jéro. Flynn wasn't as obvious, but I could tell he wasn't sure either.

"After all the excitement last night," I said, "the last thing I want is chaos at science fair. I want everything to be peaceful and calm."

Jéro gaped. He turned to Flynn. "Did he really say that?"

Flynn started laughing. "I wish I'd gotten that on video. That's the weirdest thing that's happened all year."

THE RULE IS if it's negative degrees, we have to have recess in our homeroom teacher's classroom.

"G. Grandin versus E. Garcia." The class tournament of paper-clip badminton was up and running and hugely popular, and Jéro was reading off the day's matches. "J. Johnson versus T. Tyler. R. Grant versus F. Skaar."

"Flynn's playing?" Soup asked me.

"Yeah, he joined last-minute. Today, actually."

I'd asked him if he'd wanted to play during math that morning, and he'd gotten this look of utter joy and said, "Me? *Yes!*"

"Rats," Soup groaned.

"No, it's okay, he's actually cool—"

"Nah, I just mean, he's going to win. If he's half as good at badminton as he is at soccer, he'll flatten us all."

Alex came over. "Want to play?" I said.

Soup said, "It's the All-Class Paper-Clip Badminton Open. We're the tournament directors. It'd be a late registration, but we could get you in—"

"No thanks. I'm teaching the triplets the basics of paper dolls." Alex tilted her head at me. "If you know what I mean."

"Wait. What *do* you mean?"

"You want to join us?"

What *did* she mean?

I glanced at the triplets. They were already snipping at colored paper. I couldn't decide whether to be suspicious.

"Come on, Soren. It's not the same without you."

The three badminton matches were already under way, and the rest of the class was gathered around the competition desks, chanting and clapping. "We've got to help keep stats," Soup reminded me. "And do crowd control, ref any close calls . . ."

He was right. I was needed. "Sorry," I told Alex. "Maybe later?"

She shrugged. "Sure. Maybe."

CHAPTER FORTY-NINE

FOR AN EARLY dinner before science fair, Dad heated up some leftover lasagna.

"You look nice, Soren," said Mom. "Very unusual."

"SOREN GROOM!" chimed in Ivan. He had a coloring book about royal weddings, and he thought wearing a tie meant you were getting married.

"Never," I told him.

"Aren't you excited to present your project?" said Mom.

"Yeah."

"You don't sound very excited. Nervous?"

"I guess so," I said. *Bothered* was more like it. *Preoccupied.* What was going on with Alex and the triplets and the paper dolls?

Flynn came downstairs. He was wearing blood-red dress pants, a shiny gray shirt, and a silver bow tie. "Wow," said Mom. "Very, um, different."

"Thanks!" said Flynn.

"DODGE, SOREN!" yelled Dad.

Fortunately, I have the self-protective instincts of a gazelle on the savanna. I ducked, and a clump of lasagna sailed over my head. Ivan chortled. "I'll run you guys over to school," said Mom, glancing between Ivan and my crisp white shirt.

"I'll come early too," said Ruth, pulling on her backpack.

"The audience doesn't need to be there for another hour," Mom said. "You don't want to stay here with Dad and Ivan?"

"Nah," said Ruth. "I'll be a sixth grader someday. I want to watch them set up so I can start thinking about my own project."

Dad stood and applauded. "What forethought!" he cried. "What a stand against procrastination! I hope you're taking notes, Soren."

Ruth was a bigger procrastinator than anyone. Unless Dad made her, she never started projects until the night before. She didn't even *think* about Christmas presents until December 24. Sometimes stores were already closed and she had to wrap stuff from her junk drawer.

She was up to something.

"Ready?" said Mom.

"Ready," said Ruth and Flynn.

"Yeah," I said, "I'm ready too."

"I FORGOT ALEX WAS VISITING!" said Mom in the school lobby. "Did you see her at school today?"

"Yep." She was with the triplets again. I waved, but they didn't see me.

280

"I wonder how long they're staying," said Mom. "We should have her and her mom over for dinner. And the Andrezejczaks, too."

"Mm-hmm."

"Let's go set up," Flynn told me.

"Yeah," I said, not taking my eyes off Alex and the triplets. Ruth had joined them. They were in a tight circle. All you could see was ponytails and backpacks.

Okay. It was official. They were definitely up to something.

"Come on, Soren," said Flynn. "We have to get everything ready before the judges arrive."

We set up our board and fish tank in the zoology section of the gym. The triplets came in to set up their projects. Alex and Ruth followed. I kept an eye on them. Over in chemistry, Ms. Hutchins was yelling at Freddy, who was sheepishly rubbing a towel over a large puddle of what smelled like gasoline. In psychology, Lila and Jéro were fighting over the angle of their board. "Come check out our ballista," Tabitha called to me from engineering. It was ten feet long.

"In a sec," I said.

"It works so well that Chloe's dad wants to buy it off us for deer season," said Billiam.

I'd lost track of Alex and Ruth. Ms. Hutchins opened the doors, and the parents and siblings and judges streamed in. "I'll be right back," I said to Flynn.

"You can't leave!" he said. "Our first judge is coming!"

"But—I'm worried—"

"Focus!" hissed Flynn. "Here she is!"

I straightened my tie. Dr. Adams approached. She's been my pediatrician all my life. "Why, hello, Soren," she said in the exact tone she uses when I'm naked and wrapped in paper on the exam table. "And you are . . ."

"Flynn. Flynn Skaar. I'm Soren's cousin."

"It's a pleasure. Now, tell me about your experiment."

We hadn't practiced, but it went well. "Would you do anything differently," said Dr. Adams, "if you were doing this experiment again?"

"I'd love to have more cockroaches!" I said. Flynn jabbed me. "Ouch—what? I *like* cockroaches. They make great pets. And the more the merrier, right?"

Dr. Adams made some marks on her clipboard. When she left, Flynn said, "Did you have to mention the biggest problem with our experiment?"

"What do you mean?"

"The fact that we only had two cockroaches. Sample sets of one. It's a huge flaw. I was hoping she wouldn't notice."

"Oh."

"So when our other judge comes, how about you don't point that out?"

Parents were milling around the gym. Judges were peering at clipboards. Kids in ties and dresses were gesturing at graphs. *Some* kids.

Some kids, it seemed, were missing.

"I have to check on something," I said.

"You still can't leave!"

"I'll be back in five seconds." Before he could protest more, I wove through the crowd to psychology. "Jéro!" I said. "Where's Lila?"

"I don't know. Bathroom, maybe? It's awesome. She told me I wasn't allowed to speak when the judges came around, but hey, she wasn't here, so—"

I was gone, ducking and dodging my way to earth science. "Tori!" I said. She and Olivia had done something about the hardness of rocks. "Do you know where Olivia went?"

Tori rolled her eyes. "She had to nervous-pee. If you'd ever been in a play with her, you'd remember that every time—"

I sprinted off. Engineering was my last stop. If Tabitha wasn't there, I'd know.

"Billiam!" I panted. "Where's Tabitha?"

He gave me a slow look. "Why do you want to know?"

"Just tell me!"

Billiam can be kind of a jerk. If you want something fast, he takes his time. Finally, he said, "I don't know."

"Thanks, so helpful—"

"She went out that door. A while ago now. Fifteen minutes, maybe."

AHHH! Fifteen minutes? You could do a lot in fifteen minutes. "Okay. Thanks."

I ran back to zoology, getting a lot of dirty looks from parents and judges along the way. "Flynn," I said, "I've got to step out."

"But we have another judge coming any minute now!"

"I'll be back as soon as I can."

"You're leaving me to defend our project alone?"

"I know. I'm really sorry. But it's an emergency."

Images flashed through my head: Ruth on the video chat with Alex. Ruth following the triplets up their driveway after school. The five of them hunched together, the murmurs, the backpacks . . .

Flynn's eyes narrowed. "You're trying to prank science fair, aren't you?"

"No!"

"I'm supposed to believe that?"

"Flynn." I stared into his eyes. "Please. I know you don't trust me—but please. Believe me. Give me a chance. I'm not trying to prank science fair. I'm trying to *save* science fair."

He looked at me for a long, excruciating moment. "Fine. Go."

"Wait. What? You really—"

"Go. I don't know why I trust you, but I do. I'll cover for you. Go."

CHAPTER FIFTY

I HAD A detailed digestive excuse all ready, but no teacher intercepted me as I dashed out of the gym and into the empty corridors of the school.

Where had those girls gone?

I rattled the doorknobs of the kindergarten rooms. Locked, all locked. I turned down the next hallway, tried the first-grade doors . . .

Think, Soren.

I leaned against a first-grade bulletin board (HOW DID WE CHOOSE KIND TODAY?). I took deep breaths and thought.

They would have already planned the prank. The video chats, the after-school meetings, the huddles today—the planning stage was over. So if they'd all snuck out together, it was because they needed a launchpad. They needed a place to prepare supplies before their massive prank.

A private place, but a place they could get into.

I started running again. I skidded to a halt outside the tiled entrance to the two bathrooms.

The boys' was empty. Of course. I shouldn't have wasted time checking.

I paused outside the girls'. Did I dare? I'd never gone into a girls' bathroom, and I had hoped I never would.

I set a foot inside, and then I pulled it out. I couldn't do it. "Hello?" I called. "Is anyone in there?"

Goldie's mom popped out, shaking wet hands in the air. "Soren! May I help you? Did you want paper towels for the boys' room? Because they're out in the girls', too. . . ."

"Um," I said, "actually, I was looking for, um, my sister? My mom told me to find her because they need to go home early—she just got a phone call with, uh, test results, and Ruth is *very* ill, strep throat, I think, and it's so contagious that she needs to be quarantined immediately—"

"Oh!" said Mrs. Grandin, taken aback. Darn. As usual, I'd tried to lie and ended up babbling. "Goodness gracious. I didn't think anyone was in there, but let me take a look."

I waited. She came out. "Looked under all the stalls," she reported, "and it's empty as a bird's nest in winter!"

"Okay, thanks, bye!" I took off down the hall.

"Give your sister my best wishes for a speedy recovery!" she called after me. "I'll be sure to spread the word about the strep outbreak!"

Great.

I took the stairs, swinging on the banister to make the turn. On the first floor, I'd been able to hear faint noise from the gym, but the second floor was eerily quiet. I grabbed a few doorknobs just to make sure, but the classrooms were locked up here, too. If they weren't in the second-floor bathrooms, I didn't know where they'd be. I doubted I'd be able to find them in time to stop whatever they were planning to do.

I slowed as I approached the bathrooms. There was a yellow plastic sign propped on the floor: RESTROOMS CLOSED FOR CLEANING.

Hmm.

I tiptoed into the boys' room. It was clear, as I'd expected.

I hovered outside the girls' room.

There was definitely water running. It could be a janitor.

But then I heard a familiar sound. A very familiar sound. A giggle I'd been hearing for over nine years now.

I burst in.

"The girls' bathroom has a *mirror*?" I said.

And the five girls who were gathered around the sinks, who were pulling water balloons onto the faucets, and tying them, and throwing them into a tall, deep laundry hamper, which was almost full of colorful blobs—they all jumped. They shouted, "SOREN!"

CHAPTER FIFTY-ONE

"THIS IS THE GIRLS' BATHROOM," said Ruth. "You're not supposed to be in here."

"Didn't you see the sign?" said Lila. "This restroom is closed for cleaning."

"Oh, you're cleaning?" I said.

"How did you find us?" said Tabitha.

I shrugged. "I knew something was up. You didn't cover your tracks very well."

That got to Alex, I could tell. She finished the knot on her balloon with a sharp snap. "We weren't trying to hide our tracks from *you*."

"You sure were secretive, then."

"You retired. We weren't about to blab all the details to someone who'd retired."

It kind of made sense. But then I saw Alex worrying the earpiece of her glasses. She was lying. I babble; she plays with her glasses. It's like the sunrise. Couldn't stop it if you tried.

"Oh," I said, realizing what was going on. "You're still mad at me."

"Maybe I am," said Alex. "So?"

"So you left me out."

"Now you know what it feels like," said Ruth.

"No offense, Soren, but you wanted to be left out," said Tabitha. "You literally told us you were done with pranks."

But being left out stinks. Even when you've chosen it.

"Let's keep going," said Alex, checking her phone. "We only have ten minutes to finish filling these balloons. We've got to get the laundry hamper to the catwalk before the awards presentation starts."

"What about him?" asked Lila.

"I'm not going anywhere," I said.

"At this point, he'll just have to help," said Alex. "Congratulations. We're un-leaving you out."

"No, I—"

"Here's the plan. You know that catwalk above the stage? The door's only a few yards down from this bathroom." She jingled something in her pocket. "And I got the key."

"How?" I said.

"That's classified. Anyway. We fill the rest of these balloons. Then we all pull this huge hamper to the catwalk. It's going to be really heavy. Then you and the triplets go back to science fair. Ruth stands lookout, and I'll be on the catwalk by myself. The instant Ms. Hutchins starts the awards, wahoo! Look out below!"

"But everyone'll know where the balloons are coming from," I said. "You'll get caught so fast."

"I can throw a lot of water balloons in the time it takes Principal Leary to get up a flight of stairs."

"You'll get in so much trouble."

"What are they going to do?" said Alex. "Expel me?"

In the past, we'd always had one major constraint: we couldn't get caught. Suspicion and detentions, fine. Evidence and suspensions, no thanks.

But now . . .

"Leary'll tell your mom," I said.

"And I'll tell her it's her fault," said Alex. "If she hadn't made us move, I'd still be doing nice, normal pranks with you."

She had a point.

"Now let's get a move on with these water balloons."

"It's going to be out of control," I said. Hundreds of bright bulbs hurtling down from nowhere, like God had given up on locusts and decided to send a plague of water balloons instead. "It'll be chaos."

"It'll be amazing," said Alex. "Probably our best prank ever." She checked her phone again. "Enough talking. Soren, can you tie? Our fingers hurt."

I took up position next to Tabitha's sink. I tied a balloon.

This wasn't what I'd intended.

But the prank was simple. It was glorious. I was a lifelong prankster, and this was the prank of a lifetime. Saying no to this prank would be like an ice cream connoisseur saying no to the best ice cream in the world just because he was full from dinner. And water balloons were harmless. I'd tell Alex to take aim far from the science-fair projects so none of the boards would be ruined. People would get wet, sure, but people can dry.

This was the true Dream Team. This was my chance to prank with Alex and the triplets and Ruth, the five most devilishly clever people I knew. Besides, *I* wouldn't get in trouble. I'd return to the gym, and when Flynn said, "Did you save us?" I'd say, "I hope so. I tried. I did my best." And if something happened anyway, well, I'd be as shocked and angry as he was.

I tied another balloon and tossed it into the hamper. It landed with a wet plop. I wiped my hands on my dress pants. "I can't do this," I said.

"Tying water balloons is hard," said Olivia sympathetically.

"No. *This.* I can't do this prank." I thought of Flynn saying he trusted me. I thought of Dad telling me he believed in me, how he thought I could figure it out, this pranking thing, and I thought of Mom telling me to act like the person I wanted to be. "It's not fair," I said. "It's not fair to ruin science fair for everyone."

"Nobody'll get hurt," said Tabitha. "They'll just get wet."

Sometimes, wet was bad enough. "You guys don't know what it's like," I said. The spelling bee had been my fault, and I'd learned my lesson. "You don't know how guilty and awful you'll feel. I'm telling you, it's not worth it—"

"Leave," said Alex.

291

She stared me down. She'd left a water balloon attached to a spigot, and it bobbled around in the sink as it filled.

"Leave now," she said. "You were never here. You didn't see a thing."

"I can't let you do this prank," I said.

"You think you can stop us?"

I stood in front of the hamper and crossed my arms. "I'm going to try."

"No, you're not," said Alex. "You wouldn't do that to me. Because I've been waiting for this day for months, Soren. This is the only happy thing in my life right now. Moving ruined everything—"

"That's not even true!" I said. "That's just what you keep telling yourself! Alex, you *like* Minneapolis! You like paper dolls! You like Ol' Bu—you like *Sophia*!"

Alex's fists clenched. I made sure I'd squarely blocked the hamper. "Don't try to tell me the move was a good thing."

"I'm not! But it wasn't a bad thing, either. Some parts are bad, yeah—I miss pranking with you, Alex—I miss *you*, I really do—but some parts are good. You wouldn't be friends with Sophia if you hadn't moved. You wouldn't be friends with the triplets."

"You wouldn't even be talking to me," pointed out Ruth.

"I can't *believe* you're happy I moved," said Alex.

I opened my mouth to protest, but she lunged forward and shoved me. I fell back—

—butt-first—

—right into the deep laundry hamper.

"AHHH!"

It didn't hurt, because it was full of water balloons. But half of them burst and I sank way down. I was doubled up in a V shape, getting more waterlogged by the second.

"Help! Get me out!"

A pair of people hurtled into the bathroom.

Ms. Hutchins and Principal Leary.

"Uh-oh," said Ruth.

It was at that exact moment that the water pressure got to be too much for Alex's balloon, which had been bobbling around on the faucet. It exploded off. It bounced around in the sink, spraying water all the way up to the ceiling.

For the first time ever, Ms. Hutchins and Principal Leary were speechless.

CHAPTER FIFTY-TWO

FINALLY, MS. HUTCHINS got her voice back. "What in the *world*?"

The balloon in the sink sputtered merrily along. I was stuck in the hamper, trying not to move. I was worried that if I struggled, it'd tip over.

"The judges asked us why so many students were missing their partners," Ms. Hutchins told us. "So we thought we'd take a quick look around the school. And—well. Look at this."

"More sabotage," said Principal Leary. His lips were a thin line. "The rash of pranks that have marred our fine school this fall . . . I'd hoped it was over. But no. Not if you had your way."

The girls looked intensely guilty, all staring at the floor and turning red. I lurched a little deeper in the hamper. The water was still leaking out of balloons that had split when I'd landed.

"Trying to destroy science fair," said Leary, shaking his

head. "It's hard to believe you'd have so little respect for all the hard work that's gone into this event."

What was hard to believe was that Leary was saying basically the same thing I'd just said. It made me worry I'd grow up to be a principal.

"We're sorry," said Tabitha.

"No," I heard myself say. It was a total impulse. "*I'm* sorry. *You* had nothing to do with it."

"What?" said Leary.

I swallowed. I reminded myself, *Don't babble.* "It was only me," I said. "I was acting alone. They were trying to stop me."

"Soren—" said Tabitha.

I cut her off. "That's how I ended up in here," I said, gesturing at the hamper. A balloon popped at the movement, and I sank another inch. I was so folded up that my legs almost touched my face. "They shoved me down. They didn't want to resort to violence, but they had no other choice. I was about to take the balloons to the"—but I couldn't give away that Alex had the key to the catwalk—"to, um, downstairs."

Leary nodded slowly. "And these young ladies—these heroes—stopped you?"

"Right!" Oops. I couldn't sound too happy about it. I glared at the girls. "I had such a good plan, too. But they must have been tipped off. Maybe I left some evidence lying around at home, a water-balloon receipt, maybe, or . . ." *Don't babble!* "I was an idiot."

"That's not true!" said Ruth. "It was all of us! It was everyone *but* him!"

"Don't try to save me," I said. "Besides, nobody's going to believe it was you."

"Ruth, honey," said Ms. Hutchins, "I'm a little sister too, and I know it's hard to see your big brother in trouble. But you don't need to take responsibility for his actions."

"We do admire your loyalty, however," said Leary.

He whispered something in Ms. Hutchins's ear. I took the opportunity to give Ruth a threatening look. *Don't*, I mouthed.

"Nobody move," Leary told us. "The floor's very wet and slippery. We'll be right back. Your parents need to be here for this conversation."

They left the bathroom. The girls waited ten seconds, and then they turned on me. "Soren!" said Ruth, almost in tears. "You can't do this!"

"It makes sense," I said. "I get in trouble all the time. I'm known for it. But you guys, you have perfect reputations. You don't want to ruin them." I smiled, but it was shaky. I'd begun to think about what Mom and Dad would do to me when they found out. Taking the blame *did* make sense. I knew it. But I needed to remind myself why. "You'll be way more useful for future pranks if you remain above suspicion," I said.

"But it wasn't your fault," said Tabitha.

"Well. I've done a bunch of things I didn't get caught for. So it's only fair I get caught for something I didn't do."

Olivia tearfully twisted her hands together. "We've been working with you all fall," she said. "We're just as bad."

"But the spelling bee going so wrong, that was my fault. You didn't know that Ruth and Flynn would care so much."

"What about me?" said Alex. It was the first thing she'd said since they'd found us. "It should be me, Soren. It was my idea. And I was always going to get caught. That was the plan."

I met Alex's eyes and gave her a smile, as big a smile as possible for someone who's soaking wet and stuck in a hamper with their knees around their ears. "Nope," I said. "I've been waiting for this."

"What do you mean?" said Ruth.

"This one's mine," I said.

Alex shook her head. "This is so much worse than a few plastic ants."

"Then throw in that catwalk key."

"Soren—"

"Alex."

We locked eyes. Slowly, she began to grin. "Deal."

"Your moving away," I told her, "is about the hardest thing that's ever happened to me. I'm just trying to get okay with it."

"I know," she said. "Me too."

Lila stamped her foot. "This is *stupid,* Soren. We're not letting you take the blame."

"Let me," I said. "Please."

She faced me, her hands on her hips. Lila's bossy, but

I'm stubborn. I was feeling good again, and I knew I was in the home stretch. If I could convince them before the teachers came back, they wouldn't stop me—and I wouldn't stop myself—from doing the first truly nice thing I'd done for a very long time.

"If you don't let me," I said sweetly, "I'll call up your big brother. Ethan, right? I'll tell him all about what you've been up to this school year. Alarm clocks, Jim Bob, water balloons—oh, it'll be blackmail for *years*."

She twitched. "No! Don't!"

"Then keep your mouth shut."

She subsided. She tried to glare at me, but I saw the smile tickling the corners of her mouth.

"I'm only asking for one thing in return," I said.

"Anything," said Tabitha.

A water balloon popped. I sank an inch deeper. "Help me out of this laundry hamper?"

CHAPTER FIFTY-THREE

RUMORS ARE AMAZING. By the time we made it downstairs, everyone knew that I had tried to destroy science fair with a hundred water balloons. By the time Ms. Hutchins took the stage for the awards, it was a thousand, and at the end of the night, Jéro said, "I heard you built an automatic water-balloon launcher. Like a catapult, except with a motor and a robotic arm for reloading."

"Um, not quite."

"That's so cool that I'm not even mad you didn't tell me. I'm just impressed."

"Well, I didn't—"

"Sticking to your story even now, huh?" He clapped me on the back. "You're a pro."

Principal Leary had come back to the bathroom alone. He'd told us to return to the gym, because Ms. Hutchins needed to announce the awards and it was getting late. "I've already told your parents what you did, Soren," he said. "You and I will meet with them tomorrow to discuss consequences." It'd be a painful meeting, I could already tell, but honestly, right now, I was glowing.

I joined Flynn at the board. Luckily my pants were black so it didn't look like I'd had an accident. "How was the second judge?" I said.

"Not bad. He asked me about the sample-size thing, though. He said, 'Wouldn't your results mean more if you had more than one cockroach in each kind of habitat?'"

"Oh."

"But he was impressed by our detailed data." Flynn shrugged. "So we'll see." He looked me up and down. "Soup and Freddy told me you were caught with a bunch of water balloons."

"I was."

"Were you lying to me?"

"No."

"Then," said Flynn, "I won't ask you anything else." He knelt to peer into the fish tank. "The second judge said Cah and Croach were the best-tended cockroaches he's ever seen."

I puffed up with pride. "It's all in the desserts. Cockroaches are happiest when they get dessert with all three meals."

"I think I'll add Cah and Croach to my mural."

"About that," I said. "How come you have a mural of me looking stupid?"

"Huh?"

"Every time I'm embarrassed, you draw it on your wall."

Flynn still looked confused. "No. I draw happy things.

Things I like about Camelot. They cheer me up when I'm feeling cruddy."

"You drew the time I sat on poop play dough!"

"No, I drew the first time Ivan acted like he liked me."

"What about everyone ignoring me at the block party?"

"You mean everyone wanting me to take piglet pics of them?"

I fell silent. Had I missed the whole point of the mural? "Okay. What about Ms. Hutchins telling the class about the anonymous tip? Explain *that*."

"That's just a picture of science class."

"Then why is she holding a piece of paper?"

"Because she's a teacher!"

"Oh," I said.

"Are we cool, then?"

"We're cool."

Flynn stood. He squinched the knot of his silver tie tighter. "Hey. Thanks."

"For what?"

"You know." He gave me the kind of smile he usually flashes at gross food or an especially pleasing banjo chord. "For saving us."

I HADN'T NOTICED Principal Leary's necktie earlier. I'd had other things on my mind. As he stepped up to the stage, I saw that it was patterned with test tubes.

He tapped the mike. For once, it worked on the first try. "Good evening, and thank you for attending the Camelot Elementary School science fair!"

After some stuff about young minds and STEM and the curiosity inherent to human nature, blah blah, he turned the mike over to Ms. Hutchins. She started with the list of projects that received Superior, the highest designation. "Please," said Flynn under his breath, "please, please, please . . ."

Goldie and Kiyana got it, what a surprise, for *Does a Watched Pot Boil? A Scientific Investigation.*

And Soup and Evelyn got it, which actually *was* a surprise, for *What's Faster at Crawling: A Stinkbug or a Human Child?*

Flynn's shoulders sagged as the last Superior was applauded, Emily and Jeremiah's *Can People Do Math Problems Better in Peace, or While Listening to Heavy Metal and Being Poked with a Fork?*

"It was the sample-size thing," Flynn said heavily.

"That's my fault! I told Dr. Adams!"

"She'd have noticed it anyway, and the other judge saw it himself. It's all my fault. I designed the experiment."

"It's half my fault," I said.

Then we got Excellent, which was second best. Flynn cheered up considerably. "Excellent!" he said, admiring our certificate. "You know what? I'll take it."

I plastered the certificate against the fish tank to show Cah and Croach.

MOM AND DAD came over as we were packing up. "Where's Ivan?" I asked.

"He's with a few girls from your class," said Mom. "They think he's very cute."

"They aren't letting him near the engineering section, are they?"

"Well, as a matter of fact—"

I dropped the board and sprinted to Tabitha and Billiam's huge ballista. Sure enough, Ivan was toddling toward the lever, a giant grin on his face. He had already loaded the bucket with what looked to be an entire box of pre-chewed graham crackers.

"STOP HIM!" I panted.

"Oh, Soren," said Emily. "He's just a baby!"

Ivan stomped on the lever the moment before I reached him. The spring released. The spitty wad of graham crackers sailed up, up, up—

Everyone in the gym swiveled to watch as it soared through the air.

It hit the basketball hoop's backboard, rebounded, fell through, and landed on Ms. Hutchins's head.

She looked more surprised than upset as she reached up to investigate. "Oh," she said. She swiped another clod off her hair, and then gave a queenly wave to the gym of people staring at her in horror. "I'm fine!" she called. "Just another reason I'll be glad when this evening's over!"

Everyone broke into raucous applause.

"Let's see if the ballista's strong enough to shoot *him*," I said, delivering Ivan back to my parents.

"IVAN FLY!" he yelled.

We were in the parking lot on the way to our car when Mrs. Grandin ran up. "I'm so glad I caught you!" she said to Mom. "How *is* she? Sleeping, I hope?"

Ruth was carrying our board. I motioned to her, and she lifted it up to cover her face.

"Who?" said Mom. "What?"

"Your wonderful son told me about poor Ruthie's illness," Mrs. Grandin said. "Earlier tonight, when he was looking for her in the bathroom."

"Earlier tonight," said Mom. "Really."

"I was on my way out—that first-floor bathroom is so ridiculous for adults; it's kindergarten-sized, of course, the toilets about eight inches from the floor—and Soren said you'd sent him to find her. What a kind brother."

"The first-floor bathroom," said Dad. *"Really."*

"You were searching for her in quite a tizzy, weren't you, Soren?"

"Quite," I said.

"Do tell me she's being treated," said Mrs. Grandin.

"I'm sure she'll be fine," said Mom. "Thanks for asking, Gardenia."

CHAPTER FIFTY-FOUR

MOM AND DAD totally knew what had happened. I got two days of in-school suspension from Principal Leary, but they didn't punish me extra at all, and either they forgave Flynn and me for being out of bed at four a.m. or they forgot. For obvious reasons, I couldn't ask.

The one tricky thing about the meeting was when Principal Leary said, "So. I have to wonder, Soren. The alarm clocks? The piglet? Were those you, too?"

I don't know what I'd have done if Dad's lawyer half hadn't firmly collided with his protective papa-bear half.

"Ex*cuse* me," Dad said. "Are you suggesting that confessing to one crime is tantamount to confessing to *all* crimes?"

"No—er—"

"Because the fallacies therein, sir, are not only manifold but also problematic, vide Federal Rules of Evidence 404(b), and I, for one, would take serious umbrage—"

"I just—uh—"

Dad eyed him. "Yes?"

"It was just a passing thought," said Leary. "Let's move on, shall we?"

On the way out of the meeting, Dad said to me, "This confession. I assume you know what you're doing."

"Yup," I said.

"Well, don't ever do this again. But I'm proud."

"Me too," said Mom. "Soren, do you remember when Alex first left? And I told you, 'Keep doing what you like to do'?"

"Yeah . . ."

"If you're going to retire from pranking," said Mom, "you should Michael Phelps–style retire."

I hoped that didn't involve the butterfly, because whenever I try that stroke I swallow a gallon of lake water and spend the rest of the day with algae-flavored burps. "What do you mean?"

Mom put her arm around my shoulders. "Retire, and then make a triumphant comeback in a few months."

"Agreed," said Dad, putting *his* arm around my shoulders, and for a minute we stumbled down the hallway like that, giggling as our legs got tangled up. Then I saw Tabitha at the water fountain, and I squirmed out of their arms. You don't exactly want a girl in your grade to see you in a parent sandwich.

FLYNN HAD PLANNED to spend winter break in Brooklyn, but he asked his mom to come to Camelot instead. "I like it here," he told us.

306

"Really?" I said. "Don't you miss the green tea? The vintage trunk shop?"

"Soren," warned Mom.

"My mom will replenish my supply of green tea," Flynn said. "And you can only own so many vintage trunks."

This was undeniably true.

"Plus," said Flynn, "everything I care about is right here in Camelot—"

"That's so sweet," said Dad.

"My banjo, my rhyming dictionary . . ."

"Right," said Dad.

"In fact, I've written one last song for my concept album. Would you like to hear it?"

"We wouldn't miss it for the world," said Mom.

Flynn strummed. "A remix of 'Winter Wonderland'!" he cried, and began to sing.

> "Oh, the climate is dismal,
> And the coffee's abysmal.
> The nearest Thai food's two hours removed.
> Exiled to a small-town wonderland.
>
> "But the crops here are top-flight.
> There's no traffic, one stoplight.
> And what is more posh than prize-winning squash?
> Living in a small-town wonderland!
>
> "Back in Brooklyn, I was on my lonesome,
> And when I got here, I kept calling out,

307

'Don't you want to hear of where I've flown from?'
'Not at all,' you said, 'but let's hang out!'

"Now I've learned that I cheer up
At the taste of corn syrup.
My dear country folk, let's share a Coke,
Living in our hometown wonderland!"

"Is that supposed to be a subtle hint?" said Dad. He went to the garage and came back with a twelve-pack of Coke.

"That's two each," said Ruth.

"Not so fast, young lady," said Mom. "You and Soren may split a can to start."

"Speaking of sharing," said Flynn, "I've been thinking. What if Soren moves back into my room?"

"You're the guest," I said. "I don't mind another semester being crammed in with Ruth and Ivan."

"I think it'd be fun," said Flynn.

"Me too." I thought for a second. "Can we keep Cah and Croach on the windowsill? They prefer natural light."

Flynn grimaced. "I suppose."

"Don't worry," I said. "They'll never escape again."

Ivan came running into the kitchen with a present from under the tree. It was the one he was the most curious about, a package that was long and skinny and weirdly light. "IVAN OPEN!"

"Not till Christmas, sweetie," said Dad.

"If that's what I think it is," I said, "I might move out."

"Ivan's fencing instructor says he has some real talent," said Dad. "It's only right that we let him develop it."

ON THE FIRST day back to school, Ms. Hutchins was humming with excitement. "This semester, we continue our mission to think like a scientist," she said. "And you've proven you can handle advanced scientific tools!"

She whipped a sheet off a table of equipment.

"Bunsen burners!" she said.

Oh, *heck* yes.

Comeback, here I come.

Ms. Hutchins began to review safety procedures, but all I could see was the steady blue flame.

When you're *allowed* to play with fire at school—

When playing with fire is actually *the assignment*—

The possibilities were endless.

Flynn took notes. The triplets looked about as happy as I felt. "Psst!" said Tabitha. "Want to plot during recess?"

"You bet."

"Only after our badminton tournament's over," said Jéro.

I paid careful attention as Ms. Hutchins explained how to work the Bunsen burners. I didn't know yet what we'd do, but I was starting to get a few ideas.

ACKNOWLEDGMENTS

I am deeply grateful to the people whom I lived among as I wrote this book. You are the lights of my life, and very chuffing besides. Thank you, Henry, Peter, Rebecca, Emma, Lucy, Derek, and Spencer. Thank you, Mom and Dad. Thank you, Phil. Thank you, Abbey, Allison, Ariel, Desi, Ken, Liz, Nate, Peter, Rita, Rita's vomiting rooster, Sarah, and Sasha.

Erin Clarke, thank you for having faith in this book when it was only three chapters and a synopsis that was heavily centered on the Bayeux Tapestry. It has truly been an honor to work with you again. Uwe Stender, I am, as ever, grateful for your insight, hard work, and good cheer. Many thanks also to Leslie Mechanic, Karen Sherman, Artie Bennett, Alison Kolani, Kelly Delaney, and the whole team at Random House.

I cannot express the depth of my gratitude; I am fortunate to be able to try. Thank you.

KATE HATTEMER

is a native of Cincinnati, but now writes, reads, runs, and teaches high school Latin in the D.C. metro area. She is the author of two novels for young adults: *The Vigilante Poets of Selwyn Academy,* which received five starred reviews and was named a best book of the year by the American Library Association, *Kirkus Reviews,* and *Bustle,* and *The Land of 10,000 Madonnas.* Learn more about Kate on her website at KateHattemer.com.

CURRIED AWAY

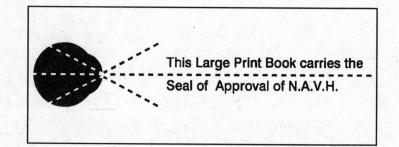

This Large Print Book carries the
Seal of Approval of N.A.V.H.

CURRIED AWAY

GAIL OUST

THORNDIKE PRESS
A part of Gale, a Cengage Company

Farmington Hills, Mich • San Francisco • New York • Waterville, Maine
Meriden, Conn • Mason, Ohio • Chicago

LIBRARY OF CONGRESS CATALOGING-IN-PUBLICATION DATA

Names: Oust, Gail, 1943– author.
Title: Curried away / by Gail Oust.
Description: Large print edition. | Waterville, Maine : Thorndike Press, a part of Gale, Cengage Learning, 2017. | Series: A spice shop mystery | Series: Thorndike Press large print mystery
Identifiers: LCCN 2017014176| ISBN 9781410499592 (hardcover) | ISBN 1410499596 (hardcover)
Subjects: LCSH: Businesswomen—Fiction. | Murder—Investigation—Fiction. | Large type books. | GSAFD: Mystery fiction
Classification: LCC PS3620.U7645 C87 2017 | DDC 813/.6—dc23
LC record available at https://lccn.loc.gov/2017014176

Published in 2017 by arrangement with Macmillan Publishing Group, LLC/St. Martin's Press

Printed in the United States of America
1 2 3 4 5 6 7 21 20 19 18 17

To Nolan Michael Brys.
Welcome to the world, little boy.

ACKNOWLEDGMENTS

My sincere gratitude to friends Craig and Sandy Granger, for being such good sports and allowing me to use their names, not in one book, but in two. Next time you make a bid at a silent auction — beware! Fran McClain, once again you came to my aid with your cooking expertise. There were moments it took all my willpower to stay at the computer when I really wanted to whip up a tasty dish from one of your cookbooks. Mike, I appreciate your persistent prodding to update my Web site. Brianna Brys, if it wasn't for you I wouldn't have heard about "crunchy parenting." Thanks for helping with the research and answering numerous questions. When it comes to cloth diapers, girl, you rock. Gratitude to Norm Francavilla, Tonawanda, New York, Police Department, Retired, for being my go-to cop. You never know what kind of questions I might serve up along with dinner when you and

Ann come for Movie Night. Also, here's a shout-out to my two fantastic editors at Minotaur, Anne Brewer, intrepid captain, and Jennifer Letwack, her trusty first mate. Thanks for steering the good ship *Curried Away* in the right direction. Jessica Faust at BookEndsLiterary, how did I get so lucky? All you lack as Superagent is a red cape. Last but by no means least, my husband, Bob, who travels by my side through all life's ups and downs. Lord knows, we've had our share, but we've never toppled off the cliff.

CHAPTER 1

"You're fired!"

I stopped chatting with the mayor's wife, Dottie Hemmings, and my ex-mother-in-law, Melly Prescott, as Reba Mae Johnson, my BFF, stormed into my shop, Spice It Up! "What's up, girlfriend?" I asked.

"Just like that!" Reba Mae snapped her fingers. "*She* fired me."

"Silly girl." Dottie giggled. "You can't be fired. You're self-employed."

"What's wrong, dear?" Melly *tsk*ed sympathetically. "Did you have an irate customer at the Klassy Kut?"

"Did a perm go wrong?" Dottie patted hair that would have qualified as a helmet in the NFL.

"Did highlights turn into lowlights?" I asked. As Reba Mae drew closer, I noted her blotchy face and reddened eyes.

"No, of course not." Reba Mae's tangerine-sized hoop earrings swayed as she stalked back and forth across the heart pine floor. "Y'all know I run the best little ol' beauty shop in Brandywine Creek, Georgia."

"But you still haven't said *who* fired you?" Dottie's inquiring mind demanded an answer.

"*She* said my *services* were no longer required. Imagine!" Reba Mae flung her hands in the air. "And after all my hard work! I'm so mad I could spit nails."

"Honey, why don't you sit down and tell us what's going on?" I motioned toward one of the stools behind the counter.

"Fine." Reba Mae flounced over and plopped down. "When I think of the hours I spent learning my lines, I want to scream. I even started teasing my hair. I haven't teased my hair since high school — no offense, Dottie," she added for Dottie's benefit. With this, Reba Mae put her head in her hands and burst into tears.

Dottie, Melly, and I exchanged worried glances. This was totally out of character for Reba Mae. She wasn't the type to indulge in bouts of weeping or histrionics. Not even when her husband, Butch, had drowned while bass fishing. Instead of wallowing in self-pity — and who would've blamed her — she enrolled in beauty school, paid off a

10

heap of credit card debt, and started her own business. She was more of a pick-yourself-up-by-the-bootstraps-and-soldier-on kind of gal. I can't remember the last time I saw my friend so . . . agitated. And that scared the bejeebers out of me.

Melly cleared her throat and gave me a look that clearly translated as: *Don't just stand there like a ninny; do something* — so I did. Perching on the adjacent stool, I rubbed Reba Mae's back in small, soothing circles like I used to do when my Chad and Lindsey were babies. "There, there," I crooned. "It can't be that bad."

"Y-yes, it c-can," she blubbered.

Dottie grabbed a fistful of tissues from a box on the counter and pushed them at Reba Mae. "Here, hon."

"Let me get you a nice glass of sweet tea," Melly offered, springing into action. "Sweet tea always makes us Southern girls feel better."

"S-Sandy Granger *fired* me," Reba Mae sobbed. Tears pooled in her pretty, golden-brown eyes and rolled down her cheeks. "I still can't believe it."

The pieces of the puzzle were starting to fall into place. Reba Mae had been over the moon ever since being chosen for the role of Truvy Jones, the outspoken, wisecracking

11

beauty shop owner, in the Brandywine Creek Opera House's production of *Steel Magnolias.* So over the moon she'd even dyed her hair Dolly Parton yellow in honor of the singer/actress who'd portrayed Truvy in the movie version.

Before I could question her further, Melly emerged from the kitchenette at the rear of the shop. "I found these in a cupboard," she said, placing a plate of cookies along with a frosty glass of iced tea on the counter near Reba Mae's elbow. "Gingersnaps always go well with sweet tea."

"Thanks," Reba Mae sniffled. "This was my big chance for folks to see me with talent for somethin' other than with scissors and a bottle of hair dye. I wanted to make my boys proud of their momma."

"Honey, your boys adore you. Clay and Caleb think you're the best momma in the universe — bar none." I nudged the glass closer. Sweet tea and sympathy were what my friend needed, so sweet tea and sympathy were what she'd get.

"You poor thing." Dottie rested her plump elbows on the counter and leaned forward. "Tell us what happened. Getting it off your chest will make you feel better."

Make Reba Mae "feel better"? More likely provide breaking news for Dottie to broadcast to her network of cronies. Nothing the woman loved more than gossip. I could almost see little antennas sprout from her beehive and twitch in anticipation.

"Did Sandy give a reason for . . . replacing you?" I asked as gently as I could. I'd almost slipped and used the word "fired." That would've resulted in yet another "gully washer," as they say here in the South.

Calmer now, Reba Mae took a sip of sweet tea. "Sandy claims I kept forgettin' to call the characters by the right names."

Nodding, I considered the possibility. "Did you?"

Reba Mae avoided eye contact with me. "Maybe, a time or two."

"Uh-huh," I said, trying to keep my tone neutral.

"Whoever heard of a woman called Ouiser — or 'Weezer,' as Sandy insisted it was pronounced? What kind of name is that anyway?" Reba Mae fired back. "Can't help it if I kept callin' her Wowser."

"Weezer, Wowser," Melly said with a forced smile. "Not much difference, if you want my opinion."

Reba Mae shot Melly a grateful look. "That's what I tried to tell Sandy. Why, I've known all these women — except Madison Winters, who plays Shelby — my entire adult life. It seems downright . . . weird . . . to call 'em by other than their Christian names."

I gave her shoulders a squeeze. "I'm sure you would've nailed it by opening night."

"Darn right I would've." Reba Mae slapped the counter for emphasis. "If Sandy isn't careful, the entire cast is goin' to mutiny. Why, just the other night, Bunny Bowtin left rehearsal in tears 'cause of somethin' Sandy said."

Dottie helped herself to a gingersnap. "I ran into Jolene Tucker at Piggly Wiggly. She told me Bunny threatened to quit, but her husband talked her out of it. Seems Dennis forked over money for Bunny's sister, husband, and their two kids to fly down from New Jersey for opening night. He said the airfare was nonrefundable."

Melly snapped a dead bloom from a pot of mums I'd set on the counter as a reminder that Thanksgiving, my favorite holiday, was only a week away. "Sandy isn't the easiest person to work with," she said, "but to be fair, as both director and producer she's under considerable pressure."

"Easy for you to say, Melly, since all you have to worry about is collecting props," Reba Mae said. "Behind Sandy's back, the rest of the cast and crew refer to her as the

14

Wicked Witch of the West. And" — she winked — "y'all know what 'witch' rhymes with."

Melly clucked her tongue in disapproval, but Reba Mae remained unfazed. "I'm just sayin' is all. . . ."

"My husband the mayor says Sandy is a real asset to Brandywine Creek. An ambassador of sorts. He calls her a marketing dynamo." Since no one else seemed interested in the lone cookie that remained on the plate, Dottie helped herself. "Harvey claims the publicity she's generating will have a positive impact on the entire town. Said it's bound to attract tourists by the busload and bring in business."

"I hope Mayor Hemmings is right," I said, tucking an unruly red curl behind my ear. "I've just increased my inventory in anticipation of an influx of playgoers."

"Not only is Bunny unhappy," Reba Mae continued, "but I saw Wanda Needmore and Dorinda Kunkel — Wanda plays Clairee, the grande dame; Dorinda plays 'Wowser' — with their heads together."

"You don't want to mess with that pair." Dottie brushed cookie crumbs from her pink polyester blouse. "Those two are the most strong-minded women you'd ever want to meet." Dorinda had raised her

15

daughter, Lorinda, single-handedly after her husband, Skeeter, ran off with a waitress from High Cotton.

"And Wanda doesn't take guff from anybody," Melly added. "She runs CJ's law firm with an iron fist."

This brought a smile to my lips. Even CJ confessed to being intimidated by his paralegal's forceful personality. "Wanda will be the first to tell anyone who'll listen that a lawyer is only as good as his paralegal. I've heard that said so many times I've been tempted to cross-stitch a wall hanging with her words embroidered on it."

"What's stoppin' you?" Reba Mae wanted to know. "It'd make the perfect gift."

I rolled my eyes. "Reba Mae, have you ever known me to be artsy-craftsy? I tried knitting once, remember? I was better at tennis, and we both know what a disaster that was."

"Yeah, I remember. You dropped so many stitches that the afghan you were workin' on had more holes than a block of Swiss cheese."

"Well, if Wanda and Dorinda are in cahoots, whoo-ee!" Dottie clapped her hands in glee. "Sandy Granger better steer clear. She's going to need eyes in the back of her head if she wants to stay out of trouble."

"Did Sandy say who was going to replace you?" There, I'd gone and done it: addressed the elephant in the room.

Silence stretched like mozzarella on a hot pizza. Dottie studied an advertisement the butcher across the square had dropped off early that morning touting a special on pork chops. Melly nervously fingered her ever-present pearls. I wished I was in Bora-Bora.

Finally Reba Mae let out a long sigh. "Mary Lou Lambert. I hate that woman's guts." When none of us had a comment to add, she continued, "Truvy Jones is a main character; she's in *every* scene. Mary Lou can't read the directions on a box of hair color without messin' up. How can she be expected to memorize pages of dialog?"

"Maybe Sandy will realize she made a big mistake firing you, and ask you to come back," I said hopefully.

"Yeah, maybe." Reba Mae grinned for the first time since entering Spice It Up! "With opening night only three weeks away, she might just do that. She'll come beggin' me to save her bacon."

"Thata girl!" Dottie beamed approval. "Don't get mad; get even."

"Good advice, Dottie. I'll keep that in mind." Reba Mae slid off the stool. "Ladies, thanks for givin' me a chance to vent. I feel better after havin' a good cry. Don't know when I've been so furious, or so hurt. For an instant, all I wanted to do was wrap my hands around Sandy's scrawny neck until she squawked like a chicken. Gotta run," she said, heading out the door.

"Better mad than sad, I always say," Dottie rattled off another cliché. "Nice talking to y'all, but I have to see Pete at Meat on Main about some pork chops. My husband the mayor sure does love his pork chops. Toodle-oo."

"Harvey Hemmings doesn't love pork chops nearly as much as Dottie loves gossip," Melly observed drily as we watched Dottie bustle across the street as fast as her short legs would carry her.

"News of Reba Mae being 'fired' will be all over town before the first chop sizzles in a frying pan," I said.

"Poor Reba Mae." Melly wagged her head. "She had her heart set on being onstage."

I nodded agreement. "If I know Dottie, the tale of her losing the part to Mary Lou Lambert will be embellished with each telling."

CHAPTER 2

Alone with only Melly for company, I reached into a drawer and removed an e-mail I'd printed out from Doug Winters, local vet and closet chef, that he'd sent the previous night. "From comments I've overheard, Sandy can be a hard taskmaster," I said.

"I thought my job as prop mistress was going to be fun, but, so far, all it's turned out to be is a headache." Melly collected the empty cookie plate and iced-tea glass from the counter. "I'll load these in the dishwasher upstairs for you before I go."

"Hmm, thanks, Melly," I replied absently, scanning Doug's list of ingredients for the third or fourth time. After months of coaxing and cajoling, Doug had finally relented and agreed to do a cooking demonstration for my customers, which was slated for tomorrow morning. I wanted everyone to know his talents extended beyond snips-

and-tucks at Pets 'R People.

Before the sound of Melly's footsteps on the stairs had faded, I plucked a small, wicker basket from a stack I kept near the counter for shoppers' convenience. I slowly cruised the freestanding shelves, picking up a jar of coriander here, a jar of cardamom there, and added them to my basket. As I did this, I was filled anew with a sense of pride and accomplishment. I loved my little shop, Spice It Up! Loved everything about it. From the gleaming heart pine floors to the exposed brick walls, but most of all — I took a deep breath and let it out — I loved the heady aroma of spices from around the globe. Long before Spice It Up! became a reality, it had been a dream. Little did my ex, CJ, suspect that when he dumped me in favor of chasing ambulances and a former beauty queen in a short skirt, I'd morph into a businesswoman. Maybe I should send him flowers as a thank-you.

Humming to myself, I proceeded to fill my basket with the ingredients Doug had requested. Spicy chicken curry happened to be one of his specialties. Although most customers would probably opt for curry powder that was readily available, Doug preferred to concoct his own version which he admitted was never the same twice.

Besides coriander and cardamom, he needed fennel seeds, a stick of cinnamon, a nutmeg, whole cloves, and gingerroot for tomorrow's blend.

I paused, then turned, at hearing the front door open. Two well-dressed women waltzed in — Sandy Granger accompanied by her pal, Vicki Lamont. The pair looked strikingly different, but they were startlingly similar. While Vicki was tall, brunette, trim, and mid-forties, her companion was average height, her hair colored golden walnut. Sandy, the older of the two, preferred card games; Vicki favored sports such as tennis and golf. Both women, however, exuded that confident, manicured, I-belong-to-a-country-club aura. The Kate Spade and Michael Kors handbags — or perhaps their designer footwear — might also have been clues.

"I don't know why I let Vicki talk me into going to lunch this afternoon when I have a million things to do," Sandy Granger said by way of a greeting. If she was harried, it didn't show. Not a single hair of her chin-length bob was out of place and her makeup was Hollywood perfect.

"You know what they say about all work, no play." Vicki waved her companion's complaint away with a flick of her wrist.

"We just had a fabulous meal at Antonio's."

"I persuaded Tony to part with some of his wonderful minestrone," Sandy said. "With rehearsals and whatnot, I don't have time to cook. Since Craig's out of town on business, there's no reason to fuss."

I'd never tasted Tony Deltorro's wonderful minestrone. The man still considered me persona non grata because of a minor misunderstanding concerning a dead body. Tony obviously held a grudge but, then again, he was Sicilian. "Ladies" — I plastered on my friendly shopkeeper's smile — "what can I help you with this afternoon?"

Sandy adjusted the silk scarf around her neck. Hermès from a trip to Paris? I wondered. "Vicki insisted on stopping to find out the time of Doug's cooking demonstration tomorrow."

"Ten o'clock," I said. "I expect a full house, so best to come early."

Vicki extracted her iPhone from her oversize handbag and keyed in the information. "Ever since the weather turned cool, I've been in the mood for bread pudding," she said after she finished. "As long as I'm here, I want some of your vanilla. Sylvia Walker raved about its flavor. She advised me to throw out the cheaper, imitation variety and splurge."

22

I made a mental note to thank Sylvia for the recommendation. Vanilla, next to saffron, happened to be the highest-priced spice in the world. "Let me suggest vanilla from beans grown on Bourbon Island, now called Réunion Island, in Madagascar. It sets the standard when it comes to pure vanilla flavor."

Sandy wandered over to a coatrack I'd discovered in Yesteryear Antiques on which I'd hung a collection of chef aprons with catchy slogans. "Bread pudding is a favorite of Craig's."

"What a coincidence!" Vicki exclaimed. "It's my favorite, too. My recipe makes far too much for one person. Why don't I wait until Craig returns home? I'll whip up a pan, then bring some over. I know how busy you are, Sandy, with the play and what-have-you. Something homemade will be a nice treat."

"Have you heard from Kenny?" I asked Vicki, reaching for a four-ounce bottle of pure vanilla extract. She and her husband had split months ago. Since then, she'd been trying to woo Kenny back with gourmet meals and Victoria's Secret. I had it on good authority the breakup was the result of Vicki's fling with a local chef, now deceased. Also on good authority, Vicki missed her

American Express Gold credit card even more than her estranged husband.

"Not a single word from Kenny since he hopped on his Harley and headed for Fantasy Fest in Key West." She gave a head toss, flinging glossy, dark locks over her shoulder. "He told me that his lawyer would contact my lawyer — or words to that effect."

"Sorry." I busied myself ringing up the sale. Vicki's announcement didn't sound promising for a Vicki-Kenny reconciliation.

"Did I hear someone mention Fantasy Fest?" Melly inquired as she returned downstairs. "Is that anything like a *Star Wars* convention?"

Sandy ceased riffling through aprons. "Ha!" she snorted. "Melly, dear, I can't believe you're so naïve. Fantasy Fest makes New Orleans's Mardi Gras seem like a child's tea party. Fantasy Fest is ten days of parades and parties — sans clothing but lots of body paint."

"Ohh . . . ," Melly murmured.

I chuckled at seeing Melly's cheeks turn rosy as Sandy's description sank home. Fortunately, further discussion of body paint and naked bodies was forestalled by the arrival of Doug Winters with Casey, my mutt of many breeds, under his arm, and his daughter, Madison. Seeing him instantly brightened my day.

Beneath a mop of prematurely silver hair, Doug's boyishly handsome face broke into a grin at his spotting a cluster of women. Chocolate brown eyes behind rimless eyeglasses twinkled with good humor. "Ladies," he said.

I smiled back, feeling a bubble of happiness well up inside me. Many folks in town regarded us as a "couple." Truth is, I'd even begun to think of ourselves that way for lack of a better term. Our coupleship, however, had suffered a serious setback since his daughter, Madison, had arrived from Chicago to live with him. Madison demanded all his free time, and Doug — out to acquit himself as father-of-the-year — gave it willingly. Every weekend, father and daughter ventured far and wide. To the best of my knowledge, the father-daughter team had thus far shopped in Atlanta, taken carriage rides in Savannah, and toured historic homes in Charleston. He'd let it drop that Hilton Head Island was the next place of interest to be explored. While I applauded the fact that Doug wanted to bond with his daughter, I wouldn't be totally honest if I didn't admit to being a little hurt by his defection.

Upon spotting me, Casey started to bark

in short, excited yaps. Doug set the squirming little dog on the floor. "There you go, boy."

Casey bounded across the shop, leaped into my outstretched arms, and lathered my face in doggy kisses.

"All right, already!" I said, laughing. "Let me see how you look after your day at a spa." Doug had recently leased space to a dog groomer from a neighboring town who came into his clinic once a week. This had been Casey's first visit to the groomer. He'd been washed, brushed, trimmed, and styled until I hardly recognized his usually scruffy self.

"I adore animals." Vicki gave Casey a tentative pat on his head, then batted her lashes at Doug in a coy gesture that predated hoop skirts. "I'm so looking forward to your cooking demo tomorrow. I plan to sit in the front row and take notes." She turned her attention to Madison. "This pretty young lady must be the daughter I've heard so much about."

Madison stepped closer to her father's side. From the pinched expression on her heart-shaped face, I could tell she wasn't happy with Vicki's flirtatiousness. Madison was a pretty girl, or least she would be if she smiled more often. She'd inherited her father's eye color, but the resemblance ended there. She was petite with delicate features and wore her long, golden-brown hair scraped back in a ponytail.

"Madison is a natural onstage." Sandy idly examined packets of recipe cards displayed on a nearby shelf. "I'd initially cast Brittany Hughes, Trish's daughter, for the role, but the girl didn't take it seriously. She was too young, too immature."

"And too interested in boys," Vicki added. "I ran into Trish at the club the other day. She's madder than a wet hen that the apple of her eye isn't going to be in *Steel Magnolias.*"

"Well, she'll just have to get over it," Sandy said briskly. "Unlike Madison, Brittany never came to rehearsals prepared and constantly missed her cues. I had no choice but to replace her."

I glimpsed the self-satisfied smirk on Madison's face before it vanished beneath her perpetual petulant expression. "Daddy," she whined, "how much longer? We need to pick up my car before the garage closes."

"Right, right," Doug said, digging into his shirt pocket and pulling out a folded piece of paper, which he handed me. "I added a few more items to the checklist I e-mailed yesterday. I want my first cooking demo to be glitch-free."

"What are you making?" Sandy asked.

"Spicy chicken curry." Doug took off his rimless eyeglasses and polished the lenses on the sleeve of his sport shirt. Satisfied they gleamed, he slipped them on again. "I like to experiment with Middle Eastern cuisine."

"I wasn't going to attend, but I changed my mind. As Vicki reminded me, all work and no play isn't good for a person. I'll encourage some of the cast and crew to come as well. A get-together outside of the theater will help create a sense of camaraderie." Frowning, she consulted her wristwatch. "Are you ready, Vicki?"

I set Casey down on the floor and handed Vicki her purchase, then watched the two friends depart.

Madison hitched the strap of her purse higher on her shoulder. "If Sandy thinks Daddy's cooking will turn the cast and crew into one big, happy family, she's sadly mistaken. If the curtain goes up before someone kills someone, it'll be a miracle."

Doug frowned at his daughter's words. Melly hugged her cardigan closer. I felt the hairs at the back of my neck prickle. Only Casey, who lounged near my feet, seemed oblivious of the tension.

CHAPTER 3

After jogging the next morning, I'd scarcely had time to shower and down a cup of coffee before I heard someone pounding on the front door downstairs. Leaving Casey in my apartment where he wouldn't be underfoot, I raced down the steps to see who was making all the racket. I hurried through my shop, switching on lights as I went, and peered through the glass. The first thing to catch my attention was the shiny black hearse parked curbside. Next Ned Feeney's face popped into view. Startled, I took a half step back. I should've known with a glossy black hearse out front that Ned wouldn't be far. Irked at myself for being jumpy, I twisted the dead bolt and let him in.

"Too early?" He smirked, pleased with himself at having frightened me.

"No, not at all," I fibbed as Ned pushed through the door with aluminum chairs tucked under each arm. Tall and lanky with a prominent Adam's apple, Ned was probably somewhere between fifty and sixty years of age. Jack-of-all-trades-but-master-of-none, he worked part-time at the Eternal Rest Funeral Home, where I'd rented the folding chairs from the owner — and county coroner — John Strickland, for a modest fee.

Ned gave me his characteristic loopy grin. "Where do you want 'em?"

I motioned toward the kitchen area in the rear of the shop. "If you'd set them in rows in front of that table at the back. I want everyone to have a clear view of Doug's cooking demo." When planning Spice It Up! I'd installed a compact, but efficient, kitchen area. My single splurge item had been a double oven. A double oven was a must-have in every Food Network episode I'd ever watched. Giada. The Barefoot Contessa. Bobby Flay. Rachael Ray. All my favorite cooks had a second oven from which to pop out the finished product. Since I planned to hold cooking demonstrations, I wanted to be able to do the same.

"All righty, then," Ned said. "I'll hop to it." He leaned the first load of chairs against the counter and scurried out for more.

No sooner had Ned disappeared out the

front when a thumping noise commenced from the back. Casey heard it, too, and increased the decibel level with his frantic barking. "I'm coming, I'm coming," I called out, and opened the door.

Doug grinned at me over a large, cherry-red-enameled Dutch oven that he held in both hands. A mesh shopping bag dangled from one arm. "Too early?"

"You, too early? Never," I countered, returning a warm smile. I eyed the box he carried. "What's with all the stuff?"

Doug followed me through the storeroom and into the shop. "I brought the finished product so I could take it out of the second oven at the appropriate time. You know, voilà! Like a magician pulling a rabbit out of a hat. I also thought it might be a good idea to have extra . . . just in case," he said.

"In case of what?"

"Fire, flood, famine. You never know what disaster might befall a poor, helpless veterinarian with aspirations of becoming a culinary superstar."

"Maybe you should consider working for FEMA or some disaster preparation agency such as the American Red Cross? Just sayin'," I added, shoving aside the basket of vegetables I'd placed at one end of the table to make room for Doug's supplies.

Doug paused when he saw my handiwork and let a low whistle. "Guess my worries were unfounded. I should've known you'd have all the bases covered. The place looks great!"

The place did, indeed, look "great." I gave myself an imaginary pat on the back. My efforts hadn't been in vain. I'd filled a wicker basket with ingredients in Doug's recipe — onions, tomatoes, garlic cloves, lemon, red chilies, and a knobby rhizome of ginger — and set it on a long, cloth-covered table. At the opposite end rested two cans of coconut milk and a carton of chicken broth. Various spices were lined up like cadets awaiting inspection at a military academy.

"Guess I don't need this stuff after all." Doug set the oven temperature on low, then slid the pricey cookware inside to keep warm until his "aha" moment. "Where's your pooch?"

"Upstairs. After a day at the doggy spa and an early-morning run, the poor little guy needed a rest." I slipped on a canary yellow apron, with a fiery red pepper and "Spice It Up!" embroidered on the bib, and tied the strings. It pays to advertise, or so I've been told.

Doug removed a Ziploc bag filled with

boneless, skinless chicken strips from his reusable shopping bag and placed it in the refrigerator. He shoved the bag of emergency supplies under the table out of sight and looked around, frowning. "Are you sure women are interested in learning Indian cuisine? What if no one comes?"

"Stop worrying." I laughed and gave him a peck on the cheek. "Wait and see; we'll have a full house. By the way, where's Madison? I thought for sure she'd want to witness her father's debut as a chef."

Doug rearranged the coconut milk and chicken broth, studied the effect, then switched them back to their original positions. "Madison reminded me someone needed to man the clinic. She promised to call my cell in case of an emergency."

The clank of metal against metal heralded Ned's return. "Hiya, Doc!" he said. "Ready for the big show?"

"Ready as I'll ever be," Doug replied good-naturedly.

"I'll have these babies set up in a jiff and get out of your hair." In Ned's haste several chairs slipped from his grasp and clattered to the floor. "Sorry, sorry," he muttered, bending to retrieve them.

"Take your time, Ned. There's no need to rush. The demonstration isn't until ten o'clock."

"Fact is, Miz Piper, I'm kinda in a hurry. I got myself a new gig."

"A new gig, eh?" I hoped his new employer realized Ned came with a warning label: Hire at your own risk. Wherever Ned went, trouble was sure to follow. Not long ago, he'd tried to install a new garbage disposal in my kitchen and wound up in the hospital with a concussion.

"Yes, ma'am." Ned lined the chairs in a haphazard row. "You're looking at the new custodian of the Brandywine Creek Opera House."

" 'Custodian' sounds pretty impressive." Doug pulled a checklist from his pant pocket and gave it a once-over.

"Yes, sirree, it sure does." Ned's head bobbed in vigorous agreement. "It's a fancied-up name for 'janitor,' but Miz Granger says 'custodian' has" — he scratched his head, searched his memory — "more class."

"Well, she should know," I replied. As unobtrusively as possible, I put a little more separation between the chairs.

"Today's my first day on the job. I want to make a good impression." Ned took off his ever-present ball cap that bore the University of Georgia logo and wiped his brow. "Miz Granger said it was up to me to keep the opera house shipshape. I'm gonna give the place a good goin' over from top to bottom, startin' soon's I return the hearse."

"Well, I'm certain you'll be very conscientious."

Ned's brow wrinkled. "I'm a bit flummoxed," he admitted. "I don't want to make any mistakes. Think I should start on the third floor and work my way down? Or start down and work my way up?"

Doug stopped scanning his list and grinned at Ned. "When in doubt, do what I do. Flip a coin."

"Great idea, Doc. I'll give that a try." Relief spread across Ned's face as he hurried off, eager to begin his new career.

Soon after Ned had left, Melly arrived with a container of bite-size cranberry-nut muffins. While Doug read, then reread, his recipe, I started coffee brewing. The finishing touches had no sooner been completed when women began filing in.

"Nervous?" I whispered to Doug.

He wiped his palms on the sides of his pants. "A little," he confessed. "It's one thing to prepare a meal in your own kitchen, another to cook with everyone observing your every move."

"Well, if it's any consolation, your demonstration — regardless of how flawed —

will be far superior to the one I attempted at my grand opening. It culminated with me drinking wine that was supposed to be used in the recipe. To make matters worse, the leg of lamb skidded off the table and landed on the floor." I could laugh about it now, but at the time I wanted to disappear.

Doug chuckled. "I've heard half-dozen variations of that story. Everyone might not agree on the exact details, but no one disputes your demo wasn't highly entertaining."

Soon the shop was filled with noisy chatter. Vicki Lamont was among the first to arrive. Flashing a bright smile in Doug's direction, she claimed a seat front and center. For some reason that I didn't choose to examine more closely, this irritated the heck out of me. Vicki liked men — attached or unattached — and made no bones about it. She was a shark on the hunt for fresh meat. I made a mental note to warn Doug.

I smiled at seeing Gerilee Barker help herself to a muffin and coffee before wedging herself between Dottie Hemmings and Bunny Bowtin. Precious Blessing, the afternoon dispatcher at the Brandywine Creek Police Department, gave me a thumbs-up as she entered and settled next to Mary Lou Lambert. Precious was accompanied by a man I assumed was Junior, one of her five brothers. Junior, she'd explained, aspired to become a chef at a four-star restaurant. The Blessing boys, I'd heard tell, were all excellent cooks. Just this past July, Bubba Blessing had won top honors at the annual barbecue festival.

"Showtime," I said in a low voice when the hands of my regulator clock indicated the hour of ten. Taking my place in front of the group, I beamed a smile. The women stopped chattering and looked attentive. The sight of all their expectant faces caused my pulse to quicken and my mouth to go dry. I recalled advice I'd once heard about public speaking and tried to picture the audience naked. *Eeuw!* That only made matters worse.

"Many of you know Dr. Doug Winters as a competent veterinarian, but he's here this morning to show he's equally skilled in the kitchen as when he's spaying or neutering your pets."

That didn't come out exactly as I'd rehearsed. Some women tittered at hearing this. Melly scowled. Out of the corner of my eye I caught Doug's grimace and felt my cheeks grow warm. Public speaking, I'd heard, is one of the most common phobias. Public cooking, for all I knew, might be another.

I cleared my throat and tried again, "What I meant to say was he's quite clever when it comes to slicing and dicing."

"Piper, dear, why not skip the introduction and let Dr. Winters show us how to prepare spicy chicken curry," Melly suggested from her post near the counter.

"Excellent idea, Melly." Grateful for the reprieve, I stepped aside, and Doug stepped forward.

"I hope I won't disappoint you, ladies," he said with a disingenuous smile guaranteed to win admirers.

"Not in the least," Vicki cooed. She crossed, then recrossed shapely legs, tanned and toned from hours on the tennis court. "I'm sure we'll be fascinated by everything you say."

"Then let's get started." Doug approached the stovetop, then proceeded to unscrew the lid of a small glass jar. "This is ghee. Add about three tablespoons into a heavy-bottomed pot."

"Ghee . . . ?" Gerilee — winner of Best Pimento Cheese Award at the county fair, three years running — repeated. "Never heard of it."

"Ghee is clarified butter. A good alternative to cooking oil," Doug explained as he measured the clear yellow substance. "It's used extensively in Indian and Middle Eastern cuisine."

"How do you make it?" Junior Blessing wanted to know.

"Make it?" Dottie sounded horrified at the prospect.

"It's not difficult, but it does take time," Doug said, addressing Junior. "Slowly melt one pound of butter over medium-low heat, being careful it doesn't sizzle or brown. Then increase the heat and bring the butter to a boil. Stir gently when the surface is covered with foam. Once this happens, lower the heat and let simmer for forty-five minutes or so, then strain through several layers of cheesecloth."

"Seems like a lot of work," Gerilee commented.

"Can't I just buy it?" Vicki whined.

"It's readily available in many grocery stores. Also check online," I advised. "Last time I looked both Walmart and Amazon stocked it."

"Amazon has everything," Precious chimed. "My brother Levi was lookin' all over for shoe goo to fix his gym shoes, and, whaddaya know, he found it on Amazon."

Doug valiantly tried to get his demo away from shoe goo and back on track. "Add two medium onions, four cloves of garlic, and ginger, all of which have been chopped. While these cook slowly, I'll tell you how I make my own special blend of curry powder."

Channeling Vanna White on *Wheel of Fortune* — minus the gown and heels — I held up each spice as Doug named it. Coriander, cumin, cardamom, fennel, black peppercorns, cloves, and mustard seed. *Ka-ching!* I could hear the ring of my antique cash register as customers rushed to stock their pantries.

"Can't we just buy it?" Vicki asked a second time.

I hurried to fill the void. "Of course you can, but let your taste buds be the judge. For those of you reluctant to experiment, or pressed for time, I sell a variety of curry powders: hot, sweet, spicy, and no salt."

Suddenly Dottie canted her head to one side. "Is that a siren?"

"Hush, Dottie, you're imagining things," Gerilee scolded.

"Don't shush me!" Dottie snapped. "I know a siren when I hear one."

As if to prove her point, two squad cars, flashing red and blue light bars and blaring sirens, screamed past Spice It Up! down Main Street. Casey's incessant barking came from the apartment above. A beeper sounded from somewhere in the audience. Junior Blessing jumped up and ran for the door.

"My brother's a volunteer firefighter," Precious announced proudly.

Dottie was the first to race to the window. The rest of the women flocked close behind. Doug and I exchanged worried glances, then joined them to see what all the fuss was about. The town's newly purchased hook and ladder rattled down the street followed by an orange and white EMS ambulance. Police cars, fire truck, and ambulance all came to a screeching halt in front of the opera house.

"Mercy!" Melly pressed her hand to her twinset-clad chest. "What do you suppose is going on?"

"Think the opera house is on fire?" Bunny asked.

Vicki peered over Bunny's shoulder for a better look. "Don't see any smoke."

Precious dug into the nether regions of her roomy handbag. "Somethin's up. Dorinda's mannin' the desk at the police station. She'll tell me what's goin' on."

"Don't bother," I said as a white van joined the vehicles already gathered. "The coroner just arrived."

41

CHAPTER 4

Ladies, start your engines. The cooking demonstration was history; the race was on. Manners were discarded as normally gracious and polite women shoved and jostled one another out the door.

I looked at Doug. He looked at me and then threw up his hands in surrender. Thoughts of chicken simmering in a savory coconut sauce evaporated. Spurred by the need to know, we hastened after our audience. As I stepped onto the sidewalk, I glimpsed Dottie Hemmings actually running in the direction of the opera house. Let me say, it wasn't pretty what with all the jiggling and bouncing. But I had to hand it to her. What the woman lacked in athleticism she more than made up for with determination.

Businesses had come to a virtual standstill. Customers and shopkeepers alike had left the stores unattended to gawk and gossip. I noticed Gerilee hustling across the street to converse with her husband, Pete, the proprietor of Meat on Main. Bunny Bowtin was in an animated conversation with Realtor Shirley Randolph. Bitsy Johnson-Jones, the clerk at Proctor's Cleaners, exchanged comments with Amber Leigh Ames. I scarcely recognized Bitsy since she'd had her tummy stapled and lost a ton of weight. Amber I'd recognize blindfolded. In less charitable moments, I refer to the former beauty queen as Miss Home Wrecker. Amber and my ex, CJ, were planning a destination wedding in the Dominican Republic over the Christmas holidays.

"I got here early this morning to review my new listings," I overheard Shirley tell Bunny. "I happened to look over and saw Ned Feeney walk up the steps of the opera house. Sandy mentioned that she'd hired him as custodian."

"Y'all know how accident-prone he is," Bunny said.

"Except for Ned, the opera house should've been empty," Shirley commented. "No one else would have had business there this time of day.

"Ned . . . ?" I gasped, unaware I'd spoken his name out loud

I felt Doug give my shoulder a reassuring

43

squeeze. Had disaster befallen Ned Feeney, the hapless, but likeable, handyman on his first day as custodian? Dread propelled my feet farther down the walk toward a knot of bystanders on the corner across from the opera house. Emergency vehicles were scattered at the curb like a small boy's Matchbox cars.

Reba Mae, out of breath and wearing the smock she used when coloring hair, ran up and joined Doug and me. "What do you s'pose happened?"

I glanced around. The firefighters congregated in front of their truck and didn't seem in a hurry to don their gear or attach hoses to hydrants. The EMTs stood near the ambulance, its rear door wide open, talking among themselves. "I have no idea," I answered, puzzled at their lack of activity.

Vicki sauntered over to join our group of spectators. "I heard Pete tell Gerilee that McBride jumped from his cruiser the instant it came to a rolling stop."

"Shirley at Creekside Realty claimed McBride had his gun drawn," Dale Simons, local pawnbroker and owner of Dale's Swap and Shop, volunteered in his raspy smoker's voice. "Said she saw it plain as day."

"Gun?" Dottie squawked from nearby. "Who has a gun? Should we take cover?"

44

If I hadn't been so worried about Ned, I'd have rolled my eyes. I swear, the woman had ears like a bat. Comments started coming from all over, including left field. Everyone, it seemed, was suddenly eager to voice an opinion.

"Think McBride should call out the SWAT team?"

"Does Brandywine Creek even have a SWAT team?"

"I heard it was a hostage situation?"

Hostage situation? Now I did roll my eyes. Who in their right mind would hold Ned Feeney hostage? Hadn't anyone been paying attention when I announced the coroner's van had arrived?

"Maybe Precious was able to find out something," Doug offered, sounding like the voice of reason in a world gone weird.

Half turning, I saw Precious drop her cell phone into her purse as she approached. "Out with it, girlfriend," I ordered. "Tell us what you found out from Dorinda."

Precious's round, dark face creased in a pout. "All Dorinda would say is that a body was found. That woman can be tight-lipped as a clam when it comes to givin' out information even to me, a coworker. Imagine!"

Dottie's eyes widened in alarm. "A body?"

45

"Male or female?" I asked.

Precious shrugged, the effort straining the buttons on the knit shirt stretched across her generous bosom. "Dorinda didn't say."

"Didn't or wouldn't?"

"Knowin' Dorinda, my bet's on 'wouldn't.' Ask me, I think she's goin' through the changes. Mean as a snake at times. I try to stay clear."

Doug stuck his hands in his pant pockets and surveyed the crowd. "Uh-oh," he murmured. "Brace yourself, Piper. CJ has you in his sights."

Doug, bless his heart, had my back. He knew I was often ambivalent when it came to CJ Prescott, my ex-husband. We'd — make that *I'd* — come a long way, baby, from the early, bitter days of our divorce. We'd established a relationship of sorts that was mostly civil, but I was far from perfect, and sometime I forgot the "civil" part.

"Hiya, Scooter. What's cookin'?" CJ nearly blinded me with flash of teeth whiter than God ever intended. Any brighter, I'd need Ray-Bans.

I cringed at hearing the irritating-as-fingernails-on-a-chalkboard nickname. "Hey, CJ," I said, forcing a smile.

"Might've known I'd find you in the thick of things." CJ adjusted the French cuffs peeking from the sleeves of his navy blue blazer. I immediately recognized the monogrammed gold cuff links I'd given him for his fortieth birthday.

"Aren't you too busy with a trip and fall than to spend time rubbernecking like the rest of us?" I inquired sweetly. If sarcasm was a sin, I'd repent later.

"Nah," he said with a shake of his head. Sunlight glinted off hair as blond as a model's on a box of Clairol. On more than one occasion, Reba Mae and I had questioned whether Clairol was precisely where that shade originated. "For a handsome amount, my client agreed to settle out of court for his pain and sufferin'."

"Nice," I said for lack of a better response.

"Don't know about y'all," Precious spoke up, "but I'm tired of waitin' and wonderin'. I'm ready for some action." She turned to me. "You game?"

"Always," I said. "Lead the way."

That was the only encouragement Precious needed. "Cut me a path," she bellowed. "Law enforcement comin' through."

Before Doug or CJ divined my intent, I was right on her heels as she cut a swath through the looky lous. Technically, I'm not certain if Precious's job as afternoon dispatcher and girl Friday at the Brandywine

47

Creek Police Department qualified her as law enforcement. But no one stopped us. Apparently no one wanted to tackle a plus-size woman hell-bent on bulldozing her way through a crowd. Seeing Precious Blessing in motion recalled Charlton Heston, aka Moses in *The Ten Commandments,* parting the Red Sea. Cecil B. DeMille could have learned from her. The trick was in the attitude: Move it or lose it.

I couldn't help but observe that while the firefighters and EMTs milled about aimlessly, police officers were conspicuously absent. The thought no sooner crossed my mind when Sergeant Beau Tucker emerged from an adjacent side street, buttoning his uniform on the run.

"Beau's coverin' the midnight shift. Probably just rolled outa bed," Precious explained, before yelling, "Hey, Beau! What's the lowdown?"

He poked the last button through its hole. "Aw, shucks, Precious. You know I can't comment without the chief's okay. McBride would skin me alive."

"C'mon," Precious wheedled.

"Want me to land in a heap of trouble? Chief assigned me crowd control," he said, giving me the stink eye. Obviously he hadn't forgiven me for his once being on probation for leaking details of a case. "Sorry, Piper, no civilians allowed. You'll have to stay on the other side of the street."

I felt like stomping my foot like a two-year-old. "What's the big deal, Beau? We both know the news will be all over town before noon."

His chubby face took on a mulish expression. "Chief McBride gave me strict orders not to talk with anyone — especially you. I'd hate to place you under arrest for interfering with an investigation."

Arrest? "Fine!" I snapped. I didn't need a Jumbotron to get the message. I knew when to walk away, when to run. In this instance, I compromised and jogged. My cheeks burned like fire, the curse of being a redhead. Feeling as though half the town had witnessed my comeuppance, I lowered my head and beat a hasty retreat to rejoin Doug and Reba Mae. CJ, thankfully, had wandered off to chew the fat with some of his cronies.

"Hey, honeybun, any news?" Reba Mae asked.

"No," I admitted, "but I can't help wonder. Ned Feeney was going to the opera house after dropping off folding chairs at my place. Shirley saw him go in, but, to my knowledge, no one has seen him since."

49

"I'm sure your worry is for nothing," Doug tried to assure me. "Wait and see; Ned will turn up any minute and be just fine."

Reba Mae shook her head in agreement, the movement making her chandelier-style earrings sway. "Doug's right, you know. No one would want to harm Ned. Why, he never did nothin' to nobody."

"You're probably right." I rubbed my arms to ward off the November chill. "But if Ned's fine, why did McBride enter the opera house with his gun drawn? Why did he call the coroner?"

We fell silent. Waiting. Watching. Meanwhile, Beau popped the trunk of a patrol car and removed a spool of yellow crime-scene tape. My stomach churned as I watched him wind it around the shrubs and trees in front of the three-story brick edifice. The Brandywine Creek Opera House was now designated an official crime scene.

Suddenly a radio inside one of the emergency vehicles crackled to life. At a command from a garbled voice, the EMTs sprang into action. One of them toted an orange box large enough to hold tackle for a bass-fishing tournament, while the second trotted alongside him. I watched, scarcely daring to breathe as the pair disappeared into the building.

Five minutes later, the pair emerged escorting a dazed-looking Ned Feeney. One of the men urged Ned down on the back bumper of the ambulance; the other slipped an oxygen mask over Ned's pale, drawn face.

I felt more confused than ever. There was still the matter of the coroner being called to the scene. Added to that, the police showed no signs of leaving. If Ned wasn't the victim, who was?

As though sensing my gaze on him, Ned looked across the street and saw me. He lowered the oxygen mask, then waved. "Hey, Miz Piper," he called. "Guess you're not the only person who finds dead people."

Some claim to fame. I tried to smile but couldn't. "Finder of dead people" was a title I'd gladly relinquish. "You okay, Ned?" I called back.

"Good as can be after finding poor Miz Granger deader 'n a doornail. I think the opera house ghost done her in."

CHAPTER 5

"Sandy? Dead?"

"Good gracious!" Dottie exclaimed, stunned by the news.

I, too, was having trouble wrapping my brain around the fact. Only yesterday, Sandy'd been in my shop. She'd been chatting with Vicki about bread pudding. *Bread pudding!* Certainly there couldn't be a more benign topic? She'd planned to come to Doug's cooking demo. In all the commotion, I'd failed to register her absence.

Doug frowned and dug his hands even deeper into his pockets. "Wonder what happened?"

I looked for Precious, hoping she'd gotten the inside scoop and could shed some light on the subject. Precious, however, was nowhere around. I assumed her services had been required elsewhere.

Dale Simons scratched his shiny bald head. "Must've been an accident."

Dottie was quick to jump on the "accident" bandwagon. "Sandy might've fallen down the stairs like that poor fella did in Melly's basement a while back."

The fella Dottie referred to hadn't suffered a simple fall, I wanted to remind her. He'd had help. Instead, I held my tongue. No sense dredging up the recent past with its painful reminder of Melly's close call with a prison jumpsuit. But what *had* happened to Sandy?

Questions circled in my brain like turkey buzzards on the hunt for roadkill. Sandy's sudden death didn't make sense. She was relatively young to die from natural causes. Not impossible, but improbable. As far as I knew, she was in excellent health. I'd heard her boast about perfect blood pressure and low cholesterol. In addition, she led an active lifestyle, keeping physically fit with aerobic classes three times a week and golf on weekends.

Stranger still, I mused, was Ned's comment that the opera house ghost was responsible for her demise. The legend of the opera house ghost was a poorly kept secret in and around Brandywine Creek. The most popular theory involved a lowly mill worker who had an ill-fated romance with an actress. The man habitually sat in the third-floor balcony and watched his love from afar. When he finally summoned the courage to profess his feelings, he was cruelly rejected. Despondent, he committed suicide. To this day, a lone chair is reserved in his memory on the third-floor balcony. Playgoers and cast members throughout the ensuing decades have reported unexplained sounds such as humming, applause, or that of someone pacing. Luckily, I had no firsthand knowledge.

Reba Mae tugged on my shirtsleeve. "The police have been in there an awful long time. Think they suspect foul play?"

"Hush, Reba Mae!" I darted a look around to make sure no one overheard her remark. "That's how rumors get started. No sense rushing to conclusions."

"S'pose she *was* killed," Reba Mae persisted. "Think her husband Craig might've done it? On TV, it's always the spouse."

"You watch way too much TV," I said.

"Hmph!" Reba Mae sniffed. "Everyone oughta have a hobby. TV's mine."

"Craig always struck me as a model husband," stated Dottie, who'd been uncharacteristically quiet.

Reba Mae wasn't easily detoured. "What if he's hidin' a deep, dark secret? What if inside he's a simmerin' cauldron of rage just fixin' to bubble over?"

"How do you come up with these things?" I stared at my friend in amazement. "Ever think of switching careers to writing crime novels?"

Reba Mae shrugged. "Can't help it if I'm gifted with a fertile imagination. One of these days, I just might try my hand at crime writin'. Make myself a pile of money while I'm at it. How hard can it be?"

"Probably a lot harder than it looks."

Doug, who had been exchanging comments with Dale Simons, turned toward us. "Madison mentioned Sandy's been under a lot of stress lately with not only directing, but producing, the play. Stress can cause a lot of nasty side effects."

"What sort of side effects?" Reba Mae demanded.

"High blood pressure for example, which can lead to heart attack or stroke."

"Weren't neither of them things."

Our heads swiveled at the sound of Ned's voice. We'd been too engrossed in our conversation to notice Ned had discarded the oxygen mask and ambled over. The EMTs were too busy gabbing with a firefighter to notice that their patient had absconded.

"Was the silk scarf around her neck that

done it," Ned announced, his tone matter-of-fact.

"Scarf . . . ?" The fine hairs along my nape stood at attention.

Reba Mae's hand flew to her throat. "Neck . . . ?"

"Right pretty scarf it was, too," Ned continued. "Someone wrapped it around her neck real tight, cuttin' off her air."

Doug studied Ned with a critical eye; then his medical training kicked in. "Ned, you don't look well. Maybe you need a little more of that oxygen the EMTs were giving you."

Ned dismissed the suggestion with a shake of his head. "Don't need any more air out of a tank," he said. "Some of the old-fashioned kind supplied by Mother Nature oughta do the trick."

Impulsively I looped my arm through his and drew him away from the crowd and the excitement. "How about we take a nice little stroll? I know a park bench that would be a perfect spot to sit a spell. Some peace and quiet is just what you need right now."

I darted a glance over my shoulder and, except for Doug and Reba Mae, no one seemed to be paying us any mind as the two of us made our getaway. Everyone was too busy speculating or gossiping to be bothered watching two figures retreating in the direction of the town square. Ned and I took a seat in the shadow of a lone Confederate soldier, rifle at the ready, who guarded the town with sightless eyes. It was peaceful here. Sunlight filtered through the leafless canopy of willow oaks overhead. A gray squirrel scampered off, its cheeks fat with acorns.

From our vantage point, Brandywine Creek looked postcard pretty. With Thanksgiving right around the corner, the town reflected the holiday season. Fall wreaths with bright orange and gold plaid bows decorated lampposts. Businesses had carried out the theme with displays of colorful pumpkins and gourds in their windows. Americana at its finest.

Except for a dead woman in the opera house.

I turned to Ned. He appeared shaken and pale after his ordeal. He sat slumped forward, his head in his hands. "Do you want to talk about it?" I asked quietly.

Ned's Adam's apple bobbed up and down as he swallowed noisily. "Chief said I wasn't s'posed to talk about it."

"That's all right. You don't have to talk if you don't want to."

"Talkin's good for folks, ain't it?" he asked

after a lengthy silence.

Leaning back, I rested an arm along the back of the bench. "Way I see it, talking is the reason the good Lord created psychiatrists."

"Havin' a real person — someone not a cop — hear me out would sure take a load off my mind. Guess I could think of you as my therapy person." He speared me a hopeful look. "Chief can't fault me for talkin' to my therapy person, can he?"

Chief of Police Wyatt McBride could and, moreover, probably would. The guy was a stickler for protocol — especially when it came to murder investigations. For the time being, though, I kept my opinion to myself. If Ned was troubled and needed a sympathetic ear, far be it from me to deny the poor man solace. "Don't let that worry you, Ned. Go ahead if you like; tell me what happened."

He rested his palms on his knees, scuffed the toe of his sneaker in the brittle grass. "Seein' Miz Granger like that, then hearin' the ghost walkin' around downstairs, would be enough to send lesser folk to the loony bin."

"If it's any consolation, you and I are members of the same elite club."

"What club is that, Miz Piper?"

"The Finders of Dead Bodies Club. We members share a certain kinship, a bond. Who better to understand what it's like? The shock, disbelief, horror." *And the nightmares,* I added silently, but Ned would soon discover that fact for himself.

"Damn straight!" He slapped his knee for emphasis.

I stared up at the bright blue sky and saw a wispy vapor trail left by a jet probably bound for Hartsfield Airport in Atlanta. My sluggish conscience stirred to life. What I was doing was wrong. I never should have lured Ned away from the crime scene without McBride's consent. I rationalized, telling myself I was acting out of friendship — not curiosity. Although, to be honest, I *was* curious. Curiosity, to my way of thinking, is a more commendable trait than nosiness.

"You know how I was all conflicted. Should I start at the bottom and work my way up? Or start at the top and work my way down? I was havin' trouble makin' up my mind. I woulda flipped a coin like Dr. Doug suggested, but I left all my change at home, so I did the next best thing. I compromised by starting in the middle; Miz Granger said not to touch anything on the stage, so I just gave it a quick look around."

59

"Then what?" I urged when Ned seemed reluctant to continue. Taking off his ball cap, he shoveled his fingers through thinning mouse brown hair. "Figured I'd do the balcony next."

"And . . . ?"

He studied the logo on the bill of his cap as though he'd never seen it before. "And that's when I found 'er. Sittin there, nice as you please. In the same chair reserved for the ghost. At first, I thought she was sleepin' or maybe restin'. I didn't want to startle her, so I gave her a nudge on the shoulder. Just a little one, and said, 'Hey, Miz Granger. Nice day, ain't it?' "

I sensed what was coming next. Goose bumps pebbled my arms as a cool breeze drifted through the naked branches.

"Before I could stop her, Miz Granger toppled out of her chair and landed *kerplunk* on the floor. I could tell by her face she was a goner. The color put me in mind of eggplant. Never did care much for eggplant. Not even when Momma used to fry it up for supper."

I sat, my arms wrapped around myself for warmth, trying to digest everything Ned had told me. Sandy Granger had been viciously murdered. Strangled with her own scarf. But when? Why? And, most important, by whom? I thought back to yesterday and the complaints I'd heard about her management style. So what if she was a hard taskmaster, a woman with high expectations, one who wanted everything perfect for a play she was producing? That certainly wasn't reason enough to be killed. Or was it?

"So there you are!"

Ned and I both jumped at hearing the angry baritone close behind us.

Ned's head automatically swiveled toward the sound. "Uh-oh."

I didn't have to look to identify the source. I mentally braced myself for the confrontation I knew was forthcoming.

Chief Wyatt McBride's long legs ate up the distance that separated us. He stopped in front of the wrought-iron bench and glowered at us. "Feeney, I warned you not to discuss the case with anyone until you made a formal statement."

"I-I, er," Ned stammered, clearly discombobulated by an irate police chief.

I rose to my feet, nonplussed by McBride's obvious irritation. I'd seen that stormy expression on his face before and refused to be intimidated. "Ned needed a few minutes to collect himself. It isn't every day one finds a dead body. It's traumatic. Shame on

61

you, McBride, for bullying him."

"I'm not 'bullying' him," McBride retorted stiffly.

McBride towered over my petite frame by nearly a foot, but I stood my ground. Dark hair, laser blue eyes, movie-star handsome features, he could have been the poster boy for Internet dating. Lonely widows and divorcées — make that any woman with a drop of estrogen — would respond in droves. Computers would crash. Networks would fail.

I gestured toward Ned. "Can't you see the man's upset? Cut him some slack."

"I thought my instructions were clear. I told you to stay put." McBride directed his words to Ned, the reprimand razor sharp.

Poor Ned, he looked ready to crumple like a cheap suit. Taking the initiative, I placed my hands on my hips ready to do battle and huffed out a breath. "Now wait just a cotton-pickin' minute before you go throwing your weight around, McBride. It'll get you nowhere."

"I've got a murder to deal with. You had no right to sequester him."

I flung my hand out. "You call this sequestering? We're smack-dab in the middle of the town square. We couldn't be more unsequestered if we'd tried."

McBride took a deep, calming breath and released it. When he spoke again, he modified his tone. "Ned, I'd like you to come down to my office while the details are still fresh in your mind."

"Okeydokey," Ned responded, less frightened now, and eager to please. He climbed to his feet and replaced his ball cap. "Miz Piper, you're a real nice lady for hearin' me out. I'm feelin' much butter since you let me get everythin' out of my system. You'd make a real good therapy person once you set your mind to it."

"Thanks, Ned," I said, and smiled. "Anytime you need to talk, I'm here for you."

"Therapy person?" McBride muttered as he left with Ned. "Just when I thought I'd heard it all."

CHAPTER 6

"What a mess!" I viewed the aftermath of Doug's aborted cooking demo from the threshold of Spice It Up! Folding chairs were no longer in neat rows but strewn helter-skelter. Jars of spices huddled at one end of the table like refugees from a storm. The cash register squatting on the counter issued a silent rebuke about the lack of sales. I'd counted on chicken curry cooking up a batch of cash to boost my end of the month totals. Only the basket of colorful vegetables added a note of cheer to the otherwise bleak scene.

"Good thing I remembered to turn off the stove before dashing out, or I'd've ruined one of my best pots," Doug commented from behind me, sounding as deflated as I felt.

It was hard to mourn the death of cookware — even pricey Le Creuset — with the coroner's van parked down the block. While relieved Ned Feeney hadn't been the victim, I was still reeling from the fact that Sandy was dead. And not ordinary dead. Dead with a silk scarf tight around her neck. In spite of Ned's conviction that her death was the handiwork of the opera house ghost, I was certain the perpetrator was flesh and blood. Sighing, I began the task of setting the shop in order.

Doug's cell phone jangled. The jaunty, toe-tapping tune contrasted with the doom and gloom I was experiencing. "It's Madison," he said, reading the display. The phone pressed against his ear, he walked toward the rear of the storeroom, which provided a modicum of privacy.

I started with the chairs and leaned them against the far wall for Ned to return to the mortuary later. Although I tried not to be obvious, I kept sneaking glances at Doug, who paced as he spoke into the phone. I didn't know Madison well, but the girl struck me as high maintenance. She was aloof, often rebuffing friendly overtures or refusing invites from those her age. She expected her father to be at her beck and call. Quite honestly, I'd been happy when she'd joined the cast of *Steel Magnolias*. Playing the role of Shelby gave Madison not only a creative outlet but also a chance to interact with various cast and crew members. In my humble opinion, it wasn't healthy for a young woman to be so attached to her father to the exclusion of all others.

"Don't worry, sweetheart," I heard Doug say. "I'm on my way."

I stopped stacking chairs. "Anything wrong?"

Doug clipped his phone back on his belt. "Madison heard about Sandy from a fellow cast mate. She's hysterical. The poor girl is scared out of her wits."

"I can't say I blame her. Sandy's death has come as a shock."

Doug raked his fingers through his short, prematurely gray hair, making it stand on end. "I saw you wander off with Ned. Madison said the rumor making the rounds is that Ned bludgeoned Sandy with a broomstick."

I stared at him aghast. "That's ridiculous!" I said, regaining my power of speech. "Ned wouldn't bludgeon a June bug, much less a human being. He quit a job at Bugs-B-Gone because he hated killing defenseless roaches."

Doug started for the door, then turned. "Madison mentioned that except for an argument between Wanda Needmore, CJ's paralegal, and Sandy, nothing out of the ordinary transpired at rehearsal last night. Does Ned have any idea when Sandy died?"

"Ned's a handyman, not a medical examiner." Scooping up an armload of spices, I returned them to the shelves. "I hardly think that qualifies the guy to determine time of death."

"Right, right. Stupid question," Doug said, extracting car keys from his pocket. "Goes to show how upset I am. It terrifies me no end to think of Madison rehearsing at the opera house while a homicidal maniac lurks in the wings."

I slid a jar of the cumin next to the coriander. "Aren't you being a little melodramatic?"

"Since I moved to Brandywine Creek, the crime rate has gone through the roof."

"That's not fair." I set a bottle of fennel seeds on the shelf with more force than necessary. "Every city — big, little, or medium — has crime. No city is exempt."

He paused, one hand on the doorknob. "I'm beginning to wonder if I should relocate. I can't risk my daughter's safety."

Doug's words gave me a jolt. Were they simply a knee-jerk reaction to Sandy's death? Or had he already given some thought to moving elsewhere? No way could a small town like Brandywine Creek compete with suburban Chicago, where he had lived before moving to Brandywine Creek. But all this time, I'd assumed he enjoyed the slower place, the friendly atmosphere, of life in rural Georgia. I wasn't ready to examine the effect a move of his might have on me. Like Scarlett O'Hara, I'd worry about that later.

"I'm certain McBride will quickly have the guilty party in custody," I said with more conviction than I felt. Experience had taught me that guilty parties don't come with a neon arrow pointing in their direction.

"We'll see," he said as he stepped out the door.

"Wait," I called after him. "What do you want me to do with the chicken curry?"

"Keep it," he tossed over his shoulder. "Freeze it; give it away; do whatever you please. I don't want it. Keep the chicken strips, too."

"All righty, then," I muttered, borrowing an expression from Ned's phrase book. You didn't have to hit me over the head with a brick to see that Madison's well-being ranked higher than chicken curry. I admired Doug's devotion to his only child, I really did, but sometimes I felt ignored. Selfish of me, I know, but there you have it.

Once the spices were in their proper places, I took the basket of veggies from the table at the rear and moved it to the counter up front. Next to it, I placed the copies of Doug's recipe for spicy chicken curry. Maybe some stragglers would drift in and be tempted to give it a whirl — and purchase turmeric or cardamom in the process. I had stepped back to study the effect when Bunny Bowtin sailed in accompanied by Dottie Hemmings and Mary Lou Lambert. Mary Lou, a plump blonde with yellow curls, hung back to hold the door open for Marcy Boyd, formerly Marcy Magruder. Marcy maneuvered a double-wide stroller through the narrow opening with an ease born of much practice. Inside the stroller, two infants, one swaddled in pink, the other in blue, slumbered peacefully.

"Ladies," I said pleasantly. "What can I help you with?"

The three looked at Bunny, apparently the appointed spokesperson. As best I could recall, this was the first time Bunny had stepped foot inside Spice It Up! She never cooked, and bragged the only things she made were reservations. She and her husband, Dennis, were close friends of the Grangers. More attractive than pretty with shoulder-length chestnut hair swept back from a narrow face, she'd been set to play M'Lynn, *Shelby's* wealthy, socially prominent mother, in *Steel Magnolias*. A perfect example of typecasting.

Bunny didn't waste time on pleasantries. "It's our understanding you had a discussion with Mr. Feeney."

Her words were more accusation than statement. "Yes, I did," I replied cautiously. "Naturally, Mr. Feeney — Ned — was shaken. He needed time to compose himself before speaking to Chief McBride." I omitted the part about Ned being spooked by the opera house ghost.

"That's right neighborly of you, Piper" — Dottie elbowed Bunny aside — "but is it true Sandy was shot with a .38?"

"Shot?"

"The town's fairly buzzing with rumors," Mary Lou confessed. "I heard Sandy might've been poisoned — cyanide."

First strangled with a silk scarf, next bludgeoned with a broomstick, then shot with a .38, and now poisoned? I shook my head in amazement. The gossipmongers were grinding out rumors at an alarming rate.

Bunny looked down her long, aristocratic nose at me. "We need to know if we should take precautions."

"Precautions?" I repeated.

Marcy, a wispy dishwater blonde, bent down and adjusted a blanket over one of her babies. "You know . . . *precautions.*"

"Things like buying a handgun," Dottie supplied helpfully.

Mary Lou nodded. "Or applying for a concealed-weapons permit."

Bunny pursed her thin lips. "I was thinking of less drastic measures. Something more along the lines of a self-defense course for women."

"A self-defense course sounds like a good idea," I agreed slowly, "but I'm not sure why you've come to me with this."

"Because, dear, you're the most logical person to get the chief's ear," Dottie explained with a wink.

"Me? Why?" I gasped. My vocabulary seemed reduced to monosyllables. I hoped the condition wasn't permanent.

Marcy tucked a strand of hair that had fallen loose from her ponytail behind one ear. "My husband, Danny, told me you and Chief McBride are buddies."

"Buddies?" I almost laughed out loud but caught myself in the nick of time. Was this a trick question? What other rumors had been brewing? I wondered. "Circumstances have thrown us together on occasion, but I'd hardly classify Chief McBride and me as *buddies*," I said, trying to explain my relationship with McBride. Granted I found the man attractive, but he was out of my league. I preferred a steady, quiet, dependable sort like Doug Winters, rather than one with lady-killer looks and a reputation to match.

"Whatever." Bunny dismissed my objection with a flick of her wrist. "Don't overlook the fact that when it comes to crime you have some experience."

Dottie wagged a pudgy finger at me. "You nearly bought the farm a time or two, dearie. My husband the mayor went on and on about your close calls."

"My being held at gunpoint once or twice doesn't guarantee McBride will agree to a self-defense class," I protested. "Besides, Dottie, you're married to the mayor. You should have him approach the chief with your idea."

"Oh, honey," Dottie said, laughing, "the mayor and I made a pact never to discuss politics or business. It's the reason we've stayed married for nearly fifty years."

Bunny's expression hardened. "After talking among ourselves, we decided you were the most likely person to approach Chief McBride with our idea."

"You won't know unless you at least try, Piper," Marcy said, her voice cold. Under the thin façade of civility, I sensed the woman still harbored a grudge. I'd once named Danny — at the time her hubby-to-be — as a person of interest in a murder investigation. I'm not pointing fingers, but some people can't seem to live and let live.

"All right, I'll do it," I agreed, brushing an unruly red curl from my face, "but I'm not sure this is the right time. Even as we speak, the chief is probably busy putting together a list of people who might have a motive to want Sandy dead."

"Good!" Bunny snapped. "That settles the matter, but do it soon please."

Marcy, satisfied with the outcome of our little powwow, wheeled the stroller around. "It's time for me to go home. The twins will be waking up soon and want to be fed."

Mary Lou rushed to open the door. Bunny gave me a tight smile, then turned to follow her self-appointed committee.

"Ladies," I called after them, halting them in their tracks. "For your information, Sandy wasn't bludgeoned, shot, or poisoned. She was strangled with her own scarf."

"Oh no!" Bunny's face mirrored her

shock. "Not the Hermès she bought in Paris?"

Mary Lou shook her head sorrowfully. "Poor Sandy. That scarf was her favorite."

Marcy, her pale face even paler, pushed through the door and disappeared. Mary Lou and Bunny followed close behind, but Dottie lingered. "Funny thing" — Dottie idly picked up the rhizome of ginger from the basket and studied its odd shape — "I recall standing on this very spot and hearing Reba Mae go on and on about Sandy firing her. She was fit to be tied about being replaced in that play by Mary Lou."

I took the rhizome from Dottie's hand and returned it to the basket. "What are you getting at, Dottie?" I asked, though I already suspected the answer.

"Poor Reba Mae. I don't think I ever saw her so upset." Dottie smiled a smile phony as a crocodile's. "She went as far as sayin' she'd like to wrap her hands around Sandy's neck till she squawked like a chicken. You don't suppose . . . ?"

The question hung in the air like yellow pine pollen on a spring day.

"Don't even think it!" I said when I found my voice. "We all say things we don't mean from time to time. It didn't mean a thing."

"You're right, of course." She patted her

blond beehive, then waved merrily. "Toodle-oo. Harvey will be home soon and expect me to have lunch on the table."

When she left moments later, I noticed she marched in the direction of the Brandywine Creek Police Department, the opposite direction of her home. Had Dottie decided to broach the subject of a self-defense course with McBride after all? Or did that take a backseat to a more nefarious intent?

CHAPTER 7

Finally the time came to flip the sign on my door to CLOSED. I thought the day would never end. All afternoon townspeople had drifted in and out, not to buy spice, but to talk about the murder. It was small consolation that some actually purchased a spice or two. And for that I had Doug to thank. The tantalizing aroma of his spicy chicken curry that wafted throughout the shop was impossible to ignore. I encouraged folks to take home a copy of Doug's recipe. As added incentive, I gave anyone who bought at least one of the ingredients a take-and-go container of chicken curry that Doug had prepared for his "voilà" moment.

Thinking of Doug only served to remind me of his comment about the skyrocketing crime rate in Brandywine Creek. Truth be told, it hadn't been far off the mark. Sandy wasn't the first person in recent memory to fall victim to an untimely demise. No wonder women were nervous and talking about precautions and a self-defense course. My imagination stuttered at the idea of gun-toting housewives strolling the aisles of the Piggly Wiggly as they shopped for produce and cold cuts. What next? Would Brandy-wine Creek resemble a scene from *Wild, Wild West*?

I began counting the day's receipts. Suddenly Casey, who had been lounging at my feet, jumped up. His noisy barking nearly drowned out the sound of someone knocking. I refused to stop what I was doing and answer the door. Whoever it was obviously must be illiterate, since they couldn't read the CLOSED sign.

"Dang!" I said when the daily total didn't tally.

The person at the door switched to a different strategy and began pounding. Casey's nails made little clicking sounds as he trotted across the heart pine floor. His excited barking quickly became interspersed with vigorous tail wagging.

"Oh, for goodness' sake." I stopped counting tens and twenties and went to the door. Even in the twilight, which in late November fell early, I recognized Wyatt McBride. Reluctantly, I turned the dead bolt and stepped aside as he entered. I sensed immediately that his visit wasn't a social call.

Casey greeted the man with more enthusiasm than I did. Stooping down, McBride took a moment to scratch my pooch in his sweet spot behind his ears. The little dog was lost in a haze of doggy joy, rolling over, paws in the air, in a pathetic bid for more.

I regarded McBride warily. He didn't look happy — not that he should — so I returned the attitude in kind. "What do you want, McBride? It's nearly dinnertime and Lindsey will be home from the library soon."

"We need to talk."

"That sounds ominous." Tucking an errant curl behind my ear, I reminded myself I had nothing to be nervous about. But when it came to making people nervous, McBride had perfected the art. His blue eyes could turn icy; his features harden into granite. He'd mastered a stare designed to make the innocent squirm and the guilty grovel. He'd once been a hotshot detective with the Miami-Dade Police Department, but he'd returned to his roots. You can take the boy out of Georgia, but you can't take Georgia out of the boy. Occasionally a sweet as a peach drawl crept into his rich baritone.

I resumed my accounting chores, leaving McBride to trail after me. "Remember, I wasn't the one who found a dead body this time. I'm pleading the Fifth."

"Do you even know what the Fifth is?"

I thought I detected a smidgen of humor underlying the question, but I couldn't be sure. I picked up the cash and stuffed it into the green canvas bag the bank supplied. I'd count it again tomorrow when there were no distractions. "If the Fifth is good enough for the Mafia, it's good enough for me."

"How do you plead to the charge of gossiping without a license?" He raised a dark brow. "It's all over town that the victim was found strangled with a silk scarf."

"It's also all over town that Sandy was bludgeoned with a broomstick, shot with a .38, and poisoned with cyanide," I retorted. "You've been in Miami too long if you've forgotten that these crazy stories spring up faster than dandelions after a spring rain. All I tried to do was set the record straight."

"Setting the record straight is my department."

I opened the register, slid the day's receipts into the cash drawer, and slammed it shut. "If you're wondering how folks found out about the cause of death, Ned let it out of the bag before you had a chance to take his statement."

"Sorry," he sighed, pinching the bridge of his nose between thumb and forefinger. "It's been a long day."

I felt an unexpected twinge of sympathy for the lawman. "Can I offer you a cup of coffee? It'll only take a minute to brew a fresh pot."

"Thanks, another time." He took a small black notebook and pen from his shirt pocket. "I'm here on official business."

My stomach dropped to my toes in a free fall. "What sort of official business?"

"Dottie Hemmings came to my office this afternoon to report a disturbing conversation. Ms. Hemmings is willing to swear on a stack of Bibles that she heard Reba Mae threaten to strangle Ms. Granger. She's ready and willing to testify to this in a court of law."

I sank down on a stool and resisted the urge to put my head in my hands and bang it on the counter. The only thing stopping me was the fact that I didn't want to give McBride the satisfaction of seeing how upset I was. At the first sign of weakness he'd be a shark on the trail of fresh blood. "Dottie is a notorious gossip. She's also prone to exaggeration," I answered but avoided eye contact.

"That's the reason I'm here. I need you to corroborate her story. Ms. Hemmings went on to say that this conversation took place right here in your shop. According to my notes" — he consulted his notebook — " 'Reba Mae said words to the effect that she wanted to wrap her hands around Ms. Granger's throat until she squawked like a chicken.' True or untrue?"

Talk about words coming back to haunt you. "What if, for the sake of argument, she did make such a statement in the heat of the moment? Things like that are said all the time. It doesn't mean they're going to be acted upon."

McBride snapped his notebook shut. "You've just given me my answer."

I stared at him, dismay plain on my face. "I didn't say Reba Mae said those things," I protested.

"You didn't deny it either," he said as he headed for the door.

"Where are you going?" I called after him.

"Where do you think?"

My feet felt encased in lead as I trudged upstairs to my apartment. By now, McBride would be walking up Reba Mae's front walk. The man was hardheaded but sensible, reasonable, fair. He couldn't seriously suspect my friend of carrying out a threat to strangle Sandy. Her words were born of anger — anger and frustration — not malice. We've all said such things in times of stress. Why, I'd said them a time or two myself about CJ — not to mention his intended Amber Leigh Ames, aka Miss Peach Pit.

I stood in the center of the kitchen and tried to focus. Lindsey would be home soon and expect to find supper at least started, if not on the table. I remembered the Ziploc bag filled with chicken strips Doug had left behind. I'd stashed them in my upstairs refrigerator earlier when I'd come up to get Casey. They'd be perfect for a quick and easy stir-fry. A raid on the fridge produced broccoli, mushrooms, peppers, and onions.

Casey rested his head on his paws and watched from beneath the kitchen table. He seemed to sense my agitation and deemed it wise to keep a discreet distance. Careful not to lop off a finger, I vented my frustrations slicing and dicing vegetables. I'd just finished when I heard Lindsey's key in the lock downstairs followed by her footsteps on the stairs.

"Hey, Mom." Lindsey dropped her backpack on a chair and shrugged out of her jacket. "What's for dinner? I'm starving."

"Chicken stir-fry," I answered summoning a smile for my favorite — and only — daughter. Lindsey, with her blond hair and eyes the same blue gray as her father's and grandmother's, took after the Prescott side of the family. At seventeen, she was a pretty girl, on the verge of becoming a pretty young woman. By this time next year, my baby would be in college and I'd be an empty nester. I had mixed feelings at the prospect.

"I'll set the table," Lindsey offered, getting plates down from the cupboard. "All the kids at school are talking about Mr. Feeney finding Mrs. Granger. With a killer on the loose, some of my friends are going to start carrying pepper spray."

Housewives *and* teens? Armed and dangerous? I shuddered at the prospect as I added chicken strips to the oil I'd heated in a skillet.

"Sean's dad is going to take him to the gun range for target practice," she confided, referring to Sean Rogers, star quarterback and her current heartthrob.

"Chief McBride is hard at work on the case. Wait and see. He'll have the guilty party behind bars before Thanksgiving."

Lindsey looked at me doubtfully. "Thanksgiving is only a week away."

"Yes, I know." I set a package of rice in the microwave, a busy woman's time-saver. "Not only will Thanksgiving be here, but so will your brother. I can't wait. I'm making each of you your favorite desserts — pumpkin pie for you, pecan pie for Chad."

"Knowing Chad, he'll spend the entire time with his nose in a book."

My son, Chad, Chandler Jameson Prescott IV, was enrolled at the University of North Carolina at Chapel Hill. He was the student; Lindsey, the socialite. "You know he has to keep his grade point average up to get into med school," I reminded her.

It wasn't until we were seated at the table eating when a sudden thought occurred to Lindsey. "Mom, doesn't Madison Winters drive a Miata convertible?"

I scooped up a forkful of rice. "Doug found it for her on eBay. Said it was a steal."

"Last night I got up to check a text message that had come through late and happened to look out the window. I thought I saw Madison's car drive past."

"Madison was probably going home after play practice."

"That's what I thought, too, before I saw the time. It was nearly midnight."

Before I could question Lindsey further, Reba Mae clambered up the steps and burst into the kitchen. "You told me to use this in case of an emergency." She held up a key I'd once given her. "Well, honeybun, this classifies as an emergency. A humdinger of one."

Lindsey hopped up from her chair. "Here you go, Miz Johnson. Take my seat."

"Thanks, hon." Reba Mae plopped down as though her legs had suddenly turned to pudding. "I need to talk to your momma."

"No problem," Lindsey said cheerfully. "Don't mind me. I'll just clear away these dinner dishes."

"I'll clean up," I interjected. "Lindsey, don't you have studying to do? SATs are in a couple weeks." I didn't need to be a brain surgeon to know Lindsey was dying to be in on the discussion. Typical teen, typical female, she wanted to learn all the details firsthand.

"Mom!" she moaned theatrically. "I have been studying. My brain needs a rest."

"Well, rest your brain in your room listening to music," I replied in my mother-knows-best tone of voice.

"Whatever." Lindsey grudgingly obeyed, snatching her backpack as she went and motioning for Casey to join her.

I stole a look at Reba Mae. My BFF's face was drawn, her expression tense. Dinner dishes, I decided, could wait till later. Occasions like this called for a stiff drink. I wished I stocked something more potent than white wine. Perhaps like Wild Turkey, CJ's favorite Kentucky bourbon. In this case, however, a nice glass of wine would have to do. Reaching into the fridge, I pulled out a bottle of Riesling, twisted off the cap, then took two wineglasses from the cupboard and poured us each a glass.

"Here, girlfriend," I said, handing one to Reba Mae and grabbing the wine bottle. "Let's adjourn to the living room for our conference."

On the way, I peeked into Lindsey's room. My girl sat cross-legged on her bed, earbuds securely in place, swaying to a beat of the music only she could hear. Casey lay curled at her feet, head resting on his paws. He opened and closed one eye in a doggy wink when he saw me.

"McBride paid me a visit," Reba Mae said without preamble.

Taking a seat next to her on the sofa, I set the bottle on the coffee table, then sipped my wine and waited for her to continue. Reba Mae's referring to McBride by his surname rather than the more casual "Wyatt" spoke volumes.

"You've got to help me, Piper. I swear if you don't I'm gonna be arrested for murder." Reba Mae's hand tightened around the stem of her wineglass. "McBride thinks I killed Sandy."

CHAPTER 8

"I don't care if orange *is* the new black," Reba Mae wailed. "Sure as shootin', Piper, if you don't help me, my goose is cooked."

I reached over and squeezed her hand. "Of course I'll help. We just have to put our heads together and figure this thing out." Brave words but, to borrow a cliché, easier said than done. Owning a spice shop didn't make me a detective. Granted, I'd gotten lucky a couple times, but luck isn't always around when you need it.

"But how?" Reba Mae sniffled, her pretty soft-brown eyes tear-bright. "What will become of my boys if their momma's hauled off to jail?"

"Calm down," I soothed, trying to talk my BFF down from a figurative ledge. "We'll think of something. Don't lose sight of the fact that we're two reasonably intelligent women."

"My last shred of intelligence flew out the

window the instant McBride brought out his little black book and started askin' questions."

"I'm sure McBride was merely following up on a conversation Dottie was only too eager to report." I made a mental note to give Dottie a piece of my mind next time she sailed into my shop. What a blabbermouth. Shame on her for throwing Reba Mae under the bus.

Somewhat calmer now, Reba Mae took a gulp of wine. "Maybe I was angry at Sandy," she admitted, "but other than wishing her a root canal, I never bore the woman any physical harm. It probably was unchristian of me to wish things like her play bein' a flop. Or dream about her havin' a come-to-Jesus moment and realizin' Mary Lou was a total moron. Then she'd come beggin' me to save her bacon."

"It's only natural you'd feel that way." Kicking off my shoes, I settled back into the cushions, propped my feet on the coffee table, and crossed my legs. "Losing the part of Truvy Jones was a huge disappointment. Anyone with a backbone would've been upset and said things they didn't mean."

"Dang straight!" Reba Mae nodded emphatically. "And then to be replaced by Mary Lou of all people — a ditz who can't follow directions on how to open a box of cereal. If that don't take the cake, I don't know what does."

Leaning forward, I picked up the bottle of wine and topped off our glasses. While I still sipped mine, Reba Mae downed hers, probably too distracted to even taste it.

"McBride thinks I'm guilty as sin." Reba Mae stared glumly into her empty wineglass.

"I'm sure McBride thinks nothing of the kind. He's only doing his cop thing," I told her, although defending McBride made me feel disloyal. "He knows you'd never harm a flea."

"A flea isn't what got itself harmed."

"It's not like you to be such a pessimist," I chided.

"McBride grilled me like a T-bone at a backyard barbecue." Reba Mae shuddered dramatically. "Asked me when I last saw Sandy? Wanted to know what we talked about? What she was wearin'? Can I account for my whereabouts?"

"Can you?" I asked. "Account for your whereabouts?"

Reba Mae's gaze wandered to a photo in a silver frame on the coffee table, a picture of my son and daughter taken on Tybee Island several years ago. Both children were tanned and smiling after a week at the beach. Neither of them had an inkling their family unit was about to burst at the seams.

"Reba Mae," I prodded when she didn't respond to my question. "Can you account for your whereabouts the night Sandy was killed?"

"Criminy!" she said, her laugh sounding forced. "I told 'im I was home alone. If I'da known I needed an alibi, I'd've been hangin' with the crowd at the VFW drinkin' beer and watchin' football."

"What about your boys?" I persisted, referring to her twenty-one-year-old twins, Clay and Caleb, who still lived at home. "Can they vouch for you?"

Reba Mae shrugged. "Clay was shooting pool at a buddy's. Caleb claimed he had some paperwork to catch up on at the garage. I must've been sleepin' like a baby, since I didn't hear either one of them come home."

"Sandy didn't strike me as being popular with the cast and crew. From comments I heard, her management style rubbed some people the wrong way. Think real hard, Reba Mae. Who did she antagonize?"

"Better get yourself some writin' paper, honeybun, 'cause it's gonna be a long list," Reba Mae said as she drew up her legs and tucked them under her.

After rummaging through a drawer of an end table, I located a pad and ballpoint pen, then returned to my spot on the sofa. "It's simply a matter of elimination, so let's get started."

She pointed at my notepad. "I'd put her husband Craig at the top of that piece of paper."

I frowned. "Sandy mentioned Craig was away on a business trip."

"Don't you ever watch the Lifetime channel?" Reba Mae regarded me in disbelief. "The husband's *always* the culprit. Don't matter if the couple's married, separated, or divorced; nine times out of ten, it's the husband that killed the wife."

To appease my friend I wrote Craig Granger's name at the top of the page. Craig never struck me as the murderous type, but then I'm not a devotee of the Lifetime channel.

"Hmph!" Reba Mae snorted, refilling her glass. "Away on business? A likely story. He coulda come back. Last time I checked there were planes, trains, and automobiles."

I tapped the pen on the pad of paper. I could almost feel the cogs in my brain start to grind. "Other than Craig, can you think of anyone in the cast who might've killed Sandy?"

Reba Mae made a broad sweeping motion with the hand that held the wineglass. I breathed a sigh of relief when the wine sloshed side to side but didn't spill. "Might as well put all their names on your list. Every single one had a gripe of some sort."

"Okay," I said, pen poised. "Start at the top."

"Now you're cookin'." Reba nodded her approval so vigorously her earrings bobbed. "Like I mentioned yesterday, Bunny Bowtin stormed out of rehearsal in tears after she and Sandy exchanged words. Bunny said that she wasn't comin' back. After talkin' to her husband, however, she musta had a change of heart."

"What happened between Bunny and Sandy?" I asked. "I thought they were good friends."

"They were — at least until Bunny got the part of M'Lynn. Bunny complained Sandy constantly criticized everythin' she did. Bunny thought Sandy was pickin' on her. She's not used to havin' someone tell her what to do. If there's any bossin' to be done, she likes to be on the doin' end."

I wrote down *Bunny Bowtin*. What Reba Mae had told me made sense. Both members of the country-club set, Bunny and Sandy were accustomed to being waited on and not having their wishes challenged. Then, all of a sudden, Bunny's role had reversed. Bunny was forced to take orders from a woman she considered an equal. That, understandably, could be cause for resentment. But murder? That was a stretch.

"Who else?" I prompted.

Reba Mae's face squinched in concentration. "Wanda Needmore and Dorinda Kunkel talked openly about quittin'. They claimed Sandy was overbearin' and obnoxious. I wouldn't want to tangle with either of them."

I dutifully added Wanda and Dorinda to my list. "Do you think Dorinda is capable of violence? She works for the police department of all places. I'd think she'd be a model citizen after watching a steady stream of miscreants parade past her desk."

"Dorinda's got a temper. I heard from a good source that when she found out Skeeter, her deadbeat husband, was cheatin' on her with a waitress at High Cotton, Dorinda took a shotgun and nearly blasted him to kingdom come."

My eyes widened in shock. "She shot him? Why isn't she in jail?"

"She missed — accidental-like on purpose — but the buckshot hit the wood frame of the screen door. Ol' Skeeter got so many splinters from all the wood flyin' he looked like a porcupine. The floozy he'd been seein' had to take him to the emergency room."

"Wasn't Joe Johnson, your husband's uncle, sheriff back then?"

"Yep, but Uncle Joe let Dorinda off with a warnin'. Her daughter Lorinda was just an infant at the time. Guess Uncle Joe felt sorry for her. He hired Dorinda on the spot knowin' she needed to support herself and her baby once the skunk ran off."

I added Dorinda Kunkel to my list. "Joe Johnson has a heart of gold."

"And Dorinda's strong as an ox," Reba Mae added, waggling a finger at my list. "I bet she could bench-press as much as Mc-Bride."

McBride — hot, sweaty, and ripped — bench-pressing? That was an image I didn't want to dwell on. I cleared my throat. "Who else?"

"Oh, be sure to put Mary Lou's name on that list of yours," Reba Mae said.

"Mary Lou?" I cleared my throat again in an effort to clear my mind of McBride half-naked. "The woman hasn't been in *Steel Magnolias* long enough to argue with Sandy."

Reba Mae gave me a pitying look. "Don't take long. Gerilee Barker is the stage manager. When Gerilee came in for a perm, she told me she heard Sandy talkin' on the phone about replacin' Mary Lou. What if Gerilee wasn't the only one to overhear the conversation?"

I dutifully wrote *Mary Lou* on the growing list. One by one, we'd have to check each person for motive and alibi. I hoped we'd quickly be able to whittle our list down to two or three viable candidates. "While you're at it, you might as well check out Marcy Boyd and Madison Winters. Everyone, even Madison, the apple of her daddy's eye, had a beef of some sort with Sandy."

"Great," I muttered as I reached for my wine. "So many suspects, so little time."

I woke up early the next morning and went for a run with Casey trotting obediently alongside me. Dark clouds swirling overhead predicted a storm in the offing. The dingy sky reflected my gloomy mood. I'd tossed and turned all night, waking up every couple hours, worrying that my BFF was a person of interest in a murder investigation. It was unfortunate that words uttered in the heat of the moment could have such a far-reaching impact. And Reba Mae's alibi — home alone — didn't help her case. I'd watched enough episodes of *Dateline* and *20/20* and read enough thrillers to know "home alone" was a better movie than an alibi. I wished either Clay or Caleb had been around to verify their mother's whereabouts once and for all.

Upon reaching my apartment, I scooped dry dog food into Casey's dish, then showered and dressed. I decided on dark brown slacks and, in contrast to the dreary weather, added a bright pumpkin-colored sweater with dolman sleeves. Chunky gold earrings, I hoped, made the look less casual.

I was enjoying a second cup of robust Ethiopian coffee when Dottie Hemmings entered Spice It Up! "Piper, I rushed right over. Have you heard the latest?"

I didn't even bother to set my cup down. I wasn't feeling kindly toward the woman who'd sicced McBride on my friend. "Can I help you?"

"Gracious, no." Dottie laughed. "I'm not here to shop. You should know I'm not much of a cook."

"Then why are you here?" I asked, putting frost in my voice.

Dottie seemed impervious to the sudden chill. "I wanted you to be among the first to know that my husband the mayor convened the town council for an emergency session."

Curiosity trumped willpower, and she succeeded in gaining my attention.

Dottie smiled a smile reminiscent of the Cheshire cat. "As a result of their meeting, Chief McBride's holding his very first press conference."

"Press conference? Whatever for?" Now I did set my cup down. From what I knew about McBride, he liked to keep his cards close to his vest. He was a regular Scrooge when it came to divulging details of an active case. I knew that for fact. Since he'd been hired chief of police, I'd tried bribery, cajolery, and blatant nosiness to pry information from him — all to no avail.

Smiling coyly, Dottie smoothed the ruffle of a flowered blouse peeking from the jacket of her purple polyester pantsuit. "Phones have been ringing off the hook in the mayor's office since word spread about Sandy's death. Calls from all over the state — Augusta, Athens, Atlanta — demanding more information. I wouldn't be surprised if CNN sends a reporter."

A sharp stab of foreboding turned the bran muffin I'd eaten earlier into a brick in my stomach. "Why all the publicity?"

Dottie shrugged a plump shoulder. "Seems the Grangers are well connected. They happen to know a lot of influential people. They're even on a first-name basis with a Georgia state senator."

"When is this press conference supposed to take place?" I asked. "And where?"

"On the courthouse steps, promptly at noon." Dottie fished her cell phone from the large handbag draped over one arm. "The council demanded McBride reassure the townspeople that the culprit will soon be behind bars. Let folks know they can get a good night's rest and can quit locking their doors."

Dottie's words made it clear that McBride was being pressured to make an arrest before he even had time for a thorough investigation. That wasn't the way he operated. Needing to busy myself, I picked up a box and slit open a package the UPS driver had delivered late yesterday. "I hope you don't think Reba Mae will turn out to be the *culprit* behind bars."

Dottie had the grace to flush. "I have no idea what you're talking about."

"Oh, I think you do!" I snapped, daring her to deny the charge. "You know exactly what I mean. You couldn't wait to rush over to the police department and tell McBride about an innocent comment you overheard."

"Oh, that." She waved a plump hand. "I

simply couldn't ignore my civic duty. I felt obligated to report anything that might have a direct bearing on a crime."

I stopped unpacking the shipment of spices and folded my arms across my chest. "All you did was land a good person in a heap of trouble. Reba Mae had nothing to do with Sandy's death. Why, you've had a standing appointment at the Klassy Kut ever since it opened. You should know better than to think Reba Mae guilty of such a thing. Shame, shame, shame, Dottie Hemmings!"

"Hmph! So that's the thanks I get for being a concerned citizen." Dottie studied her cell phone for messages, then dropped it back into her handbag. "My motto is to serve and to protect."

"I believe the motto is 'to protect and to serve,' " I said as I removed an invoice from the box I'd just opened. "Before you took possession of that motto, it belonged to the police department — and to the best of my knowledge you aren't on the force."

"Whatever." Dottie turned on her heel and marched out.

One less person on my Christmas card list, I thought as I watched her depart. At the rate I was losing friends and acquaintances, I'd save a bundle on postage stamps. I reached for my cell phone and dialed Reba Mae.

CHAPTER 9

I didn't even feel a teensy twinge of guilt at closing Spice It Up! at noon. Other merchants along Main Street seemed to suffer from the same lack of remorse. I trailed after Shirley Randolph from Creekside Realty. Across the square, Gerilee Barker waited patiently as her husband, Pete, arranged the hands on a WE WILL RETURN sign at Meat on Main. Like a colony of ants, all of us headed in the same direction. Not even the prospect of rain, sleet, or hail could undermine our determination to attend Brandywine Creek's first honest-to-goodness press conference.

Thunder rumbled in the distance, an ominous reminder of an impending storm. One look at a sky the color of tarnished pewter and I wished I'd remembered an umbrella. I never seemed to have it handy when I needed it. To the best of my knowledge, the pink-flowered umbrella I'd had for years had yet to be subjected to its first drop of rain. Stopping on the corner of Main and Elm streets, catty-corner from the courthouse, I looked both ways as I'd been taught from childhood. A rusty pickup lumbered past followed by a news van with WAGT stenciled on the side. Apparently Dottie's information that the Augusta station intended to cover the details of Sandy's death was accurate.

I was about to step off the curb when I glanced down Elm Street — and did a double take. It took me a moment to pin a name on the attractive woman who stood smoking a cigarette outside Proctor's Cleaners. She was dressed in dark-washed jeans and a scoop-necked sweater. Then recognition dawned. Bitsy Johnson-Jones. The rumor mill had churned out gossip that Bitsy'd had her tummy stapled. The results were amazing. Makeup and a new hairdo with plenty of blond highlights completed the transformation.

"Bitsy!" I exclaimed as I walked toward her. "I almost didn't recognize you. You must have lost eighty pounds."

Bitsy blew out a plume of smoke. "Eighty-two."

"You look fabulous!" I gushed. And she did. Who knew all that pretty lurked behind the plus-size clothing?

"Thanks," she said, flicking ash on the sidewalk.

I gestured to the crowd gathering on the courthouse lawn. "Aren't you going to the press conference?"

"Nah, I don't dare. Mr. Proctor would have a conniption if I closed the cleaners. From here, though, I should be able to see and hear what's goin' on." She took another drag from her cigarette. "Too bad about Miz Granger, isn't it?"

"Yes, it is." A gust of wind blew a strand of hair across my cheek, and I shoved it back. "Did you know her well?"

"Not really, but she seemed nice enough." Bitsy kept her gaze fixed on the courthouse lawn. "Last time Miz Granger dropped off her dry cleaning, I told her I wanted to be part of the play she was putting on."

"Did she take you up on your offer?"

"No. Said she was real sorry, but all the parts were cast."

"That must have been disappointing." Vicki Lamont gave me a finger wave as she hurried past us but didn't stop to chat.

"It was even more disappointing since I'd already memorized the lines of several characters," Bitsy continued. "I told Miz Granger I'd make a good understudy, but

104

she said she had everything under control."

I was beginning to doubt the wisdom of initiating the conversation. Now that I had, I found it difficult to make a getaway without appearing rude. I scanned the crowd across the street and found my excuse standing at the edge of the crowd. "Sorry, Bitsy, I promised to meet Reba Mae. Don't want to keep her waiting. Nice talking to you."

"Sure." Bitsy dropped her cigarette butt to the sidewalk and ground it beneath her heel. "Nice talkin' to you, too."

I cut a diagonal swath from the cleaners to the courthouse just ahead of a news van with the familiar CNN logo splashed across its side. The dignified courthouse, dating back nearly one hundred years, anchored one end of the town square, the opera house the other. The courthouse was built in the neoclassical Greek Revival style with four imposing white pillars, and the mayor liked to remind folks that its brick was made from Georgia red clay. A podium had been set in a prominent spot at the top of the courthouse steps.

"Hey, girlfriend," Reba Mae greeted me. "For a minute or two, I thought you were gonna miss all the hoopla."

"You're crazy if you think I'd miss Mc-

Bride's TV debut," I said as we worked our way nearer the front.

A crowd had gathered for the event. News of the press conference had spread quickly. As Melly was fond of saying, there was telephone, telegraph, or tella-Dottie. People clustered in small groups on the lawn to gossip and speculate. Most of them I recognized by face if not by name.

Reba Mae nudged me in the ribs. "Isn't the blonde over there primpin' a reporter on Channel Twenty-Six?"

"Looks like her," I said, craning my neck for a better view of the woman. The TV station WAGT happened to be the NBC affiliate out of Augusta, which broadcast locally on Channel 26. "CNN's here, too."

"Probably a slow news day."

"Maybe," I said doubtfully. "Sandy and Craig must have loads of friends in high places."

We scooted aside to let Bob Sawyer, reporter for *The Statesman,* Brandywine Creek's weekly newspaper, stake out a better camera angle. "I didn't even have to reschedule my next client," Reba Mae confided. "Shelly Ann Bixby beat me to the punch. Soon as Shelly Ann heard there was gonna be TV coverage, she called to cancel. She wants to be available in case she's asked to do one of those in-depth interviews. You know the kind where a reporter randomly picks someone from the crowd and asks, 'How well did you know the victim?' "

"Yeah, I see them all the time. Most of those interviewed are clueless."

"Guess a former baton twirler like Shelly Ann never tires of wantin' to be in the limelight. The leaves have been showin' their backsides all mornin'," Reba Mae said, changing the subject. "That's a surefire sign it's gonna rain."

As if to prove her point, a rumble of thunder rolled through, the sound a little louder than before. Seconds later, the bell from St. Mark's Episcopal Church over on Sycamore Street tolled the hour of twelve. Right on cue, the courthouse doors swung open and out marched Mayor Harvey Hemmings followed by Wyatt McBride. The pair was followed by members of the city council and police officers Beau Tucker and Gary Moyer. Council members huddled on the left; police, on the right. Their deliberate positioning reminded me of choosing sides in a child's game of Red Rover. Or, worse yet, a town divided.

"Judging from his expression, McBride doesn't look happy," I whispered. "Holding this press conference goes against the grain."

"The mayor is used to gettin' his own way. Doesn't like to take no for an answer," Reba Mae whispered back.

Harvey Hemmings, a short, rotund man with a head shaped like a bowling ball, stepped to the podium. A fringe of gray hair circled his mostly bald head like a laurel wreath and a gray caterpillar of a mustache crawled across his upper lip. His chest seemed to visibly swell with self-importance as he surveyed the crowd and spied the news crews. "Testing, testing," he said, leaning into the mic.

"Oh, for goodness' sake," Reba Mae muttered. "Just get the show on the road."

"Hurmph!" Hemmings, apparently satisfied with the sound system, cleared his throat, then addressed those assembled, "Ladies and gentlemen, so good of y'all to come on such short notice. On behalf of the town council and myself, I'd like to welcome any visitors among you to our fair city. We only wish that it was under happier circumstances. I'd like to personally invite each and every one of you to return in the future and enjoy all the amenities Brandywine Creek has to offer."

"Sounds like a campaign speech," I muttered under my breath.

Reba Mae tugged her sweater tighter

around her body. "Harvey probably campaigns in his sleep."

"How do you explain the rash of murders in your town, Mayor?" an attractive brunette in slacks and a blazer wanted to know. She bore a striking resemblance to a new hire on another of the Augusta affiliates, but I couldn't be sure which one.

"Why, ah, I'd hardly describe what happened in those terms, young lady."

From the way her expression turned rigid, she didn't appear happy at being called a young lady. "Mayor, you can't deny Ms. Granger's murder isn't the only violent death to occur in Brandywine Creek's recent history."

"I'm not tryin' to deny any such thing . . . ," Hemmings sputtered.

"Mayor" — the blonde from Channel 26 consulted her notes — "according to the station's files, a local chef was found stabbed to death in his restaurant, Trattoria Milano, last spring. Is that true?"

"Yes, yes, but that case was closed, and the alleged murderer is awaiting trial." The mayor's round-as-a-dinner-plate face flushed pink as a newborn's. "The restaurant's under new ownership. Even has a new name — Antonio's. Y'all should drop by for lunch. Be sure to order cannolis for dessert.

They're homemade."

"Mayor . . . ?" This interruption came from the reporter from CNN, a handsome young dark-skinned male I'd seen on television a time or two. "Isn't it also true that in July a woman was bludgeoned by a brisket during your annual barbecue festival?"

"True." Harvey Hemmings took a snowy linen handkerchief from his pocket and blotted sweat from his brow. "I'll have you know that the case was solved by the time the last pitmaster pulled up stakes and hightailed it to the next town on the barbecue circuit."

"What can you tell us about the latest murder?" called the intrepid Bob Sawyer.

Before the mayor had time to respond, the CNN guy intervened, "One of my coworkers informed me Brandywine Creek is getting quite a reputation. He described it as the Cabot Cove Syndrome."

"Uh-oh," I murmured. Reba Mae and I exchanged glances. Once upon a time, we were huge fans of the *Murder, She Wrote* series. Cabot Cove, as aficionados are aware, was the fictional home of Jessica Fletcher. Each week, regular as clockwork, a citizen was murdered. And each week, the ever so clever Mrs. Fletcher would solve the crime.

"Sorry, y'all," the mayor apologized. " 'Fraid I don't know what that means."

"Idiot!" Reba Mae scoffed. "That means he doesn't want to comment."

"Time's come to turn your questions over to Brandywine Creek's chief of police, Wyatt McBride." The mayor in his eagerness to escape further questioning bumped the mic, causing it to screech so shrilly that it set everyone's teeth on edge.

McBride, his expression hard as stone, stepped forward. His icy gaze swept over the onlookers and gawkers, calm, cool, and collected as you pleased. I had to hand it to the man. He wasn't easily rattled by microphones, cameras, or a pack of fervid reporters.

"Good afternoon," he said, his voice a pleasant baritone. "My statement will be brief. The body of Ms. Sandy Granger, a resident of Brandywine Creek, was found yesterday morning at approximately ten fifteen A.M. by Mr. Ned Feeney, custodian of the Brandywine Creek Opera House. The cause of death appears to be strangulation. The coroner places the time of death between the hours of ten o'clock and midnight the previous night, which has been con-

111

firmed by the medical examiner in Atlanta. Her husband has been notified and is returning from a business trip in London, England. My department requests that anyone who might have seen anyone or anything suspicious come forward."

Questions flew through the air like projectiles.

"Can you describe the murder weapon?"

"Do you have any suspects?"

"Did Ms. Granger have any enemies?"

"No comment. This is an active investigation." McBride stepped away from the mic. His tone left no room for argument. The CNN guy seemed chagrined but reluctant to pursue the issue. The girl reporter from Augusta followed his example and also remained silent.

"Dang!" Reba Mae cried. "Just my luck! There goes my theory about the husband bein' the killer. Craig wasn't only out of town, but out of the country. That's sure not how it works on TV."

"Cheer up, Reba Mae," I said. "Try to think of it as one suspect eliminated."

"Yeah, I guess," she grumbled.

"Don't sound so glum." I gave her a friendly jab with my elbow. "We still have plenty of names on our persons of interest list."

"Folks, don't rush off. I have an important announcement to make." Mayor Hemmings wasn't quite as eager as McBride to back away from the spotlight. Rubbing his pudgy hands together, he quickly moved forward before the crowd could disperse. "Mr. Granger wanted y'all to know he's offerin' a ten-thousand-dollar reward for information leading to the arrest and conviction of his wife's killer. A hotline's bein' established right this very minute."

I saw McBride's eyes widen a fraction before his cop mask slipped firmly into place. I'd bet my last jar of saffron this was the first he'd heard of any reward — or any hotline. He didn't look pleased at the prospect.

Heads bobbed as people raided their memory banks for stray details that might lead to a hefty addition to their checking accounts. I had no doubt the line wouldn't be merely hot, it would be steaming. I sent up a prayer that one or two "tips" would lead suspicion away from Reba Mae and down a different path.

"One last item, folks," the mayor was saying. "The opera house is considered a crime scene and is off-limits. Production of the play *Steel Magnolias* has been suspended indefinitely."

"I've heard enough," I said, turning away.

"Me, too," Reba Mae echoed. "I've got a cut and color due in five minutes."

Reba Mae headed toward the Klassy Kut while I started to return to Spice It Up! Vicki Lamont fell into step next to me. "Poor Craig," she crooned. "He must be devastated. I think I'll bring him a casserole."

I mustered a thin smile. "I'm sure he'll appreciate your thoughtfulness." *And the thoughtfulness of a dozen other women,* I said to myself. The casserole-to-the-grieving-widower brigade had commenced. I wondered if I should ask Vicki to suggest that Craig clear out his freezer for the onslaught of home-cooked dishes.

"Do you suppose anyone will come forward to claim the reward?" Vicki asked. "Ten thousand dollars is a lot of money."

"Hmm," I murmured, only half listening to Vicki's ramble. I was too worried about Reba Mae to think about the reward money. Pressure was on to find a killer.

Craig might have had a solid alibi, but did everyone else on our list? No time like the present to do a little sleuthing. "See you later," I said, veering in the opposite direction and leaving Vicki staring after me with a puzzled expression.

CHAPTER 10

I took a shortcut and ducked through the narrow passage that separated Yesteryear Antiques from Second Hand Prose. The space was barely wide enough to accommodate one not very large person. I certainly wouldn't recommend the route to anyone subject to claustrophobia. I wasn't claustrophobic, but, even so, I was happy to emerge from the tight confines into the open expanse of the vacant lot behind Spice It Up!

I jogged across the lot to my VW Bug parked at the curb, climbed inside, and drove off. I could just as easily have walked to my destination, but driving was faster and gave me less time to reconsider my plan. I shuddered to think of the lecture McBride would give me if he suspected what I was up to. Doug would sing the same tune if he got wind of it. But Reba Mae was in the top slot on McBride's list of suspects.

What kind of person would I be if I didn't help a friend in need? I wouldn't be able to sleep nights. I wouldn't be able to look at myself in a mirror. That wasn't how I rolled.

If I had to start scratching names off the list, someone had to be first, so I selected Wanda Needmore, CJ's paralegal, for no special reason except that she was CJ's paralegal and the person on the list I liked least. Wanda had been cast in the role of Clairee Belcher, a widow and grande dame, in *Steel Magnolias,* yet another brilliant example of typecasting. Madison had let it drop to her father that Wanda and Sandy argued at rehearsal. And furthermore, Reba Mae had said Wanda and Dorinda had been so disgruntled that they'd been on the verge of staging a mutiny. Yes, Wanda bore further scrutiny and now was as good a time as any.

The law office belonging to CJ and his partner, Matt Wainwright, was located in a handsome Victorian-style home near the historic section. The elaborate gingerbread trim and wood siding had been painted various shades of sage, sand, and cranberry. In warmer weather, wicker rockers and trailing Boston ferns welcomed clients as they mounted the steps of the wraparound porch. Knowing CJ's taste, I was certain he'd have preferred a more contemporary setting for his practice, one more in keeping with his newer, "hipper" image. His business partner, however, had persuaded him that the current location was ideal to attract the sort of clientele they wanted. There was no sign of CJ's Lexus or his partner's Bimmer in the drive, which had been widened to accommodate clients and personnel. I assumed the Honda Accord belonged to Wanda. Parking my Beetle behind her car, I hurried inside. In less than a half hour I was due to reopen my shop. My mission here shouldn't take long.

The reception area was deserted. I assumed the young woman — I couldn't recall her name — who currently served as receptionist/ secretary was at lunch. I remembered from my tenure as the "boss's wife" that Wanda's office was down a short hallway and on the left. Farther down were a small conference room, an even smaller break room, and a restroom. CJ and Matt occupied two spacious offices at the rear of the building that overlooked a flagstone terrace and sloping lawn. In the spring and summer, the firm often utilized this area for hosting cocktail parties — none to which I'm invited. CJ's soul mate, Amber Leigh Ames, now has the title of hostess with the mostess. During my reign as CJ's wife, the hors d'oeuvres were homemade. Amber keeps the caterer's number on speed dial.

Through the partially open door of Wanda's office, I could see her on the phone. At my knock, she looked up and then signaled me to enter. "I'll need a copy of the deposition," she continued her conversation with the party on the other end. "Fax it first thing tomorrow morning if you want Mr. Prescott to file a motion on your behalf."

I sank down in the cushy upholstered chair opposite her desk and waited for her to complete the call. Not much had changed in her office since my last visit. Same pale blue walls, same white wainscoting. Same family photos. Wanda hadn't changed much either. She wore her steel gray hair in a flattering bob, kept her makeup to a minimum, and preferred skirts to pants. My guesstimate put her in her early sixties. She had been CJ's paralegal ever since he started his practice. Three years ago, Wanda had lost her husband, Yancy. He'd retired early to enjoy life only to suffer a massive heart attack while playing golf. Who said life was fair?

Her conversation completed, Wanda gave me a smile that waffled between polite and not quite friendly. "Piper, I'm surprised to see you here. CJ didn't mention you stopping by. What can I do for you?"

"I hope I'm not interrupting anything important," I said, returning the smile. "I realized we hadn't seen each other in some time so decided on a spur-of-the-moment visit."

Wanda raised a perfectly arched brow, one, not both, in a gesture I'd like to emulate. "I like to use this time when everyone is at lunch, and the office quiet, to get caught up on things."

I shifted my weight. Suddenly the comfy chair wasn't as comfy as it had been minutes earlier. I'd have to be thick as a brick not to get the message. She was clearly letting me know she valued her peace and quiet and didn't care to squander it in idle chatter with the boss's ex. "Actually," I said, trying a different tactic, "I hoped to find CJ. I don't suppose you'd know if he's heard from our son recently? I'd like to know what Chad's plans are for Thanksgiving."

"I'll have CJ call you when he returns from lunch." Wanda scribbled a note on a memo pad. "Is that all?"

I refused to take the hint and slink away quietly. "Were you aware that the mayor called a press conference for noon today? I'm surprised I didn't see you there."

"Why would I be?"

I shrugged. "Since you were part of the cast of *Steel Magnolias,* I assumed you'd be interested in finding out the details surrounding Sandy's death."

"Naturally I'm interested, but some of us have work to do. I'm sure I'll hear the details sooner or later."

Was she insinuating I had nothing better to do than satisfy my curiosity? I decided to overlook the sly insult. "I understand Mayor Hemmings and the town council issued Chief McBride an ultimatum: Put an end to the rumors regarding Sandy's death and find her killer — or else."

Wanda stared at the phone as though willing it to ring and end my visit. "Or else what?" she inquired politely.

"I'm assuming McBride's job is on the line unless he makes an arrest quickly." I drummed my fingertips on the chair's armrest. I didn't like to dwell on that possibility. McBride often irritated, provoked, or challenged me, but for some reason I liked knowing the man was around. "It's almost as if the mayor holds him personally responsible for the town's recent . . . misfortunes."

"Hmm." Wanda cast a surreptitious glance at her wristwatch.

"McBride asked the public's help finding the killer."

"What else did the chief have to say?"

"He kept his comments brief but said the coroner was able to estimate the time of death, which was confirmed later by the medical examiner in Atlanta." I watched Wanda carefully for a reaction but didn't see one. Was she really as indifferent to a woman's death as she appeared?

"And what time did the murder take place?" Wanda might as well have been asking if I preferred my coffee with cream and sugar.

"Most likely occurred between ten o'clock and midnight."

"I see," Wanda said. "That means Sandy must've been killed shortly after rehearsal ended."

"That's the present theory," I agreed pleasantly. "Did you go straight home after rehearsal?"

She gave me a tight-lipped smile. "I hardly think that's any of your business."

"You're right, of course, it isn't my business, but it will be McBride's. I assume he'll question everyone connected with the play." I could tell from the surprise that flickered across her face that I'd finally succeeded in capturing her interest. "McBride also mentioned the cause of death."

Wanda fiddled with the long gold chain around her neck. "Let me guess," she said. "Did one of the cast members lace her latte with cyanide?"

"No," I said when I recovered my voice. Her total lack of empathy had caught me by surprise. "Sandy was strangled. I take it you didn't care for her."

Wanda leaned back in her executive chair, the picture of composure. "I had no idea when I auditioned for the part of Clairee that Sandy would turn out to be such a bitch. Dorinda Kunkel and I both considered quitting and leaving her scrambling to replace us this late in the game. It would've served the woman right. Other than Madison Winters, Dorinda and I were the only ones in the entire cast who had our lines down cold."

"Mayor Hemmings announced a ten-thousand-dollar reward and a hotline for information leading to the arrest and conviction of the killer."

"I doubt either of them will turn up anything useful," Wanda said airily.

"Why do you say that?" I asked, puzzled by her attitude.

"Wait and see. People will be blinded by dollar signs and conjure up useless trivia that will keep the police chasing their tails." She edged aside the sleeve of her blouse and, for the second time during my brief visit, consulted her wristwatch. "Don't you have a business to run?"

My cheeks stung at the rebuke. I rose to my feet and started to leave. At the door, I paused and turned. "Since you weren't at the press conference, you might like to know that Mayor Hemmings announced *Steel Magnolias* has been canceled."

"It's just as well. At least now, everyone is free to spend Thanksgiving with their families. Sandy demanded rehearsals first, family second. Trust me when I say that did not go over well. To put it mildly, everyone involved with the production was extremely irate. I don't remember the last time I heard so much grumbling." Wanda reached for the mouse and clicked on a computer file, effectively dismissing me.

I replayed my conversation with Wanda Needmore as I drove back to Spice It Up! My impromptu visit hadn't been a total bust, I concluded. I'd come away knowing Wanda heartily disliked Sandy. I'd also learned that most of the cast and crew were unhappy at the prospect of spending Thanksgiving weekend at rehearsals. Although that in and of itself didn't constitute a motive for murder. Interestingly, Wanda had neatly evaded my question about her alibi the night Sandy was killed. Very interesting indeed. The woman was hiding something, I could feel it in my bones. But what?

CHAPTER 11

I'd no sooner slipped the sunny yellow apron with its red chili pepper over my head when Melly breezed through the front door. "Piper, are you sick? Have you come down with something? Dottie said the flu is going around. Why, only the other night Dwayne Roberts had Madge rush him to the emergency room."

I proceeded to tie the apron strings. "I'm fine, Melly. No need for worry."

"I drove by your place earlier and saw the CLOSED sign in the window. You can imagine my shock. Where have you been all this time?"

"I might ask you the same question," I replied. "Where have *you* been?"

I watched, amused, as a delicate pink suffused her cheeks. "Cot invited me for lunch at the country club," Melly admitted.

Judge Cottrell "Cot" Herman, a widower, had recently stepped down from the bench after a long, distinguished career. As a young man Cot had been "sweet" on Melly — and, in my humble opinion, he still was. It was fun watching a romance blossom between my starchy ex-mother-in-law and the stodgy old judge. "You two are becoming quite an item these days," I teased.

Melly examined her fresh manicure. "Nothing wrong with two people our age enjoying each other's company, is there?"

"No, nothing at all," I said, trying to hide my smile.

"Not to change the subject, dear, but what could be so important that you closed your little shop in the middle of the day?"

"Mayor Hemmings called a special meeting of the town council early this morning. They insisted McBride hold a press conference regarding Sandy's death."

Melly set her purse on the counter, a surefire sign she planned to stay awhile. "I hate to be critical, but locking up in the middle of the day is no way to run a business. With the holidays right around the corner, I'd think this would be your busiest time."

"I doubt any person the least bit inquisitive would choose shopping for cinnamon over attending Brandywine Creek's first-ever press conference. A conference complete with television vans and news crews," I added.

"Television?" Melly's hand automatically flew to her already smooth pageboy.

"CNN and two stations out of Augusta." I took the feather duster from under the counter and began to make the rounds of the shelves with Melly close at my heels.

"My, my, I had no idea our little town merited so much attention from outsiders. Harvey Hemmings is going to be extremely unhappy if they show Brandywine Creek in a bad light. According to Cot, Harvey's letting it be known that he regrets hiring Wyatt McBride as the new chief of police. CJ tried to warn him, but he didn't listen. No, Harvey can be bullheaded."

I swept the duster over a row of baking spices and made a mental note to order more whole cloves. "CJ and McBride haven't been on good terms since high school when McBride was chosen over him as captain of the football team."

"True," Melly agreed. "Even as a youth, McBride was too big for his britches. He had a certain arrogance about him in spite of his trailer trash background."

I refrained from comment. Melly had harbored a grudge against McBride ever since a suspicious death in her basement had turned into a homicide and she was a suspect. Nothing I could say would change her mind.

"Harvey reminds everyone who'll listen that there were never any serious crimes when Joe Johnson was chief." Melly shook her head. "Not a single murder in all those years."

"The citizens of Brandywine Creek ought to be happy they found a candidate with McBride's qualifications," I pointed out. My supply of ground ginger was dwindling thanks to a rash of baking for the holidays. Note to self: Reorder ginger from my supplier along with whole cloves.

Melly scowled. "Since when did you start championing Wyatt McBride?"

"Good question," I replied lightly. "Someone must've planted a chip in my head while I was sleeping."

"No need to be flippant, dear. It doesn't become you."

Since when? I wondered. I stopped dusting at the sound of the front door opening. Melly and I both turned as Bunny Bowtin entered.

"I'm not going to beat about the bush," Bunny announced without preamble. "Piper, I've just come from lunch with friends. We're all anxious to learn whether you've approached Chief McBride with our idea for a self-defense course."

"Um, no," I muttered. "I haven't had a chance."

"No one feels safe," Bunny said. "Everyone's afraid they'll be the next victim."

"Cot wants to buy me a handgun," Melly confessed. "One small enough to keep in my purse."

This was said so matter-of-factly that I nearly dropped the feather duster. "I hope you refused."

"Absolutely," Melly replied primly, then beamed. "But wasn't that the sweetest thing? He wants to protect me."

"You won't feel very protected, Melly, if you shoot yourself in the foot." My spate of housekeeping chores postponed, I marched over to the counter and stowed the duster in its usual spot.

Bunny trailed after me. "I'm driving to a sporting-goods store in Augusta first thing tomorrow for pepper spray. I'm taking orders. Would you like me to get you one?"

"You should take Bunny up on her offer, Piper," Melly said. "Pepper spray would be a good thing to carry while you're out jogging."

"Exactly." Bunny was quick to jump on the pepper spray bandwagon. "You never know when some lunatic is going to leap out of the bushes and attack you."

"The closest I ever came to being attacked was when Mrs. Pomeroy's bulldog jumped the fence and tried to get it on with Casey." At the mention of Mrs. Pomeroy's bulldog, Casey, who had been asleep in the back room, perked his ears and thumped his tail on the floor.

"The dog was in heat," Melly explained for Bunny's benefit. "Myra and her husband wanted to breed the animal one more time before having her spayed. They made enough money from the first litter to pay for a cruise."

"This is a serious matter!" Bunny slammed her purse on the counter for emphasis. "Piper, on behalf of the women in Brandywine Creek, will you approach Chief McBride and demand he establish a self-defense class? We're counting on you."

Demand? Even on his good days, I doubted McBride would be in any frame of mind to accept a demand — and I'd be willing to bet this wasn't a good day. "I'm busy," I said. "Why don't you go?"

Bunny twisted the strap of her purse. "He makes me nervous," she confessed. "Did you notice how even the reporter from CNN stopped asking questions?"

"I'd go myself," Melly chimed, "but Mc-Bride doesn't like me any more than he likes CJ."

"Oh, all right already. I'll go, but I'm not making any promises." As Melly and Bunny watched with satisfaction, I tugged off my apron, grabbed my purse from under the counter, and slipped into my trench coat, which had been on a hook by the back door.

"No hurry, dear," Melly called after me. "Take as much time as you need. I'll be happy to watch the shop."

As luck would have it — bad luck, that is — the skies opened when I was halfway to my car. Rain came down in torrents, drenching me within seconds. As usual, my umbrella was at home, high and dry in a corner of the closet. Its perfect record of never getting wet was intact.

Water streamed down my face and dripped from my hair by the time I burst through the door of the Brandywine Creek Police Department. Once inside, I shook myself like a wet dog, sending water droplets flying over the institutional gray linoleum. Dorinda Kunkel sat at the front desk but didn't look up from the stack of papers she was sorting through. "Chief's busy," she snarled. "Take a number."

Dorinda's scowling countenance re-inforced Precious's opinion about her coworker's prickly disposition. Well, I'd dealt with bad-tempered people before, so I wasn't about to let that deter me. "I'm here to talk to Chief McBride. I won't take much of his time."

Dorinda grunted. "That's what they all say."

I took a seat on one of the wood benches that ringed the small waiting area. Unless you were partial to *Field & Stream* or *Car and Driver* — which I'm not — the magazines on the end table looked dated and uninteresting. "Would you please let the chief know I'm here?"

"Soon as he's off the phone," Dorinda said. "You here about the reward?"

"Uh, no."

"Good. Phone's been ringing nonstop since the mayor announced it. Damn fool idea, if you ask my opinion. All it's doing is bringing out the crackpots and looney tunes." The papers now sorted and in a neat stack, Dorinda started banging away on the computer keyboard.

I hoped I'd never get on Dorinda's bad side. She'd be a force to be reckoned with. Especially after hearing about her episode with a shotgun. And her ability to bench-press. Shotguns plus amazing strength plus bad temper equaled suspicion. "Say, Dorinda" — I casually brushed rain droplets off my trench coat — "are you disappointed *Steel Magnolias* has been canceled after all the time you invested?"

"Nope!" She sent a document to the printer. "Don't like to speak ill of the dead, but Sandy took all the fun out of being in a play. The woman was a slave driver. I was about to throw in the towel. Matter of fact, Wanda and I talked about a revolt. The whole cast was up in arms after her last edict."

"It must've been pretty bad?"

"It was." Dorinda applied a stapler to the documents like a carpenter with a nail gun. "Sandy insisted we rehearse over Thanksgiving weekend. Even threatened to schedule a rehearsal on Thanksgiving Day."

"That couldn't have made her very popular."

"It didn't. I could've cheerfully strangled the woman myself. I told her, no way, Jose. Thanksgiving's family time. Sandy was crazy as a betsy bug if she thought I'd miss my grandbaby's first Thanksgiving."

"Hey, Miz Dorinda," Ned Feeney said as he pushed through the door carrying a large utility table. "Where do you want this?"

"Conference room, down the hall on the left." Ned hurried off. With the table held in front of him like a shield, he didn't even notice me sitting there.

"Chief wants to set up a temporary command post." Dorinda turned away to answer the phone. "Interesting, Alvertie," I heard her say. "I'm sure Chief McBride would love to hear about your dog barking his head off. His first available appointment is five thirty." Her call finished, Dorinda saw that the red light on the intercom no longer flashed. "Chief's done with his call. Better grab a minute while you can. I can guarantee the quiet won't last."

I took a deep breath to fortify myself. On the short drive over, I'd rehearsed what I'd say to McBride when the chance presented itself: "The women in town fear for their lives. They want you to arrange a self-defense course." I repeated these two sentences as a mantra and I approached McBride's office. All he could do was say no, throw me out of his office, or laugh in my face. If this was multiple-choice, I'd pick all of the above.

I poked my head in the door. "Busy?"

McBride frowned at the sight of me dripping on his threshold. "Don't tell me," he said. "You're here about the reward."

"Is 'Here About the Reward' the department's new slogan?"

His mouth twisted in a wry smile. "No, but it would be appropriate."

Not waiting for an invite, I plunked myself down in the chair opposite his desk. I felt a drop of water trickle down the back of my neck.

"Is it raining out?" he asked, all innocence, as he took in my hair, which was now a riot of corkscrew curls. "You ought to invest in an umbrella."

"I have an umbrella," I replied as haughtily as a person could when looking like a drowned rat. "I actually own two, but I take special care never to subject them to moisture."

"As much as I'd love to discuss the weather, I've got a hotline to set up and a murder to solve." He drummed his fingers on a manila folder in front of him. "What brings you here?"

Before I could reply, a trio of men dressed in work clothes trooped down the hall. The leader had a coil of black cable looped over his shoulder; the other two carried various and sundry tools and equipment.

"The telephone co-op agreed to install a couple extra lines to handle the load till things quiet down," McBride explained, his expression grim.

"Do you think a hotline will yield any useful information?"

"Who knows?" McBride shrugged. "There's always a possibility, but in the meantime, it's keeping me from launching a thorough investigation of my own. My men will be running around like chickens with their heads cut off tracking down false leads, chasing down rumors, and listening to tales either exaggerated or fabricated. I'd love to see the mayor's face when he sees the department's overtime."

"I know you're busy, so I'll make this brief," I said, and launched into my spiel.

"Great idea," McBride readily agreed after my pitch. "I'll put it on my agenda soon as I find a killer."

Was that sarcasm in his tone? I wondered, but forged ahead. "I don't think that'll go over with the ladies. Some want to buy handguns. Bunny Bowtin is shopping for pepper spray. Knowing Bunny, she'll buy enough to supply the entire garden club. It's not unreasonable for women to want to feel confident that they can protect themselves."

"I'm not disagreeing with you, Piper," he said. "I'm just saying it's bad timing. All my resources need to be focused on finding a murderer. That has to be my number one priority."

While I'd been hesitant at first to be the spokesperson for a self-defense class, somewhere along the line the idea had taken root. Women had a right to feel safe whether from muggers, rapists, or abusive husbands. Simple techniques taught by a professional could save a life. "Think of this as possibly preventing a murder," I said with renewed passion.

"I'll give your proposition serious thought soon as the present situation is resolved. Now," he said, "I need to work on doing just that."

I blew out a breath knowing further debate would get me nowhere. But I was by no means finished. *I'll be baaack,* I thought silently in my best Arnold Schwarzenegger impression.

"Hey, Chief. Hey, Piper." I looked up to see Precious Blessing's generous figure fill the doorway. Precious clutched printed forms in one hand, a fistful of pens in the other. "Just wanted you to know, Chief, I'm reportin' for duty. Dorinda's out front tendin' to your appointments. I'm gonna be workin' the phones. Gerilee Barker volunteered to help. Said she'll bring along her niece. They oughta be here right quick."

"Thanks, Precious," McBride said. "Tell the men from the phone company where you want 'em installed."

"Yessir." Precious saluted and disappeared.

I started to leave, too, but paused. "I have a tip, McBride, that won't require reward money. When your investigation begins in earnest, pay special attention to the cast and crew of *Steel Magnolias.* Sandy's management style won her more enemies than friends."

"Duly noted," he replied absently, reaching for a file folder.

"Duly noted" wasn't good enough, I thought as I tugged the collar of my trench coat around my ears and prepared to battle the elements. Ten thousand dollars notwithstanding, McBride would be wise to heed my advice. If he wasn't going to investigate the cast, I'd just have to do it myself. This wasn't the first time I'd had to take matters into my own hands.

CHAPTER 12

Closing time. Finally! I'd looked forward to this moment more than grade-schoolers looked forward to recess. My mood wasn't helped any by the fact that the sun had failed to make an appearance. An abundance of blue skies and sunny days was what I liked best about living in the South. Today reminded me of a dreary winter day in Detroit.

I'd just stepped back inside Spice It Up! after hauling trash to the Dumpster when my phone rang. I dug it out of my pocket and smiled at seeing my son's name and image on the screen. "Hey, honey," I greeted him. "How's my boy?"

Chad probably cringed at hearing me say that, but oh, well. No matter what his age, he'll always be my "boy." These days, I answer his calls with motherly pride mixed with trepidation that he'll ask for a donation to his Living-Well-at-College Fund. In addition to books and tuition, money was always needed for clothes, entertainment, and dining out. For some reason I didn't comprehend, Chad tended to ask me before his father even though CJ's bank account wasn't perpetually strained like mine.

"I'm fine, Mom, but school keeps me really busy. The professor for Organic must think we're all grad students. Half the class is flunking."

"I hope you're not among them."

"No way," he said.

"Good to hear." I could almost picture the smile that was so like his father's.

"I'm hanging in there but only got a B on my last quiz."

Bs weren't part of Chad's vocabulary. Lindsey, on the other hand, was perfectly content skating through classes with Bs and Cs.

"I've barely started a paper for Anthropology that's due tomorrow," Chad continued.

I sat down on a stairstep and absently stroked Casey's head. "With Thanksgiving only a week away, you'll be able to relax and unwind while you're here. It'll be a nice break."

"Um, Mom . . . ?" Chad cleared his throat. "I don't know how to tell you this, but . . ."

The hesitation in his voice caused my mom alarm to buzz. Worst-case scenarios tumbled through my brain like towels in a dryer. Did he intend to drop out of school? Was he head over heels in love and wanting to get married? Had he spent his tuition money playing online poker? "What's wrong, honey?" I managed as calmly as I could.

"Promise you won't get mad or upset?"

"Promise."

I could hear his deep breath all the way from Chapel Hill. "I'm not coming home for Thanksgiving," he said.

"Not coming home?" I echoed. If I hadn't been sitting already, my knees would've buckled. "Next to Christmas, Thanksgiving is your favorite holiday."

"I'm sorry, Mom. Thanksgiving recess is only five days long and exams start the same week we get back. I can better use the time off to hit the books."

I knew Chad had his heart set on being accepted by one of the country's top medical schools — and he knew how much I wanted him to succeed. So what could I say? I smothered my disappointment and said, "I understand. Do you plan to stay on campus?"

"I, um," he hemmed and hawed. "A friend

of mine came up with a great idea. His parents own a beach house on the Outer Banks."

A chain of barrier islands off the coast of North Carolina is my son's preferred destination for a favorite holiday?

"Kyle said the place is virtually deserted this time of year," Chad continued, unfazed by my silence. "It's the ideal spot to get some serious studying done. If we need a break, we can take a long walk on the beach to clear our heads."

"As for Thanksgiving dinner, there's always frozen dinners," I said, trying to make light of the situation even though I felt crushed.

"Kyle said a diner nearby is open 24/7 and serves home-cooked meals. Besides," Chad added, "it's not as if it's really family time since Dad left. Nothing's the same. You and Dad even sold the house where we grew up. When I do visit you, I end up sleeping on the sofa."

Ouch! That hurt. My boy would make a wonderful surgeon someday. He'd just sliced straight into my heart with one precise incision. But I couldn't deny the truth of his words. Everything *had* changed. We were no longer the same family. I felt dangerously close to tears but didn't want

142

him to know. "I know how important your grades are, but I'll miss you all the same. Christmas will be here soon, and we'll have plenty of time to get caught up. Unless . . ." — I paused as an unpleasant thought occurred to me. "— you're planning to attend your father's wedding in the Dominican Republic."

"No way, Mom," Chad retorted. "Gotta run. Love you."

"Love you, too," I said, but he'd already disconnected.

Heartbroken that my son wasn't coming for Thanksgiving, I picked up Casey and set him in my lap. My throat felt clogged with unshed tears. "Looks like we'll have one less plate at the table this year."

I'd no sooner set Casey on the floor when Lindsey called to ask if it was okay if, instead of coming home for dinner, she met with her study group for pizza and to review material for SATs. They were a good group of kids, so I said yes. The teens seemed earnest about scoring well, and all of them planned to go on to college, even Brittany Hughes whose primary goal was to be on the cheerleading squad of a football team playing in a bowl game. Rose, Cotton, Orange, Sugar, Peach, or Fiesta, Brittany didn't care as long as there was a pom-pom to wave.

A lonely evening stretched ahead of me. Casey cocked his head and gave me a look as if to ask, *So now what are we going to do?* I thought briefly about calling Reba Mae but remembered she was meeting with a rep from a beauty-supply company. Casey thumped his tail on the floor, a hopeful gleam in his button-bright eyes.

"Want to go for a ride, boy?" I asked.

Casey was at the back door, his little body wriggling with anticipation, before I could collect my purse and trench coat and snap on his leash. Before leaving I dashed upstairs for the remainder of the chicken strips I'd stored in the freezer. Even though Doug said to keep them, I'd use them as an excuse for my visit. I wanted to find out whether he was still serious about relocating because of Brandywine Creek's recent upsurge in crime of the homicide variety. My mind balked at thoughts of him leaving. I didn't want to believe it. Doug had become an important part of my life, and I didn't want to lose him.

Once in my Beetle, I followed Old County Road out of town. Doug's home/animal clinic was a neat, low-slung ranch-type building on the outskirts of town. His living quarters occupied one end, the clinic the other. I parked in an area designated for clients, got out of the car, went up the front walk with Casey prancing alongside me, and rang the bell. A porch light switched on, casting me in its jaundiced glow. I felt myself being scrutinized through a peephole. Peepholes always made me feel as if I was auditioning. Should I break into song? Maybe do a little soft shoe? Instead, I smiled, opting for friendly and harmless.

At last Madison Winters opened the door. "Piper!" she exclaimed, her tone less than cordial. "Dad didn't tell me you were coming?"

"Mind if we come in?"

Casey's cheerful tail wagging sealed the deal, and Madison reluctantly stepped aside, admitting us into a small tiled foyer.

"Who is it, Madison?" Doug called from the direction of the kitchen.

"It's just Piper, Dad," she called back.

Doug emerged, his shirtsleeves rolled to the elbows, a dish towel slung over one shoulder. His face lit with pleasure at seeing me, making my heart do a happy dance.

"Hi there," he said, wearing a big smile. "This is a nice surprise. Everything okay?"

"Everything's fine." I smiled in return and handed Madison the Ziploc bag of frozen poultry parts. "I thought you should have what was left from the aborted cooking demo."

"That wasn't necessary. I wanted you to keep it." He moved in to give me a kiss but stopped when he caught Madison's disapproving frown. "Madison and I just finished dinner and were about to have a cup of tea. Care to join us?"

Tea? When had Doug become a tea drinker? Coffee had always been his beverage of choice. I caught a gleeful sparkle in Madison's dark eyes and had my answer. The switch to tea had been another of Doug's ploys to bond with his daughter. I applauded his efforts, but switching from coffee to tea? Every relationship needed boundaries.

"I'm usually a coffee drinker, but tea sounds lovely." I experienced a weird vibe that Madison had hoped I'd refuse.

"Here, let me take your coat." Doug helped me off with my trench coat, then hung it in the guest closet. An action that had always felt comfortable now seemed awkward under Madison's scrutiny. At this point, Lindsey would have politely excused herself, but not Madison. The girl stuck to Doug's side like a burr. She wasn't about to let some woman — *moi* — worm her way into her father's affections. No, she wanted

146

them all to herself.

I trailed behind Doug. Bypassing the dining area, we went into a spacious gourmet kitchen with a center island. He'd kept the original maple cabinets but installed granite countertops and upgraded to high-end appliances. A nook with a bay window held a table and four chairs. Two china teacups and saucers rested on place mats while a kettle burbled merrily on the back burner of the gas range.

"How do you like your tea?" Doug asked, getting another teacup from the cabinet. "Sugar, cream, lemon, honey?"

"Just plain," I said. "Anything I can do?"

"We don't need help." Madison poured hot water over tea bags in a pretty china pot.

Doug smiled apologetically to take the sting out of his daughter's words. "What Madison meant is that we do this every night. We have our routine down pat."

"I'm sure you do," I replied, taking a seat at the table. The phrase "two's company, three's a crowd" ping-ponged through my head. After having felt like the main attraction in Doug's life, I didn't relish being part of the "crowd." I didn't like it one bit. I couldn't rid myself of the notion that our relationship was about to derail.

Doug produced a doggy treat from a tin on the island for Casey, who accepted it gratefully and settled at my feet. I waited until Doug, Madison, and I were seated and the tea poured before proposing an idea. "I don't know why I didn't think of this sooner, but, well, I wondered if you two would care to join me for Thanksgiving dinner? It'll be just Lindsey and me, but we'd have turkey with all the trimmings."

Madison kept her gaze fixed on her steaming cup. Doug shifted in his chair. "Ah, Piper, as much as we'd love to accept your invitation, I've made reservations for Madison and me at a lodge I've read about in the North Georgia Mountains. It's supposed to have a fabulous Thanksgiving buffet along with a variety of planned activities for their guests."

"That sounds amazing, and no more than I deserve for a last-minute invitation." I smiled, but it took Herculean effort. So much for spending more quality time with the man in my life. Suddenly the holiday looked even grimmer. Deciding to sulk later, I changed the topic. "I didn't see either of you at Chief McBride's press conference."

"By the time we heard about it, it was already too late." Doug stirred a spoonful of sugar into his Earl Grey. "What did Mc-Bride have to say?"

I blew on my tea, then took a tentative sip. "The chief kept his comments brief. Who, what, when, where, but no why."

"Did the ME establish the time of death?"

I nodded. "Somewhere between the hours of ten and midnight."

Doug let out a low whistle and turned to his daughter. "That's cutting it pretty close, isn't it, sweetheart?"

"Mmm-hmm," Madison mumbled.

"The night of the murder, Sandy kept the cast rehearsing till late," Doug explained, vertical frown lines forming above the bridge of his nose. "It was around midnight before I heard Madison come in."

"Ah, so that's why Lindsey saw your Miata around that time." I bravely ventured another sip of the scalding brew.

"Mmm, I guess." Madison pushed back from the table. "If you'll excuse me, I need to return a phone call."

Doug and I watched her go, puzzled at her abrupt departure. Something about the time line seemed . . . off. Wanda and Dorinda were workingwomen and had to get up early for their jobs. I was finding it hard to believe that the two outspoken ladies wouldn't have objected to rehearsal lasting close to midnight. But what reason would Madison have to lie?

Doug poured more tea into our cups. "I was happy when Madison got involved in *Steel Magnolias.* She's been slow to make friends in Brandywine Creek. That's one of the reasons why I spend so much time with her — even though it means less time for us."

"Family first, I always say." I placed my hand over his and squeezed gently. "Your daughter is having difficulty adjusting. It's only natural you'd want to help. That says a lot about your character."

Behind rimless lenses, his chocolate brown eyes seemed troubled. Turning his hand, he linked his fingers with mine, his expression somber. "Piper, I have a favor to ask."

I nodded slowly, not sure what was coming next. Was this where he told me we should just be friends? That he needed his *space*? Were we breaking up? I already felt an aching sense of loss at the prospect. Clearing my throat, I said, "Ask away."

"I realize this is going to be contrary to my previous advice and warnings," he began, "but I'd like you to try to get to the bottom of this — find the person responsible for killing Sandy. You're resourceful when it comes to solving crimes. I'm convinced you can help. Madison tries to put up a brave front, but I know she's really frightened by what happened. I'm afraid she's going to pack her bags and move back to live with her mother."

This was a 180-degree turnaround from his usual telling me to mind my own business. To leave the detective work to the professionals. Nothing like applying pressure. First Reba Mae, now Doug. Who did they think I was, Nancy Drew? How on earth was I, a simple shopkeeper, supposed to find a vicious killer when I couldn't find people to join me for Thanksgiving dinner?

"I can't make any promises, Doug, but I'll keep my eyes and ears open."

"Thanks," he said, releasing my hand and leaning back. "I can't tell you how much I'd appreciate any help."

"What are friends for?" I took a sip of tea, which by now had grown tepid.

"There's something else," he said hesitantly.

Had I dodged one relationship bullet, only to be wounded by a second? Red warning flags flapped like crazy. "What is it?"

Doug avoided looking at me and, instead, fiddled with the edge of the place mat. "I've been doing some soul-searching. Madison has practically become unglued by this whole thing with Sandy. I think it would be wise if we slow things down between us — at least temporarily. My daughter requires my undivided attention right now. You have children of your own, so I'm sure you'll understand."

I swallowed a lump in my throat that felt the size of a basketball. My eyes stung with tears, and I blinked them away. "Of course, Madison needs to come first."

I shoved back from the table, and Doug walked me to the door, where, after helping me on with my coat, he turned me to face him. "You're the best," he said, giving me a chaste kiss on the forehead.

As though sensing my glum mood on the ride home, Casey rested his head on my thigh as if to confirm he also thought I was the best. If I was the best, why did I feel the worst? A lone, traitorous tear rolled down my cheek, and I impatiently brushed it aside. There would be time enough for tears later; right now I had a murder to solve.

CHAPTER 13

I woke up early the next morning feeling reenergized. While I slept, my subconscious had formed a plan to coerce — "persuade" might be a more diplomatic term — Mc-Bride into conducting a self-defense class in a timely manner. I wasn't asking for the moon. An hour of his precious time, two at the most. Some friendly advice. A few rudimentary maneuvers. A little kung fu; throw in some karate. Was that too much to expect?

Popping out of bed, I raced to my laptop. Casey opened one eye, stared at me quizzically, then resumed his snooze at the foot of the bed. He seemed to deduce, and rightly so, I wasn't about to go jogging. Instead, I sat down at the computer and drafted a basic, straightforward petition, leaving plenty of room for signatures.

While I waited for the petition to print, I gave more thought to my idea. My goal was to collect as many names as possible in the shortest amount of time. To accomplish this, I needed to lure women into my shop in droves. I picked up a pencil and absently tapped it against the desktop. Baked goods, something sweet and fragrant, usually worked like a charm. And coffee, lots of coffee. The answer came to me like the proverbial bolt out of the blue. I tossed the pencil aside. I'd make a pan of gingerbread. Perfect with the holiday season upon us. The spicy aroma of cinnamon, ginger, and cloves would draw people off the street.

Still in my jammies and humming to myself, I creamed sugar and butter, then added an egg and dark molasses. In another bowl I whisked together flour, baking soda, and the spices before adding them to the creamed mixture. I'd bake the gingerbread in the downstairs oven for the maximum olfactory assault. In the meantime, I threw a coat over my pajamas and took Casey out for a quick walk and let him do his business. When I returned, I fed my furry friend, showered, dressed, and downed a bowl of cereal.

An hour later, the spicy scents of gingerbread and fresh-brewed coffee permeated Spice It Up! I'd just opened the oven door and slid a knife into the center of the gingerbread to test for doneness when Bunny Bowtin charged in.

"Well, did he agree, or didn't he?" she demanded.

Satisfied when the knife came out clean, I removed the gingerbread from the oven and set it on a rack to cool. "Good morning to you, too, Bunny."

"You did talk to him, didn't you?"

"I assume by 'him' you're referring to McBride." I felt dowdy in jeans and a loose-fitting sweater next to Bunny. The woman was dressed impeccably, as always, in tailored black slacks, crisp white blouse, and tweedy wool Chanel jacket. Her jacket wasn't the only Chanel in evidence. Oversize sunglasses with black frames bore the recognizable CC logo on the stems. "What's with the dark glasses? Did the sun finally decide to come out?"

"A migraine!" she snapped. "I'm finally recovering, but bright light hurts my eyes."

"I expected you to call last night to see how my meeting with McBride went. Care for a cup of coffee? The beans are from Guatemala." At her nod, I grabbed two cups and poured some for each of us.

"Thanks." Bunny accepted hers with a grateful smile. "I planned to phone, but Dennis invited business associates over for

155

drinks and, well, you remember how that can go from your years with CJ. Drinks turned into dinner at Antonio's, then more drinks after dinner. I was dead on my feet by the time the evening ended."

"Yes, I remember those days," I said, taking a cautious sip of the hot coffee. I recalled them but didn't miss them. During such evenings, I had limited myself to a single glass of wine, nursing it to make it last. Not everyone, I'd observed, had developed the same skill set.

"Dead or alive, Sandy manages to find ways to make my life miserable. Dennis was on the phone with the airlines for hours yesterday. Practically everyone in town knows he bought tickets for my sister and her family to attend my stage debut. When the ticket agent told him the tickets were nonrefundable, he asked to speak to a supervisor. The supervisor finally agreed to send him a voucher, but we'll have to redeem it within a year."

"Mmm," I murmured as I headed for the front of the shop. "How do you plan to use your voucher?"

Bunny, holding her cup with both hands so as not to spill, trailed after me. "After a lengthy discussion, Dennis and I decided we'd use it to travel to Punta Cana for CJ and Amber's wedding. We've never been to the Dominican Republic, but we've heard the beaches are simply fabulous."

"I thought you'd stopped by to ask what McBride had to say about our idea." Talking about McBride's refusal to hold a self-defense class was preferable to discussing CJ's impending nuptials.

"What other reason would bring me here? You know I seldom cook," she said. "Now, what about Chief McBride? Is he willing to hold a self-defense class or not?"

Setting my coffee aside, I arranged copies of the gingerbread recipe on the counter next to the clipboard holding the petition. I hoped customers would find the samples so tasty they'd want to make it themselves and purchase a spice or two along the way. "McBride said he'd put it on his agenda — his words, not mine — *after* he finds Sandy's killer."

"Hmph!" Bunny snorted. "No telling how long that might take when we have a clear and present danger in our midst."

"A clear and present danger?" I mused. "Wasn't that the name of a book, or was it a movie? Both maybe?"

"No need for flippancy, Piper. This is a serious matter that needs to be addressed." Bunny placed her cup next to mine and removed her sunglasses.

I was shocked at the woman's appearance. Last night's wining and dining and her subsequent migraine had taken their toll. No amount of concealer could successfully disguise the dark circles under her eyes. "McBride," I said, "insisted that now is bad timing, especially since he has reward money and a hotline with which to contend."

"I'm not buying the I'm-too-busy excuse. Unless Chief McBride comes around — and quickly — I'm going to file a complaint before the mayor and town council."

"That won't be necessary. I've come up with a plan. Ta-da!" I smiled slyly as I pushed the petition toward her and handed her a pen. "Put your signature right below mine."

"A petition!" she exclaimed. "Piper, you're a genius." After reading it through, she scrawled her signature. "Be sure to keep me in the loop of how this is progressing."

"One more thing, Bunny," I said as she started to leave. "Do you remember what time rehearsal ended the night Sandy died?"

"Why, of course I remember. I was M'Lynn. It ended about nine thirty or quarter to ten."

That's odd. Only last night, Madison told

me rehearsal had ended closer to midnight. "Did you go straight home?"

"Straight home and into a bubble bath." With this, Bunny shoved her sunglasses back in place and waved good-bye. "Now I'm off to Augusta to empty the shelves of pepper spray."

I stared after her, my coffee forgotten. Why the discrepancy between Madison and Bunny on the rehearsal time? One of them was obviously lying, but for what reason?

Dottie sniffed the air as she came into the shop. "Mmm, something smells yummy. I just had to come inside and see what you had cooked up."

"Gingerbread," I answered with a stiff smile. If the woman's conscience was troubling her for dropping a dime on Reba Mae, her cheerful demeanor didn't show it. She seemed oblivious of the pain and suffering she had caused my BFF. "Care for a slice?"

Dottie giggled. "Thought you'd never ask. And I'll take an extra piece, if you don't mind, for my husband the mayor."

Dottie and Harvey Hemmings were notorious moochers. Ladies from the Methodist church, I'd heard, hid their choice baked goods after funerals to prevent the pair from loading up goody bags. Since he was the mayor, people tended to look the other way while they filled Ziploc bags or Styrofoam containers. I don't know this for fact, but I'd be willing to wager Dottie and Harvey were the original Meals on Wheels.

"What's the occasion?" Dottie asked, accepting the gingerbread.

I eased the petition closer, laid a pen alongside. "Signature, please."

Her penciled brows puckered in a frown. "What's this?"

"I've started a petition for a self-defense class. If enough women —"

"Say no more," Dottie interrupted. "I'll spread the word." Pen in one hand, gingerbread in the other, she scribbled her name beneath Bunny's.

With Dottie spreading the word, I didn't have to resort to Facebook or Twitter or take out an ad in *The Statesman* in order to advance my cause. "Another slice?" I offered, feeling magnanimous.

Dottie opened her mouth, but before she could reply Reba Mae stepped in. "I had a no-show so followed my nose. . . ." Seeing Dottie, she trailed off.

"Reba Mae?" I gasped. My BFF was a chameleon. For weeks she'd worn her hair teased and dyed Dolly Parton yellow to "immerse" herself in the role of Truvy Jones in

Steel Magnolias. With stardom no longer on the horizon, she'd changed hair color again, this time to a flattering honey blond that complemented her pretty brown eyes. The style was different, too, no longer teased but softer and with bangs. "Practice makes perfect," I said with a grin. "I love your new look."

She smoothed her new do self-consciously. "Best I can recall, this is the closest to my natural color. Truth is, it's been so long I'm not sure I remember my God-given color."

Out of the corner of my eye, I saw Dottie swipe another piece of gingerbread, wrap it in a napkin, and tuck it into her shoulder bag. "It looks real nice, Reba Mae," Dottie said, brushing crumbs from her fingers. "You ought to consider keeping it that way for more than a month or two."

Hands on her hips, Reba Mae advanced slowly, but the older woman held her ground. "Shame on you, Dottie Hemmings! Quit actin' all friendly-like. You couldn't run to the police fast enough and tell 'em I threatened to strangle Sandy."

"You can't fault a body for doing her civic duty." Dottie stuck her pug nose in the air, the portrait of righteous indignation. "Now, if you'll kindly excuse me, I need to see a butcher about a pot roast."

Together, Reba Mae and I watched her scurry across the square toward Meat on Main. "I didn't know the old biddy could move so fast," she said.

"I didn't know she could cook."

"I stopped by for some turmeric. I used the last makin' curry. Tonight I'm tryin' a new recipe for chicken cacciatore." Helping herself to a slice of gingerbread, Reba Mae perched on the edge of the counter and crossed her legs. "At least Dottie had the decency to cancel her standin' appointment at the Klassy Kut. Must be worried I'll use the wrong formula for hair dye and she'd end up bald as a billiard."

"When you've finished eating, put your John Henry on the dotted line. Figure if I get enough signatures, McBride will have to show us weaker sex how to defend ourselves." After getting her a small jar of the peppery spice and since there weren't any customers at the moment, I cut myself a small wedge of the gingerbread I'd yet to sample. Between forkfuls, I explained about visiting Doug and the explanation Madison had given for coming in late the night of the murder. "Either Bunny or Madison is lying about the time rehearsal ended, but I'm not sure which one."

"You've come to the right person for your

answer." Reba Mae licked her fork clean. "I recently found out that Madison and Caleb have started seein' each other. My boy picked her up after rehearsal, and they drove to one of those chain restaurants down by the interstate for a late bite."

"Well, for goodness' sake, why didn't she say so? Why the secrecy?"

Reba Mae shrugged. "Who knows what goes on in that girl's head? Caleb got the impression she doesn't want her daddy knowin' about 'em just yet, my boy bein' a mechanic and not a brain surgeon."

"Doug's not like that," I protested.

"Some daddies are real peculiar when it comes to guys datin' their baby girls."

"Still . . ." I stacked the dirty plates and cutlery in a pile to be washed.

Reba Mae wiped her fingers on a paper napkin, then wadded the napkin and lobbed it into a nearby trash basket. "Seein' how Madison has a solid alibi, guess we can cross her name off our list."

"Speaking of alibis," I said, "I talked to both Wanda and Dorinda yesterday. Wanda refused to tell me where she was between ten and midnight. Between the phones ringing nonstop and workmen parading in and out, I never did get a chance to ask Dorinda."

The regulator clock on the wall bonged the hour. At the sound, Reba Mae sprang off the counter. "Better run. Dorinda's my last appointment of the day. I'll worm an alibi out of her if I have to resort to my special brand of waterboarding. That's when I duck her head in the shampoo bowl until she's ready to holler uncle."

For a long while, I sat quietly, thinking of the mystery that surrounded Sandy's death. Although Craig Granger and Madison Winters had solid alibis, it didn't mean there was a shortage of suspects. Wanda Needmore hadn't been forthcoming, so she merited a more thorough investigation. Then there was Bunny Bowtin. Her earlier comment told me resentment still simmered below her well-groomed surface over mistreatment at the hands of a former friend. What other suspects would I find when I dug deeper?

All day long I'd listened to women express a variety of opinions and theories about what had happened. I'd even heard some hair-raising tales of the resident ghost. But Sandy hadn't been killed by a ghost. There was a living, breathing, flesh and blood monster in our midst.

And I intended to find him — or her.

CHAPTER 14

It was late in the day. I'd just finished washing the dishes that customers had used when Mayor Harvey Hemmings strolled into Spice It Up! He stood in the center of the shop, hands stuffed into his pockets, and rocked back on his heels. "Nice little place you have here," he said. "Nothin' fancy, but nice."

"Mayor, this is quite a surprise. What can I do for you?" I dried my hands on a dish towel, set it aside, and stepped forward to greet him.

"Heard good things from Dottie. Been meanin' to stop by and check it out for myself."

Spice It Up! had been open since spring, but Hizzoner hadn't seen fit to grace it with his presence until now. *What's the occasion?* I wanted to ask but didn't. "I'd offer you a slice of gingerbread, but all I have left are crumbs."

"Hee-hee," he chuckled, patting his tummy. "My wife keeps me well supplied with sweets."

"Is there anything in particular I can help you with?"

"You're a clever one, Piper." He smiled, showing a mouthful of small, yellowed teeth. "Your idea of starting a petition was pure inspiration. Wish I would've thought of it myself, but it will be more effective coming from a woman."

"Thank you," I said warily, waiting for the other shoe to drop.

"I'm afraid our chief of police can be hardheaded. McBride tends to be out of touch with what the public wants — or expects. He forgets who's paying his salary."

"I'm sure Chief McBride is doing the best he can under the circumstances."

"Yes, yes, of course." He nodded agreeably, his head bobbing up and down like a woodpecker on steroids. "It's those very *circumstances* that brought me here today. I wanted to talk to you about the latest . . . tragedy . . . that hit our fair city."

"All right," I said slowly, "but I don't know how I can be any help."

"Don't be so modest, my dear. You've been instrumental in the past when it came to ferreting out culprits who have committed unspeakable acts here in Brandywine Creek."

"I own a spice shop," I reminded him. "I'm not a licensed private investigator."

Hemmings glanced around furtively to make sure we were alone, then lowered his voice. "I'm here to make you a business proposition."

I tipped my head to one side and studied him. His pink, cherubic face didn't reveal the thoughts going on behind it. "What sort of proposition?"

"I'd like to offer you an incentive in exchange for you doing a little snooping."

"Snooping!" I said louder than intended. "I'm not a snoop."

"Shh." He held a finger to his lips. "Perhaps 'snooping' wasn't the best word choice. Forgive me, dear, I didn't mean to offend you. It's only that you're more open-minded, more creative, than Chief McBride. I'm merely asking that you keep your eyes and ears open. Should you hear anything or see anything that might bring this case to a close sooner rather than later, the city would be happy to reward you."

"Naturally, I'd go to Chief McBride if I find anything that needs further consideration." Judging from the look on the mayor's face, I didn't think this was the response he wanted to hear.

"Naturally," he repeated. "Don't forget there's a hefty reward for information leading to an arrest." He made a sweeping gesture with one hand. "Ten thousand dollars would go a long way in fixing this place up real nice. Make it more . . . modern."

I bit my tongue — I literally bit my tongue — to keep from saying something I'd later regret. He sounded so much like my ex-husband I wanted to scream. I loved my brick walls, exposed ductwork, handcrafted freestanding shelves, and heart pine floor. My shop looked exactly the way I wanted it to look.

"I can even recommend a good contractor. He'd be happy to put up some Sheetrock, cover the bare brick, box in that ductwork. I'd put in a good word" — he winked — "maybe have him give you a nice discount."

I counted to ten, then counted to twenty. "Mayor Hemmings," I said, keeping my temper on a tight leash, "I like Spice It Up! the way it is."

"Well then, little lady, you could use the extra cash for a nice vacation. I'm always hearing folks brag about going on one of those fancy cruise ships that boasts populations bigger than Brandywine Creek."

"I get seasick." I went behind the counter and started sorting credit card receipts in the hope he'd take the hint and leave, but no such luck.

"In that case, honey, I'm in a position to grant certain additional incentives."

I stopped sorting and stared at him aghast. "Are you offering me a bribe, Mayor?"

He did his best to appear affronted, but his acting ability wouldn't win him the role of an extra in a cast of thousands. "My dear young lady, the word 'bribe' isn't part of my vocabulary. I simply wanted to offer a token reward as a show of the town's appreciation."

"Sorry if I jumped to the wrong conclusion." I tried to sound sincere as I placed Visa receipts in one pile and MasterCard and Discover in another.

Hemmings sauntered over to watch. "Hmm . . . there are different incentives I could offer. I was thinking along the lines of, say . . . removing the no-parking ban on Main Street after six P.M. You'll no longer have to go through a vacant lot to get to your car. That should make your life easier. Also, the chamber of commerce is commissioning a marketing firm to design a new brochure. Your quaint little shop would look mighty fine on the cover. Probably draw loads of tourists. We need to band together," he went on, oblivious of my simmering temper, "and put an end to all the negative publicity these killings have rained down on us."

Before I could frame a suitable response Madison Winters entered. She hesitated when she recognized the mayor whose life-size photo adorned a window at the chamber of commerce, as well as the public library and city hall. "I . . . uh . . . can come back another time."

"No, don't leave," I implored, perhaps a shade too hastily. "You're not interrupting. Mayor Hemmings and I just concluded our business. I don't believe the two of you have been introduced."

"My, my," the mayor said when introductions were over, "all the way from the Windy City. I hope you're finding Brandywine Creek to your liking and plan to make it your permanent home."

Madison shoved aside a strand of hair that had escaped her ponytail. "I haven't decided yet."

"What's not to like?" Harvey beamed his best vote-for-me smile. "Can't compare with a city the size of Chicago, but you gotta admit we don't have traffic problems."

Chuckling at his own wit, he wandered out.

"What brings you into town, Madison?" I asked when the door closed behind Hizzoner.

She withdrew a slip of paper from the pocket of her jeans. "My father wanted to know if you received fenugreek in your last shipment."

"Ah, yes," I said, coming out from behind the counter and taking it off a shelf. "Not a lot of call for this particular spice, but your father likes to experiment. Don't tell me; let me guess. He's making yellow curry?"

"Dad said fenugreek would be an excellent addition to a recipe he has for chicken. I'd never heard of it before," Madison admitted, digging her wallet out of her purse.

"Fenugreek is used in dishes of southern India," I explained as I rang up the sale and bagged it. "It's actually a member of the bean family. The seeds are hard enough to break a tooth. Once ground, however, the seeds release a flavor similar to nuts and butterscotch, but it's more bitter than the aroma leaves one to believe."

"Whatever," she said, handing me a five-dollar bill.

I could see my tutorial on fenugreek had

been wasted. It wasn't the first time I'd gone on and on about a certain spice and in the process bored my audience comatose. Time for a change of subject. "Reba Mae stopped by earlier," I said casually. "Too bad you missed her."

"Daddy mentioned that the two of you were best friends."

I wasn't quite ready to hand the fenugreek over until I had a couple questions answered satisfactorily. "Why did you lie to your father about the time rehearsal ended the night Sandy was killed?"

Madison tried to snatch the spice from me, but I held the bag out of reach. "What makes you think I lied?" she challenged me.

"Bunny Bowtin told me rehearsal ended between nine thirty and nine forty-five, not close to midnight like you told your father. If you'd rather, I can confirm the time with other cast members. I'm sure they'll be happy to tell me the truth. What are you hiding, Madison?"

"Nothing!" Madison glowered at me. "If you must know, I went with Caleb Johnson for a bite to eat. I called him when rehearsal ended, and he picked me up. He dropped me off at my car afterwards, and I came straight home. No big deal."

I gave Madison the bag with the fenugreek

and opened the cash register to make change. "Where do you usually park while you're rehearsing?"

"In the small lot behind the opera house. That's where most of us park." She stared at me for a long moment, lips pursed, then seemed to reach a decision to come clean. "Look, Piper, I was afraid Daddy might object to my going out with Caleb. The two of us met and got talking when I brought my Miata in for an oil change. Caleb's a nice guy, and really cute, but Daddy would prefer someone with a college education — engineer, lawyer, med student. You know how fathers are."

I didn't, not really. My father had been a blue-collar worker in an auto plant in Detroit. All he ever wanted was for me to marry a man I loved. That had been good enough for him and my mother. They'd celebrate their fiftieth wedding anniversary next year.

"Caleb and I are just friends," Madison continued. "It's not like we're boyfriend and girlfriend. Besides, I don't want Daddy to read too much into my dating Caleb. It would cut into our time together." Madison dropped the change into her purse, turned, and left the shop.

Heaven forbid that Madison adjust to her

new environment. I struggled not to resent the girl for driving a wedge between her father and me. She was young, I reminded myself. Nothing in her life thus far had prepared her to cope with the violent death of someone she knew personally. But I'm far from perfect. Even as I decided to be more patient, more understanding, resentment wriggled through my resolve.

I had walked to the door, intent on locking up for the night, when a face peered back at me. "Reba Mae!" I said, clutching my chest. "You scared the daylights out of me."

"Sorry, hon." She waltzed in, carrying a pizza box. "Decided I'd share my news over pizza and a nice glass of wine. I brought enough pizza to share with Lindsey in case she's home."

I locked up behind my friend and switched off the lights as we made our way toward the stairs. "Linds was home long enough to take Casey for a run in the park before taking off again. She and her buddy Taylor are working on a school project."

"Ah, yes, I remember. Those days are gone in the blink of an eye."

"That's the truth."

We trooped upstairs, where Casey treated Reba Mae to a lavish display of affection, wagging his tail and bouncing around, making her smile and stoop down to pet him. I scooped dog food into his dish and gave him fresh water. Next I brought out two wineglasses and a bottle of wine. Reba Mae, who knew my kitchen as well as her own, got out the plates.

"No need to waterboard Dorinda Kunkel after all. Wouldn't you know, she has a rock-solid alibi for the night Sandy was killed," Reba Mae said after we'd devoured our first slice of gooey pepperoni and mushroom pizza at the kitchen table. "She and her daughter, Lorinda, took her sick grandbaby to the emergency room with an ear infection."

I sighed as I took a second slice. "Another one bites the dust — which translated means another name scratched off the list. As for the cast, we still need to confirm the alibis for Wanda, Bunny, Mary Lou, and Marcy."

We'd polished off the last of the pizza and taken our wine into the living room when Lindsey bounded up the stairs. "Hey, Mom. Hey, Miz Johnson. I just saw Sergeant Tucker getting out of a police car out back."

"Did you speak to him?" Reba Mae's hand visibly trembled as she set her wineglass on the coffee table. "Did he say what he wanted?"

Lindsey scooped Casey into her arms. "He said he'd already been to your house, Miz Johnson, but no one answered the door. He asked if I knew where you might be, so I told him you were probably talking to Mom."

Just then a fist pounded on the door downstairs. Her eyes distended with fear, Reba Mae rose unsteadily to her feet. "I got a sick feelin' in my stomach that has nothin' to do with the pizza we just ate."

CHAPTER 15

"I'm not here to make an arrest," Beau explained to Reba Mae from outside my back door. "Chief wants me to bring you down to the station for further questioning."

"Did he say why?" I asked, pressing for details. In the light spilling out of Spice It Up! I could see that Beau's usually jovial expression was absent.

"No, ma'am, he didn't say."

Beau and CJ were poker-playing buddies. I'd known the man for years. His more formal "ma'am" spoke volumes about the seriousness of his request. I placed my hand on Reba Mae's shoulder for reassurance.

Reba Mae wrapped her arms around her waist. "What does the chief want to talk to me about? Can't he come to the house where we can discuss things real civil-like over a nice glass of sweet tea?"

Behind me, I sensed Lindsey inching

closer. Casey, on full alert to potential trouble, crouched at our feet, a low growl humming in his throat. Beau shot him an uneasy glance and hitched his utility belt higher around his belly.

"Don't worry, Reba Mae." I gave her shoulder a squeeze. "McBride most likely only needs to tie up a few loose ends. With the hotline and all, he probably can't get away from his office."

"You can ride with me or follow on your own, but it wouldn't be a good idea to keep the chief waitin' with the mood he's in."

"I'll drive you," I said to Reba Mae, then addressed Beau. "Go ahead; we'll be right behind you."

Reba Mae's lower lip quivered, and she looked ready to burst into tears. "I swear on Butch's grave, I never laid a hand on that woman."

"Chief just wants to talk," Tucker said gruffly, then turned and walked toward his patrol car.

"Don't worry, Reba Mae." I grabbed a sweater off a hook by the door. "We'll get this sorted out."

"Mom, what can I do?" Lindsey asked worriedly.

"Call your father and have him to meet us at the police station." I raced upstairs, my internal engine in overdrive, and grabbed my purse, car keys, and cell phone. Lindsey had completed her call to CJ by the time I ran back down. "Give Clay and Caleb a call. Let them know what's happening with their mother."

"I'm on it." Lindsey gave Reba Mae a swift hug. "It'll be fine, Miz Johnson. You wait and see."

Reba Mae swallowed back tears. "Thanks, sweetie. Tell my boys not to worry. Their momma's gonna be right as rain."

Reba Mae and I hurried down the trail in the hard-packed earth behind my shop to my VW. "Try not to read too much into this, Reba Mae," I said in true cheerleader fashion, trying to sound more confident that I felt. "McBride's most likely talking to everyone a time or two."

"I suppose," Reba Mae said as she climbed into the passenger seat but didn't sound convinced.

I slid into the driver's side and switched on the ignition. "Remind McBride, flat out, you didn't mean anything when you said you wanted to strangle Sandy. It was a comment said in the heat of the moment. After all, it's not as if you have anything to hide."

Reba Mae stared straight ahead, her mouth set in a line. She didn't say a word.

I darted a sidelong glance at her as I turned onto Lincoln Street. Her silence unnerved me. "Reba Mae." I spoke in a hushed tone. "Please tell me you don't have anything to hide — or do you?"

Reba Mae swallowed noisily but didn't confirm or deny. It was as if she had suddenly been struck dumb. She either had suffered a stroke or was guilty of withholding information from her BFF — *moi.* Oh, boy! To quote an old movie: Fasten your seat belts; it's going to be a bumpy night.

I didn't speak again on the short ride to the police department. First my body and now my brain shifted into overdrive. What secret was Reba Mae keeping from me? We told each other everything and had since our babies were in diapers. At least I thought we had — until tonight.

Precious acknowledged our arrival with a nod that made the beads in her black braids clack together. Judging from her expression, her sunny optimism had taken a leave of absence. "Chief's waitin' on you, Miz Johnson. Go right on back. Piper, Chief said if you came along you were to wait out here."

I caught Reba Mae's sleeve before she started down the hall to McBride's office. A hallway I'd come to think of as the "walk of shame." "Don't say a word until CJ gets here," I advised. "Remember, you have the right to have an attorney present. You have the right to remain silent."

"Anything you say can be used against you in a court of law," Precious volunteered.

Her face pale, Reba Mae nodded grimly and slowly walked toward McBride's office.

"Coffee?" Precious offered. "I have a feeling this is gonna be a late night."

"Sure, coffee sounds great." I accepted the Styrofoam cup from Precious and slumped down on one of the hard wood benches to wait.

"Those durn phones been ringin' day and night. I swear I can hear 'em in my sleep." As if to prove her point, the phone rang again, and she transferred the call to the newly established command post. "Gerilee and her niece been working those lines like pros. Even sent out for food. McBride said to put it on the expense account. We're already over budget on overtime. Once they knock off for the night, it'll be up to me to log in callers."

I wished I'd had the foresight to bring reading material — and a seat cushion. I was leafing through a year-old issue of *Field & Stream* when CJ steamed through the double-glass doors. My ex'd had a serious makeover since we met as camp counselors in northern Michigan. He'd been a Southern charmer with sun-bleached hair who'd swept this li'l Yankee off her feet. Much to my parents' dismay, I'd dropped out of school my senior year of college to support him through law school. Now he was slick as a newly waxed floor and still oozed charm he could turn on and off like a spigot.

"Hiya, Scooter." He grinned, showing off a mouthful of pearly whites.

"Hey, CJ. Reba Mae's in need of your legal expertise."

"Lindsey phoned as Amber and I were about to sit down for dinner. What's up?"

"McBride had Beau bring Reba Mae in for questioning in Sandy's death."

"The man can't seriously think Reba Mae guilty of anythin' other than puttin' hair rollers too tight."

"Sandy replaced Reba Mae in *Steel Magnolias*. Understandably, Reba Mae was upset and happened to make a remark that could be misconstrued. Dottie Hemmings overheard it and, after Sandy was killed, ran straight to McBride."

"What kind of remark you talkin' about?"

I shifted my weight on the hard seat. "She said she wanted to wrap her hands around Sandy's neck — or words to that effect."

CJ let out a low whistle. "That it?"

"I'm not sure." I flung the magazine aside. "She's acting kind of weird. I've got the feeling she's holding something back."

"Appreciate the heads-up." CJ nodded thoughtfully. "Good thing you had Lindsey give me a call. I've been brushin' up on criminal law. Plan to diversify. I want to be known as more than a stereotypical trip 'n fall, fast-settlement attorney."

"Glad to hear you have higher aspirations." I made a shooing motion with my hands. "Now quit wasting time. Go do your lawyer thing."

He tugged on the lapels of his navy worsted blazer, shot his cuffs, and straightened his tie. He turned to Precious, who had been shamelessly eavesdropping on our conversation. "Please notify Chief McBride that Chandler Jameson Prescott the Third is here to represent Ms. Reba Mae Johnson."

"Go on back. Chief's waitin' on you." Precious rolled her eyes behind his retreating back. "How long were you married to the guy?"

I retrieved the magazine. "Long enough."

The Johnson boys were the next to arrive. "Hey, Miz Prescott," Clay said, "got here fast as we could."

"I was showerin' when Lindsey called and

didn't hear the phone," Caleb explained. "Clay stopped to pick me up on his way here."

"Glad you boys came." Standing, I gave each one a hug even though they were so tall I had to stand on tiptoe, then sat down again. Seemed like yesterday that I was wiping their snotty noses and bandaging scraped knees along with Chad's, then treating the three of them to chocolate-chip cookies.

"I was out working on the chief's place." Clay took a seat next to me. McBride, I knew, had purchased a fix-it-upper outside of town and was busy renovating. Clay's experience in construction made him a logical choice for doing most of the grunt work.

Caleb ran his fingers through his longish hair. "What's up? What's Momma doin' in a police station?"

Scooting over to make room, I patted the bench and motioned for him to sit. I explained the situation best I could, leaving out my suspicion that their mother was keeping a secret. Best not to give them even more cause for concern.

"We're not leaving here without her!" Clay declared when I finished my recitation.

Caleb nodded in agreement. "Even if it takes all night."

Reba Mae was right to feel proud of her sons. Identical twins, the boys were strapping six footers with chestnut hair, their daddy's hazel eyes, and athletic builds. They were fond of sports, beer, and girls and adored their mother. They lived at home while holding down jobs and attending a technical college part-time.

From time to time, Precious would glance our way, wag her head sympathetically, then return to her work. An hour crawled by, then two. *Field & Stream* lay open in my lap. I no longer pretended an interest I didn't feel in fly-fishing. Clay sat hunched forward, hands between his legs, his gaze fixed on the gray-speckled linoleum. Caleb rested his head against the wall, eyes closed. From his casual pose, one might think he was sleeping, but I wasn't fooled. His young body so close to mine was tense as a drum.

After what seemed an interminable amount of time, I heard a door open and the sound of voices. This was the cue needed for Caleb, Clay, and me to surge to our feet. Even Precious quit tapping away on her keyboard. At last Reba Mae, followed by CJ, emerged from the hallway. CJ whipped a monogrammed handkerchief from his blazer and offered it to her. Reba Mae accepted it, wiped her eyes, and blew her nose. I was relieved not to see any wrist jewelry in the form of handcuffs.

"Momma, what's goin' on?" Clay asked.

"You okay, Momma?" Caleb said almost simultaneously.

"Your momma's fine — for the time bein'," CJ answered, "but I'd advise her not to speak with that sumbitch without her attorney present. Her attorney bein' me." He thumped his chest for emphasis.

Aware that Reba Mae and my ex were more often sparring partners than allies, I raised a brow. "You sure on that score, Reba Mae? If you'd rather, we can find you a real lawyer." I shot CJ an apologetic glance. "Nothing personal, CJ, but you're out of your element in a homicide case."

Reba Mae paled at the word "homicide" but smiled bravely. "I'm fine with CJ lookin' out for me. This is bound to blow over 'cause I did nothin' wrong."

"Make that almost *nothin'*, darlin'," CJ said, shepherding us out of the police department and toward our vehicles. "McBride's mighty unhappy about you lyin' to him about bein' home alone the night of the murder."

"Momma!" Clay exploded. "Why go and do a fool thing like that?"

Caleb tugged the collar of his jacket higher

around his ears. "Cripes, Momma, you drilled 'always tell the truth' into us since we were knee-high."

"I know, I know. It was a dumb thing to do," Reba Mae cried, "but I got scared! I knew how bad it would look after that dumb remark I made about wantin' my hands around Sandy's throat till she squawked like a chicken."

Caleb and Clay groaned in unison.

"How did McBride discover you weren't home alone?" I asked Reba Mae as CJ jumped into his Lexus and prepared to make his escape.

"Blame it on that blasted hotline," she grumbled.

CJ switched on the ignition. "An anonymous tipster. The caller swore they saw Reba Mae walkin' near the opera house on the night of the murder."

"An anonymous tip . . . ?" I echoed.

Sniffling, Reba Mae started toward Clay's pickup. "Someone has it in for me. I looked around real good when I left the opera house but didn't see a single soul."

This time it was my turn to groan.

CHAPTER 16

Word about Reba Mae's session with Mc-Bride spread through the town like a California wildfire. Though we hadn't talked since leaving the police station the night before, I vowed first chance I had I'd rake her over the coals for not telling me the whole truth and nothing but the truth. In the meantime, however, I had a business to run.

News had also spread about my petition. Today I'd gotten up even earlier than yesterday and baked a double batch of Melly's famous gingersnaps. Spice It Up! was redolent with the wonderful scents of ginger, cloves, cinnamon, and cardamom. I'd added some crystallized ginger, sometimes called candied ginger, for an extra zing. I'd even swiped a small piece to nibble.

I was pleased to see the petition filling up. I'd no sooner finished slipping another sheet on the clipboard for additional signatures when Doug strolled into Spice It Up! Seeing him never failed to bring an automatic smile to my face. But my smile quickly faded, pushed aside by the memory of our last encounter. "Hey there," I said as I came out from behind the counter to greet him. He looked very put-together in a casual sort of way in a heather green half-zip sweater and plaid shirt. "You're looking very *GQ* this morning."

"Hey yourself," he said.

"What brings you into town in the middle of the day?"

"I thought this was where the bake sale was being held." He scratched his head, pretending to look perplexed. "I could've sworn I smelled gingersnaps all the way from the clinic."

"Guilty as charged. I've resorted to using baked goods as bribery to lure people into the shop." I indicated the clipboard next to the cash register. "Care to add your name?"

"So this is the petition everyone's talking about?" He quickly scanned the text, then signed.

"I'm keeping my fingers crossed it will have the desired effective on McBride," I said. "When he put the idea for a women's self-defense course on the back burner, I decided to take matters into my own hands.

The women are scared. They don't want to wait to get the ball rolling."

Doug raised a brow. "Does McBride know about your petition?"

I avoided his question by rearranging spices on a nearby shelf. "Most of my customers aren't familiar with mace or mahlab, but I'm encouraging a few of the more adventurous cooks to give them a try. How about taking a jar home with you?"

"I'm wise to your change-the-subject tactic whenever you want to avoid a particular topic — and no, I've never heard of mahlab," he confessed. "What is it?"

I showed him the label. "It's made from the pits of tart black cherries that are ground into flour. The flavor has a hint of almond, which makes sense since cherries and almonds are kissin' kin, as they say here in the South."

"Sold," he said. "You know me; I'm fearless in the kitchen."

"I wish all my sales were that easy." I took the mahlab to the register. "You still haven't told me why you're in town."

He handed me his credit card and waited patiently for me to run it though the machine. "I needed a couple items from Gray's Hardware. While I was there, Mavis mentioned she has a potential buyer for the store."

"Mavis must be overjoyed at the prospect. Rumor has it she wants to move to Florida to be closer to her sister." I returned Doug's Visa.

Doug took off his eyeglasses and polished the lenses on the sleeve of his sweater. "I'm taking Madison away for the weekend. I think a change of scenery might be just what the doctor ordered."

"Sounds nice." I carefully placed the jar of mahlab into a bag. "Where are you thinking of taking her?"

"Atlanta. I'll close up the clinic at noon tomorrow; then we'll drive over. *Jersey Boys* is playing at the Fox. I managed to locate tickets."

I cringed to think what Doug must have paid a scalper for tickets. He'd talked once about taking me to see *Jersey Boys* when it returned for a limited engagement. Guess my turn would have to wait. *Don't even go there, Piper,* I warned. *This is no time for a pity party with you as guest of honor.* The play probably wasn't as good as everyone claimed anyway, I rationalized. What was so great about a show featuring a rock band popular in the sixties and seventies? As a last resort, I could always rent the movie version from Netflix. I forced a smile and said, "I'm sure Madison will love it."

He inspected his eyeglasses for any stray smudges. "I thought we'd spend the night, next day do some retail therapy at Lenox Square, then have dinner in Buckhead before heading back."

"Sounds like a perfect weekend getaway. You might even be able to get an early start on your Christmas shopping."

He slid his glasses back on. "While at the mall, I'd like to visit one of those jewelry stores that sell those charms all you women are so crazy about."

"Pandora?"

"Yes, I think that's the name of the place. Madison lost one of those dangly things from a charm her grandmother had given her. A little gold key attached to a silver heart. She thinks she might've snagged it on a set at the opera house during the last rehearsal."

"If so, maybe Ned Feeney found it while cleaning his first day as custodian. I'll ask the next time I run into him."

"Thanks, I'd appreciate that."

A wave, a smile, and he was gone, leaving me feeling out of sorts. A friendship that had once seemed so effortless now felt strained and awkward. Maybe when Sandy's killer was found things would revert to the way they were. Maybe . . .

Since I was experiencing a temporary lull in business, I decided to phone Reba Mae. She never needed much persuasion to meet after work for dinner and margaritas. This time was no exception. We agreed to meet later at North of the Border. I'd no sooner disconnected when Ned ambled in.

"Hiya, Miz Piper." He thumbed up the bill of his ball cap. "Mr. Strickland over at the Eternal Rest is missin' some of his fold-in' chairs. I was in a dither after findin' poor Miz Granger that day. Wondered if I might've left a couple here by mistake?"

"No, I would've seen them." I held out the plate of cookies, and he took two. "Did you check at the police department? They borrowed chairs when they set up a command center."

"Thought I'd check with you first." He bit into a cookie. "Don't tell no one, but Miz Kunkel scares me. Always looks like she's about to bite my head off."

"Ned, when you cleaned at the opera house did you happen to find a tiny gold key that might have come off a charm bracelet?"

"Well, let me think," he said, tugging an earlobe. "Matter of fact, I did find an itty-

193

bitty key. Nearly forgot about it. Picked it off the floor backstage near some plywood."

"It sounds as though it might be the one Madison Winters lost." I offered him another cookie to help jog his memory. "Remember what you did with it?"

"Put it in the lost and found box in the front office. That's what Miz Granger told me to do when she hired me."

"Good thinking, Ned. Madison will rest easier knowing it's in a safe place."

"Can't be no safer place than the opera house what with yellow crime-scene tape strung around it like lights on a Christmas tree. Wonder if Chief ever replaced the lock on the back door. It's older'n Methuselah. Jiggle it just right, the door pops open. See ya," he said, snatching the lone cookie on his way out.

"See ya," I echoed. I wondered how long McBride planned to keep the opera house off-limits. The crime-scene techs from the Georgia Bureau of Investigation had long since come and gone. The building ought to be released soon. Pity Mayor Hemmings had suspended theatrical productions until further notice.

I dialed Pets 'R People to tell Madison her charm was safe, but the call went to voice mail. Rather than leave a message, I'd try to reach her later with the news. Next I refilled the plate with cookies and brewed a fresh pot of coffee. Throughout the remainder of the afternoon, women streamed in and out. I was quite pleased at the dozens of names I'd accumulated thus far. Tomorrow, being Saturday, would probably be the busiest day of the week. By day's end, I should have enough signatures to impress a reluctant McBride. Should he prove obstinate, I was prepared to present copies of the petition to Mayor Hemmings and the town council.

It was close to closing time and the shop empty of customers when I belatedly remembered a purchase I'd made last weekend. I'd driven out into the country and stopped at a farm stand where I bought an assortment of gourds and small pumpkins along with some homemade jams and jellies. With everything that had happened since, I'd completely forgotten about them. But it still wasn't too late to set them out and lend Spice It Up! a more Thanksgiving atmosphere.

I was half-hidden behind a large cardboard box I'd taken down from a storeroom shelf when it was suddenly snatched from my arms. My eyes widened at the sight of an angry Wyatt McBride confronting me.

"Care to tell me about this petition of yours?" he growled.

"If you'll kindly set my gourds on the counter" — I summoned calm and casual in the face of fuming and furious — "you'll find the petition there, too. Feel free to read and sign."

Stalking to the counter, McBride dropped the box of gourds on it with a resounding thud. "I had to hear about the petition from the mayor's wife, Dottie. The woman went on and on about the number of signatures you've managed to collect. I thought she'd never leave my office."

I removed an odd-shaped green and yellow gourd from the box. "Last I checked, taking up a petition didn't require a permit."

McBride's frown darkened into a scowl. "Ms. Hemmings said you were bribing folks with coffee and cake. This some kind of marketing ploy?"

"You're starting to irritate me, McBride." I set a round, white-and-green gourd next to its sibling. "Don't come to me with your high-handed, Mr. Hotshot Chief of Police attitude, and try to bully me."

That seemed to take him aback, but he quickly regained lost ground. "I thought I made myself clear. I'm not opposed to organizing a course, but I've got my hands full right now."

I blew out a breath. "Look, McBride, I'm not asking for a liver transplant. All we need is an hour or two of your time."

"My day doesn't come with *extra* hours."

"It *can't* wait. The time is *now* — the need is *now.*" I gathered the remaining gourds in my arms to distribute among the shelves of spices. "Should another woman get attacked or assaulted in the meantime, it'll take far more of your precious time. And could even cost you your job."

One of the gourds dropped from my arms and, before I could catch it, rolled across the floor. I started after it, but McBride was quicker. He snatched it up, cradling it in one palm as though trying to gauge its weight. I watched his face but was unable to read the thoughts.

"Understand I only agree to this on one condition. To be effective, self-defense can't be a single class but a series of classes. Do you think you ladies are ready to make the commitment?"

"Ready as we'll ever be, McBride." I hoped I wasn't speaking only for myself.

"All right then, you win," he said at long last, carefully placing the runaway gourd on a shelf behind him. "Monday night. Seven o'clock. High-school gym. Spread the word."

He turned and left without another word, leaving me staring after him, surprised and confused by his about-face. As I placed the colorful gourds and small pumpkins in strategic locations around my shop, it occurred to me that Monday was the start of Thanksgiving week. McBride, the wily bastard, had scheduled it that way on purpose to call my bluff. He was counting on the fact that women would be too busy with holiday preparations to attend a self-defense class. He'd then be able to proclaim to the mayor — and anyone else who'd listen — that he'd made an effort to co-operate, but attendance was sparse.

But he was wrong. I'd wager my last jar of pumpkin pie spice against his shiny gold badge that we'd have a full house Monday night. Bring it on, McBride.

CHAPTER 17

Business at North of the Border was bustling, but then again, it was a Friday night. If a restaurant doesn't bustle on the weekend in a small town, it might as well post a GOING OUT OF BUSINESS sign in the window. I arrived late, and Reba Mae waved at me from a back booth. She'd evidently arrived early to get a head start on a frozen margarita. On the way to join my friend, I stopped to exchange a few words with Pete and Gerilee Barker. Not even the incentive of having a butcher for a husband and choice cuts of meat at her disposal could entice Gerilee to cook when she could have a sizzling platter of fajitas appear before her like magic.

I'd no sooner slid into a seat across from Reba Mae when Nacho, owner and our favorite waiter, appeared, menus in hand. "What will it be, senora?"

I pointed at the frosty margarita. "I'm having what she's having."

Reba Mae raised her glass in a toast. "I'm drinkin' a gallon of these things tonight," she said as Nacho scurried off. "I need a brain freeze."

The gaily colored sombreros hanging on the walls and peppy mariachi music coming over loudspeakers contrasted sharply with Reba Mae's glum expression. "Honey, if this is happy hour, you should ask for a refund."

"Wish I'd had one of these last night. Maybe it would've frozen my tongue so I wouldn't have blabbed to Wyatt. Should've listened to CJ and kept my big mouth shut."

"That's a little like locking the barn door after the cow ran off."

We fell into silence as Nacho returned. After delivering my margarita along with the requisite basket of tortilla chips and salsa, he promised to be back shortly and disappeared.

"Thanks, by the way, for givin' CJ a heads-up. Without him makin' objections every five seconds, things coulda been worse."

"CJ has aspirations of broadening his horizons." I dunked a chip into salsa and savored the taste of cilantro. "I think he envisions himself giving sound bites in front of TV cameras on the courthouse steps."

Ignoring the chips, Reba Mae took another swallow of margarita. "Think I should hire me one of those Perry Mason type lawyers?"

"Let's hope it doesn't come to that. If and when it does, maybe Melly's boyfriend, Cot, can make a recommendation. Cot presided from the bench for as long as I can remember. He'd know who's good — and who isn't."

Reba Mae's mouth tightened. "There goes my life savings. Right down the tubes."

"Don't put the cart before the horse." The instant the words came out I wanted them back. Where did these stupid clichés come from? I wasn't raised on a farm. I grew up in Detroit. The Motor City. Motown. Yet, I was talking about horses, cows, and barns. Sheesh!

I was grateful for the reprieve from my own idiocy by Nacho reappearing, order pad in hand. I ordered a beef burrito while Reba Mae requested a taco salad. When he left for the kitchen, I directed my attention to Reba Mae. "You drove home with your boys last night, so we didn't get a chance to talk. Care to tell me about what happened with McBride?"

Reba Mae stirred her slushy margarita with a straw. "Lizzie Borden would've gotten a warmer welcome."

"It couldn't have been all that bad," I said but didn't even convince myself. I'd sat across from him once in an interrogation room and knew he was relentless.

"The whole time we talked, I felt he was takin' my measure for the latest in prison attire." Reba Mae sampled a chip and salsa, then shoved the basket of chips aside and slouched in a corner of the booth. "All I wanted was one last chance to convince Sandy to let me play Truvy Jones. Surely she must've discovered Mary Lou can't memorize a dang grocery list. Knowin' Sandy was always last to leave after a rehearsal, I hung around until everyone left. I thought I could reason with her, coax her into giving me a second chance. Instead, she complained she was fed up with everyone and their brother beggin' for parts. She said she already had a friend lined up for the role."

"What did you do then?"

"Did the only thing I could —" She shrugged. "— thanked her for her time and walked home."

"How did Sandy seem when you left her?"

"Do you mean was she breathing or had she turned blue? Well, the answer is no! She was fine."

"Reba Mae, shame on you. You know that's not what I meant," I scolded. "Was Sandy acting strangely, like she was nervous — or maybe scared?"

"No, none of the above. You're beginnin' to sound like McBride. He asked me those same questions."

"Nice to know he and I have something in common," I said drily. I traced the condensate on my margarita glass with a fingernail. "Reba Mae, do you realize you were probably the last person — except for the killer — to see Sandy alive? The killer could easily have been hiding in the shadows, biding their time, waiting for just the right moment to make his, or her, move."

Reba Mae sat up straighter, hugging her arms around her waist, and shivered. "That gives me the willies."

I leaned closer. "The killer might very well be the person who called in the anonymous tip. Can't think of a better way to get away with murder than point the finger in someone else's direction."

Our conversation ended when Nacho arrived with our orders. I didn't waste time digging into my burrito, but Reba Mae toyed with her taco salad, moving lettuce and tomatoes around like checkers on a board. Abruptly she stopped pretending to eat and aimed her fork at a spot over my left shoulder. "Don't turn around," she cautioned as my neck started to swivel in that direction.

"How am I supposed to see what you're pointing at if I don't look?"

"It's the devil himself. And he's not alone."

"McBride?" I speared another piece of burrito. "So what if he's not alone? What's the big deal?"

"He's with a woman," Reba Mae whispered. "Looks like he's on a date."

"So," I said, trying to sound casual, "who's he with?" It shouldn't come as a surprise that McBride dated. He had every right to see whomever he wanted, whenever he wanted, and how often he wanted. It was no concern of mine.

"You'll never guess in a million years," she smirked.

"Take pity on me. I don't have a million years."

"Shirley Randolph."

"Shirley . . . ?" Now I did turn. Fortunately for me, the couple was studying menus and didn't notice me gawking. McBride, I noted, had traded his starched navy blues for jeans and a black T-shirt and bomber jacket.

"Whoever heard of wearin' a short skirt and stilettos to dinner at a Mexican restaurant?" Reba Mae said, voicing her disapproval of Shirley's attire. "The exception bein' you've got your sights set on a certain man. I hate when women are obvious. Makes it look bad for the rest of us."

"They're both single." I took another bite of my burrito to demonstrate my disinterest. "No reason they shouldn't be seeing each other."

"Wyatt could have his pick of any woman in town, but far as I know, he hasn't dated since movin' here — and not because he lacks opportunity."

"McBride's personal life is none of my business." No longer hungry, I abandoned the burrito in favor of my margarita.

"Vicki was in hot pursuit of McBride after her marriage went kaput and Kenny rode off on a Harley. McBride, bein' smarter than the average bear, didn't take the bait. If you believe Vicki's version, a chief of police in a small town doesn't earn enough to keep her in the lifestyle to which she's grown accustomed. She's on the prowl for a man with a hefty portfolio — and one who isn't afraid of lavishin' some of that portfolio on her."

"Hey, you two." Reba Mae and I looked

up to find Gerilee, a sturdy, no-nonsense type who kept her permed hair a ruthless shade of brown, standing next to our booth. "Here, hon, I want you to have this," she said, handing Reba Mae a crumpled paper napkin.

I craned my neck and saw a message scrawled across it in black ink. "What is it?"

Gerilee darted a glance toward the register and seemed satisfied that her husband, Pete, was still waiting in line to pay. "It's the name of the lawyer my nephew Jimmy, Betty's youngest, used when he got in trouble with the law." She pitched her voice low even though no one was within earshot. "He got Jimmy off with probation and didn't charge an arm and a leg like some of those fancier lawyers."

Reba Mae opened her mouth to speak. "I —"

"No thanks necessary. Glad to help." Gerilee turned and rejoined her husband.

Reba Mae stared at the wrinkled napkin in disbelief, then shook her head, making her earrings sway. "I feel so dang helpless. I don't know if I should laugh or cry."

"Neither." I twirled the stem of my empty margarita glass. "It's time we become proactive. Stop twiddling our thumbs."

"I could kick myself for gettin' into this

mess," Reba Mae wailed. "As if it wasn't bad enough to threaten Sandy — even though I didn't mean anythin' by it — I had to make matters worse by lyin' to McBride about bein' home alone."

Nacho dropped off our checks. Before Reba Mae had a chance to reach for hers I grabbed both. "My treat," I told her when she started to protest. "I've got an idea."

"Uh-oh," Reba Mae said, frowning. "I've seen that expression on your face before — and it usually spells trouble. What devious plan is whirlin' around that brain of yours? Out with it, honeybun."

Smiling, I crooked my finger and beckoned her to follow me. "Come along, girlfriend, and you'll see for yourself."

There was no way to avoid McBride's table on our way out. He looked up as we passed. I acknowledged him and his date with a polite nod. He returned the nod, equally polite; Shirley smirked. For an instant I was tempted to wipe the smirk from her face but smiled instead and continued on my way.

Once our tab was paid and we were on the sidewalk, I looped my arm through Reba Mae's. "I think this is a good time for a field trip."

"Field trip?" Reba Mae dug in her heels.

"What sorta trip you talkin' about?"

I gave her arm a gentle tug. "I'm thinking it's a perfect night to tour Brandywine Creek's star attraction."

"The opera house?" Reba Mae stared at me in disbelief. "Now?"

"Seeing as Chief McBride is occupied by the Realtor of the Month, I can't think of a better time for a little backstage visit. I suggest walking, since my car stands out like a —"

"— gecko green VW?" Reba Mae completed my sentence. "I'm not sure this is a good idea. Isn't that place still off-limits?"

"Nothing ventured, nothing gained." I prodded Reba Mae to get her moving.

"What do you think we're gonna find that the crime-scene techs didn't?"

"We won't know until we find it, will we?"

I tugged my collar higher against the November chill. The night was cold and dark. Clouds scudded across the sky, often obscuring the moon. Elms and maples, bereft of their leaves, waved their skeletal branches as we hurried down the sidewalk.

"I want to go on record as sayin' this wasn't my idea. What if we get caught?"

"Don't be such a sissy! We're not going to get caught. In and out. Easy peasy."

"Okay, smarty-pants, but how do you

propose we get inside?" Reba Mae hitched the strap of her purse higher on her shoulder.

"Getting in should be a no-brainer. Ned mentioned the lock on the back door is ancient."

"Ned's right about the lock." Reba Mae cast a nervous glance back toward North of the Border. "All you have to do is give it a good jiggle and the door swings open. It's how I entered after rehearsal that night."

We reached the square and, seeing Main Street deserted, we cut a diagonal swath toward the opera house. A plastic bag, caught by a gust of wind, pinwheeled across the street and into a gutter. Crime-scene tape had come loose from its moorings in several places and flapped in the night breeze. The building stood before us, solid as a fortress and just as forbidding. I almost suffered a change of heart. Perhaps Reba Mae was right about this not being a good idea. But Reba Mae's freedom hung in the balance. There was too much at stake to turn back.

Hugging the shadows, we walked quickly along the side of the building and rounded the corner into a small parking lot with cracked concrete. A rusted light fixture with a low-wattage bulb hung over the door.

Reba Mae hovered so close her breath fanned my ear. "Do you suppose it's true what they say about murderers returnin' to the scene of the crime?" she asked.

"Well, let's hope if that's true they chose another night." I jiggled the handle and, like predicted, the door opened.

CHAPTER 18

The rear door of the opera house opened into a service area. I foraged through my purse and withdrew a small penlight I'd started carrying.

"There's a stairway on the right that leads to the main floor," Reba Mae whispered although there was no one around to hear. "If you go up the stairs, you can walk straight down the aisle through the auditorium. Beyond that is the lobby with the box office and manager's office. To the left of where we're standin', there's a shorter flight of steps that leads backstage."

"We'll check backstage before we leave." I found myself whispering, too. "At the moment, I'm more interested in the third-floor balcony where the body was found. What's the best way to get there?"

"There's an elevator off the lobby, but if you want my opinion, it's creepy. Might quit on us. Let's take the stairway."

We took the stairs on the right. At the top was a door marked EMERGENCY EXIT, which opened into the auditorium. I paused for a moment to get my bearings. The stage was behind me and rows of vacant seats in front. "Was Sandy in the balcony when you spoke to her?"

"Nuh-uh." Reba Mae pointed. "Over there, onstage, inspecting sets that still needed a coat of paint. The finished sets are supposed to resemble the inside of a beauty shop."

I started down a side aisle with Reba Mae nipping at my heels. The theater had a dusty, musty smell. I'd been in the opera house on occasion, but tonight the place had an alien, unwelcoming feel. The sooner we looked around and were out of here, the better I'd like it.

"Imagine! After firin' me, Sandy asked if she could borrow my salon chair. What did she expect my clients to sit on while I'm cuttin' and highlightin'? That woman had some nerve — not that I'm one to speak ill of the dead," she added hastily.

"I hope you told her no."

"Not exactly," Reba Mae hedged.

I shoved through a set of wide double doors and into a small lobby. The elevator and the stairs Reba Mae suggested we use to reach the balcony were to the left. "Translate 'not exactly.' "

"I might have said somethin' along the lines that if she'd rehire me I'd consider her request."

"You need to grow a backbone, Reba Mae. Need to say good-bye to Truvy Jones, move on with your life."

"Soon as I'm no longer a prime murder suspect, I plan to do just that."

The steps, swaybacked from decades of use, emitted soft groans as we crept upward. I felt rather than saw Reba Mae shudder. We passed the landing for the second-floor balcony and continued onward. The stairs terminated in a narrow hallway with a series of closed doors. The beam of my penlight swept over a wainscoted wall with framed photographs of celebrities taken in their heyday, then moved downward to follow a strip of carpeting, threadbare in spots, that marched down the center of the floor.

"Isn't that Fanny Brice?" Reba Mae asked, gesturing to a particular photo, her tone reverent. "I read an article about her once. Sandy told the cast that tourin' companies from New York used to stop here on their way to Atlanta."

"Hmm, could be. All I know about Fanny Brice was from a movie starring Barbra

Streisand." The last door was festooned with yellow tape. One end drooped to the floor where it had been trampled on. "X marks the spot," I quipped.

"You first." Reba Mae practically hugged my backside.

I approached cautiously. Fine, black dust — fingerprinting powder? — clung to the doorknob and surrounding area. Seeing this stifled any lingering qualms I might've had. Who killed Sandy and why? I wanted answers. And something here at the scene of the crime might possibly be a clue to that person's identity.

Not wishing to get fingerprinting powder all over my hands, I used a tissue as a barrier between the knob and my hand, then stepped inside. The beam of my penlight played over the interior of what resembled a private sitting room, more opera box than a balcony seat. Heavy red velvet draperies trimmed in gold braid were swagged on either side of the box. The furniture, comprised of a small Victorian-style table and four chairs, appeared to be genuine antiques. One chair, however, sat somewhat apart from the others. I assumed this was the chair, as tradition dictated, reserved for the resident ghost.

"Can we go now?" Reba Mae asked.

"In a minute," I replied absently. I examined the small space, hoping against hope to find a clue others had missed. I wished I could risk turning on an overhead light but didn't want to take the chance. Additional fingerprinting powder coated the chairs and railing. *Can fingerprints be taken from fabric, expensive silk scarves in particular?* I wondered. But what good are fingerprints unless they match ones already on file? Most people go through their entire lives never being fingerprinted.

I aimed the beam on the deep gouges on the wood floor that looked fresh. "What do you suppose Sandy was doing up here?"

"Darned if I know," Reba Mae said. "This part of the theater isn't used anymore, but it gives you a bird's-eye view of the stage."

Ka-chuk! Ka-chuk!

Startled, Reba Mae and I both jumped at the loud metallic noise that erupted from the bowels of the opera house. Reba Mae clutched my arm. "What was that? Think it's the ghost?"

"It's an old building," I replied as my pulse slowly settled into a normal rhythm. "Probably the furnace kicking on."

"R-right, right," she stammered. "Lots of folks reported hearin' strange sounds. Think

Sandy's ghost will come back to haunt this place?"

"I don't believe in ghosts."

"Me neither" — Reba Mae inched closer — "but you gotta admit roamin' around in the dark is kinda . . . spooky."

"We're done here," I said finally, disappointed by our lack of success.

Back on the main floor once again, I remembered Madison's charm. "Madison Winters lost a little gold key from her bracelet that night. Ned said he found one that matches the description and put it in the lost and found box in the office. Long as we're here, I thought we'd take a look."

"Can't we do it another time? Maybe in broad daylight?"

"It was a gift from her grandmother," I added for good measure, knowing Reba Mae's soft spot for her meemaw.

"Fine," she agreed reluctantly, "but let's make it snappy."

Apparently nothing of value was kept in the front office, so the door was unlocked. It opened with token resistance when I used my hip to give it an extra nudge. I breathed a sigh of relief when I spotted a shoe box labeled LOST AND FOUND on top of a file cabinet. Taking it down and placing it on the desk, I rummaged through the flotsam

216

and jetsam: sunglasses, lipsticks, mismatched gloves, ballpoint pens, two handkerchiefs, and, in the corner, a tiny gold key on a silver chain. "Got it!" I cried triumphantly, holding it up for Reba Mae to see.

"We done yet?" Reba Mae asked plaintively.

"Honestly, you remind me of how the kids used to sound when we drove to Michigan to visit my parents. By the time we reached the Ohio state line, I was close to losing my sanity. Let's check one more thing and then we're out of here. I'd like to see what a stage looks like from up close and personal."

Reba Mae heaved a sigh worthy of a martyr about to be burned at the stake. "All right, but it's nothin' special. I could draw you a picture."

The stage was accessed by three shallow steps on either side. The stage itself was much larger than I envisioned. Most of it, however, was taken up with sheets of plywood, partially painted, partially sketched, stacked along a far wall. Tools and buckets of paint were scattered here and there. A half-dozen plastic storage bins were heaped with props such as pink sponge rollers, curling irons, hairbrushes, capes, smocks, and cans of hair spray. I'd turned to leave when an item on the floor, half-hidden behind a vintage hair dryer, caught my eye. A script lay splayed open. I stooped to pick it up and noted that on page after page certain lines were highlighted in pink, others in yellow. Two separate roles? Truvy and Annelle? Someone had to be a glutton for punishment for all that memorization.

"Someone must have forgotten her script," Reba Mae said, peering over my shoulder. "Okay, you've had your look at a stage; now let's get out of here."

Bang!

Reba Mae let out a strangled scream. I felt her fingernails bite through the sleeve of my jacket. "That was a gunshot if I ever heard one," she said. "Let's beat it."

I didn't need further persuasion. Snooping through the darkened opera house was proving to be a cardiovascular workout. My heart rate must have doubled. Reba Mae and I ran — not walked, but ran — to the nearest exit, which in this case happened to be the rear door through which we'd entered earlier. Upon reaching it, I immediately realized where the sound had emanated. The cause for alarm hadn't been a gunshot, but rather the door's locking mechanism had failed to catch. The door stood ajar waiting for the next strong gust of wind to send it slamming against its frame.

Upon seeing it, Reba Mae reached the same conclusion. "It didn't have me fooled for a second," she boasted. "I've been around hunters all my life. I can tell a gunshot from a slammed door any day of the week."

"Reba Mae Johnson," I said through gritted teeth, "one more fib like that and your nose is going to grow long."

I felt an instant's relief at stepping out of the building and into the crisp night air. A reprieve that was cut short by the sight of a familiar figure lounging against a Ford F-150 pickup.

"Opera house offering private ghost tours?" McBride drawled.

"We had a big dinner and needed to walk off some calories," Reba Mae ad-libbed, not caring about the length of her nose.

"Ah, a little nighttime stroll. That explains it." He pushed away from the truck and sauntered closer. "Don't tell me, let me guess, you ladies got all tuckered out from all the exercise and decided to take a shortcut through a crime scene?"

"Why are you loitering here in the dark, McBride?" I slipped my penlight into the pocket of my jacket, hoping he wouldn't notice. "Your date finish early?"

"It was business, not a date," he said with

a thin smile. "I didn't think you cared."

"I don't," I said, perhaps a shade too hastily. I hoped he couldn't see my telltale blush in the dark.

Legs braced, he hooked his thumbs in his belt loops. "I could bring you ladies in, charge you with breaking and entering."

"We entered, but we didn't break nothin'." Reba Mae ended her protest when I jabbed her ribs.

"How did you know where to find us, McBride?" The adage "the best defense is a good offense" popped into mind. "Don't try to tell me you were standing in a deserted parking lot late in November waiting for the ice-cream truck to come along."

"Security camera." He raised a hand and pointed to an object mounted on an overhang above the door. "I had one installed day after the murder. Precious saw you on the monitor. She worried you girls might get into mischief."

"I've had about all the *mischief* I can tolerate for one night," I said, "so unless you're going to press charges, we'll be on our way." I hooked my arm through Reba Mae's and urged her to get a move on before McBride made good his threat.

After only a couple steps Reba Mae stopped and turned. "Hey, Wyatt, the real reason for the security camera — true or not, do killers really return to the scene of the crime?"

He stood tall, a formidable figure, under the feeble light thrown by the low-watt bulb. "Don't believe everything you see on TV, Reba Mae; that usually only applies to serial killers."

Reba Mae opened her mouth to speak, but no sound came out. I drew her away, but not before I saw a smile flit across McBride's handsome face.

CHAPTER 19

Shortly before noon the next day, Vicki waltzed into Spice It Up! "What's the occasion?" I asked, eyeing the fashionable cherry red boiled-wool jacket and dark-washed jeans that clung to her long, shapely legs.

"I'm out of that fancy cinnamon you sell." Vicki flipped her low ponytail over her shoulder. "I've been slaving over a hot oven all week."

"You . . . baking?" I came out from around the counter and plucked a small jar of cinnamon from the Hoosier cabinet, then, on second thought, replaced the smaller jar with a larger one. "Are you having a party?"

"Parties — at least the type I'm accustomed to throwing — are expensive. Kenny is being a regular Scrooge in our divorce negotiations. If I don't watch my budget, heaven forbid, I'll have to find a job." She shuddered at the prospect.

"That's terrible," I said with mock sincerity. I doubted the woman had ever worked a day in her life. "I've been told that the chamber of commerce has a position open."

Vicki arched a brow. "Maybelle Humphries' old job?"

"Maybelle Mahoney now," I said, returning to the counter. "She and Tex were married recently in Las Vegas."

"Ah, yes. Tex Mahoney, champion pitmaster. Who knew despite the plain-Jane exterior our Maybelle would snag her Prince Charming — and a wealthy one at that." Settling her large handbag on the counter, Vicki riffled through the contents.

I waited patiently for her to produce a credit card. "So, if you're not having a party, why all the baking?"

"I've been bringing goodies over to Craig. Poor man. Even a grieving widower has to eat. I keep reminding him of the importance of keeping up his strength during trying times. I'm certain Sandy, bless her heart, will rest easier knowing her man is well fed. After all, what are friends for?" She finally located and surrendered her Visa.

Yes, what are friends for, I wondered silently, *if not to ply bereaved spouses with baked goods — especially if that spouse happens to be attractive and wealthy?*

"I made Craig bread pudding yesterday,"

Vicki said. "I remembered Sandy saying that was his favorite dessert. Today I'm bringing him an apple pie and blueberry-nut bread."

"I'm sure he appreciates your efforts." I ran her credit card through my machine and returned it to her.

"Craig has a lot of friends — important, influential people — who stop by with condolences. I even met a state senator, but" — she giggled — "I neglected to tell him I voted for his opponent."

For someone who had just suffered the loss of a close friend, Vicki seemed unusually cheerful and upbeat. Strange, she appeared more focused on the widower's well-being than Sandy's demise. Was it possible Vicki had her sights set on becoming the next Mrs. Craig Granger? And what lengths would she go to in order to make that a reality?

"Is there going to be a funeral?" I asked while waiting for the receipt to print.

"I haven't asked." She put on a sad face. "No sense bringing up painful subjects. Craig needs to get on with his life. I suggested a round of golf might be good therapy. Tennis was another option. I even offered to be his partner in mixed doubles. Exercise is a form of grief therapy, you know."

"Really?" I said, hoping my skepticism didn't show.

"I might've heard that on *Dr. Phil.* I watch his show faithfully every day."

I bagged the cinnamon and handed it to her. "If exercise is grief therapy, maybe Craig should sign up for a half marathon."

"I'll be sure to mention that." She turned to leave, then hesitated. "Oh, I almost forgot, Bunny said to sign your petition."

I slid the clipboard with the petition across the counter. "Here you go."

"Monday!" she exclaimed at seeing the notation I'd penned across the top of the clipboard with the date, time, and place of the self-defense class. "Why do you suppose McBride scheduled it so close to Thanksgiving? Women will be trying to get a head start on preparations — things like cooking, cleaning, and manicures."

"Manicures?" My gaze flew to my short, unadorned nails. Call me crazy, but having my nails freshly manicured was never top priority when it came to executing a holiday meal. "It's a wild guess on my part, but I think McBride planned it that way on purpose, hoping for a small turn-out. He can tell the mayor he responded to our request in a timely manner, but the women really weren't interested after all."

225

Vicki signed her name with a flourish. "Well, Thanksgiving week or not, I plan to attend. It might be the only chance I'll ever have to be up close and personal with Wyatt McBride. Lord knows, I've sent out enough signals, stopping short of being a hussy, to telegraph my interest, but the man ignored all my hints. You don't suppose . . . ?"

"Don't suppose what?" Her insinuation struck me as so ludicrous that I burst out laughing. "Vicki, just because a man doesn't flirt with you doesn't mean you should question his sexuality. In all likelihood, it's simply a lack of chemistry. Or he's busy tending to law and order."

"I suppose," she said, "but I've been flirting since middle school and have perfected it into an art form. If there's any blood flowing in a man's veins, I usually get a response."

"Well, in McBride's case I think you need to find a different target."

"Perhaps." She lifted one shoulder in a casual shrug. "Shirley Randolph mentioned McBride's been coming into Creekside Realty to visit. I may be a master flirt, but Shirley's a close second. Who knows, maybe she and McBride will become an item — provided the mayor and council don't release him from his contract. See you Monday."

After Vicki left, I replayed our conversation. I'm not sure which tidbit I found more upsetting — Shirley and McBride becoming a twosome or the thought of McBride losing his job. I mentally put the brakes on thoughts racing through my brain like a runaway freight train. McBride was a free agent. Who he saw — and what happened with his job — was absolutely no concern of mine. I'd reacted because Shirley and Wyatt seemed totally unsuited for each other. McBride struck me as a chips, dip, and a beer sort of guy, while Shirley favored caviar and champagne. It was hard to overcome such vast differences. One or the other would realize this eventually and was bound to get hurt. As for McBride's position as chief of police, Brandywine Creek benefited from his experience as a Miami-Dade detective. He'd be hard to replace.

"Hello, dear," Melly sang out as she entered. She was accompanied by Cottrell "Cot" Herman. By no means handsome, with craggy, irregular features, the retired judge exuded an air of authority. Dark, deep-set eyes peered out from beneath shaggy brows.

I smoothed my curls into submission as I

went to greet them. "Hello, Melly. Judge."

Melly glanced around the shop and frowned. "No customers? Shouldn't that worry you?"

"Of course it worries me, Melly," I replied. "Especially since I ordered extra stock in anticipation of *Steel Magnolias* bringing in busloads of tourists. When it came to marketing and promotion, Sandy is . . . was . . . gifted."

"That she was," Cot agreed, his voice sonorous, his tone solemn. "Only the other night over cocktails, the mayor described Sandy as Brandywine Creek's ambassador at large."

Melly nodded. "Harvey praised Sandy for her 'off the beaten path' strategy. She even garnered the play a blurb in *Southern Living.*"

"The mayor is determined to bring whoever's responsible for this heinous crime to justice." Cot brushed a shock of iron gray hair off his forehead only to have it fall back seconds later.

"I only hope an innocent party isn't caught up in the rush to justice," I said.

"Reba Mae, bless her heart, is right in the middle of all the controversy." Melly fingered the strand of pearls around her neck. "Harvey mentioned that Chief McBride brought her in for questioning."

"Melly, you know Reba Mae nearly as well as I do. Surely you don't think she had anything to do with Sandy's death."

Melly didn't meet my eyes. "Of course not, dear, but you have to admit it doesn't look good."

"Melly's right, you know; it doesn't look good for your friend." Cot rubbed his chin. "Rest assured, Chief McBride will conduct a thorough investigation. He'll want an airtight case before making an arrest."

Arrest? I felt my heart drop to my knees. I drew in a shaky breath to steady myself. Once my heart was lodged in my chest where the good Lord intended, my resolve to help prove Reba Mae's innocence hardened even more. Most of the cast of *Steel Magnolias* had an issue of one sort or another with Sandy. All I had to do was discover which one had reached their boiling point. Easy, right?

Melly twisted her strand of pearls around her index finger. I studied her quizzically. "Melly," I ventured at last, "is anything wrong?"

"No, no, I'm fine. Absolutely fine," she replied, perhaps a shade too quickly. "Why do you ask?"

"Because whenever you're nervous or

upset you have a habit of playing with your pearls. Over the years, I've come to regard them as worry beads."

Cot gave Melly an affectionate smile. "I've noticed the same telltale trait, my dear."

I folded my arms across my chest and looked Melly in the eye. "All right," I said, assuming my best no-nonsense tone. "No more beating about the bush. Tell me what's bothering you." Melly cast an uncertain glance at Cot, who, in exchange, nodded his head in encouragement. "I've been tempted to call the hotline myself," she confided.

I blinked in surprise. "Whatever for? Did you see or hear anything suspicious?"

"No, a little odd is all." Melly ceased torturing her pearls and patted them into place. "On the night of the murder, bridge at Mavis Gray's ended late. As Cot drove me home, we noticed Wanda Needmore turning down Main Street. I thought it strange for her to be out and about at that hour when she had to be at work bright and early the next day. Wanda always opens CJ's law office. And one other thing struck me as unusual."

"Melly!" I snapped. My lack of patience earned me a disapproving scowl from Cot. With an effort, I tempered my tone. "Other than the late hour, what else did you think out of the ordinary?"

Melly's brows drew together in concentration. "Wanda, as you know, is always neat as a pin, every hair in place. Well, she looked . . . disheveled."

"Hmm, interesting." That was unusual and not like the prim and proper Wanda Needmore I'd known for years.

"There's something else you might not be aware of," Cot interjected. "Wanda filed a complaint against Sandy on the day of the murder alleging breach of contract. Only reason I'm telling you this is because it's a matter of public record."

"Sandy, I've been told, threatened a countersuit," Melly said. "Wanda prided herself on never being a defendant in a lawsuit. She must have been livid."

"Do you know what the breach of contract stemmed from?"

"Not all the details, but it had something to do with a property dispute," Cot explained. "Wanda wanted to purchase a tract of land that Sandy owned on which to build a retirement home. She thought it was a done deal, but Sandy apparently reneged when she got a more lucrative offer."

Melly placed her hand in the crook of Cot's arm. "Anyway, dear, that's not what brought Cot and me here this afternoon."

Cot placed his larger hand over Melly's. "I've asked Melly to accompany me on a European river cruise — and she accepted."

My jaw dropped — literally dropped — at hearing this. "B-but what will people think?" I stammered.

"Don't get any fool notions in your head, young lady," Cot warned. "We'll have separate staterooms."

My eyes darted from one face to the other and found them smiling and happy. Did people their age still have sex? *Of course they do,* I answered my own question. *They're not dead.* "That's wonderful," I managed.

"It's called a Christmas Market Cruise." Melly beamed. "Twelve days on the Danube from Budapest to Prague. It's something I've always wanted to do, and when Cot broached the subject I couldn't agree quickly enough."

"Have you told CJ?"

Melly's smile dimmed. "That's our next stop. We wanted to use you as our sounding board, see how the idea went over."

"Sort of take it on the road before opening on Broadway," Cot said, patting Melly's hand.

"Isn't it exciting?" Melly asked, her cheeks

flushed with pleasure. Not waiting for an answer she continued, "Cot and I are spending Thanksgiving at his daughter's home in Buckhead. He wants me to meet his family."

I smiled as I gave her a hug. "I'm sure they'll approve of their father's . . . friend."

Minutes later, I watched the couple leave, arm in arm. I didn't remember ever seeing Melly so happy she was almost giddy.

The two lovebirds, however, had given me more to think about than romance in the golden years. The information about a lawsuit involving Wanda and Sandy had been a revelation. That would explain the argument Madison mentioned. Furthermore, Wanda had refused to tell me if she'd gone directly home after rehearsal the night of the murder. Instead, she'd told me to mind my own business. What was the paralegal trying to hide?

CHAPTER 20

Not long after Melly and Cot left to break the news of their impending river cruise to CJ, business turned brisk. Melly would have been pleased at the rate merchandise disappeared from the shelves. With Thanksgiving right around the corner, spices, not gift items, were by far the most popular items. Some of my customers preferred sage for their stuffing recipes; others insisted poultry seasoning, a blend of many spices including allspice, marjoram, and thyme, resulted in the most flavorful dressings. Two women waged a lively debate over which spices worked best in sweet potato pie. Both agreed cinnamon and vanilla were must-adds but differed on whether to use ginger or nutmeg.

While ringing up orders, I asked customers who hadn't done so already to sign my petition. Even though McBride had consented — albeit grudgingly — to holding a self-defense class, I wanted to impress upon him the number of women who believed in its importance. I reminded everyone to spread the word. Seven o'clock sharp in the high school gym.

The two sweet potato pie aficionados had no sooner departed, each convinced her recipe was by far superior, when Gerilee approached the register looking uncharacteristically uncertain. "What's wrong, Gerilee? Anything I can help you with?"

She took a small jar from her basket and glared at the price sticker. "What you're asking for one half gram of saffron is highway robbery. I've half a mind to report you to the Better Business Bureau."

I handed her my cell phone. "Report away."

Ignoring my offer, Gerilee transferred her glare from the price tag to me. "I've been trying to convince myself for the last five minutes that ordinary white rice will taste perfectly fine with the curried chicken I'm fixing for company, but . . ."

"But saffron rice will taste even better," I said with a knowing smile.

"Let's just say Christmas came early." Gerilee plunked the saffron on the counter with finality. "For the life of me, I can't understand why this stuff is so dang expensive."

"Harvesting is labor-intensive," I explained as Gerilee placed jars of both hot and sweet curry powders next to the saffron. "The violet saffron crocus or roses, as they're called, are picked at dawn. Workers remove three red stigmas from each one, where they're toasted over a low fire. An acre of land yields only five to seven pounds of the finished product. Therefore, the expense."

Nodding, Gerilee grumpily accepted my explanation. "I thought I'd experiment and fix Doug's chicken curry recipe for Pete's dinner tonight."

"You'll have to let me know how it turns out," I said as I made change from the cash she handed me. "Saffron is also great in paella and risotto. By the way, do you plan on coming to McBride's class on Monday?" I asked as she turned to leave.

"Wouldn't miss it."

"Be sure to wear comfortable clothes," I called after her.

Mary Lou Lambert passed Gerilee on her way in. "Comfortable clothes for what?"

The woman didn't frequent Spice It Up!, so I was surprised at seeing her. Mary Lou possessed a pretty face, a plump figure, and

236

brassy yellow hair. Her pale blue eyes blinked open and shut like a china doll I'd once found under the Christmas tree. "Hey, Mary Lou," I said. "How can I help you?"

"Someone, I forget who, told me I should stop in and sign your petition."

"It's right here." I slid the clipboard toward her. "Even though Chief McBride has already agreed to hold the class, I'm still collecting names."

She picked up a pen and hastily added her signature. "The same person who told me about the petition also told me where and when, but I've been so discombobulated lately I can't remember which end is up."

"Monday at seven. The high-school gym."

"This Monday?" Her eyes opened and closed as she processed the information. "That close to Thanksgiving? What if no one comes?"

"I'm optimistic we'll have a good turn-out." But I'd heard this question voiced so often that I was beginning to have doubts. What if I was wrong? What if no one came? I'd not only look foolish; I'd feel foolish. And McBride would have the last laugh. I could almost hear his I-told-you-so ringing in my ears.

"What kind of comfortable clothing?" Mary Lou wanted to know. "Will sweatpants work? My jeans are getting a little tight. I think I accidentally washed them in hot water."

"Sweatpants will be fine."

Reaching inside a squishy leather bag, she produced a shiny pink gizmo. "Look what Bunny bought me. It also came in green and purple, but pink's my favorite color."

I leaned forward for a closer look. "What is it?"

"Pepper spray," she said, dropping it back into her purse. "And it works really well, too."

I studied her quizzically. "How do you know? Have you tried it?"

"Well." She giggled. "Not on purpose. I accidentally pushed a little doohickey by mistake and some squirted out. Good thing my poodle wasn't any nearer. As it was, Fifi's poor little eyes watered all day."

"Hearing about Sandy must have come as a shock," I said, making a clumsy stab at interrogation.

Mary Lou's head bobbed up and down. "I haven't slept a wink since it happened. Not a single wink. I even had to buy concealer to cover the dark circles under my eyes. Who knows who might be next? My husband's keeping a loaded shotgun by our bed."

Pepper spray *and* a loaded shotgun? But I couldn't fault Mary Lou and her husband for being nervous. In a town where people seldom locked their doors, its citizens no longer felt safe. "Are you disappointed *Steel Magnolias* has been canceled?" I asked in an attempt to steer the conversation away from weapons.

"No!" she declared. "I'm glad it's been canceled!"

"What do you mean? I thought Truvy Jones was a plum role."

Tears welled in her big blue eyes. "I overheard Sandy talking to someone on the phone when she didn't think I was around. She was planning to replace me with a friend of hers with acting experience. Sandy told her she'd be perfect. To name her price."

"I'm sorry. That must have been upsetting." I reached for a box of Kleenex near the register and offered Mary Lou a tissue.

"Upset?" She dabbed at tears that threatened to spill down her cheeks. "I wasn't upset — I was angry. So angry I had steam coming out of my ears. I knew I shouldn't keep on listening to Sandy talk, but I couldn't help myself. Do you know what she said next?"

"No," I said, shaking my head. "What did

she say?"

"She told whomever she was talking to that I was the inspiration for every blond joke ever told. I got so mad, I started crying." She dabbed and sniffled. "I really, really tried, Piper. Truvy Jones has lines on every single page. It's not my fault I couldn't remember the exact words and the cast kept missing their cues."

"Of course it wasn't your fault. The cast needed to step up." I cringed at listening to myself being an enabler.

"That's the same thing I said to my husband," Mary Lou said, reaching for another tissue.

The woman had readily admitted to being furious with Sandy. Had Mary Lou been so enraged that she'd grabbed the scarf around Sandy's neck and pulled tight? And what's more, did Mary Lou have an alibi for the time in question?

"I'll bet you went straight home after rehearsal and told your husband that Sandy was being mean to you," I said, then held my breath waiting for her to confirm or deny.

"You bet I did." She tossed her soggy tissues into the wastebasket. "But first I thought I'd better calm down. Hank has a short fuse and doesn't like seeing me upset.

See you Tuesday night," she said as she left.

"Monday, not Tuesday," I corrected but wasn't sure she heard me — or would remember if she did. Just because Mary Lou was a ditz didn't mean she wasn't capable of murder. Being a criminal didn't require membership in Mensa. Her alibi required further investigation before I crossed her name off my persons of interest list.

"What's happenin' on Monday?" Amber Leigh Ames, a statuesque brunette, remarked as she sauntered in.

Amber's chief claim to fame was being a former runner-up in the Miss Georgia pageant. Her second-greatest achievement was snagging a man, who at the time happened to be my husband. CJ claimed he needed his "space" — a space filled by Amber and her medically enhanced assets. "Are you here to sign my petition?"

Amber flipped a glossy mahogany tress over her shoulder and gave me a saccharine smile. "CJ told me all about your little project. He thinks it's a hoot, knowin' you're buttin' heads with his old nemesis, Wyatt McBride."

"Well, as long as you're here, why not add your name?" I offered her a pen.

"Whatever," she said, "long as I'm not required to attend. I don't engage in activities that require me to break a sweat — or ruin a manicure. A former beauty queen has a certain image to maintain." She signed the petition, her signature so large it took up two lines.

Since business had slowed to a trickle, I took a feather duster and started to make the rounds of the freestanding shelves. "I know you don't cook, and if the petition didn't bring you, why are you here?"

"Truth be told, Piper, I'm here on Lindsey's behalf," she said as she watched me dust.

I stopped what I was doing to stare at her. "Lindsey?"

Amber put on a sad face, an expression she no doubt practiced — and perfected — in front of her bathroom mirror. "Understand, I'm doin' this as a favor. That sweet girl doesn't want to hurt your feelin's, so I offered to explain the situation for her."

I gritted my teeth. "What 'situation' are you referring to?"

"Thanksgivin' is next week. Someone needs to have the gumption to speak up and that someone might as well be me. Lindsey would prefer to have Thanksgivin' dinner at the country club with CJ and me. We'd told her our invitation included her boyfriend, Sean Rogers, and his father."

First Chad, now Lindsey? "I see . . . ," I managed, but speech was difficult with the wind knocked out of my sails. With an effort, I resumed dusting, my actions more mechanical than purposeful.

Amber trailed after me. "We invited Lindsey ages ago, but she's been procrastinatin', especially since Chad's no longer comin' home. The club called today, however, and needs a head count. The manager asked how many in our party, so I need to give him an answer."

"By all means," I said, swallowing the lump in my throat. "If Lindsey wants to join you and CJ for dinner at the club, she has my blessing."

"Great." Amber beamed the toothy smile that had won her a satin sash and rhinestone tiara. "I thought you'd see it in the right light. It would be mighty lonely here with only the two of you." She waggled her fingers. "Bye-bye."

It's going to be mighty lonely for me, too, I thought grimly, abandoning my housekeeping chores. A tear rolled down my cheek, and I impatiently brushed it away. This would mark the first time since my marriage to CJ years ago that I'd have no one to cook for on Thanksgiving. But it wasn't the end of the world. I'd deal with it —

somehow — when the day came.

The best medicine I knew of to fight depression was to keep busy. I needed to focus all my attention on finding a killer. The list of suspects was long, with many names still to be eliminated. Mary Lou had intimated she'd gone home to her husband with her complaints.

But her slight hesitation before answering puzzled me.

I didn't know how to go about proving or disproving Mary Lou's alibi, so, for the time being, I decided to concentrate on an easier target. Marcy Boyd, the young mother of twins, was another person of interest. Marcy might prove simpler to rule out since she had no obvious motive for wanting Sandy dead. And with two babies, I assumed she'd be in a hurry to return home as soon as rehearsal ended. However, since I was working under the theory Sandy had antagonized the entire cast — and for the sake of thoroughness — Marcy needed to be excluded as a possible suspect.

The regulator clock on the wall announced closing time. But my day wasn't finished. There was still work to be done if I wanted to clear my BFF's name. I decided to pay Marcy a surprise visit in the near future.

CHAPTER 21

Before I set my plan into motion, I'd taken Casey for a walk. When I returned, I learned Lindsey and Sean were going to the movies with friends. I leaned against the doorjamb of her bedroom, arms folded, and watched her try on, then discard, one sweater after another while Casey lounged contentedly at the foot of her bed.

"What do you think? Is the pink too baby-ish?" she asked, holding the sweater up for my inspection.

"I always think you look pretty in pink." I half smiled, remembering Mary Lou's pepper spray gadget. "Some never outgrow their fondness for the color."

Her decision made, Lindsey slipped the sweater over her head and started to apply makeup. "About Thanksgiving, Mom, I'm really sorry. I didn't want to hurt your feelings especially after Chad bailed."

"I only wish you'd told me yourself rather

than have Amber drop the bomb."

"I know how much you love to fuss, but think how much easier it'll be this year not having to prepare a big dinner." She swept rosy brown eye shadow on her lids, then reached for the eyeliner.

"Preparing a special dinner for my family isn't work; it's a labor of love."

"Now you can spend the entire day in pajamas curled up on the couch, watching the Macy's Thanksgiving Day Parade without having to stuff a turkey. Instead of football games on TV, you can pig out on those old movies like *Miracle on 34th Street* you used to make Chad and me sit through."

"I thought you loved *Miracle on 34th Street.*"

"Mo-om," Lindsey wailed. "It's so ancient it was first made in black and white."

"It's a classic." I staunchly defended my longtime favorite.

"Sean was so . . . excited . . . when Dad invited not only him but his father to join us for Thanksgiving dinner at the club." Leaning toward the mirror, she swiped mascara on her lashes and replaced the wand in its silvery tube.

"Your father can be quite generous." *When it suits his purposes,* I thought. My ex-

246

husband could also be wily and manipulative. CJ had known exactly what he was doing by inviting Sean *and* his father.

"People around here consider Sean's dad an outsider," Lindsey said. She picked up a hairbrush and pulled it through her long blond hair. "This could be an awesome way for Mr. Rogers to make some business contacts, to network. Maybe get on a first-name basis with important people."

"Mmm," I murmured. Lindsey had a big heart. I didn't know whether I should be proud of my girl for wanting to help her boyfriend's father or furious with CJ. To paraphrase a quote from another of my favorite movies: He'd made an offer she couldn't refuse. I could cheerfully strangle him for his machinations. Then I brought myself up short. Should CJ turn up dead — especially choked to death — I'd be the number one suspect. Isn't it always the spouse? Or, in this instance, the ex-spouse?

Lindsey caught my expression and paused in the act of applying lip gloss. "If it really bothers you, Mom, I can call Dad and cancel."

Was I being a doormat? Should I put my foot down? Insist my daughter spend the holiday with me? It was speak now or forever hold my peace. I didn't want either

Chad or Lindsey to view me as a needy, demanding mother. No, I'd rather have them see me as an independent and loving parent who placed their desires ahead of her own. My decision made, I blew out a breath and said, "It's all right, Linds. Spend Thanksgiving this year with your father and Amber — but with one stipulation."

"Okay." Lindsey nodded warily.

"I don't want to hear that the cuisine at the country club is better than mine."

Laughing, she turned and gave me a hug. "Promise. No one makes a better sweet potato casserole than my mom."

"My pumpkin pie is world-class, too," I reminded, hugging her back.

"Absolutely the very best."

Our lovefest was interrupted by a knock on the back door, alerting us to Sean's arrival. Casey barked to notify us he'd heard it, too.

"I won't be late," she said as she grabbed a light jacket and hurried off.

"Have fun," I called after her.

Minutes later, a car door slammed. Next I heard Sean's Impala start, then fade as they rode off.

The apartment was engulfed in silence.

I switched the light off in Lindsey's bedroom and wandered into the living room with Casey trotting at my heels. Sinking down on the sofa, I picked up a foodzine and idly flipped through the glossy pages. But images of holiday treats and sumptuous party buffets failed to capture my interest. My mind was too busy scrambling for the best way to approach Marcy Boyd and ask about her alibi. Two heads were always better than one at solving problems of this magnitude, so I did what had become second nature. I reached for the phone and dialed my BFF.

"Hey, honeybun," she greeted me. "You caught me goin' out the door."

"What's up?" I sensed my plan for enticing her cooperation with pepperoni, mushrooms, and lots of gooey mozzarella evaporating. "Hot date tonight?"

"Don't I wish." She let out a theatrical sigh I could hear from blocks away. "When it comes to a 'hot' date, I'd settle for lukewarm."

"Is everything all right?"

"Right as rain," she replied with a cheerfulness that sounded phony. "I'm on my way over to Aunt Ida's. The poor thing is still recovering from hip surgery, so I told her I'd help make the mincemeat for pies. In exchange, she promised to confide her secret ingredient."

I absently petted Casey, who, after being deserted by Lindsey, had curled up on the sofa next to me. "Mincemeat, eh? Well, then, that explains why you bought a jar of crystallized ginger and a whole nutmeg."

"Aunt Ida swears neither of those is her secret weapon. Sorry, hon, but I have to run. I don't want Aunt Ida to think I'm not comin' and startin' without me. It would be just like her to overdo and get a setback."

After I hung up, I picked up the TV remote but set it down. I needed something more mentally stimulating than reruns. And what could be more stimulating than trying to solve a real-life murder mystery? Rising from the sofa, I went to the end table and brought out the persons of interest list Reba Mae and I had drafted what seemed a decade ago.

Time for a quick review. I plopped down on the sofa again and studied the names. Craig, Dorinda, and Madison all had rock-solid alibis for the time of the murder. Bunny Bowtin insisted she'd gone straight home, as did Mary Lou. In the latter's case, I'd detected a slight hesitation. I put checkmarks next to both Mary Lou and Bunny — checkmarks meaning further investigation was warranted. Wanda Needmore had been deliberately evasive when questioned, so I put a checkmark — and, for good measure, added a star by her name. Wanda definitely merited a more intensive scrutiny, especially in light of the litigious relationship between her and the vic, aka Sandy. The single cast member I hadn't contacted thus far was Marcy Boyd.

I sat in my much-too-quiet living room lost in thought. Marcy had been given the choice role of Annelle, a beauty shop assistant. She and I hadn't been on the best terms ever since I *suggested* that Danny, her then husband-to-be, might be responsible for the murder of a local chef a while back. It was time the young woman put it behind her. It wasn't healthy to harbor a grudge. I got up so suddenly that I jolted Casey from his nap.

The hands on my wristwatch indicated it was only seven thirty. The early hour afforded plenty of time for me to scratch another name off the list. Danny Boyd, on the one hand, managed the Pizza Palace and, as it was Saturday, the busiest night of the week, he'd probably be at work. Marcy, on the other hand, would be home alone tending to the couple's two-month-old twins. Tonight could prove an excellent opportunity to question Marcy about her whereabouts for the time Sandy was killed.

Up until now, I'd been negligent in cooing over the babies. My bad! No time like the present to correct the situation. As an apology of sorts, I neatly arranged leftover cookies on a plate and covered them with plastic wrap. Grabbing my purse along with the cookies, I headed out the door.

Though I'd never been there before, I'd heard from Gerilee that Danny and Marcy were renting a small bungalow from her uncle on the outskirts of town. Turning right on Pine Street, I slowed to a crawl and squinted through the windshield trying to read house numbers in the dark. I finally made out the numerals 764 mounted above a mailbox by the front door. Grass, brown and bristly as a welcome mat, covered the postage-stamp-size yard. Flowers dead and awaiting burial filled clay pots on either side of the steps. An older-model Ford sat in the cracked side drive.

I was starting to have second thoughts about my idea and wished I had Reba Mae along for backup. Parking at the curb, I grabbed the cookies, exited my car, and marched up the walk, being careful not to trip on the uneven cement. I felt butterflies flutter in my stomach and scolded myself for being the least bit nervous. What could possibly go awry visiting a young mother of twins? Unless, that is, she had a proclivity for wrapping silk scarves around the necks of unsuspecting women.

Since the doorbell didn't seem to be in working order, I knocked, once, twice, then three times. Moments later Marcy answered the door wearing an infant in a cloth sling draped across her chest. At first all I noticed was the baby's bald head peeking from the top of the sling. It took me a second longer to register Marcy's tearstained face and smudged mascara.

I held out the plate of cookies. "I'm sorry. Is this a bad time?"

She accepted the offering and stepped aside for me to enter. "What do you want?"

"I . . . um . . . realized I hadn't stopped by to visit you and the babies." Once inside, I took a closer look at Marcy. The woman seemed to have taken more pains than usual with her appearance. Her wispy, dishwater blond hair hung in limp curls around her narrow face. Lipstick and eye makeup transformed plain into . . . less plain. A skirt and blouse had replaced her usual T-shirt and jeans.

"Who is it, honey?" Danny emerged from what I assumed was the kitchen. Without the scruffy goatee he tended with limited success, he could've passed for a teenager.

Like his wife, he carried an infant, this one strapped into a baby carrier resembling a reverse backpack with tiny blue rocket ships.

"Piper came over to surprise us with cookies." Marcy set the plate on a nearby coffee table. "Isn't that thoughtful of her?"

Danny adjusted his John Lennon–style glasses, then patted the baby carrier in the region of the baby's bottom. "When we heard the knock, we hoped you were the babysitter coming to tell us she'd changed her mind and could sit with the twins after all."

"Out with it, Piper!" Marcy demanded, her pale gray eyes sharp and shrewd. "Tell us the real reason you're here — and don't try to pull the wool over our eyes by saying this is merely a social call."

My earlier feeling of dread returned, this time in spades. Uneasy, I tucked a curl behind one ear, stalling for time. "I, um, I'm doing a little investigating. I wondered what you did after rehearsal the night of the murder."

Marcy's lips curled but without mirth. "You want to know if I have an alibi."

Danny stepped nearer to his wife and rested a hand on her shoulder. "You don't owe her an explanation. The only one you have to answer to is Chief McBride."

A smile curved Marcy's mouth, this one genuine. "Danny, I think we're looking a gift horse in the mouth. We can go to your cousin's birthday party after all. Piper has kindly consented to babysit the twins."

My tongue twisted, fumbling for words, but nothing came out.

When she saw my dismay, her smile broadened into a grin. "Come into the nursery with me while I explain how we do things. Danny and I are into crunchy parenting."

Crunchy parenting? Why did the sound of that make me skittish? Babies were still babies, weren't they? The only "crunchy" I was familiar with came in an orange bag labeled cheetos.

Five minutes later, after a set of hasty instructions, I waved as Marcy and Danny backed out of the drive. Marcy had been so eager to leave that she hadn't even taken time to repair her eye makeup. All I needed to do was babysit two infants for a couple hours. Danny assured me they'd sleep the entire time. In exchange, Marcy would supply easily verified alibis not only for herself but also for one other person of interest.

I'd raised two children of my own, and they'd not only survived but thrived. How hard could it be?

CHAPTER 22

How hard could it be?

No sooner had Marcy and Danny departed when those five little words came back to haunt me. Danny had started to elaborate on crunchy parenting. Before Marcy had shushed him he'd rattled off items such as cloth diapers, breast milk, and baby wearing. Well, the baby wearing certainly explained the cloth sling Marcy wore and the backpack-like contraption Danny had strapped to his chest. Somehow, they'd magically disconnected the sleeping infants from their carriers and placed them in matching cribs.

I'd just lowered myself onto the sofa when I heard a baby cry. I sprang up and raced to the nursery before he — or she — could wake its sibling. The girl baby — Jillian? — her face screwed up and beet red, was obviously unhappy and not shy about letting me know. I scooped her up, held her against my shoulder, and swayed back and forth, hoping she would find the motion soothing. "Shh, shh," I said, darting an anxious glance at the infant in the adjacent crib.

That's all it took — one look — for Jillian's twin to join the chorus. The boy's cries were even lustier than his sister's. I feared the neighbors would report the racket as disturbing the peace. How in the world did Marcy manage to comfort not one, but two, unhappy babies? With one crying pitifully and the other howling his lungs out, they nearly drowned out the sound of a knock on the door.

"Be right back," I told Infant Number Two, who I think Marcy said was named Jackson, as I rushed to answer the door.

After fumbling with the dead bolt, I swung the door open. Looking official in crisp navy blues, Wyatt McBride stood on the stoop, his hand poised to knock again. His eyes widened fractionally when he saw me holding a squalling infant before his bland cop mask slipped into place. "What are you doing here?"

"Who said there's never a policeman around when you need one? Don't just stand there, McBride," I said. "Come in, come in."

The second he stepped across the threshold I thrust the baby into his arms and wheeled in the direction of the nursery. "Wait!" McBride shouted. "Don't leave —"

Little Jackson lay in his crib, arms and legs flailing, crying mightily. I picked him up, held him, patted his back, but the volume increased in intensity.

McBride, clutching the baby girl awkwardly, watched from the nursery's doorway. "What's wrong with them? Are they sick?" he asked, his expression bordering on panic. "Should we call a baby doctor?"

I wanted to smile at the sight of McBride struggling with little Jillian. No, actually, I wanted to laugh out loud at seeing a man accustomed to confronting dangerous criminals on a regular basis completely out of his element with a twelve-pound bundle of baby girl. I felt a little tug on my heartstrings, too.

"I think the situation calls for less drastic measures," I said, raising my voice to be heard above the noise. "Let's try changing them first. They might be wet."

McBride nodded. "How do you find out if they're wet or not?"

"You do the diaper test." I unsnapped several fasteners on Jackson's sleeper and slid a finger inside the diaper. I repeated the action on his sister with McBride assuming the role of skeptic. "Yep, they both need a diaper change."

"Oh no," he protested. "Changing diapers wasn't part of my job description."

"Don't be a wuss, McBride. It's not rocket science." I set Jackson down on a changing table. "All you have to do is follow my lead."

I searched the room, looking for the familiar box of disposable diapers, but when I didn't see one my self-confidence took a nosedive. Instead of disposables, I discovered baskets stuffed with tiny panties in whimsical prints and bright colors that were lined with absorbent cotton cloths. Cloth diapers? Was this what Marcy meant by "crunchy parenting"? As Bob Dylan sang, the times they are a-changin'. I felt adrift in a world where everything old became new again. *What next?* I wondered distractedly. *Polyester leisure suits?*

Gamely I grabbed one of the newfangled diapers and, after a false start, wrangled with the snaps and Velcro fasteners to get it in place on a squirming infant. Mission accomplished, I blew out a breath and picked up Jackson. "See, McBride, nothing to it. Piece of cake."

McBride placed a whimpering, wriggling Jillian on the changing table and unsnapped her flowered diaper cover. Immediately he wrinkled his nose in disgust and turned his head. "It wasn't bad enough she wet. Now she pooped and just put her foot in it."

I laughed at seeing him so disgruntled. "That's what baby wipes are for, Pops. Here," I said, feeling magnanimous. "I'll trade babies with you."

McBride happily accepted charge of Jackson in exchange for his odiferous sibling. "I don't see baby powder anywhere," McBride said. "I thought that's what parents used when changing diapers."

I'd noticed its absence, too. "Not all of them apparently. Maybe they worry it might damage babies' lungs should they inhale any."

McBride bounced and jiggled, but the baby he held wasn't easily mollified. Reaching over, I handed McBride a pacifier from the changing table's side pocket. "See if he'll take this."

Jackson responded by spitting it out, informing us in no uncertain terms that that wasn't what he wanted. In the meantime, Jillian tried to squeeze her entire fist into her tiny mouth. When this failed, her face scrunched up and she began a reprise of her earlier aria.

"I think they're hungry."

"Look, Piper, maybe we should call their

parents. Tell them to get home. That this is an emergency."

"Don't be a spoilsport." I stuffed the soiled diapers into a cloth bag hanging from the changing table that I assumed was used for that purpose. I left the nursery followed by McBride cradling the unhappy Jackson in the crook of his arm. "This is probably Danny and Marcy's first night out as a couple since the babies were born. Let them have some fun."

"Changing diapers. Feeding babies. Once this gets around the department, my officers will snicker behind my back. I've got a tough-cop image to maintain."

"Make yourself comfy." I ducked my head in the direction of a plaid recliner in front of a flat-screen television and went in search of sustenance.

From the kitchen, I could hear Jackson practicing vocal calisthenics. Fortunately, before running off Marcy had told me where to find the babies' bottles. I returned to the living room in short order and handed one to McBride along with a spit-up diaper from a stack on the coffee table.

"Now what?" he asked.

I settled myself in a corner of the sofa. "Do what comes naturally. Feed the hungry child."

Neither twin needed any encouragement to latch on to the bottle's nipple and start sucking. McBride and I sat for a spell, savoring the blessed silence.

He gave me a nod of approval. "You sure didn't waste any time preparing formula."

"It isn't formula. It's breast milk."

"Ohh! . . . You know, don't you," he said after a lengthy pause, "that this is above my pay grade? By the way, do these rug rats have names?"

"The one in pink is Jillian. Your bundle in blue is Jackson."

"Jack and Jill?" McBride's face broke into a grin, causing the dimple in his cheek to make a rare appearance.

"Cute, huh?" I grinned back at him. "You have a God-given knack for child care, McBride. If push comes to shove, you could always supplement your income babysitting."

He zoomed a look at me from his laser blues. "You never explained why you're here."

I was reluctant to admit I'd been bribed to babysit. It wasn't this girl's first rodeo. If he knew I'd come tonight to ask Marcy about her alibi, I'd be subjected to another of his stay-out-of-police-business lectures. "Strictly a social visit," I said glibly, then volleyed his question with one of my own. "What brought you knocking on the Boyds' front door? Here on official business?"

"Sorry. You know I can't comment on an active investigation."

"Can't blame a girl for trying." I wiped milky residue from the baby's chin. "C'mon, McBride, loosen up. Have you made any progress on the case? Did the hotline bring in any leads other than an anonymous tipster claiming to see Reba Mae?"

"Reba Mae lied through her teeth about being home alone. It took a hotline to ferret out the truth. She finally admitted she'd gone to the opera house for the sole purpose of confronting Sandy about a part in a play."

I shifted the baby from the crook of my arm to my shoulder and thumped her on the back. "Reba Mae didn't kill Sandy. You know it as well as I do. Are you even looking at other suspects?"

"I have to follow where evidence leads. I can't decide on a person's guilt or innocence based on whether I like them or not." McBride eyed me suspiciously. "Why are you hitting that child?"

I heaved an exaggerated sigh at his ignorance. "It's called burping. You might want to do the same with Jackson."

"I don't do burping."

"Give me a break, McBride. Burping is second nature for most guys."

"Jackson's not finished eating. What if I take his dinner away and he starts crying all over again?"

Jillian let out a dainty burp and resumed feeding. "Burp the baby, McBride," I said, "or the poor kid will end up with a tummy ache."

McBride raised the baby to his shoulder, but before I could advise him on the use of the spit-up diaper little Jackson dribbled a stripe of curdled milk down the back of McBride's pristine navy blue shirt.

"Oh-oh!" I stood abruptly, juggling Jillian in one arm, her bottle wedged under my chin, and started dabbing at the stain.

"What's wrong? What are you doing?"

"I'm wiping off baby spit-up."

McBride surged to his feet and craned his neck to view the damage.

"Umm, McBride, I don't know how to tell you this, but . . ."

"But what?"

I caught my lower lip between my teeth to keep from smiling. I pointed to a dark splotch on his pant leg. "I think the diaper leaked."

He stared at the infant who was now sleeping angelically, then down at his soiled uniform. "I can't conduct an interview covered in pee and spit-up. When Marcy gets home tell her I'll be by tomorrow to speak with her."

"Tomorrow's Sunday," I reminded him.

"I'll make an exception."

We tiptoed into the nursery and gently, so as not to wake the sleeping twins, placed them in their respective cribs. After quickly changing Jackson's soggy diaper I walked McBride to the door. "Don't worry, Mc-Bride," I said. "Consider your image secure. Your secret's safe. I promise I won't breathe a word about your misadventure in babysitting."

He reached out, caught my chin between his thumb and forefinger, and tilted my face up to his. "I'll hold you to it," he said, his voice a husky baritone.

Then he turned and strode down the walk toward his cruiser. I stared after him, half-dazed. For a moment — a very brief moment — I thought he might kiss me. A traitorous part of me wished he had. I reminded myself of Doug, a wonderful, caring individual, and instantly felt disloyal. Resolutely I closed the door on both Mc-Bride and my wayward imaginings.

The remainder of the evening passed uneventfully. Needing something to pass the time, I sorted through a pile of gossip magazines on the coffee table. At the bottom of the stack was the script for *Steel Magnolias.* I flipped it open and saw Marcy's lines highlighted in yellow. This reminded me of the script I'd found onstage at the opera house. *Steel Magnolias* was a deeply moving play, I mused, showing women at their finest. Pity Sandy's production had ended before it had begun.

True to their word, Marcy and Danny returned a few minutes after ten o'clock. "How were the babies? Did they sleep for you?" Marcy asked, slipping out of her coat.

Danny dug into his pant pocket for his wallet. "What do we owe you?"

"I'll take care of it, honey," Marcy said. "Why don't you take a peek at the twins while I say good night to Piper?"

At the door, Marcy dropped her voice so Danny wouldn't hear. "You wanted to know if I had an alibi for the night Sandy died. Well, I do," she said almost defiantly, "and so does Mary Lou. After rehearsal, we went to High Cotton for karaoke night. I'm not drinking alcohol since I'm breast-feeding but thought I was entitled to a night out."

I couldn't believe what I was hearing. "*Both* you and Mary Lou were at High Cotton?"

"Check with the bartender; he'll back up my story. It was after midnight when we left. Mary Lou and I rocked the place singing 'R-E-S-P-E-C-T' by the Queen of Soul herself, Miss Aretha Franklin."

With this, she shut the door in my face, leaving me standing on the front porch. My mind worked trying to process what she'd told me. If Marcy was telling the truth, she'd just eliminated not one, but two, persons from the suspect pool. But I couldn't simply take Marcy's word. For the sake of thoroughness, I intended to check out their alibis myself. *Karaoke night, here I come.*

And the tune I'd likely be singing was "Another One Bites the Dust."

CHAPTER 23

Sunday morning dawned crisp and clear. I postponed my usual housekeeping chores in favor of jogging. I donned a pair of gray sweats, tucked my hair under a knit cap, and clipped Casey's leash to his collar. Casey, knowing we were about to get us some exercise, instinctively stretched his legs. I left a note for Lindsey in case she woke up before we returned and wondered if we'd been abducted. I slipped my cell phone into a pocket along with a house key and off we went.

The thermometer hovered near the fifty-degree mark, but the day promised to be a beauty once it warmed up. After a few preliminary exercises to loosen tight muscles, my trusty mutt and I started out slow, then picked up our pace. Forty-five minutes later, feeling pleasantly fatigued yet invigorated, I slowed to a walk near Cloune Motors not far from my home. The garage was owned by Diane Cloune and operated by Reba Mae's son Caleb. The previously owned car business no longer existed, but the garage, under Caleb's mechanical wizardry, continued to thrive and supply Diane with a steady income. The expansive concrete lot that had once been crowded with vehicles sporting FOR SALE signs was currently empty except for a lone car — a shiny red Mazda Miata — that I recognized as belonging to Madison Winters.

In the course of my run, a shoelace had come untied. Casey and I seemed to have separate agendas. As I bent to retie my shoe, he wandered the length of his leash to relieve himself on the tire of Madison's car.

"Bad dog," I scolded. "Can't you find a tree?"

Casey ignored me. He was more intent on sniffing and snooping.

"C'mon, boy." I straightened and lightly tugged his leash. "Let's go."

Casey didn't budge, which was unlike his agreeable furry self. I was the stubborn half of this duo, not my pet. "What's wrong, pal?"

I walked over to see what had him enthralled and immediately spotted the problem. The car was sitting lopsided, lower on the passenger side than the driver's. Along with the realization came a sick feeling in the pit of my stomach. Two of the tires were flat. Not just ordinary flat, but flat as in having been punctured by a sharp object in a malicious act of vandalism. *Who could have done this? And why?* I wondered.

I took out my cell phone and dialed the police.

As luck would have it — bad luck — McBride answered the phone. I explained the situation, and he told me to sit tight, he'd be right over. My next call was to the Johnson residence. Reba Mae picked up on the third ring, and I gave her the condensed version of what had happened. She said she'd relay the message to Caleb. I killed minutes waiting for McBride by doing some stretches and leg lifts to keep my calf muscles from seizing.

McBride drew up at the curb and got out of a patrol car. I was surprised to see him in his go-to wardrobe of jeans, dark T-shirt, and bomber jacket. "Don't tell me little Jackson christened your last clean uniform last night?"

His mouth twisted in a semblance of a smile. "Matter of fact, he did. Been working long hours lately. Haven't had a chance to pick up my uniforms from the dry cleaners." He strolled over to the Miata, stooped down, and examined the puncture marks in the sidewalls of the tires.

"What do you think?"

"I think someone took out their aggression on a piece of rubber." He clicked off a series of photos with his cell phone. "Don't suppose you happen to know who this car belongs to?"

"Never underestimate the power of a woman, McBride," I said rather smugly. "It belongs to Madison Winters."

Just then Caleb Johnson braked to a stop and hopped out of his pickup. He shook his head in disbelief at seeing the damage. "What the . . . ?"

"Seems someone has it in for foreign sports cars — or its owner." McBride took out a notebook and began writing.

Its owner? Surely Madison didn't have an enemy who'd perform such a vicious act on her car.

"This is my fault." Caleb tunneled his fingers through his longish hair. "I wanted to keep the car locked inside the garage where it would be safe but let Madison talk me into keeping it outdoors instead. She wanted to stop for it on her way home from Atlanta today."

"I assume the 'she' you're referring to is

Madison Winters?" McBride asked, pen poised.

"Doug took Madison away for the weekend," I explained. "His daughter's very upset about the murder. He hoped a change of scenery might help."

Squatting down, Caleb stared dolefully at the ruined tires. "Madison insisted it would be easier this way. Save her a trip into town. She said her daddy had a full schedule at the animal clinic tomorrow and needed her help."

"Judging from the look of her tires, Ms. Winters isn't going to be driving anywhere right quick." McBride walked to the rear of the vehicle and wrote down the number of the license plate. "Have you had trouble with vandals before this?"

"No, never." Caleb ran his hand over the cuts in the rubber. "I'll have to call around, find out who stocks these babies. It'll take days if I have to special order."

McBride nodded. "Do you know anyone who might do this to Ms. Winters' vehicle?"

Caleb's head jerked up. "You saying Madison's car was targeted — not a random act by dumbass kids?"

"Covering all the bases." McBride's expression gave no clue what was going on behind that cop mask he wore. "I did a quick check before coming over. No recent reports of tires slashed."

Casey, who had been sitting quietly at my feet, barked, tired of being ignored.

Bending down, I rubbed behind my little dog's ears. "Casey deserves the credit for spotting the slashed tires. If not for him, the damage might not have been discovered until Madison came for her car."

"I'll note his contribution in my report," McBride said, turning his attention to me. "You and your dog were first on the scene. Did you see anyone coming or going? Any cars?"

I racked my brain for answers, but Sundays in Brandywine Creek tended to be quiet. This morning had been no exception. "No, to both questions. I guess people are either at church or sleeping late."

"Sergeant Tucker is playing Dr. Phil to a couple with an ongoing domestic dispute. When he checks in, I'll have him dust for prints. Caleb," he said, "since you worked on her car we'll need yours, too, in order to exclude you."

"Prints are already on file." Caleb stood, hands jammed into the back pockets of his faded jeans, and rocked back on the heels of his worn work boots. "Day I turned twenty-one I applied for a firearms license,

273

and fingerprinting, as you know, is one of the requirements. Momma insisted I get a carry permit. She worries about me running a business and working late."

Typical Reba Mae, I thought, smiling. "Your momma's always looking out for you and your brother."

"She sure is, Miz Prescott," Caleb agreed. "Momma's a damn fine woman. I dare anyone to say different."

I detected a hint of belligerence underlying Caleb's words directed at McBride. Caleb was primed and ready to defend his mother's honor should the need arise. Can't fault a boy for believing in his momma.

McBride chose to overlook Caleb's tone. "Ms. Winters needs to be informed of the vandalism. Do either of you have her number?"

"I do," Caleb volunteered so readily McBride raised a brow.

"They're friends," I said, hoping to spare Caleb embarrassment.

"Have her drop by the department tomorrow in case I have questions for her." McBride snapped his notebook shut and slipped it into his bomber jacket. "I didn't notice any security cameras. They'd make a good investment."

"It's not my call. I don't own the place."

"Well, if the time comes, let me know. I can give you the name of a person who's done work for the department."

Caleb and I watched in silence as McBride returned to his squad car and pulled away from the curb. Caleb was the first to speak when the cruiser was no longer in sight. "I really liked Chief McBride when I first met him. Especially because he remembered my daddy from high school. Now that he's treating Momma like a common criminal, it's all I can do to be polite."

I felt my heart twist in sympathy for the young man I'd known since he was a child. He was so angry, frustrated, and confused that I could feel tension humming through him like electricity about to spark. "The chief is only doing his job. I'm sure, deep down, he knows your mother wouldn't hurt anyone."

He thrust out his jaw. "McBride can't be very bright if he thinks Momma killed Miz Granger. Sure will be a relief when this whole mess gets sorted out."

"Amen," I said as we parted ways.

Home again, I fed Casey, then showered. Lindsey was awake by the time I finished dressing, so I made an omelet for each of us.

"SATs are a week from Saturday," she said, taking a bite of toast.

"Try not to stress over them," I advised. "Do the best you can. No one is going to compare your score with Chad's."

"My GPA isn't all that great, but I'm crossing my fingers I'll be able to get into a good school. I still want to be a physical therapist — or a nurse."

I refilled my coffee cup. Physical therapy or nursing was the longest Lindsey had ever stayed focused on a career. In the past year, her career goals had bounced between veterinarian, videographer, and journalist. "You can always attend junior college like Clay is doing while you bring up your grades."

"I suppose." Lindsey rose from the table, cleared the dishes, and put them in the dishwasher. "Is it okay if I hang out at Taylor's? Her dad just bought this amazing TV — seventy-eight inches, LED curved screen. Taylor said the color is awesome. They're video streaming on Netflix."

"If that's the case, be sure to bring popcorn."

After Lindsey had deserted me in favor of larger-than-life characters on a bigger-than-ever TV screen, I made a pot of vegetarian chili that I could reheat on weeknights. It was simmering on the back burner when Reba Mae came for a visit.

"I brought you a jar of Aunt Ida's renowned mincemeat," she said. "It should be enough to make a nice pie." She set the mincemeat in the refrigerator, took out two diet sodas, and made herself comfortable at the kitchen table.

I popped the tab on the can she handed me. "Thanks, I'll keep it to use at Christmas. This year I'm spending Thanksgiving by my lonesome."

"Oh no, hon, that's not right," Reba Mae protested. "Why not join the Johnson clan for dinner? You know most of us already. Aunt Ida and Uncle Joe would be happy to set another place at the table."

I gave my chili a stir, then took the chair opposite her. "I appreciate the offer, Reba Mae, but I'm going to take Lindsey's suggestion and spend the day gorging on parades, football games, and old black and white movies. Besides, it'll be nice to spend the entire day in pajamas with my feet propped up." *Liar, liar, pants on fire.*

Reba Mae took a swig of her soda. "Put that way, honeybun, you're makin' me jealous."

"Did Caleb tell you someone slashed the tires on Madison's car?"

She shook her head, sending the gold hoops in her ears dancing. "Who would do such a crazy thing? Think it mighta been kids with too much time on their hands?"

"Wish I knew," I said. "McBride said there haven't been reports of similar incidents."

"What's this world comin' to?"

"I hope that's a rhetorical question and you don't really expect an answer." I ran an index finger down the frosty side of my diet soda. "You'll never guess what I did last night."

"Shoot me. Put me out of my misery." Reba Mae leaned back, arms crossed. "Don't tell me the man of your dreams flew you to Paris on his private jet for a night on the town. And you didn't even think to send your BFF a selfie with the Eiffel Tower in the background. Shame, shame, shame."

"Close but no cigar." I smiled at the fantasy she'd created. "I paid Marcy Boyd a surprise visit and was . . . persuaded . . . to babysit while she and Danny went to a birthday party. Seems cloth diapers are back in vogue along with something called crunchy parenting."

"I like my crunchy served with salsa and margaritas."

"Me, too, girlfriend." I raised my can in a toast. "I looked up crunchy parenting, sometimes called attachment parenting, when I came home last night."

"Well, what are you waiting for? Enlighten the ignorant."

"Best I can tell it involves cloth diapers with cute little covers, breast milk, and carrying infants in slings or backpacks. Some parents advocate co-sleeping. It has to do with bonding and being emotionally available."

"Did I ruin my boys 'cause I wasn't crunchy enough?"

"They seem okay to me, but then I went and 'ruined' my kids, too." I smiled slyly. "And that's not all. You'll never believe who showed up to help me watch the twins."

"Prince William? I read in *People* magazine he changes nappies for the wee royals."

"Not a prince . . ." I paused for maximum effect. "None other than Wyatt McBride."

"No kiddin'." Reba Mae looked appropriately impressed. "Seein' that would have been worth the price of admission."

"For my trouble, Marcy told me where she was the night of the murder. She claims she and Mary Lou went to High Cotton after rehearsal for karaoke night."

"And you believed her?"

I shrugged. "I'm not sure. I think their alibis merit further investigation. How about

279

after McBride's self-defense class tomorrow night we pay High Cotton a visit? I haven't been to a karaoke night since college."

"Time for a refresher course." Reba Mae raised her soda and we clinked cans.

CHAPTER 24

As a rule Mondays tended to be on the slow side, but today had proved an exception. All morning customers filed in and out. Pinky Alexander introduced me to Lisa, her daughter-in-law, who had arrived from Seattle along with Pinky's son to spend the week. Pinky was over the moon when the couple announced they were expecting her first grandchild. Her daughter-in-law, a foodie, oohed and aahed over my selection of spices.

"My mother-in-law raved about your friend's spicy chicken curry!" Lisa gushed. "She gave me the recipe, and I'm going to serve it when it's our turn to host gourmet club."

"I told Lisa you stock several types of curry powder, but she insists on making her own," Pinky said.

"I prefer mine ultra-fresh." Lisa looped one of the small baskets I kept for customers over her arm. "Point me in the direction of your seeds — cardamom, cumin, coriander, and fennel."

While Lisa shopped, Pinky examined an array of gift boxes I had assembled yesterday afternoon. In addition to my more popular spices, some contained a packet of recipe cards or a colorful tea towel. "I was reluctant to tell Lisa and Mike about our town's recent murder for fear they'd cancel their trip. She's coming with me to the self-defense class tonight, but only to observe."

"That's great," I said, mentally adding Lisa's name to the expanding list of those who planned to attend. "I'm sure McBride will give us some good tips on personal safety."

Lisa's selections combined with a gift box of baking spices Pinky purchased for a Secret Santa present would make a nice addition to the day's total. I was enjoying a temporary lull and had just finished a peanut butter sandwich when Madison breezed in, jacket flapping open, ponytail swaying.

"I want to thank you," she said in a rush. "Caleb told me you were the one who reported my tires slashed."

Dusting off crumbs, I wiped my fingers on a paper napkin. "No thanks necessary.

I'm only sorry it happened."

"Because you noticed it when you did, Caleb was able to locate a dealer online yesterday who happened to have my tires in stock. They were delivered this morning, and Caleb put them on as soon as they arrived. My car's good to go."

I studied the girl surreptitiously. In spite of her weekend getaway, she seemed pale and drawn. She'd been horrified by Sandy's murder. Madison was young, barely out of her teens. Until now, I'd been more resentful than sympathetic. Shame on me. Time for an attitude adjustment. Would the tire-slashing incident send her over the edge? Have her packing her bags? "Do the police have any leads on who might have vandalized your Miata?" I asked quietly.

Madison fidgeted with a button on her jacket. "Chief McBride said it could be an isolated random act."

"Is that what you think?"

"I don't know . . . maybe." She tugged and twisted the hapless button some more.

What aren't you saying? My intuition told me something was amiss. "Madison, I know we're not close, but I'm here for you if you ever want to talk."

I expected her to tell me to mind my own business, but she surprised me. "If I tell you a secret, promise you won't breathe a word of it to my dad. I don't want to scare him."

"Promise."

She worried her bottom lip with her teeth, then blurted, "I think I'm being followed."

"Followed?" Whatever I expected to hear, this wasn't it.

"I know it makes me sound like a victim in some stupid stalker movie." She tried to sound nonchalant, but the nervous flutter in her voice betrayed her.

"What makes you think you're being followed?"

"It's not as though I've actually seen anyone." Madison shifted her weight from one foot to the other. "It's more a feeling of being watched. I can't help wonder if it might be the same person who slashed my tires. Maybe they don't like me because I'm new in town. Or maybe they're jealous because I drive a sports car."

"Oh, honey, I'm so sorry." I reached across the counter and rubbed her arm consolingly. "This might be nothing more than your imagination playing tricks. A perfectly understandable reaction considering a woman who befriended you was brutally killed. But, to be on the safe side, pay close attention to your surroundings until the vandal is apprehended."

She smiled thinly. "That's the same advice Chief McBride gave me."

Suddenly I remembered the charm I'd retrieved from the opera house. I pushed a key of the cash register, and a drawer rolled out with a merry jingle — a tune I privately thought of as dance music. "Here," I said, handing her the tiny gold charm I'd retrieved, "this ought to cheer you up."

"You found it!" Madison rounded the counter separating us and practically smothered me in a hug, then, embarrassed by her uncharacteristic display of emotion, stepped back. "I never thought I'd see this again. It's part of a gift from my grandmother. Where did you find it?"

"Ned Feeney discovered it when he cleaned the opera house. Sandy had instructed him to put any lost items in a box in the front office."

Madison's fingers closed tightly around the object as though she was afraid it might disappear. "I thought the opera house was off-limits."

"It was. It is, but . . ."

Madison waited patiently for me to continue.

"Reba Mae and I — well, maybe me more than Reba Mae — thought we'd check out the scene of the crime. A fresh set of eyes and all that. I hoped we might spot something law enforcement missed."

"Did you?" Madison carefully relegated the cherished item to a zipper compartment of her purse.

"Except for Reba Mae being spooked by the opera house ghost, our visit was uneventful. Unless you include being caught red-handed by Chief McBride. We're lucky he didn't arrest us for trespassing."

Madison nodded knowingly. "The chief strikes me as the type who'd lock you up and throw away the key. I bet he has a pit bull for a pet."

"Nope," I said, grinning. "Believe it or not, he adopted a feral cat. He named her Fraidy."

Madison laughed at this. "As in 'don't be a fraidy cat'?"

"One and the same," I said, walking with her to the door. "McBride's holding a self-defense class tonight at seven in the high-school gym. Why not join us?"

"I'll think on it. And, Piper, thanks for letting me vent — and returning my charm."

Some say that no good deed goes unpunished, but, in this instance, I'd take my chances.

By six forty-five the parking lot at Brandywine Creek High School was rapidly filling up. I felt a keen sense of satisfaction at seeing all the sedans, compacts, SUVs, and a smattering of pickups. If anyone had won rights to I-told-you-so, it was me, not McBride.

Reba Mae scuffed the asphalt lot with the toe of her purple sneaker. "I'm not sure I shoulda come, seein' how Mr. Police Chief views me as the person folks need protection against."

"Nonsense." I slung an arm around her shoulder. "Quit being such a pessimist."

"Nothin' in the murder suspect handbook calls for perky."

"Hey, don't forget after class we're going to have ourselves a good time. A glass of wine, some music, a little interrogation. What more could you ask for?"

"I guess," Reba Mae grumbled. "Remember, you're buyin' the first round."

We joined the group of women who streamed toward the gym. As we neared the side entrance to the high school, I spotted Bitsy Jones loitering between a late-model Ford and a minivan. "Hey, Bitsy," I called. "You coming in?"

Bitsy fired up a cigarette. "Yeah, sure. Soon as I finish my smoke."

I waved. "See you inside."

Reba Mae lowered her voice as we contin-ued on our way. "Bitsy claims cigarettes help cut down on food cravings. The day I did her highlights, she was in and out so many times for smoke breaks, I needed a revolvin' door. Took twice as long as it should've."

"Surely you're exaggerating."

We passed through a corridor lined with glass display cases filled with trophies for various sports. Photos captured teams past — young men, boys really, in football gear, clutching basketballs or holding bats and catcher's mitts. I wished I had time to search for McBride's face among them. As captain and star quarterback of his high-school football team, he'd led his squad to regionals. CJ had been on the team, too, but from all accounts his performance had been lackluster.

"I considered orderin' pizza since it was so late," Reba Mae continued, "but knew if I did Bitsy would break out another pack of smokes and I'd be there till midnight."

"You have to admit, Bitsy looks hot."

"Smokin'," Reba Mae agreed, and we both burst out laughing.

We were still laughing as we shoved through the gym's double doors. I caught a whiff of sweat and testosterone that not even

Pine-Sol could obliterate. High-school gyms, I concluded after a cursory glance, hadn't changed much since I'd been a teenager: bleachers stacked along each wall, basketball hoops and scoreboards on either end, polished wood floor. Someone, probably McBride, had placed a large blue mat in the floor's center. I estimated two dozen women were ready and waiting for the class to begin. Reba Mae and I mounted a couple rows in the bleachers to join Precious Blessing.

Precious scooted over to make room for us. "Thought you girls might unfriend me for bein' a snitch and reportin' you for sneakin' around the opera house."

"No harm, no foul." I slipped out of my jacket, feeling inordinately pleased with myself for using a sports expression.

Reba Mae set her purse by her feet. "Don't worry, Precious. You were only doin' your job."

"I worried whoever killed Miz Granger might be skulkin' around. Then there's those durn ghost stories. Ghosts can give folks heart attacks. Didn't want to chance that happenin' to either of you nice ladies."

"Good to know you're lookin' out for us, Precious," Reba Mae said. "For the record, snoopin' was Piper's idea, not mine. I just went along for protection. Kinda like a bodyguard."

I rolled my eyes. "Fine bodyguard you'd make. You'd trample me in a heartbeat in your hurry to get out the door."

I swept my gaze over the crowd. Bunny Bowtin, Vicki Lamont, and Shirley Randolph were dressed in formfitting stretch pants as though they'd just come from yoga class. The other women for the most part wore loose clothing. Pinky was proudly introducing her daughter-in-law to her friends. Other familiar faces in the crowd included Gerilee, who was gabbing with Sylvia Walker, Lindsey's Language Arts teacher, and Trish Hughes. Bitsy, one of the last to arrive, took the remaining space on the bottom bleacher. I noticed she'd failed to score in the dress code department. Instead of loose or functional, she'd chosen a hot pink knit top, skintight jeans, and ankle boots with three-inch heels. I didn't see Madison so assumed she'd had second thoughts about attending. Mary Lou wasn't present either.

At seven o'clock on the dot, the door leading to the locker rooms swung wide and McBride strode out followed by Officer Gary Moyer. Though both men were in uniform, McBride carried with him a commanding presence that easily marked him as the alpha male. He stationed himself in front of the bleachers, feet slightly apart, hands clasped behind his back. The room grew so still I could hear the tick of the shot clock.

"Good crowd on short notice," he drawled. "Thought y'all would be home baking pies."

An uncertain titter went up from the audience.

"Police officers call it a gut feeling; women call it intuition. I can't stress strongly enough the importance of paying attention to subtle warning signals. That little tickle along the back of your neck or twinge in the pit of your stomach. Pay attention to it. Fear can be the gift that keeps you safe." Assured he had everyone's attention, he went on, "Self-protection allows a person to prevent, identify, and avoid violence. Self-defense is what you do when that isn't enough. Self-defense is what we're going to focus on tonight."

I noticed women nodding their heads.

McBride walked back and forth in front of the bleachers as he talked. "When you find yourself in a confrontation, you may only have seconds to react before being overpowered. Once the situation turns physical, it's hurt or be hurt. Aim for parts of the body where you can do the most damage in the least amount of time. Places such as eyes, nose, ears, neck, groin, knee, and legs."

Motioning for Officer Moyer to join him on the blue mat, McBride proceeded to demonstrate techniques for disabling an attacker. In spite of the subject matter, my thoughts drifted. I looked at the faces of the women surrounding me, all paying rapt attention to McBride. Was Sandy's killer present among them? Or absent?

"What if an attacker comes up behind us?" Vicki wanted to know.

McBride smiled his approval. "I'm glad you asked."

With Officer Moyer playing the victim and himself as the assailant, McBride demonstrated several basic techniques to ward off an attacker. I must have left my concentration back at Spice It Up! because my attention wandered again. I'd ruled out most cast members — and tonight I'd check out the alibis of two more — but a few names remained on the list. Bunny, who'd been hurt and humiliated by Sandy, swore she'd gone straight home and into a bubble bath after rehearsal. How could I prove or disprove this? Vicki Lamont, though not a cast member but the deceased's best friend, was happily wooing the recent widower with golf and goodies. Then there was Wanda Needmore. The paralegal had motive and stubbornly refused to answer my questions.

"Let's see if you ladies were paying attention," McBride said from the floor. "I need a volunteer."

Hands waved in the air like a field of daisies in a breeze. Ignoring them, McBride leveled a finger at me.

"Me?" I squeaked, jolted back to the present.

"You," he said in a tone that brooked no further argument.

CHAPTER 25

"Damn, girl, you sure got all the luck," Precious chuckled, giving me a playful poke as I clambered down from the bleachers. "I traded hours with Dorinda in order to see my boss in action and he picks you."

I felt everyone's eyes on me and my cheeks burned. "What do you want me to do?" I asked when I joined McBride on the blasted blue mat.

"Turn around," he ordered gruffly.

"If Piper isn't willing, I'll be your partner!" Vicki shouted out.

Sheesh! Could the woman be any more obvious?

"No!" Precious cried. "Pick me."

All the women laughed, albeit a trifle nervously. Being partnered with McBride had its advantages and disadvantages. He had a reputation for being tall, dark, and dangerous. Tall and dark were okay, but a prudent woman should avoid dangerous like the plague.

"Turn," he repeated.

Gamely I did as instructed and turned my back. Moyer assumed a position slightly behind us and to the left.

"Officer Moyer's job will be to offer advice and criticize technique," McBride explained.

I wiped damp palms on the sides of my pants and wished I'd paid closer attention to McBride's lecture rather than zoning out trying to solve a murder.

"Nervous?" McBride's baritone rumbled in my ear, soft enough not to be overheard by the rest of the women.

"Nervous," I replied, licking my dry lips. "Why would I be nervous?"

"Perhaps because your mind wasn't on the lesson?"

I heard the smirk in his voice, and it irritated me. "So what are you going to do, McBride? Send me to the principal's office?"

"Piper is going to be the victim," he addressed those gathered, "and I'll pretend I'm the assailant. If you recall, the rear stranglehold is one of the most common used by muggers."

My pulse quickened as McBride's arm slid around my throat. I felt his breath, light as a feather, against my ear. His hold tightened marginally. Instinctively I pulled McBride's elbow, needing more breathing room. I didn't know if it was his proximity — or my vulnerability.

"You have only seconds to react before your assailant renders you unconscious," Moyer counseled. "Tuck your chin into the crook of his arm. Now raise your arm and strike. Ribs, groin, head."

Graceful as a ballerina, McBride shifted his weight and avoided my blows with embarrassing ease.

"Lift the attacker's elbow and pull on his wrist," Moyer coached from outside my field of vision. "Turn, step back, and slip out of his hold."

I did as he instructed and drew in a deep gulp of air, happy to be free.

"You forgot a step!" Pinky shouted.

"What . . . ?" Frustrated, I shoved a riot of messy curls out of my flushed face.

"You forgot the part where you break the perp's elbow," Gerilee offered helpfully.

"You know — put the guy out of commission while you make your getaway," Bunny reminded me.

"Nuh-uh." Precious wagged her finger. "Break the chief's elbow, girl, and he'll charge you with battery."

Reba Mae, I observed, kept any comments to herself. She was too intent on flying under McBride's radar to risk drawing his attention by smarting off. For a while tonight, I thought she'd change her mind and decide not to come. She wasn't keen on the prospect of spending time in the man's company. In the end, though, she'd put on her big-girl panties and accompanied me.

"Isn't there a way for a woman to break free without ruining her hairdo?" Vicki simpered, stopping short of fluttering her lashes like a Georgia belle.

"Ladies, when your life is at stake worry about hair later," McBride replied sternly, apparently inoculated against blatant flirts. I started to return to the bleachers, but McBride placed a hand on my shoulder, waylaying me. "The bear hug defense is another technique that could be useful. It assumes your attacker is bigger and stronger than you."

"Big like you and little like Piper." Precious nodded, clearly enjoying herself. "This I gotta see."

Turning me so I faced away, McBride wrapped his arms around my waist, tight but not too tight, and pinned my arms to my sides. Part of me wanted to wriggle away from the hard body pressed against me. A traitorous part wanted to snuggle closer. In hindsight, Vicki would have been a better candidate for this maneuver.

Moyer studied our posture from several angles. "Widen your stance, Piper. Keep your knees slightly bent and your hips lower than your attacker's," he directed. "Now raise your arms, palms up, to create resistance. Tilt your hip —"

Memory kicked in. I hooked my opposite leg around McBride, reached down and grabbed him behind the knees, straightened, and flipped him. I executed the movement with a precision that surprised me.

And surprised McBride even more.

He lay flat on his back, staring up at me, eyes wide, and I knew I was in deep doo-doo. Prudence had never been my strong suit.

Released from its stunned silence, the gym erupted in a burst of cheers. Even Reba Mae and dour Officer Moyer cracked smiles. I bowed to a standing ovation, then offered my hand to help a flabbergasted McBride to his feet. There would be time to seek asylum later.

"I think you ladies have the general idea." McBride brushed the dust from his uniform. "Let's pair up and practice."

It didn't come as a shock when no one chose me as a partner.

"You might not shine when playing golf or tennis, honeybun, but when it comes to self-defense, you rock," Reba Mae congratulated me as we climbed into my VW and headed for High Cotton.

Class had ended after a reminder from McBride to develop our situational awareness. No more texting or phoning while walking to parked cars. "Stay alert," Moyer had added, "stay alive." I planned to do all of the above.

Trading the highway for a dirt and gravel road, I turned into the parking lot of the bar and grill. A neon sign flickered above the door advertising beer and burgers. The place wasn't much to look at — inside or out — but the beer was cold and burgers juicy. High Cotton hosted its fair share of Saturday night brawls, and the bartender was said to have Brandywine Creek Police Department on speed dial. Definitely not a joint to impress a first date, but the locals loved it. And so did the younger crowd from neighboring towns.

Upon entering, Reba Mae and I stood just inside the door to give our eyes time to adjust to the dim light. Patrons lined the bar two deep while a bearded man in a Kid Rock T-shirt was kept busy filling mugs with draft beer.

"Who knew karaoke was this popular," Reba Mae said, gazing around in amazement.

"I don't hear any music, so the DJ must be on a break. Let's find a place to sit and question the bartender about Marcy and Mary Lou when he isn't quite as busy."

We threaded our way through the mostly twenties crowd to a vacant booth for two at the rear. I recognized a few faces but not many. We didn't have a long wait before a girl who was barely legal drinking age with multicolored hair and ripped jeans approached our table. "What can I getcha?"

I never knew when the need to interrogate might strike, so I smiled pleasantly at the girl to communicate that I was a fan of yellow, purple, and blue striped hair. "I'll have a Riesling."

"Riesling?" She snapped her gum. "Don't know that one. We have Bud, Bud Light, Miller Lite, Heineken, Corona, Michelob, and Yuengling. Want bottle or draft?"

I kept my smiled pinned securely in place. "Riesling isn't beer; it's wine."

"Never heard of it," she replied looking bored. "As far as wine goes we only have red or white."

"Then I'll have white."

"Make that two." Reba Mae toyed with one of her dangly earrings. "Why do you s'pose Mary Lou and Marcy ended up here after rehearsal? Mary Lou's not a singer. Heard she was kicked out of church choir 'cause she's tone-deaf."

"Marcy and Mary Lou probably needed a girls' night out. Rehearsals were getting stressful. Both of them were unhappy with Sandy's management style, and they wanted to unwind before going home."

"Marcy deserves a break. Twins can be a handful." Reba Mae ceased fiddling with her earrings and slouched in a corner of the booth.

Our waitress returned with two glasses of wine and a small bowl of pretzels. "DJ's about to start up again. If you ladies have a request, you better get it in."

As if to prove her point, a trio of women picked their way through the crowd to the small stage that doubled as a dance floor Saturday nights. "This fine group of song-birds from Walmart is about to entertain you with a Carrie Underwood hit, 'Before He Cheats,' " the DJ announced into a mic.

Reba Mae raised her glass, took a sip, and made a face. "Bet they concocted this stuff

301

in the cellar after a crash course on wine makin'. Seein' how the bartender's busy, whatdaya say we ask the waitress if she remembers the pair, then let's blow this pop stand?"

I took a cautious sample of my wine. "Best idea I've heard all night."

Reba Mae flagged the girl down as she was about to pass our table. "By any stretch of the imagination did you work last Monday?"

"I'm here every friggin' karaoke night." She tucked the tray she carried under her arm. "I know the lyrics of each stupid song backward and forward till I hear them in my sleep."

"We wondered if you might remember a couple women who were here last week. The two would've come in late — ten o'clock or thereabout," Reba Mae said.

A brain cell fired in my cranium and a memory burst out. "I think they might have requested 'R-E-S-P-E-C-T' by Aretha Franklin."

"Yeah, I remember." The girl's jaws worked her wad of gum, causing it to crack and snap. "The older one had canary yellow hair teased and sprayed stiff as a plank. The skinny one kept showing everyone baby pictures on her phone."

"Sounds like the pair," I said. "I don't suppose you recall what time they left?"

"Remember that, too," she said scowling. "The DJ usually quits at midnight, but they bribed him into one more song. The skinny one with the babies wasn't half-bad, but the yellow-haired gal couldn't carry a tune in a bucket."

"Thanks for your help," I told her. I left a generous tip on the table and Reba Mae and I slid out of the booth a short time later, our wine virtually untouched. "Now that we've confirmed Marcy's and Mary Lou's alibis, we can focus our attention on Bunny and Wanda. I also wondered about Vicki. She wouldn't be the first person to commit murder because of envy — or greed."

"My money's on Wanda. Never did care for that woman," Reba Mae commented. "She's too uppity if you want my opinion."

"Granted, Wanda seems the most likely candidate for Who Killed Sandy, but I'm not willing to place all my hard-earned cash on the odds-on favorite. Sometime it's the long shot — the dark horse — that wins the race."

We wove through patrons that formed a ring around the bar. The Walmart women were leading the patrons through a lusty chorus that would have made Carrie proud.

We were almost at the door when I did a double take. Sitting at a small table, Wyatt McBride and Shirley Randolph shared a plate of chili cheese fries. My earlier elation at having flipped the lawman on his backside gurgled down the drain like bathwater.

CHAPTER 26

Parsley, sage, rosemary, and thyme.

The tune of a classic folk song drifted through my head nonstop. The Tuesday before Thanksgiving brought a steady stream of customers into Spice It Up! Hot-ticket items seemed to be spices needed for new recipes or to add pizzazz to family favorites. I hoped the surge in business was a harbinger of sales in the weeks leading up to Christmas. Soon I'd need to plan ahead for the quieter months of January and February. Spring arrived early in the South. By late February, daffodils would make an appearance. January's weather, though, tended toward the unpredictable with even an occasional light dusting of snow. January might be an ideal time to lure customers into my shop with Reba Mae's Hungarian goulash. It was impossible to ignore its mouthwatering appeal. First, though, I'd have to convince Reba Mae to part with her grandmother's recipe. And even then, Reba Mae couldn't very well perform a cooking demonstration if she was behind bars.

I'd just finished placing an order with a supplier when Mary Lou entered the shop.

"I'm not much of a cook, but my sister insists everyone bring a dish Thanksgiving," she announced. "I'm fixing a boxed dessert from the cake mix aisle at Piggly Wiggly. The directions say a sprinkle of cinnamon is optional. Everything came in the box except the cinnamon. You'd think it would be included, but no. Someone must have forgot to add it."

I walked over to the Hoosier cabinet where I kept the baking spices. "I carry several varieties, Vietnamese, Chinese, and Ceylon."

"Since I'm fussing, I want the best sprinkling cinnamon you carry."

"This one is extra fancy." I plucked a jar from a shelf. "Vietnamese cinnamon is the richest and sweetest. It's also the strongest of the cinnamons, so don't overdo your sprinkle."

"Thanks, Piper." Mary Lou fumbled through her wallet for cash. "I'm awfully busy right now, but I plan to come tonight."

I accepted the ten-dollar bill she handed me and made change. "What's going on tonight?"

"Silly." Mary Lou giggled. "The self-defense class in your petition."

I slid the cinnamon into a bag. "That was *last* night, Mary Lou."

"Last night?" she moaned. "I thought it was tonight. Hank really wanted me to go. He said Chief McBride needs to earn his salary seein' how he can't keep the town safe from thieves and murderers."

I wondered how many others shared Hank's opinion. Until her alibi had checked out last night, Mary Lou had been a viable person of interest for that crime. I was curious to know why she went to a bar instead of straight home after the final rehearsal. I had my theory, of course, but I'd like it validated. "Reba Mae and I went to High Cotton after the self-defense class," I said off handedly. "Did you know Monday is karaoke night?"

"Sounds fun."

I held her purchase slightly out of reach. "Have you ever been there?"

"Um . . . once, maybe. Hank doesn't like me goin' to bars. He's afraid men will start hittin' on me."

"Our waitress recalled a woman matching your description belting out a memorable version of an Aretha Franklin hit."

Mary Lou's baby-doll blue eyes shone at what she interpreted as a compliment. "If you promise not to tell, I'll let you in on a little secret."

"Your secret's safe with me," I said, relinquishing the cinnamon.

"Rehearsal didn't go well that last night. When it ended, Marcy and I decided to blow off some steam. The twins really keep Marcy tied down these days. Her momma's good about babysittin' while she's at rehearsals, but the kids keep her runnin' the rest of the time. She wanted to kick up her heels a bit before goin' home. We stayed till the DJ quit. Don't let it get out that I was singin' karaoke. Hank would be fit to be tied."

"My lips are sealed." Although Mary Lou had nothing new to report, at least my assumption had been correct. "Hope your dessert is a success."

"Thanks," she said in a rush. "If I don't hurry, I'm going to be late for my appointment at the Klassy Kut. Since I'm no longer trying to imitate Dolly Parton trying to imitate Truvy Jones, I'm ready for a change of hair color. I'm thinking a nice strawberry blond. Hank's awful partial to strawberries."

Five minutes later, Cot and Melly strolled in. It seems these days I seldom saw one without the other. Melly, on the one hand, looked especially pretty in a lilac cashmere twinset and tailored dove gray slacks. Cot, on the other hand, managed to look rumpled even in permanent press.

"Hello, dear," Melly chirped, then looked around and frowned. "What? No customers?"

"A temporary lull," I told her, stifling a spurt of irritation.

"Hmm, if you say so." She caressed the strand of pearls around her neck. "As I mentioned before, Cot's daughter invited me to join the family for Thanksgiving. Since I'll be meeting them for the first time, I want to make a good impression."

The judge gazed at her fondly. "I keep telling you, Melly, my dear, you needn't worry on that score. With all your charms, how could anyone find fault?"

"You're always so sweet." She flashed him a smile, then turned to me. "I thought I'd bring along an assortment of spices as a hostess gift."

"That sounds like the perfect touch. If you choose the spices, I'll make up a basket tailored especially for you and deliver it to you later."

"Excellent. In case I'm not home, leave it on the porch. Cot and I are driving to

Augusta for dinner tonight to meet old friends of his." Taking one of the small customer baskets, she began to peruse the aisles. I let her roam at will knowing she was familiar with where I kept everything.

Cot lowered his voice. "I have it on good authority your friend Reba Mae Johnson is up to her neck in hot water. Evidence — though mostly circumstantial — is piling up against her. Might not be too much longer before McBride makes his move."

I felt sick to my stomach at hearing this. It was one thing to sense it, another to hear the possibility voiced out loud. "I know it doesn't look good, but —"

Taking a pen and business card from his shirt pocket, Cot scribbled on the back of the card, then handed it to me. "If your friend finds herself in need of legal counsel, have her give this man a call. He's appeared before the bench numerous times, both here and in Columbia County. He's a trial attorney, experienced in murder cases. The man doesn't work cheap, but, with the predicament your friend's in, this is no time to be penny-wise and dollar-foolish."

"Thanks," I whispered around a lump in my throat that felt the size of a baseball. I slipped the card in my apron pocket, knowing it would break my heart to give it to

Reba Mae.

Her basket filled, Melly returned and offered me her credit card.

"Don't worry about it, Melly." I set the basket aside where I'd get to it later. "You can work off the cost by helping behind the counter when Christmas gets closer."

"Giving away merchandise is no way to turn a profit, dear. You don't have to major in business to know this for fact," she said, shoving her Visa at me. "Besides, I'll be away much of the time and unable to help."

"Oh yes, the river cruise in Europe. I'd nearly forgotten." I removed Melly's selections, amused to see they were spices she used in her gingersnaps. I'd make sure to include a copy of her recipe in the gift basket for Cot's daughter. "When are you leaving?"

"Cot's travel agent just contacted him with the details. We leave in two weeks. I'm so excited. I've already started packing."

"We arrive home a few days before Christmas," Cot explained.

Melly nodded, then added, "Next we're off to the Caribbean for CJ and Amber's nuptials."

At hearing this, I felt the wedding, which had seemed on the distant horizon, loom closer. A wash of emotion — resentment, regret, sadness — threatened to engulf me before I brought myself up short. Taking a deep breath, I counted my blessings instead. Spice It Up! was turning a modest profit. My children were thriving. Yes, I reminded myself, life was good.

"A friend of mine in Atlanta is having health issues," Cot said. "He can't make it down to Florida this winter, so he's willing to rent me his condo in Boca Raton." He smoothed his mustache and shot Melly a meaningful look from under a shelf of dark brows. "I'm trying to convince your former mother-in-law to join me."

Melly shook her head. "I'd hate people to get the wrong idea. I'm still thinking it over."

"I can be very persuasive, my dear." Cot gave her a tender smile.

"So I've noticed," Melly replied with an arch look.

A short time later I watched the couple leave. A person would have to be blind not to notice the affection between the pair. While Melly's social life — and love life — had kicked into high gear, mine seemed to be faltering. Why should septuagenarians have all the fun? I missed Doug's easy companionship and the fun times we had at football games, dinner dates, and movie nights.

Sighing, I went into the storeroom and rummaged through the shelves for a perfect container for Melly's gift basket. Aroused from his nap, Casey opened one eye to watch. "Don't mind me," I told my pet. "When Lindsey gets home from school, she'll take you for a romp in the park."

Casey thumped his tail on the floor in acknowledgment and promptly resumed his snooze.

Pleased with the pretty wicker basket I'd unearthed, I returned to the counter and, since there were currently no customers in the shop, proceeded to fill it. I'd no sooner put a handful of raffia in the bottom and started arranging the spices when Craig Granger came through the door.

Since the Oktoberfest party he and Sandy had thrown last month, Craig had lost weight and aged years. If anyone ever looked in need of a hug, it was him. I came out from behind the counter and did just that, then took a step back. "Craig, I'm so sorry for your loss. If there's anything I can do, you only have to ask."

"Thanks, Piper." He ran a hand over his thick salt-and-pepper hair and sighed. "Actually, I'm here to ask a favor."

"Certainly, anything."

"I know from things Sandy said that

313

women are in and out of your shop all day. I hope you'll spread the word they can stop bringing me food. I've been deluged. My freezer is stuffed with casseroles. I can't even see countertops beneath all the cakes, cookies, and pies. As soon as I leave your shop, I'm taking the baked goods to the senior center, where they'll get used in the free-lunch program."

"The ladies mean well, Craig. They simply want to do something useful, so they cook and bake in the belief it will help in some small way."

"It's not as though I don't appreciate their efforts, Piper, but enough is enough. I'm going to Michigan day after tomorrow and don't know when I'll return. McBride promised to keep me in the loop regarding the investigation. Our family is there. My children and grandchildren are begging me to stay."

"It's understandable they'd want you close at a time like this. That might be what the doctor ordered." I winced inwardly at the cliché.

"You sound like Vicki Lamont!" he snorted. "She's been hounding me to play a round a golf or get out on the tennis court. According to Vicki, exercise is a form of grief therapy."

"She claims she heard that on *a talk show.*" I returned behind the counter and set about arranging and rearranging small jars of ginger, cardamom, and coriander under Craig's watchful eye.

"Truth is," Craig confessed, "Vicki makes me uncomfortable. She's overly friendly, too helpful." He stuffed his hands into the pockets of his chinos. "She even had the nerve to offer to pack Sandy's clothing and donate it to Goodwill."

"They were good friends — almost inseparable." I added a packet of recipe cards to Melly's gift basket.

"It's more than that. I think Vicki wanted to *be* Sandy." Craig shrugged and turned toward the door.

I stared after him, my thoughts churning. Sandy, compared to Vicki, had it all. Comfortable lifestyle. Beautiful home. Doting husband. Wealth. The Grangers traveled the world, entertained on a grand scale, and had a bevy of influential friends. What's not to envy? But after what Craig had just said, I couldn't help but wonder how strong Vicki's desire was to emulate Sandy. Strong enough to kill?

CHAPTER 27

The Detroit Lions game was on the television, the sound muted. Old habits die hard, I guess. Watching the Lions play football on Thanksgiving Day was a family tradition. It had never mattered to my father, uncles, and cousins that our favorite team lost more often than won.

I scraped the dressing I'd made into a buttered pan. Casey was under the kitchen table, alert for any tidbits that might fall his way. This year I'd decided on the old-fashioned bread and celery variety, the kind my mother used to make with parsley, sage, rosemary, and thyme. Again the lyrics from the ballad "Scarborough Fair" played in my head.

Lindsey came out of her bedroom and did a pirouette. "How do I look?"

I stood back to admire my girl, who was quickly morphing into a woman. Long blond tendrils spilled down her back and around her shoulders to frame a pretty face. Although she'd spent a considerable time applying makeup, the result looked youthful and natural and not overdone. A red knit dress and high heels added an air of polish and sophistication. "You'll make your daddy proud, sweetie."

"You look nice, too," she said returning the compliment. "That top with the big turkey on it is supercute. And the leggings and flats look comfy."

"Comfort is the rule of the day." I tossed Casey a crumb of the dressing, and it vanished like magic.

"I'm really sorry, Mom." Lindsey twirled a lock of her hair around a finger. "Accepting Daddy's invitation was thoughtless of me. I should've told him I'd rather spend Thanksgiving with you."

"Nonsense. You made your decision. Stop obsessing over it and don't let it ruin your day." Checking the timer I'd set, I opened the oven door, removed my pumpkin pie, and set it on a rack to cool. The spicy scents of cinnamon, nutmeg, and cloves pervaded the kitchen. "Don't worry about me, Linds; I'll be fine. Now that your father and I are divorced, it's only fair you alternate holidays. Next year, don't forget it's my turn."

"I won't." She munched on a piece of

celery that hadn't made it into the dressing. "I only wish you weren't spending Thanksgiving alone. Dad, at least, has Amber."

"Mmm." I moved on to scrubbing the sweet potatoes. I hardly considered Amber Leigh Ames a consolation prize, but CJ viewed the former beauty queen in a different light. With her at his side, he strutted around proud as a peacock. In my humble opinion, Pooh Bear and Sweetums, as the couple had nicknamed each other, were a match made in heaven.

"I'll bet the pumpkin pie at the country club can't compare with yours."

"If it does, I don't want to hear about it." I took a roasting chicken — a substitute for turkey — from the fridge and proceeded to wash and pat it dry.

"That must be Daddy," Lindsey said at hearing a knock on the door downstairs. "I'll get it."

She raced off as fast as her heels allowed to answer the door. There went my wish for avoiding him. In spite of my brave words to Lindsey, all day I'd tried to quash memories of happier times when we had gathered as a family around the dinner table to give thanks for blessings big and small.

It took a Herculean effort on my part, but I succeeded in tamping down nostalgia and pasted on a bright smile for Lindsey's benefit. "Hey, CJ," I greeted my ex. "Happy Thanksgiving."

CJ grinned at me from the top of the stairs. "Hey there, Scooter. How's the world treatin' you?" He straightened his silk tie and flicked a glance at the small television. "Still rootin' for the Lions, I see. You've lived in Georgia for years. Past time you switch allegiance to the Atlanta Falcons."

His hearty greeting made me want to kick him in his shin. Instead, I liberally sprinkled salt and pepper in the cavity of the chicken. "Thanks for the advice, but I'll stand with my hometown."

"Suit yourself." He sauntered over and sniffed my pie. "Smells good in here. Sure do miss the amaretto cheesecake you used to make."

"I'll send Amber the recipe."

"Don't bother." He chuckled. "That girl can't boil water. It's why we eat out all the time."

"Well, at least she knows how to make reservations."

"Heard from our son? Hope he takes time out from the books to get him some turkey." CJ shoved one hand into his trouser pocket. "Remember from the time he could talk how Chad always wanted a drumstick?"

Ignoring the invitation to waltz down memory lane, I put a bunch of fresh thyme and a sprig of rosemary into the cavity of the chicken and added half a lemon and a clove of garlic. "Chad called earlier. He and his friend are going to a diner that advertises home-cooked meals."

Lindsey, who had stood listening to our exchange, excused herself to give her reflection a final inspection.

"Even Momma raved about your Thanksgiving dinners — and you know she's picky." CJ darted a look over his shoulder to make sure we were alone. "Speakin' of the ol' gal, she's got me worried. She's got a wild hair to run off to visit Christmas markets along the Danube. What does Europe have that Macy's don't?"

"A river cruise sounds like a wonderful opportunity for your mother to visit places she's only dreamed about. I don't think I ever saw her so excited — or this happy." I wound twine around the legs of the chicken and tucked the wings into a prayerful pose.

CJ rubbed the back of his neck. "Nothin' against the judge, but Momma needs to slow things down. People are startin' to talk about the two of 'em off gallivantin'."

"Your mother is perfectly capable of deciding what's best for her." I popped the dressing, sweet potatoes, and roasting chicken into the oven. Out of the corner of my eye, I glimpsed Lindsey in the hallway chatting on her cell phone. "Say, CJ, what do you know about Wanda being involved in a lawsuit with Sandy Granger?"

He shrugged. "Don't mind sayin', Wanda sure has her panties in a twist. All her life, she's been on the suin' side, and she isn't happy the tables are turned."

"Is it true Sandy threatened a counter-suit?"

"Let me tell you, that went over like a fart in church — pardon the expression. Musta raised Wanda's blood pressure to the top of the meter."

"I'd like to stop by your office tomorrow and talk to her."

"Save yourself the trouble. Wanda took time off to visit her grandkids in Omaha. Don't expect her back till Monday."

"Ready, Daddy?" Lindsey returned to the kitchen, purse in one hand and a wrap in the other. "Sean and his father will meet us at the club. After dinner, Sean said he'd give me a ride home."

"Have fun, sweetie."

CJ gave me a jaunty salute, Lindsey a peck on the cheek; then both trooped down the stairs and left me to my lonesome except for Casey as company.

I vented my frustration on a sack of hapless potatoes. Peels littered the sink like confetti in Times Square on New Year's Eve. By the time I calmed, I realized I'd peeled enough potatoes to feed a family of four. I told myself I'd use the leftover mashed potatoes over the weekend to top a shepherd's pie.

With dinner under control, there was little left to do but wait. I abandoned the kitchen in favor of the living room, where I curled up in a corner of the sofa and patted the spot next to me, a signal for Casey to join me. Picking up the TV remote, I clicked it on and absently stroked Casey's head. "Guess we've been deserted, boy."

Casey licked my hand in a canine show of solidarity.

I stared at the television, no longer interested in players in tight blue and silver uniforms racing back and forth across the screen. I blocked out the roar of the crowd when they protested a referee's call. I had a choice to make. I could either sit alone, wallowing in self-pity, or take action. Slowly an idea coagulated out of the doldrums. When Precious's brother Junior had stopped in yesterday for marjoram, he'd mentioned that, for the first time in several years, the entire Blessing clan would sit down to dinner together. He'd gone on to report that McBride had given his staff the day off to spend with their families. In their absence, he'd volunteered to man the station.

No reason we both had to eat alone. No reason at all. Perhaps with a full stomach the man might be more inclined to share a tasty morsel or two of information. If he questioned my intentions, I'd tell him to view the meal as a peace offering of sorts for tossing him on his backside and damaging his manly pride. Casey cocked his head in confusion when I sprang off the sofa and rummaged through the hall closet for a picnic hamper.

When the oven timer buzzed, I took the items from the oven, covered them with foil, then mashed potatoes and whipped up some gravy. That done, I loaded up.

Minutes later I was at the police department and parked beside McBride's Ford F-150 pickup. The hamper was so heavy I needed both hands to haul it inside. "Yoo hoo," I yodeled in my best Dottie Hemmings fashion. "Anyone home?"

McBride appeared in the hallway. "What the . . . ?"

"Hungry?" Seeing him standing there frowning at me, I almost lost my nerve.

At last he strode over and took the hamper. "What do you have in here, bricks?"

"I don't like eating alone."

He stared at me, long and hard. I stared back, trying without success to read his thoughts. For a second I feared he might order me to leave and take my food with me. Maybe accuse me of trying to bribe an officer of the law. Or, worse yet, tell me Shirley Randolph had already provided a Thanksgiving feast.

"C'mon back to the break room — aka command central, home of the friendly neighborhood hotline."

As he started down the hallway, I let out a pent-up breath and followed.

Upon reaching a room at the far end, McBride shoved the phones and forms on a utility table aside to make space for the picnic hamper. While he did this, I slipped out of my jacket and hung it over the back of a folding chair. "Junior Blessing told me you gave your employees the day off."

"No reason they shouldn't spend the day with their families. What about you? No friends or family to fuss over?"

"Nope, I've been deserted," I said, beginning to feel more cheerful.

I began unloading the hamper while McBride watched a bit warily. Along with the food, I'd thrown in a few extras — items such as a plaid tablecloth, contrasting napkins, and a fat vanilla-scented candle. "Sure you didn't forget the kitchen sink?" he inquired drolly.

"Don't tell me a sense of humor lurks down deep inside?"

A ghost of a smile played around his mouth. "Merely making an observation."

I proceeded to haul out the food. "I didn't roast a turkey this year, but chicken is the next best thing."

"I always thought turkey was overrated."

Finally I set out plates and flatware. "Sorry" — I shot him an apologetic look — "nothing fancy, just everyday. I didn't have any use for the fine china and fancy silver, so I sold them on eBay after my divorce."

"China and silver? Also overrated." He smiled and the dimple in his cheek that I found so appealing made an appearance. "Can I help?"

I handed him a knife. "I'll let you do the honors."

While McBride carved the chicken, I uncovered the various dishes I'd brought. He took the chair opposite me and was about to dig into the mashed potatoes when I stalled him by taking his hand. Startled, he almost jerked it away.

"First," I said, "we say grace."

My heart warmed as his fingers, strong and competent, curled around mine. Bowing my head, I repeated words of thanksgiving I'd been taught as a child. Looking up, I smiled. "Now, help yourself before it gets cold."

McBride wasn't bashful about heaping his plate and diving in. I derived a simple pleasure from watching him enjoy the meal I'd prepared. Even though it wasn't elaborate, he didn't seem to mind.

"So this is what a real home-cooked Thanksgiving dinner tastes like," he said, taking a second helping of dressing. "Seems I've been missing out all these years."

I paused in the act of pouring gravy over my potatoes. "Surely you're joking."

"No joke," he said, shaking his head. "Before my mom took off, she'd spend the day either sleeping or reading a gossip magazine. She believed holidays should be a day of rest and relaxation, not spent slaving over a hot stove. In the meantime, my dad guzzled beer in the living room, then passed out in front of the TV. My sister Claudia and I had to fend for ourselves, which usually meant a frozen dinner."

I sampled the sweet potatoes over which I'd dribbled maple syrup, butter, and a sprinkle of cinnamon. "I thought you told me once that you'd been married? Didn't your wife cook?"

He sliced off the second drumstick. "Before she died in a car wreck, Tracey and I only had one Thanksgiving together. I was on duty that time, still in the army, so ate dinner in the mess hall."

"What about all the Thanksgivings since? Surely with your charm and good looks, someone would have taken pity on you."

"Lack of 'charm' has always been a short-coming of mine." He helped himself to the last of the mashed potatoes. "Usually I volunteer to work holidays. I'd grab a bite to eat at some place unlucky enough to be open like the Waffle House."

"How about a slice of pumpkin pie? Even Melly can't find fault with it."

"Let me put on a fresh pot of coffee first," he said, getting to his feet. "Be right back."

While he was gone, I packed up the dishes and returned them to the hamper. A day that had started out dismal had taken a surprising turn for the better. McBride had been more open than usual about his personal life. Against my will, I found myself drawn to him. In the distance a phone rang and I heard the low rumble of McBride's voice as he spoke to the caller. Prepared for a wait, I cut two generous wedges of pie.

Unable to sit still, I prowled the break room. In McBride's absence, I thought I'd set the room back to the way it had been before my arrival. I moved the phones back into position and picked up the stacks of papers, then paused when I realized what they were — forms used to record hotline tips.

I knew I shouldn't peek but couldn't resist. I leafed through the tips, looking for one dated a week ago. Then I found it. A person who refused to give their name reported Reba Mae near the opera house the night of Sandy's murder. A scrawled note said the voice sounded like that of a female.

"What are you doing?"

I jumped at the sound of McBride's voice. The papers in my hand fluttered from my nerveless fingers to the floor. "I, ah . . ."

"Dammit, Piper." He advanced into the room, his face dark with anger, and set the cups he held down on the table with enough force to send coffee sloshing over the rim. "I should've known you had an ulterior motive for bringing me dinner. The entire time you only wanted a chance to snoop around."

"No, that's not true," I protested, feeling on the verge of tears.

"Learn anything interesting while you were nosing around?"

I could sense from his expression he wasn't ready to believe anything I had to say. "What if that was the reason I'm here? Can you blame me for wanting to help a friend? Do you really think she's guilty?"

"Doesn't matter what I think. My job is to follow the trail of evidence."

"And your so-called trail is leading straight to her doorstep."

He didn't answer; he didn't have to.

CHAPTER 28

Bright and early the next morning, McBride stormed into Spice It Up! "All right, where is she?"

McBride's sudden arrival had the same effect as someone pressing the PAUSE button on a DVR player. The shop, which had been bustling with patrons thanks to the Black Friday rush, grew still. Everyone froze.

I excused myself from waiting on a customer and walked over to him. Standing as he was in the center of the floor, he looked like a force of mass destruction. Lindsey, who had been drafted as my assistant, sidled closer. "Mom," she whispered anxiously, "should I call Daddy?"

"It's okay, sweetie. I haven't done anything to merit a lawyer."

McBride, his expression hard as flint, hooked his thumbs in his belt and widened his stance. "Last time I checked, aiding and abetting a fugitive was still a criminal offense."

Melly, another of my "helpers," edged next to me. "Piper, dear, I'm asking Cot to come down. He'll put an end to this harassment."

"McBride, I have no idea what you're talking about. You're not making a lick of sense," I said, all the while reminding myself to remain calm and not to let him upset me.

"Don't play games with me, Piper. You'll lose."

I didn't doubt that for an instant. He'd play dirty if he had to, but he'd play to win. Lindsey and Melly flanked me on either side, ready to leap into the fray. I'd thank them later for their staunch support, but right now I had a tiger to tame. I gestured at the shop full of women who gawked unabashedly at the mini-drama being played out in front of them. "Being a man, perhaps you're not aware this is Black Friday, the busiest shopping day of the year. Please, state your business, McBride, and let me get on with mine."

He looked around, probably aware for the first time we had a large audience. "We need to talk," he growled. "Lady's choice. Here or my office?"

"I can hardly leave with the shop as busy as it is. What about the storeroom?" I suggested.

"Fine," McBride muttered. Taking my elbow in a firm grip, he hustled me toward the storeroom at the rear of Spice It Up! Lindsey and Melly followed our exit with perplexed and worried expressions. Each, I noted, held a cell phone in her hand. McBride shut the storeroom door with a finality that bordered on a slam.

"What is *wrong* with you?" I demanded the second we were alone. "Did you spoon too much macho on your Wheaties this morning?"

"Where's your friend?"

"My friend . . . ?" I raised a brow. "Unlike others in this room, McBride, I have a lot of friends. Care to be more specific?"

His breath hissed out, and I could see that instead of taming a tiger I was provoking one. "I'm talking about Reba Mae Johnson. If you know where she is, now would be a good time to tell me."

"Reba Mae? Missing . . . ?" The news came as a shock. Didn't she realize running away would make her look guilty even though she wasn't?

"Enough of the wide-eyed innocent act." McBride's laser-bright gaze, sharp enough to do surgery without anesthesia, didn't leave my face. "You know damn well what I'm talking about. I sent one of my men over to bring her in, but she's disappeared."

"What do you mean disappeared?" I asked, struggling to process all this. "She never takes Friday off. Did you check the Klassy Kut?"

"Of course we did. Who do I look like, Barney Fife? Officer Moyer found the beauty shop locked and a sign in the window big as life: CLOSED TILL FURTHER NOTICE."

"Reba Mae would never up and leave without saying something to me or her boys!" I brushed a curl off my forehead with a hand that wasn't quite steady. "Have you checked with them? The family was going to her uncle Joe and aunt Ida's for Thanksgiving dinner."

"Clay and Caleb deny knowing anything about their mother's disappearance. That leaves you as the lone traveler on the information highway."

"I swear, McBride, I have no idea where Reba Mae could be. She didn't say a word about leaving." I felt like a bug under a microscope beneath his scrutiny. "What about her car?"

"Her Buick vanished along with her. I've issued a BOLO — be on the lookout," he explained for my benefit.

I stared at a coatrack mounted on the far wall without really seeing it. "You don't think . . ." My thoughts were so jumbled, it was difficult to organize words into sentences. I moistened my dry lips and began again, "You don't think whoever killed Sandy . . . ?"

McBride looked at me as though I'd taken leave of my senses. Well, maybe I had. It's not every day a girl's BFF simply vanishes without a trace. "No," he said, allowing a trace of frustration to creep into his voice. "I think your friend got wind of the fact she was about to be arrested and is on the lam. And" — he gave me a mirthless smile — "who better than you to give her a heads-up?"

"Dear . . . ?" Melly's muffled voice came from the other side of the closed door. "Are you all right? Do you need any help?"

No, I wasn't all right. I didn't know whether to laugh or cry. Or scream. I was in way over my head — and so was Reba Mae.

McBride placed his hand on the knob but didn't open the door. "If you know where Reba Mae's hiding but don't tell me, you're in for a world of hurt."

I stood on the threshold of the storeroom and watched McBride march out. In my absence, Melly and Lindsey had summoned reinforcements. CJ and Judge Cottrell Herman formed an honor guard on either side of the shop's exit. Eyes straight ahead, McBride passed through the gauntlet without acknowledging their presence.

For the remainder of the day, I forced myself to act as though nothing out of the ordinary had transpired. Rather, I focused on my customers. Thankfully, Brandywine Creek was unusually busy with an influx of relatives visiting for the holiday. From the look of things, business was also booming at Yesteryear Antiques and Second Hand Prose. Tapping into my marketing playbook, I'd developed a little Black Friday strategy of my own. With each bottle of vanilla extract sold, a jar of sea salt could be purchased for half price. As a result, my day's total reached an all-time high — even better than the day preceding last July's barbecue festival.

After locking up for the night, I felt more wired than tired. Melly had deserted me in order to primp for an evening of bridge. Lindsey and a group of girlfriends were headed to the Augusta Mall in a quest for Black Friday bargains. To keep him from getting underfoot Casey had been cooped up in the apartment all day, and he was ready for some exercise. Truth be told, I could use a little exercise myself for stress relief. "How about we go for a run, boy?"

He thumped his tail, signaling his willingness.

I quickly changed into sweats and running shoes. I snapped on Casey's leash and picked up the day's receipts on the way. "While we're out, we'll drop these off in the night depository at the bank."

Casey barked his agreement, and we took off. By the time we reached the bank, I'd found my rhythm. I jogged in place while taking a good look around. McBride had emphasized developing situational awareness. If he could see me now, he'd be pleased to know I'd taken his advice to heart.

The area surrounding the bank was well lit with floodlights, making it bright as day. Even so, I examined the shrubbery for boogeymen. I didn't see anything suspicious, yet I had an uneasy feeling I was being watched. Goose bumps pebbled my arms. Was that the same creepy sensation Madison experienced? It didn't help any when Casey started to growl. Feeling vulnerable, I hurriedly took the money bag from the waistband of my sweats and dropped it into the slot.

As I jogged away, I tried to convince myself that carrying so much cash on my person accounted for the attack of nerves. My mind on autopilot, I turned down a residential street. Almost without realizing it, I found myself not far from Reba Mae's home. Drawing nearer, I slowed my pace, then, my mind made up, went up her front walk and rang the bell.

Clay answered the door. "Hey, Miz Prescott, c'mon in. My brother and I were just about to phone you."

Clay stood aside for Casey and me to enter. Caleb rose from a recliner when he saw us. "Don't know about you boys," I said, "but I could sure use a big hug."

I'd scarcely gotten the words out before I was engulfed in a three-way bear hug. "We're worried sick about Momma," Clay mumbled against my neck.

"Not a word," Caleb said, his voice choked. "Not a single word."

The hug over, I stepped back. "Did you search the house? Maybe your momma left a note of some kind. Hinted at where she might be."

Clay shook his head miserably. "We hunted high and low but couldn't find a thing. That's why we wanted to talk to you.

She tells you everything."

"Not this time," I said sadly. "I didn't have a clue she was planning to run off until Chief McBride burst into Spice It Up! this morning demanding I tell him where she was."

"He paid me a visit, too," Caleb said. "Came by the garage. Asked if I knew where she might be."

"Chief rolled by the construction site where I was working." Clay stuck his hands in the back pockets of his jeans. "Said if I knew anything, I'd better come clean."

"Your momma's one smart lady. I'm sure she's fine," I said, trying to reassure them as well as myself. "She might assume that with her out of the picture McBride will concentrate on finding other suspects — and she'll buy herself time."

They nodded, their expressions glum.

I wished I could say something, or do something, to lessen their worry but felt helpless. "Promise you'll let me know if you hear from her."

Casey and I left shortly afterward to walk home. The night was dark and windy, the moon hidden beneath a thick layer of clouds. Hunching my shoulders against the nip in the fall air, I quickened my step. Instead of trotting at my heels as he usually did, Casey lagged behind. "What's the matter, boy?"

My pup's uncharacteristic behavior was starting to have an untoward effect on me. I'd walked this same route hundreds of times — alone and at night — and never felt a bit anxious. McBride had lectured on the importance of trusting your instincts to avoid dangerous situations. Well, my instincts were hollering for attention. Was I being watched? Followed? To be safe, I crossed to the opposite side of the street.

I thought I heard muffled footsteps but couldn't be sure with the wind whistling through the bare branches. I stopped walking, pretending to tie my shoe, and the footsteps stopped, too. Casey twisted around and barked. I dove into the pocket of my hoodie for my cell phone and came out empty-handed. I'd forgotten it. Lights shone from behind closed drapes in some of the homes. As a last resort, I'd run up on a stranger's porch, bang on the door, and ask them to dial 911. If I was wrong and no one was following me, I'd feel like a fool. But better a live fool than a dead one.

"C'mon, boy." I tugged on Casey's leash. "Let's hurry." We walked briskly another ten feet before I cast a quick glance over my shoulder in time to see a figure melt into the shadows.

Confront your attacker; don't show fear.

"Coward!" I yelled, whirling around. My heart slammed against my rib cage. "I know you're following me. If you don't show yourself this second, I'll calling nine-one-one."

With agonizing slowness, a form materialized from behind the trunk of a tree. "Nine-one-one at your service."

I squinted into the darkness. "McBride, that you?"

Casey, bless his traitorous little heart, broke free and ran to greet his favorite lawman. McBride didn't disappoint the mutt. Squatting on his haunches, he scratched Casey's sweet spot, making the pup squirm with pleasure.

I advanced with less enthusiasm. "Why are you stalking me? Do I need to take out a restraining order?"

"When you try my patience, a restraining order might not be a bad idea." McBride rose to his feet. In the light spilling from a nearby house, I could see he was dressed in his favorite black — jeans, T-shirt, and a windbreaker with the BCPD logo.

"I bet as a child you dressed in a Darth Vader costume on Halloween. Now," I said, "why are you skulking around in the dark?

Hoping I'd lead you to Reba Mae?"

"It's called surveillance." He sauntered closer, his expression unreadable. "I drew the short straw. Moyer and Tucker are keeping an eye on the twins."

"Reba Mae and I have become quite adept at surveillance. Trust me, McBride, your technique sucks. If I was in a friendlier state of mind — which I'm not — I could give you a few pointers."

"Your friend will eventually contact you, Piper, and when she does I want to hear about it."

I patted my thigh, a command for Casey to heel. When he returned to my side, I picked his leash off the sidewalk. "Your department's time and money would be better spent looking for the real killer than harassing innocent citizens. If you'd gotten any closer without identifying yourself, I'd have blasted you with pepper spray."

I didn't bother to inform him I didn't have any. Turning on my heel, I trudged home. Black Friday had certainly lived up to its name.

CHAPTER 29

I let myself in through the back door. Unzipping my hoodie, I shrugged it off and hung it on a hook along with Casey's leash, then stomped up the stairs with Casey maintaining a safe distance. Fury emanated from me like steam from a boiler. Why was McBride being so narrow-minded? Couldn't he see there were plenty of others who might've wanted to kill Sandy? But, no, he'd zeroed in on Reba Mae and couldn't see the forest for the trees.

"Reba Mae," I said, addressing the deserted apartment, "this disappearing act of yours isn't going over well. Sure hope you know what you're doing, girlfriend."

Casey sat on the floor and watched uneasily.

I thought about making coffee, but caffeine would only make me more hyper, so I settled on herbal tea instead — soothing and relaxing chamomile. I paced while waiting for the water to heat. Thus far, all my snooping, all my sleuthing, had been for naught. I hadn't turned up a single tangible clue to prove Reba Mae had nothing to do with strangling Sandy. All I had to show for my efforts was a rapidly dwindling number of suspects on my persons of interest list.

I stopped pacing long enough to take a mug from the cupboard and a tin of tea bags. Casey got excited at the sound of me prying the lid off a container. His tail swished back and forth like a dust mop on steroids in a pathetic plea for a doggy treat. I couldn't resist the look in his soulful dark eyes. "Here, you go, boy," I said, tossing him a dental chew Doug had recommended. "Not only will that keep your gums healthy, but it's full of antioxidants and omega-three fatty acids."

Casey didn't seem the least bit interested in the benefits as he tackled his treat with enthusiasm.

When the teakettle whistled I drowned my tea bag in a flood of boiling water. This was a far cry from the civilized ritual with bone china and a delicate teapot that Doug and Madison performed nightly. I hadn't heard from Doug in days. Did he ever think of me? I wondered. Did he miss me as much as I missed him?

I moved into the living room and was about to take my first sip of tea when my cell phone jangled. I'd been distracted when I left for my run and couldn't remember where I'd put the darn thing. Its persistent ringing led me to the dresser in the bedroom. By the time I reached it, the ringing had stopped. The display read CALLER UNKNOWN.

"Telemarketers," I muttered in disgust. Who else calls at all hours? I didn't need vinyl siding, replacement windows, or my carpets cleaned. I had no desire to participate in a Nielsen survey. The world didn't need to know my TV-viewing habits. I'd done that once but had been too embarrassed to return it. Shortly after CJ announced he needed his "space," I'd fallen into a crevasse filled with tabloid talk shows. The sleazier they were, the more I watched. It was bittersweet consolation knowing some folks were worse off than me. After a period of moping, I started to climb out of the hole I'd dropped into, regained more solid footing, and switched to cooking shows. These proved my salvation. They renewed my love of cooking and revived my desire to own and operate my own business. Spice It Up! was the end result.

Perching on the edge of the bed, I blew

on my tea to cool it, then took a cautious sip. I'd no sooner lowered the mug to the nightstand when my phone rang again. I frowned at the display: CALLER UNKNOWN. Against my better judgment, I answered, "Hello —"

"Hey, honeybun," Reba Mae responded, sounding remarkably chipper for a fugitive from justice. "Since when have you stopped answerin' your phone? Coulda been the Georgia lottery callin' to say you hit it big in the Mega Millions jackpot."

"Reba Mae Johnson," I practically yelled into the phone, "where are you? The boys and I are half out of our minds with worry. McBride issued a BOLO; you know that's —"

"— be on the lookout. I know, I know, I watch cop shows all the time. Listen up, hon; I only got limited minutes on this burner phone I bought at a fillin' station."

"Burner phone?" I gasped. "Aren't those for drug dealers?"

"Yup, drug dealers and folks on the lam. Problem is, I can't stay hid forever. My clients will drop me like a hot potato if I stay away too long."

"McBride is having your boys and me watched to see if you make contact." At the mention of McBride, I sat up straighter and cast an involuntary glance over my shoulder. If he loitered outside, would he be able to spot me gabbing on the phone?

"Hey, hon, you still there?"

"Hold on a sec, Reba Mae." I scurried to the windowless bathroom, closed the door for good measure, and sat on the rim of the bathtub. "Okay, shoot."

"I'm callin' to find out what you're doin' to get me out of this predicament. You're my last chance to clear myself. I'm dependin' on you, Piper."

"What can I do that McBride hasn't done already?"

"You believe in me," she said simply. "He doesn't. Now who else is on our list? It's all a matter of elimination, right?"

"Right" — I nodded — "but there aren't many names left. I spoke with Bunny. She swears she went straight home and into a bubble bath."

"Calgon or Mr. Bubble?"

"This isn't the time for wisecracks. Limited minutes, remember."

I heard Reba Mae expel a breath. "Yeah, yeah. I remember. Check out Bunny's alibi. See if anyone can vouch for her."

"Like who — the water department?"

"Now who's being a smart aleck?" Reba Mae asked. "Who else have you talked to?"

346

"Craig Granger dropped in the other day. Seems Vicki's been plying him with home-made goodies. And hinting she'd like to be his partner for golf or tennis. Before he left, Craig made an odd comment. He said something along the lines of not only were Vicki and Sandy good friends, but Vicki wanted to *be* Sandy."

"Creepy, but Craig might be on to some-thin'. Vicki's lookin' for a replacement for Kenny. I've seen her sizin' up Doug and Wyatt. If she could find a man with a fatter bank account, even better."

"I heard her complain once that Sandy had it all — and she didn't appreciate it."

"Well, girlfriend, sounds like you got your work cut out for you. Check out Bunny and Vicki, but do it right quick. Klassy Kut to Spice Girl, over and out."

I opened my mouth to speak, but all I was left with was a dial tone. I'd been about to tell Reba Mae that Wanda Needmore wasn't in the clear alibi-wise yet either. That Wanda was not only secretive but also not forth-coming and had a strong motive.

I was still sitting on the rim of the tub, pondering my next move, when Lindsey charged up the steps.

"Mom . . . ?" she called from the kitchen. "Mom, where are you?"

"I'm right here," I said, coming out of the bathroom, cell phone in hand.

Lindsey frowned at seeing me. "You've been in the bathroom, talking on the phone?"

I gave a little shrug as though sitting on the bathtub with my cell phone for company was the most natural thing in the world. "Did you find any bargains at the mall?" I asked, although the multitude of shopping bags she held told the tale.

Her eyes lit up. "Wait till you see what I bought Chad. He'll freak when he sees it." She pawed through her spoils, then held up a T-shirt with a humorous saying that would resonate with her brother's fondness for bacon. "By the way," she said, stuffing the shirt back into the bag, "why is Chief McBride parked behind your car?"

I mentally counted to ten before answering. "Because, sweetie, the man's a pit bull with a Sherlock Holmes complex."

"Whatever," Lindsey said, gathering her purchases and reaching for her cell as she headed for her room. "I told Sean I'd call him after I got home."

My anger rekindled. So McBride was sitting out back. I returned to my bedroom and peeked through the blinds. Sure enough, there he was in a squad car behind my Beetle, plain as a wart on your nose. Was he waiting to see if I'd be stupid enough to rendezvous with Reba Mae? Or was this an intimidation tactic? His way of sending a message: Big Brother is watching. *Some "big brother,"* I thought in disgust.

Hurrying into the kitchen, I dumped the chamomile tea that had grown cold down the drain. "So much for its soothing effects," I grumbled as I brewed a pot of coffee. Who did Mr. Law and Order think he was? I didn't appreciate the notion of a guard dog monitoring my every move. When the coffee — Colombian — finished perking, I poured some into a travel mug.

I considered a sneak attack — exiting through the front door, slipping down the narrow passageway between my shop and the building next door, and coming up on McBride from behind — but abandoned the idea for a straightforward approach. I threw on my hoodie and marched brazenly, coffee in hand, across the vacant lot separating my shop from his cruiser. I smiled with satisfaction at seeing his surprise when I motioned for him to roll his window down.

"What the . . . ?"

"Here." I shoved the mug at him. "I thought this might keep you awake while you're on a fool's mission. All you're going to show for this tomorrow are dark circles under your eyes from lack of sleep."

I heard him call after me as I fled back inside but didn't turn around.

The next day was Saturday. Business had been brisk all morning. News of Reba Mae's vanishing act drew people like spectators to a circus. In a relatively short span of time my friend had turned into Brandywine Creek's very own version of Houdini. I-don't-know-where-she-is-but-while-you're-here-have-you-tried had become my sales pitch du jour. To my surprise, it worked more often than not. Around lunch-time, things had slowed to a point where I felt I could leave Spice It Up! in the capable of hands of my daughter and ex-mother-in-law for a brief period.

"Melly, I hope this isn't an imposition," I said, whipping my apron over my head and stashing it beneath the counter. "I won't be gone long, but I can't put off my errand any longer." "Errand" seemed a much nicer word than "interrogation," which was what I planned for Bunny Bowtin.

"Don't worry, dear." Melly waved me off. "Lindsey and I can handle things."

I felt overwhelmed with a sense of urgency as I ducked out the back door. I felt the weight of Reba Mae's freedom rest heavily on my shoulders. My BFF was on the lam, communicating via a burner phone. Unless I found the killer soon, her clientele would desert her like rats on a sinking ship. I didn't want that fate to befall the best little ol' beauty shop in Brandywine County.

Thankfully, there was no sign of McBride either in his truck or in a squad car. I assumed even an intrepid cop had to sleep sometime. I hopped into my VW and headed for the historic district. I'd been to Bunny's once, years ago, for a Halloween party when CJ and I had masqueraded as Hansel and Gretel. Bunny and her husband lived in a stately colonial not far from the Turner-Driscoll House, Brandywine Creek's premier bed-and-breakfast.

I wasn't certain I'd find Bunny home on a Saturday afternoon, but since I suffer from poor impulse control I took a chance. I parked in the drive next to a late-model black Camaro, made my way up a flagstone walk, lifted the heavy brass knocker, and let it fall. The door, which was painted a glossy fire-engine red, was opened by their teenage son, a high-school senior with stringy hair and acne.

I smiled, not sure whether he'd recognize me even though he and Lindsey had been classmates since grade school. "Is your mother home?"

"Yeah," the kid said. "I'm on my way out, but go right in."

"Umm, thanks."

"Mom!" he yelled upstairs. "Some lady here to see you. You're just in time to hear my parents go another round." He tossed the latter remark over his shoulder as he brushed past, leaving me standing in the foyer. The next sound was the throaty purr of the Camaro's engine as it fired up, then faded as the car backed down the drive and disappeared down the street.

Feeling like a trespasser, I waited, expecting Bunny to appear any minute.

"That's the final straw!" a male voice rang out. "First thing Monday morning, I'm making arrangements."

"Dennis, don't be this way," Bunny pleaded. "I can stop drinking any time I want. Promise, I'll quit."

I shouldn't be here, I told myself. *I should leave. Now. This instant. This is a private conversation between husband and wife.* Although my first instinct was to leave, my feet felt glued to the floor. I seemed to have stumbled into a scene from a movie I'd seen ages ago — *Who's Afraid of Virginia Woolf?* starring Elizabeth Taylor and Richard Burton as a couple engaged in marital warfare fueled by alcohol. The argument between Bunny and Dennis was just as vitriolic.

"I've had it with you. You either enter a treatment program — or else."

"But Dennis," Bunny whined. "You're never home. I get lonely."

"Sure, blame your drinking on me," Dennis said angrily. "If I hadn't gotten home early the night Sandy was killed, you could have died, too. I found you dead drunk in the Jacuzzi. You could easily have fallen asleep, slipped under the water, and drowned. And then again, last night. . . ."

I quietly let myself out. I'd found out what I'd come for. Bunny had been home alone all right. Passed out cold with a bottle of liquor for an alibi.

CHAPTER 30

"Your errand certainly didn't take long," Melly said upon my return. "I didn't expect you back this soon."

"Mom," Lindsey said after she finished waiting on a customer, "you need to make more of those cute little gift baskets. There's only two left."

"And it's time you reorder paper for your credit card machine. What would you do if you ran out?" Melly wagged her head in disapproval. "Folks don't carry cash like they used to do."

I'd worry about gift baskets and cash versus credit later. "Melly, did you know Bunny Bowtin drinks?"

"Everyone drinks, dear." She smiled at me as though I was slow-witted. "Doctors recommend eight glasses of water a day."

"No, no." I lowered my voice so as not to be overheard by a trio of women in the far corner, who were debating the merits of various types of peppercorns. "I'm not talking water; I'm talking spirits. Hard liquor."

Aghast at the notion, Melly pressed a blue-veined hand against her apron-clad bosom. "Lord have mercy, give me strength. Surely you don't mean . . . ?"

"That's exactly what I mean."

Lindsey moved closer to join the conversation. "I overheard kids at school talking about Mrs. Bowtin. Anthony's embarrassed. He hardly ever invites friends over."

I thought of the pimply-faced youth who'd run out of the house as I arrived and felt a rush of sympathy for the teen. It was bad enough to have your parents argue, but worse yet to know your mother's drinking was the root of the problem. We ceased our discussion of the Bowtin family when Amber and CJ strolled in.

Amber flashed a smile bright enough to be a lighthouse beacon. "Mother's hostin' a dinner party tonight. Her cook's preparin' a dish that calls for fennel so Mother sent us over to see if you might carry it. Fennel? Whoever heard of fennel? If folks never heard of it, how will they miss it? I tried to explain this to her cook, but the woman wouldn't listen."

CJ slid his arm around his fiancée's waist. "That's my Sweetums. Always a deep thinker."

"Fennel has been around forever." I forced a smile of my own, though not nearly as bright. "In ancient Rome, fennel was considered a symbol of prosperity and good health."

Amber smothered a yawn, which made the temptation to torture her with trivia too great to resist. My bad. "Fennel fronds resemble dill but taste much sweeter. I read that in Italy asparagus and fennel are used to make a classic antipasto that's on practically every café menu."

Amber perked up at the mention of Italy and gazed at CJ adoringly. "Pooh Bear," she cooed, "promised to take me to Italy. As soon as we get back from our weddin', I'm callin' our travel agent and havin' him make reservations. Sightseein' in Rome, museums in Florence, a gondola ride in Venice, and then shoppin' in Milan."

My blood pressure must have climbed the Mount Everest of blood pressure readings at hearing this. During the years we'd been married, I'd pestered, cajoled, begged, and pleaded with CJ for a trip to Europe. France, England, Italy, didn't matter where. But for the vacation CJ had in mind, we didn't need a travel agent. Pointing the car due east was all it took, and we'd wind up in Myrtle Beach or on Tybee Island. Once a year, I'd pack up the kids and head north to Michigan to visit my parents. Detroit might be my hometown, but its Renaissance Center can't compare with the Eiffel Tower. And eating a Coney dog smothered in chili, cheese, and onions can't compete with sipping wine in a French bistro or in an Italian trattoria.

Lindsey — smart girl — correctly interpreted the storm warnings. "Wait here. I'll get the fennel," she said, darting off.

Oblivious to gathering storm clouds, Melly's lips curved in a dreamy smile. "Being newly retired, Cot wants to indulge his love for travel. Just the other night, he showed me brochures for China and the Far East."

"Momma, you have a reputation to protect." CJ's brows beetled in a frown. "Sure hope you're not plannin' to go traipsin' all over hell and creation with him. What would Daddy think?"

"CJ, your father has been dead for years," Melly said, no longer smiling. "I no longer have to ask his permission for every single thing."

You go, girl, I silently applauded.

"If you'll excuse me, Son, I see several customers in need of my help." Head high,

Melly marched off to answer any questions the three ladies in the peppercorn section might have.

"Here's the fennel." Lindsey returned with the jar.

"Will that be all?" I inquired.

CJ took out a gold money clip and peeled off a twenty. He was old-school and preferred the flash of cash over the glint of plastic. I made change while Amber and Lindsey huddled to discuss Amber and CJ's forthcoming wedding in Punta Cana.

CJ lowered his voice and leaned in. "Heard Reba Mae took off, her whereabouts unknown."

"No comment."

"Folks are askin' why run if you've nothin' to hide?"

We locked eyes, during which I silently dared him to blink. "You've known Reba Mae as long as I have, CJ. You can't possibly think — even for a nanosecond — that she strangled Sandy."

"Everyone's capable of murder given the right circumstances. Just sayin' is all." He dropped his gaze. "Speakin' of friends, should you talk to that vet friend of yours, tell 'im I've got some documents ready for him. I can have my girl put them in the mail unless he'd rather pick 'em up. I've been tryin' to get ahold of him but no luck."

"Doug and his daughter are away for the weekend, but I'll be sure to relay the message if I hear from him." I slid the fennel into a small bag.

Her conversation with Lindsey over, Amber slipped her arm through the crook of CJ's arm. "From everythin' I hear, Doug spends all his free time with his daughter. Doesn't leave much time left over for the two of you, does it?" Amber said with false sympathy.

"Madison is having a difficult time adjusting. And Sandy's murder doesn't make things easier. Doug's putting his daughter first. I admire a father who does that."

CJ flushed at this. My jab hadn't been intentional, yet it hit its mark. CJ didn't ignore his children, but his priorities tended to get skewed.

Amber clung to CJ like moss to a rock — any closer she'd be crawling inside his shirt — and smirked. "Another little tidbit makin' the rounds is that Wyatt McBride and Shirley Randolph are an item. The two are seein' a lot of each other. Hangin' out at her office. Havin' cozy dinners at local eateries."

"I'd hardly classify chili cheese fries at High Cotton as a 'cozy' dinner, but" — I shrugged — "nothing wrong with two single people enjoying each other's company. I couldn't care less how McBride chooses to spend his off-duty time."

I was so relieved when they started to leave I practically shoved them out the door. If I was the "other" woman — which would never happen in a million years — I certainly wouldn't flaunt it in front of the ex-wife. Amber, however, must've been absent when the subtle gene was distributed. Since it was next to impossible to avoid her in a town the size of Brandywine Creek, I gritted my teeth and prayed for patience.

Later in the day, business slowed to a trickle. I sent Melly home, and Lindsey went upstairs to primp for her date with Sean. After straightening and restocking the shelves, I went into the storeroom and brought out a large box filled with Christmas decorations. Now that Thanksgiving was over, it was time to switch into Christmas mode. Tomorrow being Sunday and the shop closed, I'd devote the day to setting out decorations. Starting Monday, I'd serve customers mulled cider and home-baked cookies to put them in a festive mood.

Dottie Hemmings, a plastic dry cleaners bag draped over one arm, blew into Spice It Up! under full sail. "I didn't think Bitsy would ever stop talking. She kept going on and on about how everyone had it in for Sandy. I gathered she didn't care for the woman much herself."

"Hmm," I said as I began to unpack Christmas decorations. "I was under the opposite impression. I thought Bitsy liked Sandy."

"Speaking of Sandy, what's all this about Reba Mae gone missing?" Dottie demanded. "It's all everyone's talking about. I had to hear about it thirdhand when I'm usually the first to know. Why, it's downright insulting."

I unwrapped a ceramic snowman. "Thirdhand would be preferable to breaking news as broadcast by Wyatt McBride."

"Where is she?" Curiosity sparkled in Dottie's eyes. If she'd been a bloodhound hot on the trail, her nose would have twitched.

"I have no idea."

"Really, Piper!" Dottie wagged her head in disapproval. "I can't believe Reba Mae wouldn't tell her best friend where she hightailed it off to."

"Unfortunately, neither can McBride." I huffed out a sigh.

"Has the man been giving you a hard time, dear? Gerilee said Pete worked late at the butcher shop last night. He noticed McBride parked out back. They're wondering if there might be some hanky-panky goin' on" — she winked — "not that I could blame you. McBride's a fine-looking man. If I was younger — and single — I'd give you some stiff competition."

"Let me set your mind at ease, Dottie; where McBride and I are concerned there's no hanky-panky involved." I removed a string of hopelessly tangled twinkle lights and set them aside.

Dottie plunked her oversize carryall on the counter, a sure sign she intended to stay awhile. "Chief McBride seems to think Reba Mae's guilty. If not, why disappear?"

Wasn't that the same question CJ had voiced? I lifted an object wrapped in Bubble Wrap from the box of decorations. "Did you stop to consider Reba Mae was afraid she'd be arrested for a crime she didn't commit? Maybe she hoped the real killer would be caught during her absence? And . . ." I paused. "Maybe no concern of yours."

"Well," she huffed. "I only stopped in for a friendly chat, but clearly you're not in a friendly frame of mind. That's no way to run a business, my dear girl, especially in a small town where news of your rudeness could get around."

"I'm not your 'dear girl.' " I unwound a yard of Bubble Wrap and unearthed a Santa cookie jar I'd bought at a Christmas shop when the kids were little.

"Hmph!" Dottie picked up her carryall and flounced out, nearly bumping into Vicki on her way in.

"Excuse me," Vicki said to Dottie, her tone chilly enough to put frost on a pumpkin.

"Watch where you're going!" Dottie barked. "You nearly knocked me over."

"Believe me, if I knocked you over, it wouldn't be an accident," Vicki fired back.

Dottie's eyes narrowed in anger, her cheeks flushed. "Such insolence! No wonder you need to resort to extremes to attract a man."

"Why, you old bag," Vicki hissed.

Dottie's face went from flushed pink to bright red. "Be careful who you call an old bag."

"Ladies, please." I came out from behind the counter, afraid the two women were about to come to blows and ready to step between them. "Is that any way for friends to talk?"

"Make that *former* friends," Vicki snarled.

I looked from one angry face to the other. "Surely, there's a simple solution . . . ," I began, adopting the role of peacemaker.

"Simple?" Dottie snorted in disgust, then directed her wrath at Vicki. "Thanks to my husband's influence, I've had you removed as cochairperson of the annual Christmas party at the Children's Home. So there!" Satisfied she'd had the last word, or perhaps worried the verbal combat would turn physical, Dottie stalked out, banging the door behind her.

I stared after Dottie, puzzled by what I'd just witnessed. "In all the years I've known her, I've never seen Dottie so riled. What was that all about?"

Vicki tossed her head, sending her dark hair flying. "Dottie acts all holier-than-thou, but underneath she's nothing more than a gossipy old biddy."

"That shouldn't come as a surprise," I said as I headed back to finish unpacking holiday decorations. "Dottie Hemmings craves gossip like some women do chocolate."

Vicki raised a brow in disbelief. "Don't tell me you haven't heard what she did to me?"

"Sorry," I said. "I've had too much on my mind recently to pay attention to the rumor mill. Care to enlighten me?"

After looking to make sure no one else

was around, Vicki leaned her face close to mine. "Can you see them?" she whispered.

Decorations forgotten, I leaned, too, and studied her face for flaws. Her makeup was perfect as always. Her eyebrows expertly arched. Lipstick freshly applied. Then I spotted what some might view as a slight imperfection while others would call it a beauty mark. "Are you talking about the small mole on your right cheekbone?"

"No, not the mole," she replied impatiently. "I'm talking about the crow's-feet."

Feeling I'd just flunked Observation 101, I studied her again, more intently this time. Her skin appeared smooth, almost satiny beneath her foundation. "Maybe I need my eyesight checked, but I don't see any crow's-feet."

"Exactly." She preened. "You don't see them because I don't have any. At least not anymore thanks to the collagen injections."

"Ohh," I said, intrigued at the notion. "I've heard collagen injections are expensive — and painful."

"Both," Vicki admitted. "I've had them before. But the last time, something went wrong, and I had a reaction. Oh, nothing terrible," she explained hastily at seeing my expression, "but bad enough that I didn't want to show myself in public. My doctor recommended cold compresses until the redness and swelling subsided. By the next day, the residual effects were easily concealed with makeup."

I resumed unpacking decorations — Santas on the left, snowmen on the right — and set the empty box on the floor. "I still don't understand what your collagen injections have to do with your feud with Dottie."

"Dottie and I were supposed to meet at her house the night Sandy was killed, which happened to be the same day as my reaction."

The same night . . . ? I struggled to grasp the significance.

"I asked Dottie if she'd mind coming to my house instead so I could continue with the compresses," Vicki elaborated. "Dottie readily agreed. Personally, I think she was happy that she could eat my snacks rather than the stale cashews she usually serves. She stayed till nearly midnight. I don't think she stopped gossiping long enough to draw a breath."

My stomach dropped to my toes. Dottie had unwittingly supplied Vicki with an airtight alibi for the night of the murder. What had started out as a laundry list of suspects had slowly dwindled down to . . . one. Only Wanda Needmore's name remained. I stuffed a pile of tissue paper and Bubble Wrap into the box to be reused after the holidays. "I assume Dottie questioned the need for compresses."

Vicki nodded. "Dottie kept harping on the subject till I finally confided I'd been having collagen injections ever since Kenny left me. I made her swear not to say anything, but telling Dottie a secret is like keeping water in a leaky sieve. I've just learned she's gone and spread it all over town. Now no one can look me in the eyes because they're too preoccupied searching for invisible wrinkles and puncture sites."

I cleared my throat, wishing I could clear my frustration as easily. "I, um, you haven't mentioned what brought you here."

"Oh, right." She withdrew a sheet of paper from her designer bag and handed it to me. "The chamber of commerce is asking all the local merchants for a donation to their No Child Without a Christmas Fund. Fill in the blanks and drop the form at the chamber office by the end of next week."

It wasn't until I turned the lock on the front door and flipped the CLOSED sign that I replayed my entire conversation with Vicki. Though Vicki envied Sandy's position, wealth, and belongings, it would've been impossible for her to kill Sandy under

Dottie's watchful eye. Each time I thought a solution was at hand, I discovered it was still out of reach. Times like this called for a margarita or a glass of wine. And my BFF.

CHAPTER 31

I performed the usual end-of-day rituals. Chores like sweeping the floor, emptying the trash, and totaling the day's receipts. None of these, however, kept my mounting anxiety at bay. In my head, I could hear the imaginary ticktock of a bomb about to explode. It was only a matter of time — minutes, hours, days — before Reba Mae's hiding place was discovered and she would be arrested. She was counting on me for help and, so far nothing, nada, zip, bupkis. If this was the game Beat the Clock, I'd be the biggest loser. Correction — that title would belong to Reba Mae.

"Later, Mom," Lindsey called as she flew down the stairs and out the door for her date with Sean.

"Later," I echoed to an empty space.

Casey, who lay at my feet, stared up at me with hope gleaming in his button-bright eyes. If he could speak, he'd be asking, *Is this all there is?*

"Sorry to disappoint you, pal, but it's just you and me," I told him.

Casey thumped his tail on the floor in a canine version of understanding. I was grateful for my furry companion and wondered how I'd managed as long as I'd done without his shaggy presence. I may have saved his life once upon a time, but he'd also come to my rescue a time or two.

Time hung heavy. Pre-Madison, Doug and I usually met for dinner on Saturday evenings, occasionally taking in a movie. Recently his weekends were occupied introducing Madison to the charms of a Southern lifestyle. During those times, Reba Mae and I would meet for pizza, Mexican, or popcorn and a DVD at her home or mine. Tonight I was bored and restless. A wicked combination.

I looked at Casey; he looked up at me. "Want to go for a ride?"

Casey didn't need an engraved invitation. He beat me to the door, tail wagging the dog.

Minutes later we were in the VW with Casey riding shotgun.

I'd looked but hadn't seen any sign of McBride either in front of or behind my shop. I assumed this meant he'd given up shadowing me. Or maybe it was still too early for surveillance. At any rate, I took full advantage of my freedom and started driving with no particular destination in mind. For an instant I toyed with the notion of going to the mall but just as quickly dismissed it. No way was I in the mood to fight my way through a crush of holiday shoppers.

For a while I drove aimlessly. At one point, I found myself on Old County Road. I slowly cruised past Pets 'R People on the off chance Doug and Madison might have returned early. I could use the documents CJ had referred to as my excuse for a visit. Their home/clinic, however, was dark, so I continued roaming. Without conscious intent, I turned right onto Route 78. McBride's fixer-upper was just down the road a piece, as Southerners would say.

Heaving a sigh, I drummed my fingers on the steering wheel. Lately, McBride and I seemed to be at cross purposes — McBride trying to establish Reba Mae's guilt and me her innocence. Instead, we needed to be on the same page, share the same goal, work together to find a killer. Someone had to be the first to declare a truce, and that someone might as well be me.

A shiny black mailbox with MCBRIDE

stenciled neatly on the side marked his driveway. Squashing doubts about the brilliance of my olive-branch idea, I turned the wheel. Gravel crunched beneath my tires as I traveled down the long drive. The VW's headlight beams illuminated a small house, hardly more than a cottage — Country Southern with a dash of New England Colonial and a hint of Greek Revival.

"In for a penny, in for a pound," I muttered, braking to a halt.

My fight-or-flight instinct teetered to and fro. I had half a mind to shove the gearshift into reverse, gun the engine, and back down the drive. Too late. McBride, probably alerted by my headlights or the crunch of gravel, came out onto the wide front porch. If he was surprised by my unexpected visit, it didn't show in his expression. We stared at each other for a protracted moment.

Then, taking a deep breath, I shut off the ignition, opened the car door, and stepped into the cool, crisp fall night. Casey, not sharing my reticence, bounded out of the car and greeted McBride with a flurry of excited barks.

McBride remained where he was, thumbs hooked in the pockets of his jeans. "What's the occasion?"

I lifted my chin a notch. "Thought I'd save

you the trouble of checking up on me."

The corner of his mouth twitched in a trace of a smile. "I was just about to head over your way. See what you were up to. Maybe bum a cup of coffee."

I eyed his worn jeans, turtleneck, and well-used bomber jacket. A slight bulge at his waist told me he was carrying, and I caught the glint of gold clipped to his belt. "Is that the prescribed dress code for undercover work?"

"After last night, I thought I'd better up my game. Aim for my version of casual chic."

I stayed at the foot of the steps while Casey, the turncoat, claimed a spot alongside McBride. "I didn't realize 'chic' was part of your vocabulary."

"Lot of things you don't know about me," he countered. "Care to divulge the real reason behind the surprise visit?"

I cocked my head to one side and smiled. "Care to invite us inside?"

He lifted one shoulder in a careless shrug. "Sure, why not?" he said easily. "Just don't complain about the ambience."

I mounted the steps and McBride, a true Southern gentleman, held open the door and motioned for Casey and me to enter. A tiny foyer led into a living space furnished with a recliner and a flat-screen television. The kitchen was on my right. Nothing much had changed since my last visit: same plywood subflooring, same wood plank stretched across two sawhorses holding a toaster, salt-and pepper shakers, and his beloved George Foreman grill. The main difference was the installation of a French door in a space previously hidden behind a plastic tarp.

"No complaints about ambience, Mc-Bride, being there isn't any."

"Still a work in progress," he said. "Renovations came to a standstill when my contractor's apprentice went on strike. Clay refused to pound another nail for a man 'dumb enough' to think his momma guilty of homicide."

"Reba Mae's boys are loyal to a fault. She raised them single-handed after Butch's accident and did a mighty fine job of it, too. Ask anyone."

"It isn't Reba Mae's parenting skills that got her into this mess. Care for a Diet Coke? I might could find one if I look real hard." Not waiting for an answer, he pulled a diet soda out of an ancient fridge.

"Sure." I took a seat at a drop leaf table with chipped paint. "Looks like you moved your refrigerator off the front porch and back into the kitchen where it belongs. Is that your bid for gentrification?"

He popped the tab on a soda and handed it to me. "Here you go."

"Am I going to have to drink alone?"

"I'm on call tonight but don't see any harm in having a drink." He took a Dr Pepper from the fridge, shrugged off his bomber jacket, tossed it over the sawhorse, then straddled the chair opposite me. The shoulder harness he wore came into plain sight.

Just as I raised the can and was about to take a sip the quiet was fractured by a ferocious hissing. I jerked my head in time to see the sleek black head of a very unhappy feline peeking from what I assumed was a bedroom. Casey let out a startled *yipe* and hurtled into my lap. Soda sloshed out of the can and over my hand.

McBride twisted in his seat and ripped off a length of paper towel from a roll on the table. "Fraidy doesn't cotton to strange animals invading her space."

Even from a safe distance, I could see the animal's emerald green eyes glow with disapproval. Months back, McBride had adopted a part-feral cat with one mangled ear. Or, more correctly, the cat had adopted him. Go figure. "Perhaps your pet needs more socialization," I suggested, wiping soda from my hand. "With only you as a role model, she doesn't know how to play well with others."

"Fraidy and I are well suited. We're both comfortable in our own skins."

I stroked Casey's head before venturing into territory where fools rush in, but angels fear to tread. "Animals aren't the only ones in need of socialization. Aren't you ever lonely with no wife, no children, and only a sister with whom you rarely speak?"

"A person can be lonely even in a crowd," he replied, his eyes on mine. "Are you here in your capacity as therapy person, as Ned called you?"

I laughed at the reminder. "I'd make a terrible 'therapy' person. I have a hard enough time living my own life without advising others how to live theirs."

He smiled, the dimple-showing kind of smile I found so appealing, then turned sober again. "So if it isn't in your capacity as shrink, why are you here?"

"I'm in a sharing frame of mind, for lack of a better explanation." I took a small sip of my Diet Coke. "It bothers me that you're focused on Reba Mae to the exclusion of everyone else."

"I'm getting a lot of pressure to make an

arrest. All my leads point to your friend."

"Remember my telling you to check the alibis of the cast of *Steel Magnolias*?" At his nod, I continued, "Well, Reba Mae and I took it upon ourselves to do just that."

"And . . . ?"

"And," I said, "everyone except Wanda Needmore has a firm alibi. Quite by happenstance, I learned Bunny Bowtin was home alone — alone except for a bottle of booze and a bubble bath. Denny, her husband, wants her to go into rehab. Even though she's not in the play, I suspected Vicki Lamont for a while. She even had a motive — jealousy."

McBride took a swig of his Dr Pepper. "Wouldn't be the first time jealousy was a motive."

"Alas" — I sighed dramatically — "Vicki has an alibi."

He raised a brow. "And that would be?"

"Collagen," I replied, barely able to contain a smirk. "Dottie Hemmings can attest to the fact that she was with Vicki at the time of the murder. Vicki needed to reapply cold compresses to minimize a reaction she was having."

McBride studied the fine print on the side of his can of Dr Pepper. Then looked up, skewering me with his laser blues. "In the spirit of fair trade," he said slowly, "Reba Mae's car has been located."

I sat up straighter, nearly spilling Casey off my lap. "Where? When? Any sign of Reba Mae?"

McBride studied me like a frog under a microscope in high-school biology. "Her car was found in the long-term lot at Augusta Regional Airport. If she'd parked at a larger airport, say at Hartsfield in Atlanta, in a long-term lot, it might not have been tracked down until spring."

I took a big swallow of soda to moisten my mouth, which had suddenly turned to cotton. "That means Reba Mae could be almost anywhere. She's never been farther than Myrtle Beach for a hairdressers' convention. You think she booked a flight and took off?"

"I've had the airlines check their flight manifests, but there's no one by her name listed."

"I see," I murmured, although I really didn't. I stared through the newly installed French doors to the blackness beyond. If Reba Mae didn't drive and didn't fly, where was she?

Fraidy, the cat, crept out of the bedroom, her green eyes fixed on Casey, and rubbed against McBride's pant leg. Casey watched warily and snuggled even tighter against me. Silence, thick as taffy, was shattered by the ring of my cell phone. I fumbled to find it in my shoulder bag, which I'd placed on the floor next to my chair. A quick glance at the display showed it read CALLER UN-KNOWN. I clicked the phone off.

"Wrong number," I said cheerily. "Those darn telemarketers have been pestering me to death." Before I could drop the phone back into my purse it rang again.

"Don't mind me. Answer your phone." A thread of steel undermined his tone. It wasn't a request but a challenge. *Go ahead; I dare you,* it seemed to say.

I affected a casual shrug. "Whatever," I said, doing my best to mimic a bored teen who needed an attitude adjustment. Assuming an irritated expression, I pretended to listen to the caller. "No," I said pointedly. "I'm not interested in purchasing a back brace as advertised on QVC —"

Quick as a copperhead McBride reached across the table and snatched the phone from my fingers. "Reba Mae? Time for you to turn yourself in. It'll go much easier on you if do it voluntarily." He made no attempt to hide his anger as he returned my phone. "She hung up on me."

"What did you expect — a confession?"

"I could haul you in for obstructing justice. You told me you didn't know where she was."

"I don't." I set Casey on the floor and stood. Clearly, I'd overstayed my welcome. I could almost hear my olive branch snap in two. "Reba Mae called once before but refused to tell me where she was hiding."

"Have it your way." McBride rose, too, his expression grim. "I'll have the phone company put a trace on your calls."

"Trace away." Picking up my purse, I dropped my phone inside. "Save yourself the trouble, McBride. Reba Mae's using a burner phone she bought at a gas station."

"Burner phone?" McBride swore softly.

"Watching TV is Reba Mae's favorite pastime. She's big into reruns of *The Wire*. If you ever watched the show, you'd know it's the phone of choice for drug dealers." I started to leave but paused on the threshold. "One last thing, McBride. If I find you lurking outside my shop tonight, don't expect coffee."

As I drove away, I didn't know whether I should be mad at myself or at McBride. In hindsight, I should have followed the gut instinct he'd lectured about and stayed home.

CHAPTER 32

"Why run if she has nothing to hide?" had become a popular refrain.

Was Reba Mae aware that disappearing hadn't helped her case? Did she realize people she'd known for years were starting to question her innocence? I'd been shocked to learn her car had been found at the airport in Augusta. And to add to the mystery, McBride said her name hadn't appeared on any flight manifests. Had she taken a cab, bummed a ride, hitchhiked? Then hopped on a Greyhound or boarded a train?

After tossing and turning Sunday night, I woke up Monday with a dull headache. I downed two Tylenol, saw Lindsey off for school, tended to Casey, then showered and dressed for the day. Downstairs, I unlocked the dead bolt on the front door and opened for business.

Before I dove into decorating my shop for

Christmas — which I'd planned to do yesterday but procrastinated — I needed to jumpstart my day with caffeine. I'd just poured my second cup of coffee when Madison Winters strolled in.

"Hi, Piper." She grinned at the assortment of snowmen, Santas, and tin angels scattered willy-nilly across the counter in front of me. "Guess I know what's on your agenda today."

"Hi yourself," I said, taking another sip of liquid oomph. "You seem to be in good spirits. How was your weekend in the mountains?"

"Amazing!" She beamed. "We even went horseback riding one day. In the evening, all the guests would gather around a bonfire for hot chocolate and homemade cookies while we listened to this really cute guy play guitar."

"Hmm," I murmured. "Can't miss with cookies and hot chocolate. Add a cute guy with a guitar and you've got a winning combination."

Madison blushed. "Daddy sent me into town to pick up a contract from his lawyer. He asked me to invite you for dinner Friday night. He plans to make his signature dish — spicy chicken curry."

"I'd love to come," I said after a momentary pause. Even though Doug and I were taking things slow, it didn't mean we weren't still friends. And friends invited friends for dinner all the time. Right? "Thank your father for the invitation. Tell him I'll bring the wine."

The door opened then, and Ned Feeney ambled in. "Hey, Miz Piper." Ned bobbed his head in my direction, then turned to Madison. "Hey, Miz Winters. Who made them ugly scratches on your car door?"

"Scratches?" Madison's eyes widened and the pretty color drained from her cheeks. "What scratches?"

Ned shrugged, a mere twitch beneath his flannel shirt. "Ask me, it kinda looks like somebody wrote you a note."

Madison turned and ran toward the little sports car angle-parked at the curb with me nipping at her heels. She skidded to a halt so abruptly, I nearly slammed into her. Her hand flew to her mouth as she stared in horror at the message carved into the passenger door. "Oh no," she groaned.

I moved closer to inspect the damage. In big, uneven letters, the words "GO HOME" had been etched into the car's shiny red paint — the second act of vandalism on her Miata. If a person was deliberately trying to scare the girl, they were doing a darn fine job.

"Thought you must've known about it." Ned shoved up the bill of his cap.

I placed my hand on Madison's shoulder. "I'll call the police."

"I'll call Daddy," she said in a small voice.

"Business been slow over at the Eternal Rest," Ned mumbled, shifting his weight. "I came by this mornin' to see if you had any odd jobs for me, but I can see you're busy. I'll come back another time."

While waiting for Dorinda to answer the phone at the police department, I watched Ned lope down the sidewalk and out of sight. The poor guy obviously wasn't eager for another encounter with Brandywine Creek's finest. McBride had scared the bejeebers out of him.

Her call to her father completed, Madison wailed, "Who would do this?"

"I don't know, sweetie." I draped my arm over her shoulders.

By the time a squad car appeared five minutes later, a crowd had started to congregate. Pete Barker, swathed in a white butcher's apron, crossed the town square to find out what was going on. He wagged his head sorrowfully when he saw the scrawled message. "Don't know what's come over this town."

Patti Sue Parker, lean as a greyhound with a perfectly coiffed silver bob, *tsk*ed as she came out of Yesteryear Antiques. "Thugs," she said succinctly, raising her half-moon eyeglasses from a chain around her neck to peer at the etched words. "A perfect example of spare the rod and spoil the child."

I was happy to see Sergeant Beau Tucker, and not McBride, emerge from the police cruiser. He paused to speak into a radio clipped to his shoulder, then hitched his belt higher and motioned at the Miata. "This yours?" he asked Madison.

Swallowing hard, Madison nodded.

"If I recollect, this isn't the first time you reported vandalism done to your car." He stooped to study the damage. "Sure hope you got good insurance, young lady. Your premium's about to go through the roof. Any idea who might have it in for you?"

"N-no," Madison stammered. "I don't have a clue."

Beau withdrew a notebook and pen from his shirt pocket. "Well, someone either has it in for you or hates cars made in Japan. When did you first notice the damage?"

"Ned Feeney brought it to our attention a few minutes ago," I said in answer to Beau's question.

Madison wrapped her arms around her midriff to keep from shivering. "My father and I were away for the weekend. The car was locked in his garage the entire time."

Beau jotted down the information. "Where have you been since you got home?"

"I came into town this morning to pick up some documents for my father at his lawyer's. Other than that, this is the only place I've been."

CJ's office? I stared at the mutilated car door. If the Miata had been under lock and key like Madison claimed, it meant the damage was inflicted this morning — in broad daylight.

"Mr. Prescott wasn't there," Madison continued, "and neither was Mrs. Needmore, his paralegal, only the receptionist. Mrs. Needmore came in about twenty minutes later and apologized for making me wait. She explained she'd been at the courthouse."

Snapping his notebook shut, Beau stuffed it back in his pocket. "Don't suppose you saw anyone suspicious loitering around when you left the office?"

"No, no one," Madison said, biting her lip to keep from crying. The young woman was clearly distraught and Beau's brusque manner wasn't helping matters.

Beau used his cell phone to snap photos of the crude words carved into the passenger door and then swept his gaze over the people who had gathered to gawk and eavesdrop. "Don't suppose any of you good folks might know who did this?" The only response to his question was blank looks. "Didn't think so but had to ask. Chief's a stickler on these things."

"What next?" I asked.

"Not much to do other than file a report." Beau turned to me as our audience began to dwindle. "Reba Mae sure is somethin' else. That gal's crazy as a betsy bug if she thinks she can hide from the law."

"I'll be sure to relay the message next time I hear from her."

Beau shot me a dirty look before climbing into the police cruiser and driving away. Doug arrived minutes later. Madison flew to him and threw herself into his arms. "Oh, Daddy, I hate it here."

Doug patted her back consolingly. "It's all right, baby. We don't have to stay if it makes you this unhappy."

I watched Doug comfort his daughter with a feeling of finality. Curtain going down in Act Three of a family drama. Curtain going down on me and Doug, too.

I spent the rest of the day halfheartedly setting out Christmas decorations. Not even twinkle lights and candy canes lifted my sagging spirits. I felt myself sinking deeper and deeper into the doldrums. If the thought of losing Doug wasn't depressing enough, I could lose Reba Mae as well. Finally, I brought myself up short. The situation called for some of that old-fashioned when the going gets tough the tough get going mind-set. That pull yourself up by the bootstrap mentality. That every cloud has a silver lining frame of mind. By the time Lindsey came home from school, my resolve had hardened into a plan.

"Honey, you're in charge," I told my girl as I headed out the door. "I've got an errand that can't wait."

Wanda Needmore was my target. When it came to "straight," the paralegal had been more straitlaced than straightforward. Jumping into my Beetle, I aimed for the offices of Prescott and Wainwright, Attorneys-at-Law. Wanda's name wouldn't be eliminated unless I was convinced she didn't kill Sandy. The paralegal had been livid at the prospect of a lawsuit. As far as I was concerned, that provided motive up the wazoo. And, furthermore, Cot and Melly had reported seeing Ms. Prim-and-Proper uncharacteristically disheveled the night of the murder.

I pulled into the drive and parked next to Wanda's Honda. I took it as a good omen that other than mine, her Honda was the only vehicle present. This meant everyone either was occupied elsewhere or had already left for the day. I switched off the engine and sat contemplating the best approach. Dealing with Wanda would require a certain degree of finesse. I couldn't very well come right out and ask her if she'd killed Sandy. Better to choose a more subtle approach.

Feeling more confident after my little pep talk, I got out of the car and marched down the walk and up the steps. A large holly wreath adorned the front door, a reminder I still hadn't replaced my fall wreath with an evergreen. Since no one was around to detain me, I went directly to Wanda's office and found her seated behind her desk. She was the epitome of decorum in a tailored gray suit and white blouse. A blue silk scarf draped gracefully around her neck added the only bit of color.

"Hi," I said with a bright smile. "CJ here?"

Irritation flickered across Wanda's features as she glanced up from the documents she'd been studying. "Sorry. You just missed him."

"Oh, drat! He must have forgotten our meeting," I improvised. "Tell him I'll call tomorrow to reschedule."

"I'll do that."

Wanda resumed reading the papers in front of her, but she should've remembered I wasn't the type to be easily ignored. "I suppose you've heard the news that Reba Mae's missing," I said, adopting a conversational tone. "When McBride finds her, it's only a matter of time before she's arrested. Unless, that is, she can provide an alibi for the time of the murder."

"Hmm."

Hmm? Was that all the woman had to say?

My presence must have annoyed her, because she stopped reading to glare at me. "Piper, if you don't mind, some of us have work to do," she said pointedly.

"Did you kill Sandy?" I blurted.

She lifted a perfectly arched brow. "Excuse me?"

"Do you have an alibi for the night Sandy was killed?" I asked, throwing finesse to the winds. Subtle had never been my strong suit either. "It's general knowledge you filed a lawsuit alleging Sandy reneged on an agreement between the two of you."

"We had a verbal agreement," Wanda admitted at last. "I had a check in my hand for the deposit when she announced she'd sold the property I was interested in to a higher bidder."

I advanced farther into the room. "That must have been a huge disappointment."

"It was!" Wanda snapped. "Sandy was an ambitious, greedy woman who threatened a countersuit against me for pain and suffering if I didn't drop my complaint."

"So did you go directly home after the final rehearsal?"

Wanda's mouth tightened into a hard line. "What I do with my free time Monday nights is hardly any of your business. Now if you don't get out of my office, I'll see that you're charged with harassment."

Apparently Wanda wasn't well versed in *subtle* any more than I was, so I took my leave. As I hurried to my car, my mind worked almost as quickly as my legs. Wanda had been very specific about a certain day of the week — Monday. Sandy had been killed on a Monday. Today was also a Monday. What did Wanda do Monday nights that she wanted secret? Curiouser and curiouser.

My stakeout skills hadn't been tested in a

while. I'd miss having Reba Mae along as my trusty sidekick, but I thought I was up to the task.

CHAPTER 33

"Sweetie, why don't you ask Taylor to join you at the Pizza Palace for dinner before your study session? My treat."

Lindsey gave me a suspicious look. "You feeling all right, Mom?"

"Never better," I said, handing her a twenty.

The instant Lindsey left, her backpack slung over her shoulder, I closed up shop earlier than usual. No doubt Melly would have frowned upon my lack of business acumen, but these were extenuating circumstances. I changed into what I'd come to think of as my cat burglar costume: black jeans, turtleneck, watch cap, and, since nights had turned cool, a black zip-up fleece. Next I set about loading my supplies — Diet Coke, thermos of coffee, ham sandwich, chips, and cookies — into a duffel. No stakeout was worth its salt without snacks. I'd learned that trick from Reba

Mae. She always brought the tastiest sandwiches and juiciest gossip. Surveillance would certainly have fewer calories without her along.

Casey watched my preparations with a hopeful gleam in his eyes. "Sorry to disappoint you, pup," I told him. "This time I'm flying solo."

I patted the pocket of my fleece for the reassuring weight of my penlight and cell phone. I glanced around the kitchen a final time to make sure I wasn't forgetting anything; then, reassured I had what I needed, I left the apartment. Once outside, I stood for a moment, peering through the purple twilight for signs of McBride. He was nowhere in sight. Hoping he'd given up shadowing me, I ran to my car and, for the second time that day, headed for Prescott and Wainwright.

I parked a discreet distance down the block that afforded a clear view of their office. Wanda, I knew, was a creature of habit. Always the first to arrive, the last to leave. The second hand of my watch crept toward six o'clock, and as predictable as ever, Wanda left the office. Or was it Wanda? Leaning forward, I squinted through the windshield. Did the woman have a twin, a doppelganger? The tailored suit I'd seen her wearing earlier had disappeared and in its place were jeans and a heavy-duty leather jacket. Wanda didn't seem the type to even *own* a pair of jeans much less be seen wearing them in public. And what was with the heavy-duty leather?

Wanda got into her Honda and backed down the drive. I slouched down in my seat, but I needn't have bothered, since she turned in the opposite direction. I started to follow, keeping several car lengths behind. If I'd had an inkling I'd be doing surveillance someday, I would have opted for a less conspicuous mode of transportation than a sour-apple green VW Beetle. Maybe the next vehicle I purchased would be a nice, gray, nondescript sedan.

Instead of heading toward her home, Wanda surprised me. Leaving Brandywine Creek behind, she turned down Old County Road. About a mile or two past Pets 'R People, Wanda signaled a left turn onto a winding, narrow two-lane road. Soon after I saw the blink of her turning signal, then her taillights vanished down a rutted dirt drive. I cruised past the spot, which was marked by a mailbox that listed drunkenly to one side. What was she up to? I wondered. Except for a few scattered farms, there wasn't much out here. As soon as I could, I turned around and retraced my route. I was almost back at Old County Road when a trio of motorcycles flew past, their throaty engines wide open. In my rearview mirror, I saw all three bikes slow, then wheel into the drive with the crooked mailbox.

There was only one way to find out what was going on. I shifted into reverse, stopping just shy of the driveway in question. I parked as far off the road as possible and got out of my car. The situation called for stealth. Surveillance would best be accomplished on foot. Switching on my penlight and keeping to the shadows, I cautiously made my way down a dirt drive lined with bare-limbed trees and scrub pine.

The drive opened into a clearing. Light spilled from every window on the ground floor of a two-story farmhouse with weathered siding. A single floodlight was mounted above the door of a barn that was otherwise dark. A half-dozen motorcycles sprouted from a yard that consisted mostly of hard-packed earth. I didn't know much about motorcycles, but even to my unpracticed eye, these appeared to be king-of-the-road variety — big, shiny, and powerful. Instantly Hells Angels and the classic film *Easy Rider* sprang to mind.

I inched closer to the house for a better

look and peeked through a window into what turned out to be the kitchen. It was a large room with both men and women milling about. All were dressed in clothing similar to Wanda's jeans and leather — bikers' gear. Some held coffee cups, some beer cans, and still others to my amazement held stemmed wineglasses.

"Hold it! Don't move!" a whiskey-rough voice barked.

I froze. I literally couldn't move. Even speech seemed to have deserted me.

"Now turn around," the man ordered.

I heard the bikers chatter as they filed out of the farmhouse. Out of the corner of my eye, I saw that I was surrounded.

"Having a driveway alert system was money well spent," the whiskey-voiced man chortled. "Know right away when someone's coming."

"What in the world is *she* doing here?" I heard Wanda ask.

At the sound of a familiar voice, I began to unthaw from my flash-freeze. I turned slowly, nearly dropping the penlight when I saw a shotgun aimed at me.

"Hoyt, lower that dang thing before you give the lady a heart attack."

Another familiar voice, I thought with relief. This one belonged to Dale Simons, owner of the local Swap and Shop.

Hoyt, a burly man with a neatly trimmed gray beard, lowered the weapon and leaned it against the house. "This is private property, lady. I could call the cops. Charge you with trespassing."

My back brushed the weathered siding making retreat impossible. I licked my lips which suddenly had gone dry and floundered for a plausible explanation for my being there. My gaze swept over the unsmiling bikers in search of a friendly face. They were an older bunch than I'd anticipated. I recognized my insurance agent and his wife, CJ's chiropractor, and the assistant manager of my bank among the group. Professionals, not hooligans.

"So, is this some kind of a club?" I asked with false bravado. "Can anyone join?"

"Sorry, darlin'," Hoyt drawled. "I've seen you toolin' around town. Can't join as long as you claim a VW as your only form of transportation."

Everyone laughed at my expense, and I felt blood rush to my face.

"This is an invitation-only kind of club," Dale explained, taking pity on me. "Folks tend to misjudge motorcyclists, view them in a certain light. We're picky about who we allow in our inner circle."

The banker, whose name temporarily escaped me, nodded his agreement. "People often prejudge people on Harleys."

"Makes them think of Hells Angels," someone added.

"Or that old movie with Peter Fonda and Dennis Hopper. You know the one," Hoyt said, his forehead wrinkling as he struggled to recall the title.

I winced. Guilty on all counts. "So, Wanda," I said, getting down to business, "is this where you went after rehearsal the night of the murder?"

"Well, well, well . . . that's what all the snooping is about." Chuckling, Dale casually draped his arm around Wanda's shoulders. "If memory serves, we met at my house in town that night to plan our next road rally. Wanda got there soon as rehearsal ended."

"That meeting lasted till nearly midnight," CJ's chiropractor added. "And most of us had to get up early for work the next morning."

"Dale and I are travel buddies. Have been ever since Yancy passed," Wanda admitted, sounding defensive. "I've cultivated a certain image over the years and don't relish being a laughingstock because of my new interest."

Dale smiled fondly at his starchy companion. "If I have my way, Wanda and I will be more than travel buddies."

Wanda . . . and Dale? Who knew? A textbook case of opposites attracting.

"I trust you'll keep our . . . friendship . . . under wraps for the time being." Wanda placed her hand on top of Dale's. "Once Dottie Hemmings discovers I belong to a motorcycle club, people will be gossiping behind my back."

Hoyt twisted his head to peer over his shoulder. "Don't see your Beetle anywhere, darlin'."

"I, um, left it back on the road and walked the rest of the way."

"Let me give you a lift." The burly biker grinned, and I caught the glint of a gold tooth. "Plenty of room on my bike for a pretty little thing like you."

"Hoyt's always been partial to redheads," laughed a plump woman with streaked blond hair scraped into a ponytail.

Hoyt unstrapped a helmet from the back of a maroon Harley-Davidson parked nearby. "Here you go," he said, handing me a spare helmet. "State law in Georgia. Hop on."

The remainder of the club drifted back into the farmhouse. Hoyt donned a helmet,

400

straddled the motorcycle, and worked magic with the controls until the machine roared like a lion. It was now or never. I put on the helmet and swung on board.

"Hold tight, darlin'."

I wrapped my arms around Hoyt's ample girth and off we zoomed down the rutted drive toward my car. My first motorcycle ride ended much too quickly. I was surprised to discover I'd actually enjoyed it. I climbed down, removed my helmet, and thanked the man.

He winked. "Ever decide to turn in your Beetle for a hog, give me a call."

"Thanks," I said, and smiled. I assumed "hog" was another name for a Harley but made a mental note to Google that later.

My stakeout hadn't been a total bust. Thus far tonight, I'd been caught trespassing, stared down the barrel of a shotgun, been threatened with arrest, and passed up an invitation to become a motorcycle chick. That's the most adventure I'd had in months. And — bottom line — my last viable suspect had an alibi that could be verified by a dozen biker buddies.

It all amounted to zero progress in saving my best friend's bacon and finding the real killer. I drove back to town slowly. I blew out a breath, feeling frustrated beyond belief. If Wanda wasn't the guilty party, she'd have no reason to slash the tires on Madison's car or carve a warning into the door. A cold-blooded killer walked the streets of Brandywine Creek, free as a breeze, terrified Madison might bring their freedom to a halt. Madison, whether she knew it or not, was the key to unlocking a mystery.

A logging truck whizzed past. I shook my head and looked around, surprised to find myself stopped at the junction of Old County Road. I'd been driving on autopilot. One more stop, I decided then and there, before going home. I hit the accelerator and made a right turn.

There was no sign of either Doug's SUV or Madison's Miata when I pulled into Pets 'R People, but lights burned in the living quarters. I assumed one or both of them was home and their vehicles in the garage. It was early yet; therefore I wasn't worried I'd wake someone. Before I could reconsider I got out of my car and went up the walk. After I rang the bell and knocked, Madison cracked open the door.

"My dad's not here," she said. "He was called out on some kind of emergency. A horse or cow, I don't remember which."

"That's all right. You're the one I wanted to see."

"Me? What for?"

"Mind if I come in?"

Madison stepped aside, then twisted the dead bolt. "Daddy said to keep the doors locked and not to let anyone in, but I suppose he won't mind if it's you. I was about to have a cup of tea. Want one?" Not waiting for an answer, she turned and led the way to the kitchen.

"I really don't want tea," I said, taking a chair at the table. "I just wanted to talk to you. Someone is going to extremes to frighten you. I can't help but think this person, whoever they might be, believes you heard — or saw — something that might incriminate them in Sandy's death."

Madison filled a kettle and turned on a burner. "I've been over and over everything a hundred times. I don't know what you expect from me."

I realized I still wore the knit watch cap. Tugging it off, I ran my fingers through my matted hair. "Why don't we try to look at things from a different angle?"

She took a package of Earl Grey tea from the cupboard. "I don't know what I can tell you that you don't already know."

"Start at the beginning. Tell me everything

you remember about rehearsal that night."

She placed a tea bag in a china cup painted with dogwood blossoms. "Like what?"

Getting Lindsey to open up was like prying open a clam. I blew out a breath. "For instance, did Sandy seem upset? Angry? Nervous? Anything out of the ordinary?"

While waiting for the water to boil, Madison leaned against the counter, arms folded across her chest. With her face scrubbed clean and her hair loose, she could easily have passed for fourteen. Poor kid, I thought, she was still a child in many ways and doing her best to cope under trying circumstances.

"Sandy seemed stressed is all," she said at last. "Rehearsal didn't go well. Mary Lou couldn't remember her lines and probably qualified as the worst Truvy Jones in the history of *Steel Magnolias.* To make matters worse, the entire cast was uptight because Sandy insisted we rehearse over Thanksgiving weekend."

"It's my understanding you and Caleb went out afterwards."

"We had a bite to eat; then Caleb dropped me off at the opera house where I'd left my car, and I came straight home."

Frustrated, I twisted the knit cap in my

lap into a pretzel shape. I wasn't making any headway with my line of questioning. "Think harder, Madison. When Caleb dropped you off, did you notice anyone hanging around?"

The kettle whistled then, and she poured boiling water over the tea bag. "Nope, didn't see a soul."

Taking a seat at the table across from me, she gave an apologetic shrug. "Sorry."

"Did you hear anything, for example a car engine starting? Or maybe smell something?" I was grasping at straws, and we both knew it.

Madison frowned. "Well," she said slowly, "now that I think about, I do remember something odd."

It took all my willpower to sit still and not shake the information out of the girl. "What do you remember?" I asked, keeping my voice quiet, soothing.

"It could have only been my imagination, but . . . I thought I smelled cigarette smoke."

CHAPTER 34

Cigarette smoke?

Upon leaving Pets 'R People, I reminded Madison to lock the door behind me. As I drove toward home, my mind busily sorted through the various possibilities. This was the girl's first mention of cigarette smoke. "Smells ring bells" was something my college psych professor had once said, and for some reason it had stuck in my head. If I'd fired up a cigarette — and risked choking — would that have triggered a significant memory from somewhere in Madison's brain? I concentrated, trying to visualize the rear of the opera house. In my mind's eye I pictured an overhang above the door. The perfect spot to mount a security camera. And a place where odors could easily get trapped and linger.

Then again, the vague memory of smelling cigarette smoke might leave me no closer to solving the riddle. Elated one minute, deflated the next, my emotions were a wild roller-coaster ride.

I parked in my usual spot on the street behind my shop and took the footpath through the vacant lot to my back door. There was no sign of Lindsey's Mustang, so I assumed she was still at Taylor's. With SATs on Saturday, she was hitting the books — and hitting them hard. I'd just entered my building when the phone rang. I dug my cell phone out of my fleece and read the display: CALLER UNKNOWN, aka Reba Mae Johnson. I might've known it was her. I sank down on the stairs leading to my apartment. Far from windows and prying eyes, the stairwell seemed the safest place to conduct a conversation with a fugitive from justice. Or, in this case, a fugitive from injustice.

"Sure you're alone?"

"Positive," I said but caught myself looking around to double-check. McBride could be a sneaky devil. "You can't hide out forever, girlfriend. You need to turn yourself in."

"And then what? Develop a likin' for bracelets with chains attached?"

"We need to talk."

"Talk away, but give me the *Reader's Digest* version. I don't have unlimited minutes."

Ka-chuk! Ka-chuk!

"What was that?" I asked, but I already knew the answer. It was the noise Reba Mae and I had heard at the scene of the crime. The sound of the furnace at the opera house.

"Gotta run," Reba Mae said in a rush.

The phone went dead in my hand. I'd found my friend, but had I found her only to lose her? The sands of time were running through the hourglass faster than I could slow them. I needed to see Reba Mae, make sure she was all right, talk to her. Maybe, if we put our heads together, we'd figure out a solution.

Bounding to my feet, I exited through the door I'd just entered from and eased into the night. I released a pent-up breath when there was no sign of McBride or one of his men. Creeping along the back of the neighboring shop, I squeezed into the gap between Yesteryear Antiques and Second Hand Prose and hurried through the narrow passage until I reached Main Street. A look in either direction assured me Brandywine Creek was buttoned up tight. The statue of the Confederate soldier in the town square would be a mute witness to my escapade. Hugging the shadows, I hurried down the block and at the corner cut across to the opera house. I skirted along the side of the building and rounded the corner.

Last time we were here, our getaway had been foiled by a security camera. How had Reba Mae managed to avoid detection with a camera monitoring comings and goings? I switched on my penlight and shone it over the rear of the opera house until I found the camera under the overhang. I smiled grimly. This time it wouldn't pose a problem. Someone had sprayed black paint over the lens. Vandals, maybe, but I'd place my bet on a certain beautician with a fondness for hair dye.

More confident now, I jiggled the door handle, hoping no one had thought to replace the ancient lock. The door squeaked open on rusty hinges. "Reba Mae," I called softly as I slipped inside.

No answer.

"Reba Mae," I called again, louder this time.

Had I been mistaken? Had I jumped to the wrong conclusion? Reba Mae was superstitious — spooked by ghost tales. Maybe she wasn't hiding here after all? She could be miles away. I advanced farther into the service area. The beam of my penlight picked out a recessed door that blended into the wall so well it had gone unnoticed on our previous visit. I tugged on what was more latch than knob or handle, and the door swung open to reveal a steep flight of stairs leading to a basement.

"Reba Mae," I shouted, "this place is creeping me out. If you're down there, show yourself this instant or I'm leaving!"

Like magic, Reba Mae materialized at the foot of the stairs, her sudden appearance startling me. "How'd you find me?"

"Blame it on the furnace." Holding the penlight with one hand, the banister with the other, I cautiously descended a rickety flight of steps. Once my feet hit the bottom, Reba Mae hugged me so fiercely I worried she'd crack a rib. The hug over, I stepped back to study her. Her face was pale, her hair limp, and her clothes rumpled, but she was still able to summon a smile. "You all right?" I asked.

"I will be when I quit livin' like a bat and see the light of day."

"Even so, you look mighty good — for a fugitive."

"C'mon," she said, turning. "Let me show you my new digs."

She led me down a narrow corridor in the musty-smelling basement and toward a faint light at the far end. The basement was a warren of small rooms, most of which seemed used for storage purposes. Racks of costumes filled one; an assortment of props overflowed shelves and bins in another. One large room was reserved for tools, lumber, and painting supplies for set building. Reba Mae had selected a space in the far corner for her little nest. A small battery-operated lantern shed a feeble light, adding to the gloom rather than dispelling it.

Reba Mae gestured to a soft-sided suitcase shoved against a wall. "I took the biggest one I could find to haul my stash."

From what I could see, Reba Mae's "stash" consisted of a blanket, a small pillow, bottled water, pouches of tuna, packets of crackers, and protein bars. "What," I said in mock horror, "no Peanut M and Ms? No wine?"

"Didn't plan on doin' much entertainin'. I've come to the conclusion the opera house ghost is anorexic, 'cause she leaves my stuff alone."

"Smart move disabling the security camera."

"Ranks right up there along with me buyin' a burner phone." Reba Mae lowered herself to the blanket that she'd spread on the floor and sat Indian fashion, motioning me to join her.

"Pretty clever of you to ditch your car at

the airport," I said, squirming to find a more comfortable position on the cold cement.

"They found it already?" she said, disappointed. "I was hopin' it'd take a while."

"How did you manage to get from the airport back to Brandywine Creek?"

"I hung out for a while in Baggage Claim and overheard a couple talkin'. They were goin' to visit their daughter not far from here, so I bummed a ride. Told 'em my kids were supposed to pick me up, but they had car trouble." She plucked at a loose thread on the blanket. "Any luck findin' the killer?"

"Not yet." I drew my knees up to my chest and wrapped my arms around them. "I followed Wanda tonight, but she has a solid alibi. Believe it or not, Wanda's a member of a motorcycle club. She rides with Dale Simons of the Swap and Shop."

"No kiddin'!"

"What's more, if Dale has his way, he'd like to get hitched."

"Wanda and Dale?" Reba Mae said, shaking her head in disbelief. "If that don't beat all. But where does that leave us? Fresh out of suspects, that's where."

I shifted so I could see my friend's face more clearly. "Wanda and her Harley-riding friends weren't the only ones I visited tonight. I also had a nice chat with Madison Winters. Something she said started me thinking," I said slowly. "What if we've been wrong the whole time?"

"What do you mean — wrong?"

"What if we've been working under a false premise? All along we've assumed the killer is a member of the cast, but what if — other than Vicki Lamont — it's someone *not* in the play? Maybe we should broaden the scope of our investigation. Think outside the box."

Though Reba Mae listened, she didn't seem totally convinced. "Just what was it Madison said that's got you all fired up?"

"She remembered smelling cigarette smoke when Caleb dropped her off. Who do we know that smokes?"

"Most folks I know have given up smokin' for one reason or another, all except . . ."

"Bitsy Johnson-Jones," I said, completing her sentence. Excitement fizzed through my veins like champagne.

Reba Mae frowned. "I don't get it. Why would Bitsy want to hurt Sandy?"

"Bitsy wanted to be in *Steel Magnolias* so much she could practically taste it." I squirmed, unable to sit still. "Remember the night we were here. I found a script on the stage with not one but two roles high-lighted — Truvy Jones *and* Annelle. I didn't think much of it at the time, but it's all starting to make sense. The day of the press conference, Bitsy told me she'd memorized the lines of several characters, but Sandy insisted the parts were already cast. Bitsy even volunteered to be an understudy only to have her offer rejected. What if she heard the rumor that Mary Lou was about to be replaced and came after everyone left in a desperate attempt to audition? Bitsy has lost a ton of weight and wants everyone to notice. She craves attention and adulation. What better way to show off her new figure than being onstage? Sandy denied her that opportunity."

"Might make sense to us, but the sixty-four-thousand-dollar question is, will it make sense to McBride?"

"All we have to do is find a way to convince Bitsy to confess."

Reba Mae snorted. "Piece of cake, right?"

"Get out the dessert plates." I pulled out my cell phone. "I think I know a way."

CHAPTER 35

"You sure this will work?"

"Do you want to continue living like a bat and never seeing the light of day?"

"No, but . . ."

Persuading Bitsy to come to the opera house had been child's play. All it had taken was a single phone call — and acting talent I never knew I possessed. In the blink of an eye I'd transformed into Brandywine Creek's own — a vertically challenged, red-haired version of Meryl Streep.

"She'll be here any minute," I said. "We'd better set the stage."

We hurried up the basement stairs. I located an electrical panel backstage and threw a couple switches. Instantly the stage was bathed in light, leaving the rest of the theater shrouded in darkness. The script was right where I'd dropped it. Picking it up off the floor, I flipped it open.

"Want me to search the costume room for

a beret?" Reba Mae asked. "A beret would give you an artsy look."

"Thanks, but no thanks." I rearranged a container of pink sponge rollers and a can of hair spray next to a mock shampoo bowl. "A beret might give Bitsy the impression I'd gone Picasso and wanted to paint her portrait."

Reba Mae twisted her hands together. "My nerves are jumpin' like fleas on a hound."

"Mine, too," I sighed. If this didn't work, I was fresh out of ideas. "Let's just stick to the plan. Your job is to keep out of sight and record our conversation while I wheedle a confession out of her."

"What if Bitsy turns violent?"

"Quit worrying. I'm not wearing a scarf, am I? No way she can strangle me."

Reba Mae cocked her head to one side. "Hear something?"

"Quick!" I whispered when I heard the telltale squeak, too. "Exit stage right."

"Bitsy," I called. "That you?"

Bitsy emerged from stage left. She'd taken time to prepare for the role, with her hair done up in a bouffant style and thick makeup. She wore a loose jacket over tight jeans, which I'd come to think of as her trademark, V-neck sweater, and high-heeled

416

ankle boots. "Got here as fast as I could," she said.

"Thanks for coming on such short notice," I said, attempting to put her at ease. "It's tragic what happened to Sandy, but the show must go on. When I offered to take over as director, Mayor Hemmings agreed. As you might expect, time is of the essence. The role of Truvy Jones is yours if your audition goes well."

Bitsy smiled eagerly. "Mary Lou Lambert was a terrible choice for the part. I don't know why Sandy picked her in the first place. She never even remembers to come by for her dry cleaning."

I took a seat in a styling chair with torn red vinyl that looked as though it had been salvaged from Floyd's Barbershop in Mayberry. "Your name was mentioned as a possible replacement."

"Where do you want me to start?"

"I thought we'd start at the beginning. How about Act One, Scene One?" I removed the script from where I'd stuffed it under the chair cushions and held it out. "Look familiar?"

Bitsy's eyes widened as comprehension dawned. "Should it?" she said.

If this was the extent of Bitsy's acting talent, I could understand why Sandy didn't take her seriously. But being a terrible actor didn't make a person a murderer. I'd need to press harder if I wanted an admission of guilt. "This is yours, isn't it?"

She licked her lips. "Where did you find it?"

"Right where you left it — the night you strangled Sandy." I slid out of the chair and advanced toward her.

"What are you implying?" A tremor in her voice undermined her bravado.

"I'm not implying; I'm accusing. You learned Mary Lou was being replaced. Knowing Sandy was always last to leave rehearsals, you waited until the cast left before making one final attempt to convince Sandy you were right for the part. You witnessed Reba Mae arriving, then leaving again, before you made your move. Unfortunately, you can't act — and Sandy told you as much. You flew into a rage, and as they say, the rest is history."

"What if I did?" she spat, her fear transforming into anger. "You can't prove it."

"I'm willing to bet that you're the one who made the anonymous call about Reba Mae to the hotline." I hoped Reba Mae was videotaping our exchange. *Would any of it be admissible in a court of law?* I wondered. If not, all this would be reduced to a case of she-said, she-said. "I also think you're responsible for slashing the tires and keying 'GO HOME' on Madison Winters' car in order to scare her."

"Don't be ridiculous!" she sneered. "Why would I do that? I don't even know the girl."

This was the moment to play the trump card I didn't have, so instead I went for a big fat lie. "Madison remembers seeing someone duck around the corner when Caleb dropped her off to get her car. She's pretty sure that person was you."

"You're bluffing. If she was positive it was me, she'd have said something by now."

Any lingering doubts about Bitsy's guilt vanished. "So you *did* kill Sandy."

"Too bad your plan to send Madison back to Chicago didn't work." Reba Mae stepped out from the wings, brandishing her phone. "I'm no longer gonna be the fall guy. I have everythin' recorded right here on my cell phone."

Fury turned Bitsy's expression ugly — the same look she'd probably worn as she tightened a silk scarf around a woman's neck. Casually reaching into the pocket of her jacket, she withdrew a small revolver. "Don't act so surprised, ladies. My husband Dooley is a long-haul trucker. He gave me this for self-protection when he's on the road. If ever a situation calls for 'self-protection,' this is it."

Reba Mae inched closer and grasped my arm. "You're goin' to shoot us?"

Bitsy frowned, considering her options. "No," she said after some thought, "guns are too noisy. I have a better idea, but first toss me your cell phones. Don't want the cavalry riding to the rescue, or all this would be for nothing. And don't try my patience — I'll shoot if I have to. Dooley made sure I knew how to fire this baby."

Our phones landed at her feet with a loud clatter. "You'll never get away with this." How lame was that? I cringed at using a line I'd seen or heard dozens of times in books and on television.

Keeping the gun trained on us, Bitsy bent down, scooped up both phones, and dropped them in her pocket. Should I live through this, I'd ask McBride how to protect oneself from a frontal gun attack. Right now, however, it was a moot point.

"Now, both of you, hands in the air where I can see them." She herded us backstage and into a small dressing room, then slammed the door shut. A click of a bolt sliding home seemed to reverberate inside my brain. Reba Mae and I turned to each other in the dark.

"Is she going to leave us here to starve?" Reba Mae whispered anxiously.

"Hush." I pressed my ear to the door and heard Bitsy moving about.

The answer to Reba Mae's question came to me along with my first whiff of smoke.

"Oh, my god," Reba Mae squealed. "She's burning this place down with us inside."

I threw myself against the door and felt it shudder beneath my weight. "C'mon, Reba Mae, don't just stand there. Help me. We have to get out of here."

Smoke curled underneath the door like an arthritic finger.

I lunged at the door again, but with the same results. I darted a look at Reba Mae, who stood off to the side. "What are you doing waiting?" I cried, coughing.

"I'm using my regular phone to report a fire," she said. "I gave Bitsy my burner phone. It was nearly out of minutes anyway."

Meanwhile smoke continued to seep into the dressing room, stinging my eyes and burning my throat. It was making me mad, fighting mad. I wasn't about to allow some tummy-stapled, chain-smoking wannabe actress to permanently lower my curtain. Channeling Jackie Chan, I raised my leg in a kung fu move I'd seen in a movie. I felt the jolt all the way from my foot to my spine. Her phone call completed, Reba Mae joined her efforts with mine.

Under our combined strength, the old wood splintered and the bolt tore loose. Coughing and sputtering, we headed for the exit. Flames licked upward from a rag-filled bucket that had been set purposely close to the stage's heavy velvet curtains. Reba Mae grabbed a fire extinguisher from the wall, pointed the nozzle, and doused the flames.

"Are you crazy?" I hissed. "What are you doing? Bitsy's getting away."

"This building is about to go on the national historic register."

Not nearly as civic-minded as my friend, I yanked her by the arm. "Let's go. The fire department can handle it from here."

Outside, I bent forward, hands on knees, and inhaled a lungful of the crisp November air. Reba Mae did the same. The wail of a siren in the near distance energized me. I wasn't about to let Bitsy get away with not only killing Sandy but attempting to kill me and my BFF as well. I straightened and looked around. The night was black as pitch. No moon, not a solitary star, peeked through a thick cloud cover. Where had she disappeared?

I gazed across Main Street to the square in time to see a small flame flicker, then die.

No self-respecting lightning bugs would dare show themselves this time of year. What I'd witnessed had been the flash of a cigarette lighter. Bitsy Johnson-Jones had foolishly lingered in the square in order to have a front-row seat at the drama she'd created.

I took off running. After a slight hesitation Reba Mae sprinted after me. We dodged a police car, the first on the scene, its light bar flashing. Sirens screamed louder. "We can't let her get away," I panted, our sneakers soundless in all the commotion. "You take the right side; I'll take the left."

"Gotcha! Just like *NCIS*," Reba Mae huffed as we split up.

Ahead of me, I saw the glowing tip of a cigarette grow fainter and fainter as Bitsy's figure retreated farther into the square. I took this as my cue to pick up speed. My lungs begged for oxygen, but my veins were flooded with adrenaline.

"Stop!" I gasped.

Bitsy paused for a fraction of a second, and in that fraction of time Reba Mae sailed from the opposite direction and did a flying tackle. Bitsy jerked away in the nick of time, leaving Reba Mae holding a high-heeled boot. Bitsy scrambled to her feet but, hobbling with one boot on, one boot off, didn't get far. The next tackle was strictly mine. I brought her down to the ground with a satisfying, "Oomph!" Reba Mae, not wanting to be left out of the action, climbed on board.

"Freeze!" a familiar baritone voice shouted.

"Get them off of me — now!" Bitsy demanded.

McBride shone the beam of a powerful Maglite at the human pileup in the grass near the base of the Confederate soldier. I straddled Bitsy's waist; Reba Mae straddled her thighs while the woman cried, cursed, and threatened.

"Hiya, Wyatt." Reba Mae gave him a sassy grin. "Long time, no see."

"Ladies, you have a lot of explaining to do."

"Bitsy did it," I said, feeling triumphant. "She killed Sandy."

"And we have proof." Reba Mae held up her phone. "I recorded her confession."

McBride pulled Reba Mae and me off of Bitsy but kept his hand clamped firmly around the woman's upper arm should she try to escape. "Remind me to include the flying tackle in my next self-defense class."

"Don't bother." It was my turn for a cheeky grin. "We've got it down pat."

424

CHAPTER 36

The day was partly sunny, the temperature mild, perfect weather for an impromptu picnic lunch in the town square. Melly had consented to play shopkeeper while Reba Mae and I feasted on Italian subs. I stifled a yawn before taking another bite of my sandwich. We'd been at the Brandywine Creek Police Department until the wee hours of the morning answering questions and giving statements. "Don't know about you," I said, "but I'm going to bed early tonight."

"Me, too." Reba Mae tore open a bag of chips. "Phone at the Klassy Kut's been ringin' like crazy all mornin'. Suddenly everyone needs a trim. Or, more likely, wants to hear a firsthand account of our adventures."

"My shop's been like Grand Central Station. Sales are brisk, gossip brisker. I've already whipped up two batches of mulled cider for customers. Melly brought over a couple dozen gingersnaps she'd been saving in her freezer."

"Wait till you hear this" — Reba Mae licked salt off her fingers — "Mayor Hemmings wants to give me the key to the city. He said me reportin' the fire at the opera house as quickly as I did saved a national treasure."

"You go, girl!" I gave her arm a playful swat. "If not for you and your phone it would have been curtains."

"You got that right, honeybun, and us along with it." Reba Mae polished off her sub and balled up the wrapper.

"What else did Hizzoner have to say?"

Reba Mae's eyes sparkled. "This is the best part. He said soon as smoke damages and some minor repairs are done, the opera house will be up and runnin'. He's plannin' a press conference to let folks know Brandywine Creek is the new tourist destination for those who prefer places off the beaten path."

"That'll be great for business." I watched a gray squirrel with an acorn nearly the size of its head scamper up a willow oak.

"Look who's here," Reba Mae said, pointing at Doug, who was making his way toward us. "The guy looks pretty down in the mouth for such a nice day."

"Melly said I'd find you two here," Doug said upon reaching us. "Glad you're in the clear, Reba Mae. I never thought for a minute you were involved in Sandy's death."

"Wish I had a nickel for every time I heard that this mornin'. I could take me a nice vacation to Myrtle Beach." She cocked her head, studying Doug's serious expression. "Guess I ought to be gettin' back to cuttin' and colorin'. See you guys later."

I watched the gentle sway of her paisley print skirt as she walked away, both happy and relieved her troubles were over. Doug sat down next to me and cleared his throat. "I need to talk to you about a decision I've reached."

He had my full attention now. "Oh, oh," I said. "That sounds ominous."

He rested one elbow along the top of the bench. Behind rimless glasses, his dark brown eyes were as earnest as I'd ever seen them. "As you know, Madison has had a difficult time adjusting to life in the South. If that wasn't enough, she's been traumatized by the murder of someone she knew and the subsequent harassment."

I nodded, bracing myself for what I knew was coming next.

"Madison plans to enroll at Northwestern

for the winter term. She's going to need a lot of emotional support, and I promised I'd be there for her."

I blinked back tears, already feeling the loss. "I don't know what to say. . . ."

He took my hand and gently squeezed. "This isn't the direction I thought our relationship was heading, but I hope you'll understand. I need to put Madison's needs before my own."

"Of course, I understand." I squeezed his hand in return. And I really did. Family first was my credo, too. In fact, I admired Doug for making the sacrifice. I knew until now he'd been happy with his choice to relocate to a small Georgia town. "How soon?"

"For Madison's sake, the sooner the better. I contacted the animal clinic where I used to work, and they're willing to rehire me. I've also been in touch with a friend of a friend who might be interested in buying my practice. Madison and I will be flying up to Chicago in the next week or so to find housing."

"Time for me to relieve Melly of her duties." I rose to my feet, collected the remnants from lunch, and tossed them in a nearby trash can.

"I'll walk you back."

I nodded, not trusting myself to speak.

His plans to leave filled me with a deep sadness. Though I might not have been "in love" with the man, I was very much "in like" with him. Doug had made me laugh and listened to me whine and was a pillar of common sense whenever mine took flight. He'd be dearly missed. "Anything I can do to help," I offered, summoning a wan smile.

"It's not like I'm moving to Mars." He looped his arm around my shoulders. "There are dozens of flights out of Atlanta to O'Hare every day. Chicago's a great city, loads of great restaurants. It'll be fun to show you around."

We stopped on the sidewalk outside of Spice It Up! Not caring who might be watching, Doug pulled me in for a long kiss that was both sweet and bittersweet. Finally, we broke apart. "Good-bye, Piper," he said, his voice husky. "I'll miss you, too."

"Bye, Doug." I stood on the walk, watched him get into his Ford Explorer and then drive off. Reluctantly, I turned and went inside.

As I entered, Melly whipped off her apron and gathered her purse. "Tsk, tsk," she clucked her tongue in disapproval. "Half the town saw you and Doug kissing on the sidewalk. In my day, a public display of affection wasn't considered unladylike."

"I'll repent later," I told her, shrugging out of my sweater and into an apron.

"No need to be glib, young lady." Melly took out her compact and studied her reflection. "I'm meeting Cot for a late lunch at the country club. We're finalizing our travel plans."

It was my turn to cluck my tongue. "Tsk, tsk. Two unmarried people traveling together? In my day that was frowned upon."

Chuckling, she returned her compact to her purse. "You can be such a brat."

"What's this about you being a brat?" McBride asked as he passed Melly on his way in.

"No comment." I folded my arms over my chest and studied my visitor. "What brings you here, McBride? Did you hear the rumor I was handing out mulled cider and ginger-snaps?"

"That's just an added bonus." He snatched the lone cookie off a plate on the counter. "I thought you might be interested to know Bitsy's attorney of record has entered a plea of not guilty to voluntary manslaughter on her behalf."

"Not guilty!" I nearly exploded. "We recorded her confession. Who is this idiot lawyer of hers?"

"Bitsy hired CJ, but I think the judge is smart enough to take everything into consideration." His cookie disappeared in two bites. "I think the clincher came when CJ complimented her on her new figure."

"He's a silver-tongued devil all right." I tucked a stray curl behind one ear. "Did Bitsy admit why she strangled Sandy?"

"The woman yearned to be in the limelight. She'd been the fat girl kids made fun of her whole life. Now that she'd lost weight, she wanted their admiration. Being onstage was her golden opportunity to have everyone take notice. When Sandy refused her the part for the second time, Bitsy flew into a rage. CJ will probably argue it was a crime of passion."

"Sad, isn't it, a life destroyed for the sake of a woman's vanity?" Going to the Crock-Pot on the counter, I gave the mulled cider a stir. Immediately the shop was perfumed with the scent of cinnamon and cloves. "Sure you don't want a sample?"

"No, thanks, I'll take a rain check," he said, watching me. "Not to change the subject, but I was just over at Creekside Realty. Shirley said you and the good doctor put on quite a show in the middle of the sidewalk. Are congratulations in order?"

"You could say that." I busied myself sorting through the morning's receipts. "Doug accepted his old job back so he can be close to Madison. She plans to return to school at Northwestern."

McBride rubbed the back of his neck and frowned. "Doug's leaving Brandywine Creek?"

"Isn't that what I just said?" I asked. "How is Shirley by the way?"

"Good, she's good." McBride grinned that darn dimple-winking grin of his. "Matter of fact, we just wrapped up a deal for me to purchase the five acres bordering my land. It took a lot of finangling, what with offers and counteroffers, but Shirley pulled it together."

"So," I said slowly, my receipt sorting forgotten, "that's what all your meetings were about?"

"Yep." He brushed crumbs from his shirt, looking pleased with himself. "Guess you could say, I'm putting down roots. I'm here for the long haul, not planning to leave anytime soon."

He sauntered out with a cocky smile on his handsome face. I smiled, too. I probably shouldn't, but I liked the idea of McBride sticking around.

"Who sent you the roses?"

"I don't know," I said, putting the bloodred buds into a makeshift vase. "I searched high and low but couldn't find a card."

"Looks like you've got yourself a secret admirer."

It was opening night of *Steel Magnolias,* and we were backstage at the opera house. The show must go on, but in this case it had taken until mid-February — Valentine's Day. Lots had transpired since the November night Bitsy had confessed to murder. The minor damage done to the opera house had been repaired and a new lock installed on the stage door. In a moment of insanity I'd agreed to direct *Steel Magnolias.* Healthy and out of rehab, Bunny was ready to have the audience reaching for tissues by the poignant final scene. Lindsey had stepped in to replace Madison Winters as Shelby, the prettiest girl in town. She was rethinking becoming a physical therapist and majoring in theater arts instead. As for Reba Mae, she'd been reinstated in the coveted role of Truvy Jones. Her fellow castmates had grown accustomed to her calling Wanda Wowser instead of Ouiser.

Gerilee Barker, stage manager, spoke into a headset and her husband. Pete, the lightboard operator, dimmed the houselights.

Reba Mae nudged me toward the stage. "Break a leg, kiddo."

I stepped into the spotlight before a packed house. It felt as though the butterflies in my stomach were on amphetamines. I couldn't make out many faces beyond the first couple rows, but I did see Cot and Melly, front and center, sitting next to Craig Granger. Dale Simons was there to support Wanda and had brought along Hoyt, his Harley-riding pal. Hoyt had become a frequent customer in my shop. Seems he'd developed a penchant for cooking. He gave me a broad smile and a wink. I was about to speak when a latecomer strolled down the aisle. Wyatt McBride, handsome as ever dressed head to toe in his signature black, gave me a smile as he took his seat at the end of the second row.

"Ladies and gentlemen," I said, addressing the audience. "Tonight's performance is dedicated to Sandy Granger. Without Sandy's generous spirit, none of this would have been possible."

Suddenly the lights blinked off. I sucked in a breath. This hadn't been part of the script. What's more, I'd seen Pete in the wings, nowhere near the light board. But if not Pete, who had thrown the levers?

Just as suddenly the lights blazed back on.

Their off-again-on-again was followed by a ripple of nervous laughter from cast, crew, and audience alike. I darted a glance over my shoulder and found Reba Mae among the cast members standing stage right.

The ghost, she mouthed.

Who was I to argue?

CURRY

For trivia lovers such as myself, chicken curry, as we're familiar with in North America, isn't a new item on the menu. It was introduced in Savannah, Georgia, in the early 1800s by a British sea captain who had been stationed in Bengal, India. Apparently the sea captain shared his recipe with friends who then nicknamed the dish Country Captains Chicken. This was the name used in 1940 by Mrs. W. L. Bullard from Warm Springs, Georgia, when she served this dish to Franklin D. Roosevelt and General George S. Patton.

It may come as a surprise to learn that curry powder used in the West is radically different in the country where it originated. Cooks in India freshly grind their spices each day for use in a particular dish, making the curry powder they use much more favorable than the store-bought variety. Curry powder is a blend of up to twenty different herbs and spices, which can include: caraway, cardamom, chilies, cinnamon, cloves, coriander, cumin, fennel, fenugreek, garlic, ginger, mace, nutmeg, pepper, poppy seeds, saffron, sesame seeds, tamarind, and tumeric (which gives curry its characteristic golden color). Curry quickly loses its pungency. It will keep for 2 months in an airtight container.

SPICY CHICKEN CURRY

3 tablespoons olive oil

16 boneless chicken tenderloins (2.5–3 oz. each) cut into 1-inch pieces

Salt and pepper to taste

2 sweet onions, chopped

4 cloves garlic, crushed

1 teaspoon fresh ginger, peeled and diced

12–14 baby carrots, halved, or 2 large sweet potatoes, peeled and in 1-to-2-inch pieces

1/2 cup chicken broth

2 tablespoons tomato paste

1 cup diced tomatoes, well drained

1 teaspoon lemon juice

2 1/2 tablespoons curry

1/8 teaspoon crushed red pepper or one small red chili pepper, diced

1/2 teaspoon cardamom

1/2 teaspoon cinnamon

1/4 teaspoon fennel seeds

1/4 teaspoon dry mustard

1–2 teaspoons sugar

2 cans coconut milk (shake well)

1 teaspoon cornstarch blended with 3 tablespoons of water, if needed

Heat oil on medium in heavy-bottomed pan. Add chicken, season with salt and pepper, and partially brown. Add the onions and cook until tender. Stir in garlic and ginger and cook for several minutes longer. Next add carrots or sweet potatoes, broth, tomato paste, diced tomatoes, lemon juice, spices, and sugar. Combine well and allow mixture to come to a boil. Lower heat to simmer and stir in coconut milk a little at a time. Continue to simmer for 45–60 minutes. If necessary, thicken with cornstarch blended with 3 tablespoons of water. Serve with rice or couscous.

Yield: 6–8 servings

CRANBERRY-NUT MINI-MUFFINS

2 cups flour
1 cup sugar
2 teaspoons baking powder
1/2 teaspoon baking soda
1 teaspoon salt
1/2 teaspoon cinnamon
2 teaspoons grated orange rind
1/3 cup orange juice
1 large egg, beaten
2 tablespoons salad oil
1/2 cup water
1 cup chopped pecans
1 cup fresh cranberries, halved

Whisk flour, sugar, baking powder, baking soda, salt, and cinnamon in a large bowl.

In a second bowl, combine orange rind, orange juice, egg, oil, and water. Add all at once to dry ingredients. Stir just until well moistened. Fold in nuts and cranberries.

Bake at 350°F. in mini-muffin tins that have been well greased or lined with baking cups for 20 minutes or until toothpick inserted in the center comes out clean.

Yield: 3 dozen

GINGERBREAD

1/2 cup sugar
1/2 cup butter
1 large egg
1 cup molasses
2 1/2 cups flour
1 1/2 teaspoons baking soda
1/2 teaspoon salt
1 1/2 teaspoons cinnamon
1 teaspoon powdered ginger
1/2 teaspoon ground cloves
1/2 cup applesauce
3/4 cup hot water

Preheat oven to 350°F. Grease and flour a 9-inch square pan.

In a large bowl, cream together the sugar and butter. Beat in the egg and mix in the molasses.

In a second bowl, whisk together the flour, baking soda, salt, cinnamon, ginger, and cloves. Blend into the creamed mixture. Add the applesauce. Stir in the hot water. Pour into the prepared pan.

Bake 1 hour in a preheated oven or until a knife inserted in the center comes out clean. Cool before serving. Serve with fresh whipped cream.

Yield: 9 servings

ABOUT THE AUTHOR

Gail Oust is often accused of flunking retirement. Hearing the words "maybe it's a dead body" while golfing fired her imagination for writing a cozy. Ever since then, she has spent more time on a computer than at a golf course. She lives with her husband in McCormick, South Carolina.

The employees of Thorndike Press hope you have enjoyed this Large Print book. All our Thorndike, Wheeler, and Kennebec Large Print titles are designed for easy reading, and all our books are made to last. Other Thorndike Press Large Print books are available at your library, through selected bookstores, or directly from us.

For information about titles, please call:
 (800) 223-1244

or visit our website at:
 gale.com/thorndike

To share your comments, please write:
Publisher
Thorndike Press
10 Water St., Suite 310
Waterville, ME 04901